A Dream of Red Mansions

红 楼 梦

Saga of a Noble Chinese Family
(Abridged Version)

Written by Cao Xueqin
and Gao E

Translated by Huang Xinqu

Purple
Bamboo
Publishing

Library of Congress Catalog Card Number: 94-070302
ISBN 0-8351-2529-7

Printed in the United States of America by Purple Bamboo Publishing

Table of Contents

Foreword   v
Primary Residents: East and West Mansions with Their
          Chinese Names viii
Chapter 1 - A Poor Scholar's Tale   1
Chapter 2 - Family History of the Jia Household   8
Chapter 3 - Black Jade Meets Magic Jade 16
Chapter 4 - Xue Pan and the Murder Case 28
Chapter 5 - Granny Liu Enters the Honored Mansion . 37
Chapter 6 - Jiao Da, a Wild Servant in the Peaceful
          Mansion 47
Chapter 7 - Precious Hairpin and Her Gold Necklace . . 52
Chapter 8 - Phoenix Takes over the Household
          Management 61
Chapter 9 - Grand View Garden 68
Chapter 10 -- Aroma Plays a Trick 79
Chapter 11 -- Black Jade, a Sentimental Girl 88
Chapter 12 -- Magic Jade's Enlightenment 97
Chapter 13 -- Black Jade Buries the Fallen Blossoms . 107
Chapter 14 -- A Lovelorn Girl Falls Deeper in Love . . 120
Chapter 15 -- Magic Jade Bares His Heart 131
Chapter 16 -- Lovebird Rejects the Marriage Offer . . . 139
Chapter 17 -- Artful Cuckoo Tests Magic Jade's
          Feelings 151
Chapter 18 -- Jia Lian Secretly Marries Second Sister
          You 161
Chapter 19 -- The Death of Third Sister You 170
Chapter 20 -- Jealous Phoenix's Decoy 180
Chapter 21 -- Phoenix Kills Second Sister You with a
          Borrowed Knife 191
Chapter 22 -- A House Search in the Grand View
          Garden 199

Chapter 23 -- Skybright Dies in the Flower of Her
             Youth 210
Chapter 24 -- The Secret Trouble of Black Jade 217
Chapter 25 -- Magic Jade's Wedding in the Making . . 228
Chapter 26 -- Black Jade Rejects All Nourishment . . . 235
Chapter 27 -- The Cunning Trick of Phoenix 243
Chapter 28 -- Black Jade Dies of a Broken Heart 255
Chapter 29 -- Precious Hairpin Goes through Her
             Wedding Ceremony 263
Chapter 30 --Imperial Guards Raid the Peaceful
             Mansion 270
Chapter 31 -- The Death of the Lady Dowager and
             Phoenix 279
Chapter 32 -- Magic Jade Renounces the World 285

Foreword

Of all Chinese literary classics, the best known and most loved by the Chinese people is *A Dream of Red Mansions*. This novel was written by Cao Xueqin (1718-1763) and completed by Gao E in the mid-eighteenth century. It is a great saga about a noble Chinese family, and it consists of 120 chapters in which as many as 975 characters are portrayed. The work is a rare masterpiece of literary creation, the unchallenged model in linguistic style, and an encyclopedic reference of Chinese culture during the 17th and 18th centuries. It also contains a superb collection of poems, fables, allusions, and vivid characters.

Much of the novel is generally thought to be autobiographical, although little is known about the actual life of the author. It is known, however, that he lived in poverty. Thus it is only natural that he would voice his sufferings and attack the traditional aspects of Chinese feudal morality, political and legal institutions, the old marriage framework, and the feudal examination system. Unfortunately, he failed to finish the work by the time of his death, at age 45. Only 80 chapters of the book were copied and circulated during his lifetime. The completed novel did not come out until 1791, almost 30 years after his death.

In recent years, the unique scholarship of studying not only the linguistic and literary merits of the novel, but also its aesthetic, religious and philosophical values, has been in fashion. Scholars have attempted to interpret the book in terms of Chinese culture and traditional values as well as the conflicts of these values with modernization and Western culture.

Since the middle of the 19th century, various abridged English versions of the work have appeared in the West. Prof. David Hawkes of Oxford University in England produced his first volume of the complete translation of this classic in 1973. It was published by Penguin Books. This was followed by a full translation completed by Yang Xianyi and Gladys Yang, and published in 1978 and 1980 by the Foreign Languages Press in Beijing. However, most people may find it too difficult to read through the thick volumes of this complete translation. In view of this, while giving lectures on Chinese culture and literature in the United States (1982-1983), I made up my mind to offer a shorter version so as to serve as an appetizer for those who cannot afford the time and effort to read through the thick volumes of the complete translation.

I took liberty to omit and simplify the minor details and nonessential episodes, focusing on the chief characters' joys and sorrows, the tragic love of Magic Jade (Jia Baoyu) and his two female cousins, Black Jade (Lin Daiyu) and Precious Hairpin (Xue Baochai). I have also attempted to highlight the main lines of the story so as to present a picture of the ups and downs of this noble Chinese family in the Qing Dynasty (1644-1911). I have tried to use modern English to make this world masterpiece readily accessible to a wider circle of readers.

For my translation, I have used the complete Chinese original text published by the People's Literature Publishing House, Beijing (1982 edition), and an expurgated Chinese edition prepared by Mao Dun, the noted Chinese writer, and published by the Kaiming Press in 1935. I first worked out the details of my Chinese text and then did the English version.

I would like to express my appreciation to those international friends who have made comments and suggestions for the improvement of my typescripts. They are: Professors Wilbur Birky (US), Realene Penner (US), Madeleine Enns (Canada), and Dr. Charles Tyzack (UK). I am indebted to Juliet Yu for typing the manuscripts, Steven and Tom Huang for their assistance in proofreading the different chapters. Thanks are due to my poet friend Dr. Steve Liu (US) and Dr. Kuan Yu-chien from Hamburg University, Germany. I am especially grateful to Prof. Wang Zuoliang and Prof. Li Fu-ning from Peking University who has favored me with a preface from the perspective of comparative literature.

I should also thank Foster Stockwell and Chris Noyes for their constant efforts in promoting Chinese culture through the publication and circulation of Chinese books in San Francisco. Without the warmhearted encouragement and assistance in one way or another by the above-mentioned friends, I could hardly have completed this immense task. If my tiny effort in putting this peak of Chinese fiction into a simplified English version proves of some service to Western readers, then I have not come to this world in vain.

(Frank) Huang Xinqu
January 8, 1994
Frank Huang Research Institute
Chengdu, Sichuan, 610068 PRC

A Dream of Red Mansions has been praised as a treasure-house of Chinese culture at its height and most sophisticated stage of development. All the refinements of cultural life are minutely delineated and discerningly evaluated. The book has been time and again translated into Western languages. The best English translation is David Hawkes's *The Story of the Stone*, in five volumes (unfinished).

Since the Chinese novel is fairly long (120 chapters), the need for a simplified version is keenly felt. Professor Huang Xinqu has done an excellent job in meeting this need. The abridgment has been judiciously made and full justice has been done to the content and flavor of the original. Professor Huang has chosen what Addison calls the middle style in rendering the 18th-century Chinese classic. It is easy, flowing and delightful to read. I would like to congratulate him on his success in doing a good service to the reading public.

Li Fu-ning
Professor of English, Peking University

Primary Residents: East & West Mansions

I. The Honored Mansion (The West Mansion)

Heads of the Jia Household

The Lady Dowager (贾 母), née Shi, widow of Jia
Daishan, ruler of the Jia Household

The Seniors

Jia She (贾赦), elder son of the Lady Dowager
Lady Xing (邢夫人), née Xing, wife of Jia She
Jia Zheng (贾政), younger son of the Lady Dowager,
mistress of the Honored Mansion
Lady Wang (王夫人), née Wang, wife of Jia Zheng
and mother of Magic Jade

The Juniors

Jia Lian (贾琏), son of Jia She
Madam Phoenix (Wang Xifeng 王熙凤), wife of Jia
Lian and Lady Wang's niece, taking charge of the
Honored Mansion
Magic Jade (Jia Baoyu 贾宝玉), son of Jia Zheng
and Lady Wang
Jia Huan (贾环), son of Jia Zheng by his secondary
wife Zhao; half brother of Magic Jade
Li Wan (李纨), widow of Jia Zhu and mother of Jia
Lan

The Female Juniors

Beginning of Spring (Yuanchun 元春), daughter of
Jia Zheng and Lady Wang, and elder sister of
Magic Jade; Imperial Consort

Greeting of Spring (Yingchun 迎春), daughter of Jia
She by his secondary wife

Taste of Spring (Tanchun 探春), daughter of Jia
Zheng by his secondary wife Zhao and half sister
of Magic Jade

Jia Lan (贾兰), son of Jia Zhu, the deceased son of
Jia Zheng

Relations of the Jia Household

Lin Ruhai (林如海), son-in-law of the Lady
Dowager

Black Jade (Lin Daiyu 林黛玉), daughter of Lin
Ruhai, granddaughter of the Lady Dowager,
Magic Jade's love

Aunt Xue (薛姨妈), elder sister of Lady Wang

Precious Hairpin (Xue Baochai 薛宝钗), daughter of
Aunt Xue, Magic Jade's wife

Xue Pan (薛蟠), son of Aunt Xue, brother of
Precious Hairpin

Lotus (香菱), secondary wife of Xue Pan, kidnapped
daughter of Zhen Shiyin (甄 士 隐), a retired
scholar

River Cloud (Shi Xiangyun 史 湘 云), orphaned
grandniece of the Lady Dowager

Jia Yucun (贾 雨 村), a poor scholar claiming
relationship with the powerful Honored
Mansion

Granny Liu (刘佬佬), an old countrywoman
patronized by Madam Phoenix and the Jias of
the Honored Mansion

II. The Peaceful Mansion (The East Mansion)

Jia Jing (贾敬), son of Jia Daihua, retired to a Taoist temple

Jia Zhen (贾珍), son of Jia Jing; in his place master of the Peaceful Mansion

Madam You (尤氏), née You, wife of Jia Zhen

Jia Rong (贾蓉), son of Jia Zhen

Mistress Rong, wife of Jia Rong, also known by her childhood name Qin Keqing (秦可卿)

Grief of Spring (Xichun 惜春), daughter of Jia Jing

Old Mrs. You (尤佬娘), stepmother of Madam You

Second Sister You (尤二姐), elder daughter of Old Mrs. You, later secondary wife of Jia Lian

Third Sister You (尤三姐), younger daughter of Old Mrs. You

Qin Zhong (秦钟), younger brother of Qin Keqing; Magic Jade's classmate under the same tutor

Jiao Da (焦大), an old retainer of the Peaceful Mansion

Main Waiting Maids

Lady Dowager

> Lovebird (Yuanyang 鸳鸯)
> Amber (琥珀)
> Sister Silly (傻大姐)

Lady Wang

> Gold Bracelet (金钏)

Madam Phoenix

> Patience (平儿)

Magic Jade

    Aroma (Xiren袭人)
    Skybright (Qingwen 晴雯)
    Musk (Sheyue 麝月)

Black Jade

    Cuckoo (Zijuan紫娟)
    Snowswan (Xueyan雪雁)

Precious Hairpin

    Oriole (莺儿)
    Apricot (杏儿)

Greeting of Spring

    Chess (司棋)

Taste of Spring

    Scribe (侍书)

Pages full of absurd words
Soaked with bitter tears:
All say he is a fool in love,
But who his message hears!

Cao Xueqin

1/ A Poor Scholar's Tale

Our story begins in one of the rich and mighty quarters beyond the Imperial Gate of Suzhou, the garden city in southeastern China. It is a region of wealth and nobility. At that time an old Buddhist temple, known as the Gourd Temple, stood there in a narrow lane off Three Mile Street. Beside it lived Zhen Shiyin, a respected gentleman, and his graceful and virtuous wife, Madam Feng.

Though not rich or noble, this family was most respected in that area. Quiet and easygoing by nature, Zhen was no lover of honor or rank. He did, however, take great pleasure in tending his flowers, growing bamboo, and chanting classical Chinese poetry over a glass of wine. He enjoyed his free hours very much. There was only one thing he missed. He had no little son to rock on his knees, although he was well over fifty years in age. Fate had only granted him a three-year-old daughter, whom he named Lotus.

One day, as Shiyin was sitting idly at home, his neighbor, Jia Yucun, dropped in for a visit. Yucun was a poor scholar who originally came from Huzhou. He was, in fact, the last in a family line of scholars and officials. His parents died after they exhausted the family fortune, and left him alone in the world. Since nothing could be achieved at home, Yucun decided to set out for the capital and there take the civil service examinations so that he could be appointed to an official post. But, unfortunately, his money had ran out by the time he reached Suzhou. He had to live in the temple, earning his daily bread by writing letters for others and by copying and drafting documents. Here he met Shiyin. They soon became good friends.

The two had exchanged just a few words when a servant came in to announce the arrival of another guest. Shiyin excused himself, saying, "I'm awfully sorry, I have another visitor. Would you mind waiting here for a few minutes?"

"Please go ahead," said Yucun, rising, "I'm a frequent visitor here. I don't mind waiting."

Shiyin left the room to receive his guest, while Yucun stayed in the study passing the time by leafing through some books of poetry he found there.

Suddenly he heard a young lady coughing outside the window. He rose and looked out. It was a maid picking flowers. Although no great beauty, she had bright eyes, graceful eyebrows, and a certain charm. Yucun stared at her, spellbound.

The girl looked up just as she was getting ready to go and caught sight of Yucun. She noted that, although his clothes were shabby, he was handsome and strongly built. She quickly turned away, realizing that this must be the scholar her master kept talking about and predicting that such a person wouldn't remain long in miserable circumstances. She couldn't resist looking back at him a couple of times.

Yucun was overjoyed at this, thinking that he had made an impression on her. He decided that this girl was both wise and observant, and certainly one of the few who could appreciate him in his obscurity.

Presently Shiyin's servant came back to let Yucun know that the guest was staying for a meal. Since it would be unwise to wait any longer, Yucun departed through a passage leading to the side gate.

During the Mid-Autumn Festival, Shiyin decided to invite Yucun over for a drink. Shiyin ordered a table to be laid out in his study following the family dinner, and then he strolled to the temple in the moonlight to see his friend.

Yucun, ever since the day that the maid looked back at him twice, flattered himself that she fancied him. He constantly thought of her and, as he gazed at the full moon that night, he chanted the following lines:

Not knowing what fate is in store for me,
Sorrow often comes to this poor heart of mine.

In my sadness my brows contract with new care
Is there not one who, parting, turns to stare?
Looking backward at my shadow in the wind,
Under the moonlight, where is a friend to find?
Bright orb, if with my plight you sympathize,
Shine first over the chamber where the fair lady lies.

His hair was rumpled and he sighed deeply, as he reflected on how far he was from realizing his ambitions. In this mood, he produced the following couplet:

The jade in the box asks for a fair price,
The hairpin in the casket longs to soar on high.

Just then Shiyin arrived and overheard him reciting the couplet. "I see, you are a man of no mean ambition, Yucun," he joked.

"Oh, no!" replied Yucun. "You're too flattering. I was just reciting some lines of an old poet, that's all. How can I ever aspire so high? What brings you here?"

"It's Mid-Autumn tonight, you know. The moon festival is the time for reunions. I thought you might be feeling lonely in the temple, and so I've prepared a little wine at my humble place. I'm just wondering if you'd like to join me."

Yucun was quite pleased to accept the offer. Smiling, he said, "You've favored me with so much kindness, nothing would be better than that."

They walked together to Shiyin's house and went into the courtyard in front of the study. There they drank tea, and then they sat down at the table in the study to some choice wine and plates of delicacies. At first they sipped the wine slowly, but as they chatted and began to drink more lavishly, draining one cup after another, their spirits rose.

Yucun, eight-tenths drunk, could not suppress his joy. To the full moon he improvised a quatrain that expressed his feelings:

On the fifteenth day the moon is full

Bathing jade railings with her pure light;
Once her bright orb sails up the sky,
All men on earth gaze up at her sight.

"Excellent!" cried Shiyin. "I've always said that you are a young man who can rise in the world. These lines foretell your roaring success. Soon you will be up among the clouds. Let me congratulate you in advance."

He filled another large cup with wine. Yucun gulped it down, then sighed. "Don't think this is just drunken talk," he said, "I'm sure I can pass the exams and honor my name in the list of the chosen few; but I'm short of funds for traveling expenses and the capital is far away. I can't raise enough money to go there by just doing copy work."

"Why didn't you say this sooner?" Shiyin cut in. "I've often thought about your taking the exams, but since you didn't mention it, I didn't want to open the subject. Luckily, the civil service examinations are coming up again next year. I will consider it as a privilege to provide you with traveling expenses and funds for other things. It is the least I can do for your friendship."

He sent a servant into another room to fetch fifty ounces of silver and two suits of winter clothes. "The nineteenth would be a lucky day for traveling," Shiyin continued. "On that day you should hire a boat and start your journey westward. How delightful it will be to see you again next winter after you have distinguished yourself by coming out on top of the list of candidates!"

Yucun accepted the silver and clothes with words of appreciation and then sat down for more conversation and drink. They did not part until early in the morning. By the time Shiyin saw his friend off and returned to go to bed, the sun was already high in the sky. After he awoke, he sat down to write two letters of introduction for Yucun to some officials in the capital who might provide housing for him during his stay there.

The servant who was sent to the temple to invite Yucun to come and get the letters of introduction, however, brought back word that the monk there said Mr. Jia had left for the capital early that morning. He had asked the monk to forward a message to Shiyin, saying that scholars are not superstitious about lucky or unlucky days, but like to act according to reason. So he had no time to say good-bye in person.

Thus Shiyin had to let the matter drop.

It is true that time is quickly spent in idleness. In what seemed like a flash, the date for the Lantern Festival arrived. Shiyin decided to send his daughter, Lotus, out into the streets with a servant so that she could enjoy the sight of gay lanterns and merry fireworks. Toward midnight the servant set the little girl down on a doorstep while he went around the corner to relieve himself. When he came back, Lotus was nowhere to be seen. The servant searched desperately all night, but in vain. At dawn, not daring to face his master without the little girl, he ran away to another district.

Shiyin and his wife knew that something must be wrong when their daughter failed to come home. They sent out search parties, but all returned without finding the child. Her loss nearly drove the parents mad. They wept day and night and were almost ready to take their own lives. After a month of grief, Shiyin fell ill, as did his wife. Every day physicians and fortunetellers came to the house to care for them.

On the fifteenth day of the third month, a fire broke out in the Gourd Temple when the monk, who was cooking sacrificial food, carelessly let a pan of oil ignite. Most of the nearby buildings had bamboo fences and wooden walls, and so the flames spread easily from house to house until the whole street was ablaze. Though soldiers and civilians tried to put out the fire, it was beyond control. It raged the whole night until it burned itself out, rendering many families homeless. Shiyin's house was quickly reduced to a pile of rubble and, although the family and their few servants were lucky enough to escape, poor Shiyin could do nothing but stamp his feet and sigh in anguish.

He then decided, after consultation with his wife, to go and live on their farm. But recent harvests had been ruined by floods and droughts, and the countryside was overrun by robber bands. The government's attempts to round up these robbers only made matters worse. Thus, finding it impossible to settle on the farm, Shiyin decided to sell his land and take his wife and two maids to live with his father-in-law, Feng Su.

Feng Su, a native of Taruzhou and a relatively rich farmer, was not at all pleased with the arrival of his panic-stricken daughter and son-in-law. Fortunately Shiyin did not come empty-handed, but brought the money from the mortgage of his land. He asked Feng Su to invest it for him in some land where he could live in the future. His father-in-law agreed to do this, but tricked him by pocketing half the sum and buying just an old cottage and some poor land.

Shiyin, because he was a scholar, had little knowledge of farm management. He struggled at the task for a year or two, losing money all the time, while Old Feng complained to others behind his back that he was incompetent and lazy. Eventually Shiyin learned about this. It depressed him greatly. The shock and misfortune of his circumstances had visibly worn him down. Aging, poor, and sick, he began to look like he was about to die.

One day he made an effort to forget his sorrows by taking a stroll in the street. He tottered along, leaning on his stick. Then a wandering Taoist in straw sandals and tattered clothes limped towards him, chanting:

All men know it's nice to be immortal,
Yet to rank and fame each one scrambles:
Where are the rich and mighty now?
Their graves are but a mass of brambles.

All men know it's nice to be immortal,
Yet silver and gold they all prize.
Each day they grumble they've not made enough,
When they've enough, death seals their eyes.

All men know it's nice to be immortal,
Yet dote on the loving wives they've wed,

Who swear to love their husbands ever more,
But they're off with another, once you're dead.

All men know it's nice to be immortal,
Yet with their darling heirs they won't have done.
Although there's no shortage of fond parents,
Who ever really saw a grateful son?

At the close of this song Shiyin stepped forward and said, "Your words touched my soul to its very depths, master! May I join you, and we can go along together?"

"Fine!" said the wandering Taoist.

So Shiyin took the knapsack from the Taoist's shoulders, and then, without going back to his home, strode off into the world with the eccentric Taoist priest.

This event caused a sensation in the neighborhood and became the main topic of street gossip. When word of it reached Shiyin's wife, she gave way to a storm of tears. She conducted a thorough search for her missing husband, but he had completely disappeared. From then on, she had to live with her parents. Luckily she still had her two maids, and the three of them helped the father relieve his daily expenses by taking in sewing.

2/ Family History of the Jia Household

We must flashback here to Yucun. After receiving the traveling expenses from Shiyin, he left for the capital. As luck would have it, he passed the exams brilliantly, coming out at the top of the list, and so he was appointed prefect of the area.

His sense of pride in his unusual abilityled him to develop a superior attitude towards his colleagues and even his superiors. They hated him for this. Within less than two years, they found a way to impeach him. He was immediately dismissed from his post. His impeachment, however, gave him a chance to move back to his native town and, after that, to travel far and wide.

One day Yucun's travels took him again to Yangzhou, where he learned that the Salt Commissioner that year was Lin Ruhai. Lin had come out third in a previous Imperial Examination, and had recently been promoted to this post. One of Lin's ancestors, five generations earlier, had attained the title of marquis. The rank had been conferred for three generations, but by special Imperial favor had been extended to the fifth generation so that Lin's father had also inherited the title. But Lin, himself, made his career by taking the civil service examinations.

Unfortunately Lin was the only son in his family, and he was now over fifty years of age. His own son had died at the age of three. His wife, Madam Jia, bore him a daughter named Black Jade (Daiyu), who was both pretty and intelligent. She was now five years old and was the apple of her father's eye. Her parents decided to give her a proper education, as if she were a son.

At the time Yucun arrived in Yangzhou, the Salt Commissioner was looking for a resident tutor for his little daughter. Through recommendations of his old friends, Yucun received the post in the Lin household.

Black Jade was a delicate child. She was often accompanied by two maids, and her lessons were somewhat irregular. The job left Yucun plenty of time to relax.

Rapidly another year went by. His pupil's mother was struck by a sudden illness and died, in spite of Black Jade's devoted attendance. Black Jade immediately went into mourning, following the strict rites and ceremonies of Chinese tradition. She was overwhelmed with grief; her health went from bad to worse. She had to give up her lessons for quite some time. During this period, Yucun, feeling rather bored, began to take long walks in the surrounding countryside whenever the weather was fine.

One day he happened to come upon an old temple hidden in the luxuriant woods among hills and streams. He was glad to find a village inn nearby. He entered and was surprised to meet an old acquaintance in the tavern. This friend, named Leng, was a curio dealer whom he had originally met in the capital. The sudden encounter was an occasion for hearty drinks and a mutual exchange of gossip between these two old friends.

"Any news from the capital?" asked Yucun.

"Nothing much, really," replied Leng. "But something rather curious has happened in the house of one of your noble kinsmen."

"I have no kinsmen in the capital. Who do you mean?"

"You have the same family name, even if you don't belong to the same clan," Leng said.

Yucun was puzzled.

"I'm referring to the Jia family of the Honored Mansion (Rongguo Mansion)," Leng continued, "I don't think you need be ashamed of the connection."

"Oh, that family," Yucun laughed. "To be frank, our clan is a very large one. Since the Han Dynasty the Jia clan has spread into most of the provinces. No one can identify all the branches of the family any more. We may be in the same genealogical table, but we've never claimed any relationship. Social differences separate us too greatly."

"Don't talk like that, friend. The Ning and Rong households have declined," Leng sighed. "They are not what they used to be."

"How is that possible? They used to be a most prosperous household."

"That's true. Anyway, it's a long story."

Yucun went on, "Last year, when I was traveling through the capital, I passed the gates of their old mansions. You know, the whole north side of the street is taken up by their estates, the East Mansion (the Peaceful Mansion) and the West Mansion (the Honored Mansion) adjoining it. True, there wasn't much coming and going outside their gates, but over the wall I caught glimpses of some of the most imposing halls and pavilions, while the trees and rockeries of the gardens behind were in perfect condition. There was nothing to suggest a house in decline."

"For a Palace Graduate you're not very smart," Leng chuckled. "A centipede dies but never stops its wriggling, as the Chinese saying goes. Although they're still a cut above ordinary official families, they're not so prosperous any more. The number of members in their families is increasing all the time and their commitments are growing, while both masters and servants are so used to living in luxury that none of them seems to think ahead. Outwardly they may look as grand as ever, but inwardly they're beginning to feel the pinch. That's not the worst of their troubles. The problem is that each new generation of this noble and scholarly clan is inferior to the last."

"But I've always heard that these two families know the proper way to bring up their younger generations."

"Just hear me out," continued Leng. "It is now five generations since the Jia family was raised to the rank of Duke. In the beginning, two brothers by the same mother bore the title as a reward for their splendid services to the Emperor. The elder became the Duke of Ningguo and the younger, the Duke of Rongguo. However, the decline of this family started with the grandson of the elder brother. This grandson was so wrapped up in Taoism that he lived as a hermit in the mountains. His son, Jia Zhen, now holds the title in his place. Jia Zhen never studies, but lives for pleasure. He's turning the Peaceful Mansion upside down. Yet no one dares say anything about it. This is the reason why everything in the Mansion is going to rack and ruin.

"And in the case of the Honored Mansion, since the death of the second Duke of Rongguo, the Lady Dowager, his widow, has been the ruler. She belongs to the noble family of Shi from Jinling (present-day Nanjing). She has two sons. The elder son, Jia She, inherited the title. The younger son, Jia Zheng, was so fond of studying as a child that he became his grandfather's favorite. He once hoped to make a career for himself by taking the civil service exams, but by special Imperial favor, following the last wishes of his grandfather, Jia Zheng was exempted from taking the exams and was subsequently appointed to a post as an assistant in one of the ministries. Now he has risen to the rank of Under-Secretary.

"Two incidents are worth mentioning in relation to Jia Zheng's family. Lady Wang, his wife, bore him a daughter. Strangely enough, she was born on the first day of the first month. But here is something even more curious. Years later his wife had a son who was born with a piece of crystal-clear jade in his mouth. There were even inscriptions on the jade. Isn't that fantastic?"

"It certainly is," replied Yucun. "Such a baby is destined to have a remarkable future."

"That's what everyone says," Leng smiled cynically. "And for that reason he is the favorite of his grandmother. On his first birthday, his father tested the darling son's disposition according to Chinese custom. He put a whole bunch of toys in front of the boy so as to determine his talent and future aptitude from the choice he might make. Ignoring everything else, the boy reached for the rouge, powder box, hair ornaments, and bracelets! Thus Jia Zheng predicted that his child would grow up to be nothing better than a play boy.

"Now although the father is not very fond of the boy, to the old lady, he is everything. The boy also said the strangest things for a child: 'Girls are made of water, boys of mud,' he declared. 'I feel clean and refreshed when I'm with girls, but 1 find men dirty and stinking.' Isn't that absurd? Sooner or later he's bound to be a lady-killer."

Yucun was listening to his friend's tale with great relish.

"However, the girls in the Jia family aren't bad at all," Leng continued. "The Jias have four daughters. Jia Zheng's eldest daughter, Yuanchun (Beginning of Spring), was chosen to be a Lady Clerk in the palace of the heir apparent because of her virtues and talents. The second, Yingchun (Greeting of Spring), is Jia She's daughter by his concubine. The third, Tanchun (Taste of Spring), is Jia Zheng's daughter by another concubine. The fourth, Xichun (Grief of Spring), is the daughter of Jia Jing, the one who retired to a Taoist temple, and the youngest sister of Jia Zhen.

"The Lady Dowager is so attached to these granddaughters that she makes them study around her. They are in every way virtuous and well-behaved young ladies. For proof, look at the wife of your respected employer Mr. Lin, she is one of the sisters of Jia She and Jia Zheng."

At this Yucun was glad to respond, "I have wondered why this pupil of mine talked and behaved so differently from the general run of young ladies today. I suspected she must have had an unusual mother. If she's a granddaughter of the Honored Mansion, that explains it. What a pity that her mother passed away last month!"

"She was the youngest of the Lady Dowager's three daughters," Leng sighed. "Not one of those sisters is left. It will be interesting to see what husbands the younger generation find."

"You spoke of Jia Zheng's son being born with jade in his mouth. Has he got only one son?" Yucun asked. "And what about the venerable Jia She? Has he got any sons?"

"Jia Zheng's eldest died years ago," Leng replied. "After the birth of this boy with the jade, Jia Zheng had another son by his second wife. Jia She also has two sons. Jia Lian, the eldest, is over twenty now. Two years ago he married a relative, the niece of Jia Zheng's wife, Lady Wang. This Jia Lian has the rank of a sub-prefect. He is a man of the world, takes no interest in books, and lives with his uncle, Jia Zheng, trying to help him manage the domestic affairs. Since his marriage, Jia Lian has been pushed into the background by his wife, who is praised by everybody. I hear she's extremely good-looking and a clever talker, so resourceful and shrewd that not a man in ten thousand can match her."

After they finished their conversation, the two men paid their bill. They were about to leave when a voice from behind them called out:

"Congratulations, Brother Yucun! Fancy meeting you here! I've brought you good news."

Yucun turned and saw that it was Mr. Zhang, a native of Yangzhou. He was his former colleague who had been dismissed from his post at the same time and for the same reason as Yucun. Now living at his home, he had just received word from the capital that a request had been approved to allow the former dismissed officials to resume their offices. Mr. Zhang was now busily pulling strings to find patronage.

Once greetings had been exchanged, he lost no time in telling Yucun the good news. Then, after some hurried remarks, they parted to go their own ways.

Leng, who had listened to everything, advised Yucun to talk with his employer, Lin Ruhai, and ask him to enlist the support of Jia Zheng in the capital. Yucun agreed that this was a good plan and went home to verify the report as published in *The Court Circular*.

The next day he laid his case before Lin Ruhai.

"What a lucky coincidence!" exclaimed Ruhai. "Since my wife's death, my mother-in-law in the capital has been expecting to help bring up my daughter. She has sent two boats with a dozen servants to fetch her, but the departure has been delayed because my Black Jade has not fully recovered her health. Now this gives me a chance to show you my appreciation. I will write a letter to my brother-in-law in the capital, asking him to do all he can for you as a small return for your kindness. You don't have to worry about your expenses. I will make that point clear to my brother-in-law."

Yucun bowed politely with many thanks and asked, "May I know your respected brother-in-law's position? I don't want to be too rude or to intrude on him."

Ruhai smiled, "My humble kinsmen belong to your honorable clan. They are the grandsons of the Duke of Rongguo. My elder brother-in-law, Jia She, is a hereditary general of the first rank. My second brother-in-law, Jia Zheng, is an Under-Secretary in the Board of Public Works. He is a man of simplicity and generosity who takes after his grandfather. That's why I'm writing to him."

This confirmed what Leng had told him the previous day, and once more Yucun expressed his thanks.

"I've chosen the second day of the next month for my daughter's departure," continued Ruhai. "Would it suit both of you, if you were to travel together?"

Yucun readily agreed with the greatest satisfaction, and left with gifts and the traveling expenses Ruhai had prepared for him.

Black Jade, of course, didn't want to leave her father, but she had to comply with the wishes of her grandmother. So, parting from him in a flood of tears, she embarked in the first boat with her nurse and some elderly maidservants sent from the Honored Mansion. Yucun and two boy servants followed in the second boat.

In due course they arrived at the capital. Yucun immediately put on his best coat and went with his servants to the gate of the Honored Mansion, where he handed in his visiting card.

Jia Zheng had already received his brother-in-law's letter of introduction, and so he invited Yucun in without hesitation. Jia Zheng followed the tradition of his grandfather in being delighted to honor worthy men of letters and to help those in distress. As his brother-in-law had recommended Yucun to him beforehand, he treated Yucun extremely well and did his best to help him.

The very day Yucun presented a petition to the Emperor, he was granted a new appointment. Within less than two months he was sent to fill the vacated post of prefect close to the capital. Taking leave of his patron Jia Zheng, Yucun chose a proper day to proceed to his new post.

3/ Black Jade Meets Magic Jade

When Black Jade disembarked at the capital, she found a sedan chair and luggage carts awaiting her. They had been sent by the Honored Mansion.

She had heard a great deal from her mother about the wealth and grandeur of her grandmother's home; and during the last few days she had been impressed by the food, clothing, and behavior of the low-ranking attendants accompanying her. She realized she must watch her step in her new home. She must act with utmost prudence and never say too much, or else she might be laughed at.

After what seemed a long journey, they arrived at a street with two huge, stone lions crouching in front of a great triple gate with beast-head door knockers. A dozen servants in splendid, brightly-colored livery were waiting there. The central gate was shut, but people were going in and out of the smaller side gates. On a tablet above the central gate was written, in large Chinese characters: "Peaceful Mansion, Built by Imperial Command."

Black Jade's sedan chair was then carried through another gateway, of similar style and size, a little further up the street. This was the entrance to the Honored Mansion. The bearers put the sedan chair down, and then four smartly-dressed lads of seventeen or eighteen came, picked it up, and carried it to a gate decorated with flowery patterns carved in wood. There, the bearers withdrew. They had been followed by the maids, who raised the curtain of the chair, helped Black Jade out, and supported her through the gate. At that point several other maids, dressed in red and green, rose to greet her from where they had been sitting on the door step.

"The old lady was just talking about you," they cried. "And here you are." Three or four of them ran to raise the door curtain. A voice could be heard announcing, "Miss Lin is here!"

Black Jade entered. A silver-haired old lady, supported by two maids, came forward to meet her. She knew that this must be her grandmother. Before Black Jade could kneel down to kowtow, the old lady threw both arms around her.

"Darling! My flesh and blood!" cried the Lady Dowager, bursting into tears. The attendants were so moved that they began sobbing at this sight. Black Jade couldn't hold back her own tears. She knelt before her grandmother, and was consoled by others nearby.

A few moments later, one by one, the Lady Dowager introduced the family. "This is your eldest aunt; this is your younger aunt; this is the wife of your late cousin Zhu." Black Jade greeted each in turn.

"Now the young ladies may come," the grandmother announced. "They can be excused from their lessons today in honor of our guest from afar."

Two maids went to carry out her orders.

Presently three young ladies appeared, escorted by three nurses and six maids. The first was somewhat plump and of medium height, with icy-fresh cheeks and a nice nose—a charming sight. Gentle and quiet, she looked approachable. The second was slender, slim-waisted, and had an oval face, well-defined eyebrows, and lovely dancing eyes. She seemed elegant and quick-witted, with an air of distinction. It was probable that a glance at her would make anyone forget vulgar things. The third was not yet fully grown and still had the face of a child. All three wore similar tunics and skirts, with matching bracelets and head ornaments.

Black Jade hastily rose to greet her three cousins. After the introductions, they all sat down while the maids served tea. Much of the conversation centered on the topic of Black Jade's mother. How had she fallen ill? What medicine did the doctors prescribe? Had the funeral and mourning ceremonies been completed properly? The Lady Dowager, of course, was painfully affected by all the details.

"Among all my children I loved your mother the most," she told Black Jade. "Now she has gone before me, and I didn't even get one last glimpse of her. The mere sight of you almost breaks my heart!" Again, in her excitement, she took Black Jade into her arms and wept. The others had difficulty in comforting her.

To everyone's surprise, Black Jade seemed to have good breeding for a girl of her age. She possessed an air of romantic distinction, although she appeared too slight even to bear the trifling weight of her own clothing. Seeing how frail she was, they asked what tonics and treatment she had taken.

"I've always been like this," Black Jade said with a smile. "I've been swallowing bitter pills ever since I was old enough to take my own meals. I remember when I was three, a scabby monk came to our house and wanted to take me away to become a nun so that I might be cured. My parents wouldn't let me go. The monk told them, 'If you can't bear to part with her, she'll probably never get well. The only remedy will be for you to keep her from hearing any weeping and to prevent her from meeting any other relatives. That's her only hope of being able to lead a peaceful life.' Fortunately, no one took the talk of this crazy monk seriously. However, I have been taking health-giving ginseng pills ever since."

"That's fine," said the grandmother. "We're just having some of those pills made for us here, and I'll see that they make a dose for you."

Just then they heard peals of laughter coming from the backyard, and a voice saying, "Oh, I'm late in greeting our guest from afar."

The relatives in the room became suddenly tense at hearing this voice. Black Jade thought to herself, the people here all seem to be holding in their breaths. Who can it be that makes them react in this way?

A smartly-dressed young lady entered from behind the back room. She was surrounded by many ladies-in-waiting and maids. Unlike the others, she was quite richly dressed and glittered with jewels. She had the almond-shaped eyes of a phoenix and slanting eyebrows as long and drooping as

willow leaves. Her figure was slender and her manner flirta-
tious. Her vermilion lips were parted in a sparkling smile.

Black Jade rose quickly to greet her.

"You don't know her yet," the Lady Dowager chuckled.
"She's the terror of this house. In South China they'd call her
'Hot Pepper'! Well, you can just call her 'Fiery Phoenix'!"

Black Jade was somewhat confused as to how to properly
address the new arrival, but her cousins came to her rescue.
Even though Black Jade had never met this woman, she knew
from what her mother had told her that this must be her
sister-in-law, the niece of Lady Wang and her second uncle's
wife. Black Jade lost no time in greeting her with a smile.

Madam Phoenix took Black Jade by the hand, inspected
her from head to foot, and then led her back to her seat beside the Lady Dowager.

"Well," she said, "you are the most charming beauty in
the world. No wonder our Old Ancestress couldn't put you
out of her mind and was forever talking about you. How sad
that our poor, ill-fated cousin should lose her mother when
she was so young!" With that, she dabbed her eyes with a
handkerchief.

"I've just dried my tears," said the Lady Dowager playfully, "do you want to start me off again?"

Madam Phoenix immediately switched from grief to joy.
"Of course not. I was so carried away by the sight of my little
cousin that I forgot our Old Ancestress. I really deserve a
slapping!" Then, taking Black Jade by the hand once more,
she plied her with questions: "How old are you? Have you
started your schooling yet? What medicine are you taking?"
And then she said, "You mustn't be homesick here. If you
fancy anything special to eat or play with, don't hesitate to let
me know. If the maids or old nurses aren't good to you, just
tell me."

Next she turned to the servants and asked, "Have Miss
Lin's luggage and other things been brought in? How many
attendants did she bring with her? Hurry up and clear out a
couple of rooms where they can have a good rest."

From all of this Black Jade got the impression that this sister-in-law was the soul of the great household. Meanwhile tea and refreshments were served. As Madam Phoenix handed around the delicacies, Lady Wang asked her whether she had distributed the monthly allowance.

"It's finished," was Madam Phoenix's answer. "Just now I took some people to the upstairs storeroom to get the brocade, and though we searched for a long time, we couldn't find any of the sort you described yesterday. Could your memory have played a trick on you?"

"It doesn't matter if there's none of that sort," said Lady Wang, "just choose any kind to make your little cousin some clothes."

"I've already done that," said Madam Phoenix, "as soon as I learned that my cousin would be coming one of these days, I had the material prepared for inspection. With your permission, it can be sent over right now."

The refreshments were cleared away, and the Lady Dowager then ordered two nurses to take Black Jade to see her two uncles.

At once Lady Xing, Jia She's wife, rose to her feet and suggested, "Wouldn't it be simpler if I were to take my niece?"

"Very well," agreed the Lady Dowager, "and there's no need for you to come back afterwards."

Escorted by Lady Xing, Black Jade got into a curtained blue-lacquered sedan chair that was resting on wheels. It was apparently a long distance to the residence of her elder uncle. The sedan chair was not set down until they had passed through many courtyards and gateways.

When they stopped, Lady Xing took Black Jade by the hand and led her into a reception hall. It seemed to Black Jade that this part of the gigantic estate must be located in the mansion gardens. She had seen them through the ceremonial gates when she first arrived. The gardens contained finely constructed halls, side chambers, and covered corridors set among groups of trees, plants, and artificial rockeries.

As they entered the hall, they were greeted by a group of heavily made-up and richly dressed concubines and maids. Lady Xing sent a message to her husband, who was said to be in the study, and then invited Black Jade to be seated.

After a while, the servant returned to report, "Master says he hasn't been feeling well the last few days; and he's not able to meet Miss Lin at this time. But she should make herself at home here."

After expressing her gratitude, Black Jade rose to take leave. Lady Xing saw her out and gave some instructions to the maids, waiting there until Black Jade's sedan chair was out of sight.

When the bearers stopped and Black Jade got down from her conveyance, she was met by nurses who escorted her around a corner, through a ceremonial gate, and into a large courtyard. She looked around in astonishment. The building in front of her had five huge apartments and wings on either side. A broad, raised avenue led straight to the gate of a central reception hall. Black Jade soon learned that this was the main inner suite.

She entered the hall, and the maids in attendance served her tea. As she sipped it, she studied them, observing that their make-up, clothes, and manners were quite different from those she had seen in other families. Then, before she had time to finish drinking her tea, a maid came in and announced:

"Her Ladyship asks Miss Lin to go inside and take a seat."

Black Jade was directed by the nurses along the eastern corridor and into a small three-roomed suite that faced south. On the bed under the window was a low table laden with books and a tea service. Lady Wang was sitting there in the seat of lesser importance by the west wall. She invited her niece to sit beside her. But Black Jade hesitated, guessing that this was her uncle's seat, eventually sitting down only after she had been pressed several times to do so by her aunt.

"Your uncle is worshipping in the temple today, fasting and chanting Buddhist sutras," Lady Wang said. "You'll see him some other time. But I want to tell you about my dreadful son, a true torment in this house—a real devil. He's gone to a temple today to fulfill a vow, but you'll see what he's like when he comes back this evening. Pay no attention to him. None of your cousins dare to provoke him. Be careful not to do so yourself."

Black Jade's mother had often spoken of this cousin born with a piece of jade in his mouth. She knew Lady Wang must be referring to him.

"Do you mean my elder cousin, the one born with jade in his mouth?" she asked with a smile. "Mother often spoke of him. I know he's a year older than I am, that his name is Magic Jade (Baoyu), and that for all his mischief he's very kind to his girl cousins. How can I provoke him? I'll be spending all my time with the girls in one part of the house while my boy cousins are in the outer courtyards."

"You don't understand," replied Lady Wang, laughing. "He's not like other boys. Because the Lady Dowager is always doting on him, he's used to being spoiled with the girls. When they ignore him, he keeps fairly quiet, though he is bored. But if the girls give him the least encouragement, he becomes so elated that he gets up to all kinds of mischief. One moment he's all honey-sweet; the next, he's rude and foolish, raving like a lunatic. You can't take him seriously."

Black Jade promised to remember this. At that point a maid came in and announced that dinner was ready to be served in the Lady Dowager's apartment. Lady Wang led her niece out the back door and along several zigzag paths. On the way, she stopped to point to a dainty house. It was built in three tiers with a verandah running along its south side. Behind it was a small door leading to an apartment.

"That's where your cousin Phoenix lives," Lady Wang said, "so now you know where to find her. If you need anything, just let her know."

The old lady was already awaiting them in the dining room. Despite her modesty, Black Jade was obliged to take the seat of honor at her grandmother's left side.

The outer room swarmed with nurses and waiting maids, but not so much as a cough could be heard from there. The dinner was finished in silence. Black Jade noted that many table manners here were quite different from those in her own home. She decided she would have to quickly adapt herself to these new ways.

"The others may go now," said the Lady Dowager, as she rose from the table after the tea was served. "I wish to chat with our guest alone."

At these words Lady Wang promptly rose and led the way out, followed by Phoenix and other ladies. Then the Lady Dowager asked Black Jade what books she had read.

"I've just finished reading the Four Confucian Classics," said Black Jade, "but I'm still ignorant." Black Jade then inquired what her cousins were reading.

"They only know a few Chinese characters, not enough to really read any books," said the Lady Dowager.

These words were hardly finished when they heard footsteps in the courtyard, and a maid came in to announce, "Magic Jade is here!"

Black Jade, wondering what sort of graceless, slow-learner Magic Jade must be, awaited his entrance in eager expectation. But she was most pleasantly surprised the moment she saw him because he turned out to be such a good-looking young gentleman. His face was as bright as the full Mid-Autumn moon, his color as fresh as spring flowers at dawn. The hair above his temples was sharply outlined as if cut by a knife, and his eyebrows were jet black as if they had been painted with ink. His cheeks were as red as peach blossoms and his eyes were as bright as the wet shine of autumn ripples. She soon found out that even when he was angry he seemed to smile, and that there was warmth in his glance even when he frowned. Around his neck hung a golden chain in the form of a dragon and a silk cord of five colors from which dangled a beautiful piece of jade and a locket-shaped amulet containing his Buddhist name and lucky charm.

Black Jade was completely taken by surprise at his appearance. How very strange, she thought to herself. He looks somewhat familiar, as if I have seen him somewhere before.

Magic Jade paid his respects to the Lady Dowager and then quickly went away to see his mother, Lady Wang.

He returned before long, having changed his clothes. But he still wore the necklace with the jade and locket-shaped amulet hanging from it.

With a smile directed towards Magic Jade, the Lady Dowager said, "Fancy changing your clothes before meeting our guest! Hurry up now and greet your cousin."

Magic Jade, of course, had noticed this new cousin earlier and guessed that this charming young lady was the daughter of his Aunt Lin. He bowed to her before he took a seat. Gazing at her attentively, he soon recognized how different she was from other girls. Her eyebrows were knitted and yet not frowning, her sparkling eyes held both joy and sorrow, and her breath was soft but faint. In repose, he mused, she must be like a lovely flower mirrored in the water; in motion, like an easily-bent willow branch swaying in the wind.

"I've met this cousin before," Magic Jade declared with a smile, after he had thoroughly scrutinized her.

"You're talking nonsense," said his grandmother, laughing. "How could you possibly have met her?"

"Well, her face looks familiar; I feel we're old friends, meeting again after a long separation."

"So much the better," said the Lady Dowager, laughing. "That means you are bound to be good friends."

Magic Jade sat beside Black Jade and once more fixed his gaze on her. "Have you done much reading, cousin?" he asked.

"No," said Black Jade, "I've only studied for a couple of years and learned but a few Chinese characters."

"May I know your name?"

She told him her name.

"And your courtesy name?"

"Sorry, I have none," she replied.

"I'll give you one," he proposed with a chuckle. "As your eyebrows look half knit, what could be better than the two characters for knitted brows?"

Then he asked Black Jade if she had any jade.

Imagining that he had his own jade in mind, she answered, "No, I haven't. I suppose it's too rare for everybody to have one."

This instantly threw Magic Jade into a frenzy of rage. Tearing the jade from his neck, he flung it on the floor.

"What's rare about it?" he stormed. "It can't even tell good people from bad. What spiritual understanding does it have? I don't want this nasty thing!"

In consternation all the maids rushed forward to pick up the jade. The Lady Dowager immediately took her grandson in her arms.

"You wicked monster!" she said. "Be angry with people if you want to. But why should you throw away the one magic thing that your life depends on?"

Magic Jade, his face stained with tears, sobbed, "None of the girls here have one, only me. What's the fun of that? Even this newly arrived angel-like cousin hasn't got one. It's no good at all!"

"Your new cousin also came into the world with a jade like that," lied the grandmother to quiet him. "Out of filial piety she buried it with her mother, so that even in death a bit of herself would stay with her deceased mother. Now be sensible, my darling boy. What would your mother say if she heard about this silly behavior of yours?"

She took the jade from one of the maids and put it back around his neck. Magic Jade, convinced by his grandmother's tale, let the matter drop.

Just then a nurse came in to ask about Black Jade's quarters. "Move Magic Jade into the inner apartment of my suite," said the grandmother. "Miss Lin can stay, for the time being, in his apartment in the Green Pavilion. When winter is over, I'll arrange another place for her."

"Dear grandmother," begged Magic Jade, "let me stay in the Green Pavilion. I can sleep quite well in a side chamber. Why should I move over and disturb your peace?"

After a moment's consideration, the Lady Dowager agreed. Magic Jade and Black Jade each would be attended by a nurse and a maid, while other attendants were on night service outside.

Black Jade had brought with her only Nanny Wang, her old wet nurse, and ten-year-old Snowswan. The Lady Dowager considered Snowswan too young and Nanny Wang too old for service, so she gave her granddaughter another maid, one named Cuckoo. In addition Black Jade was assigned half a dozen maids for other light and heavy work.

Nanny Wang and Cuckoo accompanied Black Jade to the Green Pavilion where Magic Jade's wet nurse, Nanny Li, and his chief maid, Aroma, made a bed ready for him in the outer room.

That night when Magic Jade and Nanny Li were asleep, Aroma noticed that Black Jade and Cuckoo were still awake in the inner room. She tiptoed in there wearing her nightdress and asked, "Why are you still up, miss?"

"Sit down, please, sister," invited Black Jade with a smile.

Aroma sat on the edge of the bed.

"Miss Lin has been in tears all this time; she's so upset," said Cuckoo. "The very day of her arrival, she says, she made our young master flare up. If he'd smashed his jade into pieces, she would have felt it was her fault. I've been trying to cheer her up."

"Don't take it so much to heart, dear young lady," said Aroma, "I'm afraid you'll have more strange and absurd experiences with him later on. You won't get a moment's rest if you let yourself be upset by his queer manners. Don't be so sensitive!"

"Thank you, sister. I'11 remember that," promised Black Jade, somewhat calmed. Then, after a little more talking, they all went to bed.

Black Jade soon became the Lady Dowager's favorite niece, treated in every respect as well as was Magic Jade. The other cousins had to take a back seat and, by and by, Magic Jade and Black Jade became as closely attached to each other as glue and lacquer. In fact, the two became inseparable. On all matters they seemed to see things eye to eye. In the evening they went to bed in the same apartment.

4/ Xue Pan and the Murder Case

Now let's return to Jia Yucun. Shortly after he took up his post as prefect, a case of a murder was brought into his court. It involved a dispute over the ownership of a pretty slave girl who had been purchased by two different people. Neither side had been willing to give way, and one of the buyers was subsequently beaten to death. Yucun summoned the plaintiff for interrogation.

"The murdered man was my master," the plaintiff testified. "He bought and paid for the slave girl without knowing that she'd been kidnapped. The young master said he'd wait for three days before taking her home because the third day was a lucky one according to the Chinese calendar. The kidnapper, meanwhile, sold the slave girl again, this time to a member of the Xue family. When my master found this out, he went to the slave dealer to demand the girl.

"Unfortunately, the Xues are a family of wealth and power in Jinling. They lord it over everyone. A bunch of their thugs beat my master to death. After that, the murderers, master and men, made off with the slave. They disappeared without a trace, leaving only a few people behind who weren't involved in the case. I brought a charge against them a year ago, but nothing came of it. I beg Your Honor to arrest the criminals and punish these evildoers so that justice may be done and innocence triumph over wickedness. If you do this, both the living and dead will be grateful to you forever!"

"What? A murderer is allowed to go scot free? How is that possible?" fumed Yucun. He was about to issue warrants for the arrest and interrogation of the criminals' relatives, when an attendant, standing nearby, shot him a warning glance. Yucun took the hint, and dismissed everyone but the attendant.

The attendant then made haste to salute, and said: "Your Honor has risen steadily in the official world. However, I am wondering if you still remember me after eight or nine years?"

"Well, your face looks familiar, but I can't place you at the moment," replied Yucun.

The attendant smiled. "So you've forgotten the place you started from. Can you still remember your life in the Gourd Temple, Your Honor?"

At this remark, the past came back to Yucun like a thunderbolt. He remembered this attendant as one of his acquaintances in Suzhou. He was a novice at the temple.

"So, we are friends from the old days when I was hard up." said Yucun. "Old friendships made in times of poverty should not be forgotten. Since we're not in a public court, I wish you would explain why you gave me a warning glance just as I was ready to issue the warrants."

"Has no Protection List for this province been given to you since you've come to this post, sir?" asked the attendant.

"What do you mean by Protection List?"

"You know, all local officials nowadays keep a secret list of the most powerful, wealthy, and high-ranking families in their provinces. Each province has such a list. If you offend one of these families without knowing it, you may lose more than just your post. You might lose your life. That's why it's called a Protection List. This Xue family is one you can't afford to offend. There's nothing difficult about this case, of course, but your predecessor took care never to settle it because it involved a member of the Xue family. Xue Pan's guilt is obvious, but it pays to be careful."

With that the attendant took a handwritten copy of the Protection List from his pocket and handed it to Yucun. It was a catalog of the most powerful families in that district, written in poetic form. It read like this:

The Jia families,
If truth be told,
Have halls of jade,
Stables of gold.

Vast O Fang Palace,
Fit for the King of Qin.
Isn't fine enough
For the Shes of Jinling.

If the Dragon King wants
A white jade bed,
He turns to the Wangs
Of Jinling, it's said.

The Xues in their power
Are so rich and grand,
Gold is like iron to them
And pearls like the sand.

"These four families are closely connected," explained the attendant. "The punishment you mete out to one family hits all four; and the honor you show to one family is shared by the others. Anyway, they help and protect one another. The murderer, Xue Pan, is a member of one of the big four familles. Not only can he count on the support of the three other families, but he has plenty of influential friends and relatives in both the capital and the provinces. So who is Your Honor going to arrest?"

"If that's the situation, how are we to settle the case?" asked Yucun. "I take it you may know the murderer's hiding place?"

"I won't keep it from you, sir." The attendant grinned. "I not only know where the murderer has gone, but I also know the kidnapper who sold the girl, and I knew the poor devil who bought her. I will tell you the whole story.

"The murdered man was named Feng Yuan. He was a member of a modest family of local gentry. Up to the age of eighteen or nineteen he was by nature averse to women, and preferred the companionship of men. But then he became infatuated with this girl slave, and decided to buy her as his concubine. He swore to take no other wife. He took the matter so seriously that he even consulted the calendar to find a lucky day on which to take her home. How could he anticipate that the kidnapper would also sell that girl on the sly to the Xues, in order to get a double payment? But before the kidnapper could get away with this scheme, he fell into the hands of the two rivals and was beaten within an inch of his life. Both parties refused to take back their money—both wanted the girl. Then young Xue ordered his men to beat Feng Yuan to a pulp. Three days after Feng Yuan was carried back home, he died.

"Young Xue had already set the date for his trip to the capital. He decided to take the girl along, as if nothing had happened. He then set off with his household, leaving his clansmen and servants here to settle the affairs. A trifling matter such as taking a man's life didn't scare him a bit. So much for him. Do you know who the girl is?"

"How could I know?"

"Little Lotus, the daughter of your great patron, Zhen Shiyin, the one who lived next to Gourd Temple."

"Well!" exclaimed Yucun in astonishment. "So that's who she is! I heard that she was kidnapped when she was five. Why didn't they sell her before?"

"Kidnappers like this often steal small girls and raise them until they are twelve or thirteen years of age, then sell them elsewhere. Do you remember how we used to play with Lotus every day? I could easily recognize her by the red birthmark, the size of a grain of rice, that she has between her eyebrows."

"Because the kidnapper once rented rooms from me, I often saw her. One day, when he was away and she was alone in the house, I went to her and questioned her extensively. She'd been beaten so much she was afraid to talk to me. She insisted that the kidnapper was her father, and that he was selling her to clear his debts. When I tried again and again to get her to talk about her childhood, she burst into tears and said she couldn't remember a thing about it. But I have no doubt that it's her."

"The day that Feng Yuan met her and paid the price for her, the kidnapper got drunk. Lotus just sighed and said, 'At last my trials are over!' However, this world is full of disappointments. The very next day she was sold to the Xues. Xue Pan started a big fight and dragged her off by force, more dead than alive. What's become of her since, I don't know. Feng Yuan dreamed of happiness, but instead of finding it lost both his money and his life. Poor luck, wasn't it?"

"So this romance was an empty dream, a chance encounter between an ill-fated young couple. What's the best way to settle this case?"

"You were shrewd enough in the past, sir," said the attendant with a smile. "What's made you so short of ideas today? You owe your present post to the patronage of the Jias and Wangs, and this Xue Pan is related to the Jias by marriage. So why not sail with the stream and do them a good turn by dropping the matter gracefully so that you can face them in the future?"

"Hm, that sounds reasonable," Yucun replied. "Nevertheless, a man's life is involved. Moreover, I've been reinstated by the Emperor's favor. I should be doing my utmost to show my gratitude. How can I ignore the law for private considerations? I really can't bring myself just to drop the matter."

The attendant continued, "Your Honor is right, of course. But that won't get you anywhere in the world today. Remember the old sayings: 'A gentleman adapts himself to circumstances,' and 'The superior man is one who pursues good fortune and avoids disaster.' If you do as you just said, not only will you be unable to repay the Emperor's trust, you may also endanger your own life. Better think it over carefully."

Yucun lowered his head. After a long silence he asked, "What do you suggest, then?"

"I've thought of a very good plan," said the attendant. "It's this. When you try the case tomorrow, make a great show of issuing the warrants. The murderer, of course, won't be coming and the plaintiff will press the case. You can then arrest some of the Xue clansmen and servants for interrogation. Behind the scenes, I'll fix things up for you by asking them to report Xue Pan's 'death by sudden illness.' We'll even get his clansmen and the local authorities to testify to this farce. Since this trouble was caused by the man who kidnapped the girl, he must be dealt with according to the law, but no one else is involved...and so on and so forth.

"The Xues are rolling in money. You can make them pay five hundred or a thousand ounces of silver for Feng's funeral expenses. Feng's relatives are people of no importance, and all they're out of is money. So the money will shut their mouths! What do you think of this scheme of mine, sir?"

"Impossible," Yucun laughed. "I'll have to think it over carefully in order to suppress idle talk."

The consultation between the two had lasted late into the afternoon.

The next day a number of suspects were summoned to court and Yucun cross-examined them carefully. He found that the Feng family was indeed a small one and only interested in getting some money for a funeral. The case had been confused and left unsettled because of the Xue's powerful connections.

Yucun, therefore, twisted the law to suit his own purpose and passed an arbitrary judgment. The Fengs received a large sum for funeral expenses and made no further objections.

Once the case was settled, Yucun lost no time in writing to Jia Zheng and General Wang, the Commander of the Garrison, to inform them that the charge against their nephew was now dropped and so they need not worry about it any longer.

Although the scheme had been developed by the attendant who had been a novice in Gourd Temple and who had thus saved Yucun from much embarrassment, and perhaps even saved his life, Yucun was dismayed by the thought that this man might disclose certain facts about the trying days when he was poor and humble. Yucun thus later found some fault with the attendant and exiled him to a distant region.

Xue Pan, the one who had bought Lotus and had Feng Yuan beaten to death, came from a scholarly and very rich family, one that received a handsome income from the State Treasury. But Xue Pan, being an only son and having lost his father while still a child, was spoiled by his mother and grew up as a good-for-nothing. By the age of five or six he began to demonstrate extravagant habits, rough manners, and arrogant speech. At school he learned little, and spent most of his time at cockfights, in riding, or in taking pleasure trips.

Although he was appointed a Court Purchaser, he knew nothing of business or worldly affairs. He relied on his grandfather's old connections to find him a well-paid and light job in the Ministry of Finance. He left all business matters to his agents and old family servants.

His widowed mother, Madame Wang, was the younger sister of the Commander of the Garrison and the sister of Lady Wang, the wife of Jia Zheng of the Honored Mansion. Besides Xue Pan, she had a daughter two years younger than him, whose infant name was Precious Hairpin (Baochai). The daughter was a beautiful, dainty girl of great natural refinement. While her father was still alive, he required her to study, and she grew up to be ten times the better person than her brother.

Shortly before the incident involving the slave girl Lotus, the Emperor had ordered his court officials to compile a list of daughters of ministers and noted families, so that virtuous and gifted companions could be chosen for the princesses from the list.

Xue Pan, having heard of the splendors of the capital for a long time, looked forward for a chance to visit there. Now he had three reasons for such a visit: first, to escort his sister there for the selection; second, to visit his relatives; and third, to settle some official matters. His real reason, of course, was so that he could enjoy the grand sights of the great metropolis.

He prepared for the trip by packing his luggage and valuables and by choosing local specialties of every kind as gifts for relatives and friends. He then selected a favorable day for the departure and, while waiting for that day, met the kidnapper who was selling Lotus. Struck by her good looks, Xue Pan promptly purchased her. Then, when Feng Yuan demanded her back, Xue Pan ordered his bullies to beat the man to death. Quickly entrusting the family affairs to some clansmen and old servants, he left with his mother and sister for the capital. To him, a murder charge was a trifle that could be easily settled with a handful of coins.

After some days on the journey and as they were approaching the capital, word came of the promotion of his uncle, General Wang, to the post of Commander of Nine Provinces with orders to inspect the frontiers. This news was a relief to Xue Pan. He now suggested to his mother, "Although we have some houses in the capital, none of us has lived there for ten years or more, and the caretakers may have rented them out to others. Let's send someone ahead to have one of them cleaned up."

"Why go to such trouble?" his mother asked. "When we arrive, we should first call on our relatives and friends. I know what you're after. You're afraid of being under restraint, if you stay with your uncle or aunt. You'd prefer to be on your own, free to do as you please. In that case, go and find some lodgings for yourself. I've been parted all these years from your aunt, and we old sisters want to spend a little time together. I'll take your younger sister there with me. Have you any objections to that?"

Realizing that he could not talk his mother around to his plan, Xue Pan told his servants to make straight for the Honored Mansion. There Xue Pan, his mother, and his sister, Precious Hairpin, were received with the greatest cordiality. Both the Lady Dowager and Aunt Jia urged them to stay on in Uncle Jia Zheng's Pear Fragrance Garden.

The Pear Fragrance Garden was a delightful pleasure house. It was the favorite residence of the Duke of Yongguo in his old age. Small, but charming, its dozen or so rooms included a reception hall in the front and the usual sleeping quarters and offices in the back.

Each day after lunch or in the evening, Aunt Xue would walk over to chat with the Lady Dowager or to talk with her sister. Precious Hairpin spent her time with Black Jade and the other girls. She was quite happy to read, play chess, and do needlework with them. Xue Pan, however, disliked this arrangement. He feared that his uncle would control him so strictly that he could not be his own master. To his relief, after less than a month, he was able to make close friendships with Jia sons and nephews, and all the young men of fashion enjoyed his company. One day they would meet to drink, the next to enjoy flowers, and soon they included him in their gambling parties and amorous adventures. As a result, Xue Pan became ten times worse than before. And he made himself so much at home in his new surroundings that he soon gave up any thought of taking another residence.

5/ Granny Liu Enters the Honored Mansion

There were more than three hundred masters and servants living in the Honored Mansion. And, although there was not a great deal to do each day, there was always a score of things to be seen to. As the saying goes, it is easier to straighten out a skein of tangled hemp than to try to recount the strands.

One day, a humble individual, as insignificant as a mustard seed, came from three hundred miles away to pay a visit. The visitor, Granny Liu, was remotely related to this rich and mighty household. But before I tell of the visit, let me say something about her family.

Granny Liu's family name was Wang. Her grandfather was, at one time, a petty official in the capital. It is there that he came to know Madam Phoenix's grandfather, the father of Lady Wang. Eager to attach himself to the powerful Wang clan, he claimed kinship with them, calling himself Wang's nephew.

The grandfather died leaving only a grandson, Gouer. This grandson married a woman from a family named Liu. She gave birth to a son and a daughter. This family of four lived on a farm outside the capital. Because Gouer was busy tending the farm all day and his wife had a lot of housework to do, there was no one to take care of the children. Gouer, therefore, asked his mother-in-law, Granny Liu, to live with them and care for the tots.

Granny Liu was an old widow who had gone through thick and thin with no son or daughter-in-law to help her. She had tried, rather unsuccessfully, to support herself on two *mu* of poor land. She was therefore only too glad to be taken in and cared for by her son-in-law. She did her best to be helpful to her daughter's family.

When autumn came to an end and the early winter turned cold, Gouer's family suddenly realized that they had made no provision for winter. Gouer began to drink heavily in order to forget all his cares, and he tried to vent his spleen on his family. Granny Liu, however, was not going to put up with this.

"You mustn't mind me putting in my opinion, son-in-law," she advised, "but we villagers are simple honest folk who must make ends meet. Your trouble is that you had it too easy when you were young, so you're not good at family management. When you have money you don't plan ahead; when you are out of funds, you become worked up for no reason at all. Is that the proper way for a grown-up to behave? You know 'the streets in the capital are paved with gold,' but only for those who know how to lay their hands on it. What's the use of getting into a huff at home?"

"It's easy for you to jabber away," her son-in-law retorted. "Do you want me to go out and steal from someone?"

"Who's asking you to rob anyone?" she replied. "Let's put our heads together and think of something. Do you expect silver coins to come rolling in by themselves?"

"Would I have waited all this time if there was some way out?" her son-in-law snorted. "I've no relatives who live on rent, no friends in official posts. What can I do? Even if I had such friends, they'd probably cold-shoulder us."

"Don't be so sure," said Granny Liu, "Man proposes, Heaven disposes. I have thought of a chance for you. In the old days you joined families with the Wangs in the capital, and twenty years back you were decently received there. I remember calling on them once with my daughter. Their second young lady was really openhanded, very pleasant and free from airs. She's now the second wife of the second Lord Jia of the Honored Mansion. I hear she's grown even more charitable to the aged and poor. I'm sure this Lady Wang would still remember us. Why not go and try our luck?"

"Mother's right," put in her daughter. "But how could frights like us go to their gates? Most likely the gatekeepers would refuse to announce us. Why ask for a slap on the face?"

But her son-in-law was attracted by this suggestion. He laughed at his wife's objection and proposed, "Since this is your idea, mother, and you've called on the lady before, why not go there tomorrow and see how the wind blows?"

"Dear me! 'The threshold of a noble house is deeper than the sea.' Who am I? The servants there don't know me. It's no use my going."

"That's no problem. I'll tell you what to do. Take your grandson with you and ask for their steward, Old Zhou. That man had some dealings with my father and used to be on the best of terms with us."

"I know him, too," she said. "But how will they receive me after all this time? All right, I'm old enough not to mind risking a snub. If I have any luck we'll all share it." That evening the matter was settled.

The next morning Granny Liu got up before dawn to wash and comb her hair. She took her grandson with her and began the trip.

When she came to the Honored Mansion, she was too overawed by the crowd of sedan chairs and horses there to venture near to the stone lions that flanked the main gate. But, after dusting off her clothes and giving the boy some instructions, she timidly approached the side entrance. Inside, some arrogant servants, washing themselves in the sunshine, were engaged in a lively discussion.

Granny Liu edged forward and said, "Greetings, gentlemen!"

The men surveyed her from head to foot before asking where she came from.

"I've come to see Mr. Zhou, who came with Lady Wang when she was married," she told them with a smile. "May I trouble one of you gentlemen to fetch him for me?"

The men ignored her for a time, and then an old man said to the others, "Why make a fool of her and waste her time?" He told Granny Liu, "Old Zhou has gone south, but his wife is still here. Their house is at the back. Go around to the back gate and ask for her there."

Thanking him greatly, Granny Liu took the boy around to the back gate. Several peddlers had put down their wares there, and about two dozen rowdy servant boys were crowded around those who were selling snacks and toys. The old woman caught hold of one of these youngsters and asked, "Can you tell me, brother, if Mrs. Zhou is at home?"

"Which Mrs. Zhou?" the boy retorted. "We have several Zhous here. What's her job?"

"She is the wife of Old Zhou, who came with Lady Wang as her attendant."

"That's easy then. Come with me."

He walked ahead of her through the back gate to the compound where Mrs. Zhou could be found. "That's where she lives," the boy said, and then he called, "Auntie Zhou! Here's a granny asking for you."

Mrs. Zhou hurried out to see who it was, while Granny Liu hastened forward crying, "Sister Zhou! How are you?"

It took Mrs. Zhou some time to recognize her. Then she answered with a smile, "Why, it's Granny Liu! After all these years I hardly recognized you. Come on in and sit down."

Once indoors, Mrs. Zhou told a maid to serve tea. Then, after a short exchange of polite greetings, she asked Granny Liu whether she just happened to be passing by or if she had come for any special purpose.

"I came especially to see you, sister, and also to pay a visit to Her Ladyship. If you could take me to see her, that would be fine. If not, I'll just trouble you to pass on my respects to her."

Since Liu's son-in-law had once helped her husband to purchase some land, she could hardly refuse Granny Liu's appeal for help. Besides, she wanted to show her that she was someone of consequence in this household.

"Don't worry, granny," she replied with a smile. "Because you've come all this way in earnest, I'll surely help you to see the real Buddha in this household. Strictly speaking, it's not my job to announce visitors. But since you're related to Her Ladyship and have come to me for help, I'll make an exception and take in the message for you.

"Things have changed here in the last five years. Her Ladyship doesn't handle much business any more, but leaves everything to the second master's wife. And who do you think she is? My lady's own niece, the daughter of her elder brother and the one whose childhood name was Master Feng."

"You don't say," cried Granny Liu. "No wonder I predicted big things for her. In that case I must see her today."

"Of course. Nowadays Her Ladyship can't be troubled much with business, so she leaves it to the young mistress to entertain visitors. Even if you don't see Her Ladyship, you must see the young mistress, or your visit will have been wasted."

"Buddha be praised! I'm most grateful for your help, sister."

"Don't say that. 'He who helps others helps himself.' All I need to do is to say one word. It's no trouble at all." She then sent her maid in to see if the Lady Dowager's meal had been served.

The two went on chatting for some time until the maid came back to report, "The old lady's finished her meal. The second mistress is with Lady Wang."

At once Mrs. Zhou urged Granny Liu to hurry. "Come on! Our chance is now while she is having her own meal. Let's go and wait for her. Later on there will be such a crowd there on business, we'll hardly get a chance to talk to her."

Granny Liu, holding the boy, followed Mrs. Zhou by the winding ways to Jia Lian's quarters. There, Mrs. Zhou explained who Granny Liu was to Madam Phoenix's trusted maid, Patience. The maid agreed to invite them in to sit down. As they mounted the steps to the main reception room, another maid raised a curtain and a waft of perfume greeted them as they entered. Granny Liu did not know what it was, but felt she was walking on air. She was so dazzled by everything in the room that her head began to swim. She could only nod, smack her lips, and cry "Gracious Buddha!"

Patience was now standing in the east room. Casting two searching glances at Granny Liu, she greeted her and bade her be seated.

Patience's silk dress, her gold and silver trinkets, and her face were as pretty as a flower. Granny Liu almost made the mistake of taking her for her mistress. But before she could greet her as "my lady," she heard the girl and Mrs. Zhou address each other as equals and so realized that this was just one of the more favored maids.

After waiting for some time in the reception room, a group of maids ran in crying: "The mistress is coming!" Patience and Mrs. Zhou stood up at once, telling Granny Liu to wait till she was sent for.

In the distance laughter rang out. Ten to twenty serving women swished through the hall to another inner room, while two or three others bearing lacquered boxes came in and stood at the side to wait. When the order was given to serve the meal, all left except for a few who remained to hand round the dishes. A long silence followed. Then two women brought in a low table covered with scarcely touched dishes of fish and meat. Next, Mrs. Zhou came in to call Granny Liu with a smile.

Granny Liu, with the boy in hand, followed Mrs. Zhou into the hall. After some whispered advice from Mrs. Zhou, the three of them slowly entered Madam Phoenix's room.

Phoenix was nobly dressed with all sorts of ornaments. Heavily powdered, she sat erect as an angel, stirring the ashes of her hand stove to keep warm. Patience stood by her holding a small covered cup of tea on a tray, but Phoenix ignored the tea and kept her head lowered as she warmed her hands over the stove.

"Why haven't you brought her in yet?" Phoenix finally asked. Then raising her head to take the tea, she saw Mrs. Zhou with her two visitors before her. She made a motion as if to rise and greeted them with a radiant smile, blaming Mrs. Zhou for not speaking up earlier.

Granny Liu had already curtseyed several times to Phoenix who hastily said: "Help her up, Sister Zhou, she mustn't kowtow to me. Ask her to be seated. I'm too young to remember what our relationship is, so I don't know how to address her."

"This is the old lady I was just telling you about," said Mrs. Zhou. Phoenix nodded. By now Granny Liu had seated herself, and her grandson took refuge behind her. Coaxed to come forward and bow, the boy would not move an inch.

"When relatives don't visit each other they drift apart," observed Phoenix with a smile. "People who know us well would say you're neglecting us. Petty minded people who don't know us at all might imagine we look down upon everyone else."

She asked Mrs. Zhou if she had notified Lady Wang of the visit.

"I was waiting for madam's instructions," was the reply.

"Go and see how busy she is. If she has visitors, never mind. But if she is free, let her know who is here and see what she says."

After Mrs. Zhou left on this errand, Phoenix told the maids to give the boy some sweetmeats.

She was asking Granny Liu questions when Patience announced the arrival of a number of servants to report on affairs in their charge.

"I have a guest here now," said Phoenix. "They can come back this evening. Only bring in those whose business won't wait."

Patience went out, reappearing to report, "They've nothing urgent so I've sent them away."

As Phoenix nodded, Mrs. Zhou came back. "Her Ladyship isn't free today," she said. "She hopes you'll entertain the visitors and thank them for coming. If they have just dropped in for a call, well and good. If they have any business, they can discuss it with you, instead, madam."

"I've nothing special really," put in Granny Liu. "I just came to call on Her Ladyship and Madam Lian, seeing as how we're related."

"If you've nothing special, all right," said Mrs. Zhou. "But if you have, telling our second mistress is just the same as telling Her Ladyship." She winked at Granny Liu, who took the hint.

Although her face burned with shame, Granny Liu forced herself to pocket her pride and explain her reason for coming. "By rights, I shouldn't bring this up at our first meeting, madam. But as I've come all this way to ask your help. I guess I'd better speak up.

"The reason I brought your nephew here today is that his parents haven't a bit to eat. And winter's coming on, making things worse. So I brought your nephew here to ask for your help."

Granny Liu nudged her grandson. "Well, what did your dad tell you? What did he send you here for? Was it just to eat sweets?"

Phoenix smiled at this blunt way of talking. "Don't say any more. I understand."

She then asked Mrs. Zhou, "Has granny eaten anything yet?"

"We set out first thing in such a rush, we had no time to eat anything," said Granny Liu.

At once Phoenix ordered a meal for the visitors. Mrs. Zhou passed on the order and a table was set for them in the east room.

"Sister Zhou, see that they have all they want," said Phoenix, "I'm sorry, I can't keep them company."

After Mrs. Zhou had taken them to the east room, Phoenix called her back to find out what Lady Wang had said to her when she reported the visitors.

"Her Ladyship says they don't really belong to our family," Mrs. Zhou told her. "They joined families because they have the same surname and their grandfather was an official in the same place as our old master. We haven't seen much of them these last few years, but whenever they came we didn't let them go away empty-handed. Since they mean well in coming to see us, we shouldn't slight them. If they need any help, madam should use her own discretion."

"No wonder I was thinking that if we were really relatives it was strange that I didn't know the first thing about them," said Phoenix. At this point Granny Liu returned from her meal with her boy in tow, loud in her thanks.

"Sit down now and listen to me, dear old lady," said Phoenix cheerfully. "We shouldn't wait for relatives to come to our door before we take care of them. But we've plenty of troublesome business here, and now that Her Ladyship's growing old, she sometimes forgets things. Besides, when I took charge recently, I didn't really know all our family connections. Then again, although we may look prosperous, you must realize that a big household has difficulties of its own, though few may believe it. Since you've come so far today, and this is the first time you've asked me for help, I won't send you away empty-handed. Luckily Her Ladyship gave me twenty ounces of silver yesterday to make clothes for the maids, and I haven't touched it yet. If you don't think it too little, you can have it."

The talk of difficulties had at first dashed all Granny Liu's hopes, but now the promise of twenty ounces put her into a beaming smile. "Ah, I know what difficulties are," she said. "But 'A starved camel is bigger than a horse.' No matter how, 'A hair from your body is thicker than our waist'."

Mrs. Zhou tried to signal to her not to talk in this crude way, but Phoenix merely laughed and seemed not to mind. She sent Patience for the package of silver and a string of cash, which she then gave to the old woman. "Here's twenty taels to make the child some winter clothes. When you are free some other day, drop by again, as relatives should. It's growing late, I won't keep you any longer. Give my best regards to everyone at home to whom I should be remembered."

Phoenix stood up, and Granny Liu, having thanked her profusely, took the silver and cash and followed Mrs. Zhou toward the outside.

"My goodness gracious!" exclaimed Mrs. Zhou. "What possessed you to keep on talking to her about your nephew? At the risk of offending you, I must say that even if he were a real nephew you should have glossed over the matter."

"My dear sister!" Granny Liu beamed. "I was struck dumb at the sight of her and didn't know what to say."

Thus, chatting together, they reached the Zhou house and sat down for a few moments. Granny Liu wanted to leave a piece of silver for Mrs. Zhou so that she could buy sweets for her children, but this Mrs. Zhou resolutely declined. Such small sums meant nothing to her. Then, with boundless thanks, Granny Liu left by the back gate.

6/ Jiao Da, a Wild Servant in the Peaceful Mansion

When the lamps were lit, Madam Phoenix went to see Lady Wang.

With a smile Phoenix said, "Today, Brother Zhen's wife invited me to spend tomorrow with them. I haven't anything special to do that I know of."

"Even if you had, it wouldn't matter," Lady Wang replied. "She usually asks us all, but that can't be much fun for you. Since she's only invited you this time, obviously she wants you to have a little fun. Don't let her down. Even if you did have something to attend to, you ought to go."

Phoenix agreed and retired to her own room. The next morning, after Phoenix had finished her toilet, she went to tell Lady Wang that she was leaving. Then she went to tell the Lady Dowager. When Magic Jade heard where she was going, he insisted on going too. Phoenix had to agree and wait until he had changed his clothes. The two of them then drove quickly to the Peaceful Mansion.

Jia Zhen's wife, Madam You, and Jia Rong's wife, Qin Keqing, had gathered a group of concubines and maids to welcome them at the entrance gate. Having greeted Phoenix in her usual teasing manner, Madam You led Magic Jade to a seat in the drawing room.

After Keqing served tea Phoenix asked, "What did you invite me for today? If you have something nice to give to me, please hand it over quickly. I've other things to attend to."

But before Madam You or Keqing could reply, one of the ladies in waiting retorted, humorously, "In that case you shouldn't have come. Once you're here, madam, you can't have it all your own way."

Jia Rong then entered to pay his respects, and Magic Jade asked if Jia Zhen were at home.

"He's gone out of town to inquire after his father's health," said Madam You. "But you must find it dull sitting here. Why not go out for a stroll?"

"As it happens," put in Keqing, "my brother, the one whom Magic Jade was so eager to meet last time he visited, is here today. He's in the study. Why don't you go and meet him, uncle?"

"Why not ask young Master Qin to come in here?" suggested Phoenix, "Then I can see him too."

"He's shy and hasn't seen much of the world. You'd have no patience with him," Keqing replied.

"Even if he's a giant, I insist on seeing him. Don't talk like a fool! Fetch him here at once or I'll give you a good slap!"

"How dare I disobey?" Jia Rong chuckled. "I'll bring him in at once."

With that, he departed and returned with a lad of slighter build than Magic Jade, yet even more handsome. He had fine features, a fair complexion, red lips, a graceful figure, and romantic manners, but he seemed as timid and bashful as a girl. He bowed shyly to Phoenix and inquired almost inaudibly after her health.

Phoenix nudged Magic Jade delightedly and leaned forward to take the young stranger's hand. She made him sit down beside her, then began questioning him about his age and the books he was reading. She learned that his school name was Qin Zhong.

After lunch the ladies sat down to a game of cards. Magic Jade took this opportunity to leave the table with Qin Zhong and go with him into a side room for a chat. It didn't take long for the two to become good friends.

From further conversation Magic Jade learned that Qin was, at the moment, without schooling. His previous tutor had left the post some months earlier. Qin's father was old, sick, and overburdened with official duties, unable to bother much about his education. All he could do at present was to go through his old lessons. But he lacked the company of a good friend, and he thought one could learn much better in company than alone.

"Just what I think," broke in Magic Jade. "We have a school for members of our clan who can't engage a tutor. Some other relatives attend also. Since your father is concerned over this matter, why not tell him about our school when you go home today? Then you can come and study with us. I will be your classmate, and we can help each other. What could be better?"

"The other day, when my father brought up the question of a tutor, he spoke highly of this free family school here," replied Qin Zhong eagerly. "If you think I could be company for you, let's try to fix it as soon as possible. Then neither of us need waste our time. We'd have plenty of chances to talk, our parents' maids would be set at rest, and we could become real friends. Wouldn't that be fine?"

"That's no problem," reassured Magic Jade. "You can speak to your father when you get home, and I'll tell my grandmother. There's no reason why it can't be arranged quickly."

By the time this was settled, lamps were being lit. After supper, because it was dark, Madam You suggested that they send two men servants to see Qin Zhong home, and maids went out with these orders. When, some time later, the boy took his leave, she asked who was to accompany him.

"Jiao Da," said the maids, "he is tipsy again and using foul language, as usual."

"But why send him?" protested both Madam You and Keqing. "We've all those young servants who could go. Why pick him?"

"I've always said you're too soft with your servants," Phoenix's commented. "Fancy letting them have their own way like this!"

"You know Jiao Da, surely?" Madam You sighed. "Not even the master can control him, let alone your cousin Zhen. He went out with our great-grandfather on three of four expeditions when he was young, and saved his master's life by carrying him off a battlefield heaped with corpses. He went hungry himself and stole food for his master. After two days without water, when he got half a bowl, he gave it to his master and himself drank horse urine. Because of these services, he was treated with special consideration in our great-grandfather's time. Nobody likes to interfere with him now. But since he has grown old, he has no regard for appearances. He does nothing but drink, and when he's drunk he abuses everyone. Time and again I've told the stewards to write him off and not give him any jobs. Yet he's being sent again today."

"Of course I know Jiao Da. You ought to be able to handle him," scoffed Phoenix. "Pack him off to some distant farm and have done with it." She then asked if her carriage was ready.

"Everything is ready, madam," said one of the attendants.

Phoenix rose to take her leave and went together with Magic Jade, hand in hand. Madam You and the others escorted them to the main hall where, by the bright light of lanterns, they saw attendants waiting in the court yard. Because Jia Zhen wasn't there, Jiao Da was letting himself go. Roaring drunk, he was cursing away full blast as Jia Rong saw Phoenix to her carriage. He ignored all the servants' shouts to him to be quiet. Jia Rong could hardly let this pass. He swore at Jiao Da and told the men to tie him up.

"We'll ask him tomorrow, when he's sobered up, what he means by such disgraceful behavior," Jia Rong blustered.

At this, Jiao Da bore down on him bellowing still more angrily, "Don't try to lord it over Jiao Da, young Brother Rong! Not even your dad or granddad dared stand up to Jiao Da. If it hadn't been for me, and me alone, you'd have no official posts, fancy titles, or riches. It was your great-granddad who built up this estate, and nine times I snatched him back from the jaws of death. Instead of showing yourselves properly grateful, you try to lord it over me. Shut up, and I'll overlook it. Say one word more, and I'll bury a white blade in you and pull it out red!"

"Why don't you get rid of this lawless wretch?" asked Phoenix from her carriage. "He's nothing but a source of trouble. If this came to the ears of our relatives and friends, how they'd laugh at the lack of rules and order here."

As Jia Rong nodded in agreement with her, some servants overpowered Jiao Da and dragged him off, for this time he had really gone too far.

As they were taking him away, Jiao Da put forth a flood of abuse in which even Jia Zhen was included. "Let me go to the Ancestral Temple and weep for my old master," he fumed. "Little did he expect to beget such degenerates, a house full of rutting dogs and bitches in heat, day in and day out, scratching in the ashes[1] and carrying on with younger brothers-in-law. Don't think you can fool me. I only tried to hide the broken arm in your sleeve..."

These abuses scared the servants half out of their wits. Hurriedly trussing him up, they stuffed his mouth with mud and horse dung.

Phoenix and Jia Rong pretended not to have heard, whereas Magic Jade, sitting in the carriage, was rather entertained by this drunken outburst.

"Did you hear that, sister?" Magic Jade asked. "What's meant by 'scratching in the ashes'?"

"Don't talk nonsense!" snapped Phoenix, glowering. "What's come over you? You not only listen to drunken raving but have to ask silly questions too. Just wait until we get back and I tell your mother—you'll pay for this with a thrashing."

"Dear sister," apologized Magic Jade fearfully, "I promise not to do it any more."

"That's more like it, brother. The important thing, once we're home, is to talk to the old lady about sending you and your nephew Qin Zhong to school."

In almost no time they were back in the Honored Mansion.

---

[1] A slang term for adultery between a man and his daughter-in-law.

7/ Precious Hairpin and Her Gold Necklace

Now Precious Hairpin came to live in the Honored Mansion. Although not much older than the cousins, she was so polished in her manners and was so charming that most people considered Black Jade her equal. Besides, she knew how to win the hearts of the servants by her friendly and accommodating ways, whereas Black Jade was a solitary individual and went around with her head in the air. For this reason, nearly all the maids liked to be close to Precious Hairpin. Black Jade, in turn, began to feel twinges of jealousy. Hairpin, however, was completely in the dark about the matter.

Magic Jade was still a boy, too immature to discriminate tactfully between close and distant kinsmen. For him, one cousin was the same as another. Because he and Black Jade both lived in the Lady Dowager's quarters, he was closer to Black Jade than he was to the other girls, and, being closer, he had grown more intimate. But precisely because of this he sometimes offended her by being too demanding and thoughtless.

Today, for one reason or another, the two of them had fallen out and Black Jade was shedding tears again. Black Jade, in short, felt offended whenever Magic Jade said a friendly word to Precious Hairpin. This eventually led to many scenes of jealousy. Black Jade would rush weeping from the room. Then, sorry for his rough words, Magic Jade would go into her room and try to make it up. In no time Black Jade would be herself again and forgive her cousin. All this became an almost daily occurrence among the three cousins.

One day a big banquet and theatrical performance were presented in the Peaceful Mansion in honor of the relatives' reunion. Magic Jade missed his cousin, Precious Hairpin, in the crowd. He had not seen her for several days as she was now under the weather.

While the family was together enjoying the opera, he accompanied the Lady Dowager back to the Honored Mansion. There he seized the opportunity to steal off to the Pear Garden through side paths untroubled by tedious attendants and undesired watchers. Magic Jade first greeted Aunt Xue, who was sitting there distributing sewing to her maids. He greeted his aunt, who caught him in her arms and hugged him.

"How nice of you to come on a cold day like this, my dear boy," she beamed. "Come here to warm up." Then she ordered hot tea to be served.

"Is Cousin Xue Pan at home?" asked Magic Jade.

"Ah, he's like a horse without a halter," she sighed. "Not a single day does he spend at home."

"Is Hairpin better?"

"Yes, thank you. It was thoughtful of you to send a messenger over to ask how she was the other day. She's in her room now. Why not go in and see her? It's warmer there. Go and keep her company, and I'll join you as soon as I'm through here."

Magic Jade promptly rushed off to his cousin's door. It had a red brocade curtain. Lifting the curtain, he stepped inside. Precious Hairpin was sewing on the heated divan.

Magic Jade asked, "Are you better now, cousin?"

Precious Hairpin looked up and rose swiftly to her feet, saying, "Ever so much better. Thank you for your kind concern." She invited him to sit down beside her. A maid came and poured some tea. There were then conventional inquiries as to grandmother, aunts, and cousins. At last the conversation became personal. Her eyes were now fixed on the five-colored cord around his neck, the one that held the precious jade that was found in his mouth at birth.

"I've heard so much about that jade of yours, but I've never seen it. May I look at it closely today?" As she asked, she came nearer to him. He also sidled a little closer to her. He then took the cord with the jade from his neck and put it in her hand. Hairpin looked attentively at the shining thing.

It was about the size of a sparrow's egg and shone with a pinkish hue like morning clouds, smooth as clotted cream. It was covered with colored lines.

On the front of the jade was written in minute script:

Jade of penetrating spiritual power.

Under this were two lines, each consisting of four symbols, reading:

Never lose me, Never forget me,
Eternal life, Lasting Prosperity.

On the back were three lines, each of four engraved characters:

1. Drives away Evil Spirits.
2. Cures Mysterious Diseases.
3. Foretells Happiness and Misfortune.

Precious Hairpin suddenly looked at the maid, "Why do you stand there gasping instead of getting us tea?"

The maid answered with a giggle: "Those two lines seem to match the words on your locket, miss."

"Why, cousin," cried Magic Jade eagerly, "does that locket of yours have an inscription too? Do let me see it."

"Don't listen to her," replied Precious Hairpin. "There aren't any inscriptions on it."

"I let you see mine, dear cousin," he countered coaxingly.

Cornered like this, Precious Hairpin answered, "As it happens, there is a lucky inscription on it. Otherwise I wouldn't wear such a clumsy thing every day."

She unbuttoned her red jacket and took out a bright gold necklace studded with glittering pearls and jewels. Magic Jade took the locket eagerly and found two inscriptions, one on either side, in the form of eight minute characters. These read:

Never Leave me, Never Abandon me,
Fresh Youth, Lasting Bloom.

Magic Jade read this twice, repeated his own inscriptions.
"Why, cousin, this inscription of yours matches mine exactly.
Together they form a four-line stanza!"

"It was given her by a scabby monk," explained Oriole,
the maid. "He said it must be engraved on something made
of gold."

Before Oriole could say more, Precious Hairpin ordered
her to bring them some tea.

"Where did you just come from?" Hairpin asked.

But Magic Jade didn't answer. He was now close enough
to her to catch whiffs of some cool, sweet fragrance. "What
perfume have you used, sister?" he asked. "I've never smelled
this kind of perfume before."

"Perfume?" she said slowly, "I am not in the habit of
spoiling my clothes with perfume."

"Then, what is that perfume?" asked Magic Jade.

Precious Hairpin thought for a moment. "It must be the
pills I took this morning."

"What pills smell so nice?"

"Pills of cold balsam."

"Oh, let me taste some of your fragrant pills."

"Don't be silly!" she laughed. "How can you take medicine at random?"

Just then a servant outside announced, "Miss Lin is
here." In came Black Jade.

"Ah," she exclaimed at the sight of the pair. "I've chosen
a bad time to come."

Magic Jade rose with a smile and offered her a seat, while
Precious Hairpin asked cheerfully, "What do you mean?"

"I wouldn't have come, if I'd known he was here."

"I don't see what you're driving at," Precious Hairpin
said.

"Either everybody comes at once or no one comes at all,"
explained Black Jade. "If he came one day and I the next,

that would give more variety and a better distribution of our visits. You would not feel too lonely nor too surrounded by noisy people. What's so difficult to understand, cousin?"

Magic Jade noted that Black Jade was wearing a crimson camlet cloak that buttoned in front. "Is it snowing outside?" he asked her.

"It has been for a long time," the voice of one of his nurses replied outside.

"Bring me my raincoat," ordered Magic Jade.

"Wasn't I right? As soon as I come, he goes," remarked Black Jade.

"When did I say a word about leaving? I just want to get ready," Magic Jade said, trying to pacify the oversensitive cousin.

Meanwhile Aunt Xue arrived with tea and other delicacies that were prepared for them. A couple of days before, Magic Jade had spoken highly of the goose feet and duck tongues served by Madam You. So Aunt Xue produced some of her own for him to try.

"These taste even better with some wine," he hinted, smiling.

His aunt immediately sent for the best wine in her house.

"Don't bother to heat it. I prefer cold wine," Magic Jade said.

"That won't do," said his aunt. "Cold wine makes one's hand shake when writing."

"Cousin," put in Precious Hairpin teasingly, "you've the chance every day to get all sorts of knowledge. How come you don't realize why wine should be heated? Drunk hot, its fumes disperse quickly; drunk cold, it stays in your system and absorbs heat from your vital organs. That's bad for you. So do stop drinking cold wine."

Since this made sense, Magic Jade put down the wine and asked to have it warmed. Meanwhile Black Jade was just sitting there with a smile that appeared to imply a deep meaning, as she cracked melon seeds. Now her maid, Snowswan, brought in her little hand stove.

"Who told you to bring this?" demanded Black Jade. "Many thanks. Think I was freezing to death here?"

"Cuckoo was afraid you might be cold, miss, so she asked me to bring it over."

Nursing the stove in her arms Black Jade retorted, "So you do whatever she asks, but let whatever I say go in one ear and out the other. You jump to obey her instructions faster than you would if they were an Imperial edict."

Although Magic Jade knew these remarks were aimed at him, his only reply was a chuckle. And Hairpin, aware that this was Black Jade's usual way of acting, paid no attention either. Aunt Xue, however, protested:

"You've always been delicate and unable to stand the cold. Why should you be displeased when they are so thoughtful?"

"You don't understand me, aunt," replied Black Jade with a smile. "It doesn't matter here, but people anywhere else might well take offense. Sending a hand stove over from my quarters, as if my hosts didn't have such a thing! Instead of calling my maids too fussy, people might think I always behave in this outrageous fashion."

"You take such things too seriously," said Aunt Xue. "Such an idea would never have entered my head."

Towards evening, Magic Jade was slightly tipsy and he would have liked to accept Aunt Xue's invitation to spend the night in her house. But Black Jade did not like his intimacy with the Xue family. "Are you ready to go?" Black Jade asked Magic Jade at last.

He glanced at her sidewise from under drooping eyelids. "I'll go whenever you do."

Black Jade rose to her feet promptly. "We've been here nearly all day. It's time we left."

They took leave. Aunt Xue told two older servants to escort them home. Black Jade and Magic Jade thanked their hostess and made their way to the Lady Dowager's quarters.

The Lady Dowager had not yet had her supper, and was pleased to learn where they had been. Seeing that Magic Jade had been drinking, she asked him to go back to his room to rest, forbidding him to leave his room again that evening. She also gave orders for him to be well looked after.

Swaying a little, Magic Jade reached his bedroom. There his eyes fell on the brush and ink on the desk.

Skybright greeted him with a smile, exclaiming, "Well, you're a nice one. You got me to prepare the ink for you this morning, and then you wrote only three characters. Then off you went. You've kept us waiting for you the whole day. You must set to work quickly now and use up this ink."

Reminded of that morning's happenings, Magic Jade asked, "Where are the three characters I wrote?"

"Indeed you must be tipsy! When you went over to the other mansion you told me to paste them above the door, yet now you ask where they are. I didn't trust anyone else to do a good job of it so I got up on the ladder myself. My fingers were stiff with cold."

"Ah, I don't remember. Give me your hand. I'll warm it in mine."

He took her by the hand and drew her with him outside the door to look at the inscription. Just then Black Jade came along.

"Tell me frankly, dear cousin, which of the three characters is the best written?" he asked her.

Black Jade raised her eyes and read the inscription: *Red Rue Studio.*

"They're all good," she said. "I didn't know you were such a calligrapher. You must write an inscription for my room some time."

"There, you're kidding me." Then he turned to Skybright and asked, "Where is Aroma?"

Skybright curled her lips and pointed to the bed. Aroma lay there fully dressed, apparently sound asleep.

"Very early to go to bed," he remarked, laughing.

At this point a maid brought in tea and Magic Jade said, "Do have some tea, Cousin Lin."

The maids burst out giggling. "She's gone long ago, yet you offer her tea."

After drinking half a cup, he remembered something else, and asked the maid, "Why did you bring me this kind of tea? This morning we brewed some maple-dew tea, and I told you its flavor doesn't really come out until after three or four infusions."

"I did save that tea," she replied. "But Nanny Li insisted on trying it, and she drank it all."

This was really too much for Magic Jade. He dashed the cup to pieces on the floor, splashing the maid's skirt with the remaining tea. Then springing to his feet he asked, "Nanny Li! It's always Nanny Li! Who is she, anyway? Is she your grandmother that all of you treat her so respectfully? Just because she suckled me for a few days when I was small, she carries on as if she were more important than our own ancestors. I don't need a wet nurse any more, why should I keep an ancestress like this? Send her packing and we'll all have some peace and quiet."

Magic Jade wanted to go straight off to his grandmother to have the old woman dismissed. But Aroma, who had only been pretending to be asleep because she wanted to be teased by Magic Jade, now jumped up and came out to smooth things over.

She calmed Magic Jade. "So you've decided to dismiss her. Good. We'd all like to leave. Why not take this chance to get rid of all of us? That would suit us fine, and you'd get better attendants too."

Magic Jade remained silent and allowed himself to be undressed and put to bed. Very soon his tired eyes closed.

Early the next day the nephew Rong from the Peaceful Mansion arrived, accompanied by his brother-in-law Qin Zhong. The old lady was just as charmed by the young boy as were the other ladies of the house. He was kept for lunch and loaded with gifts on leaving. She considered Qin Zhong a suitable companion and schoolmate for Magic Jade. So she gladly agreed that he should be accepted into the family school.

"You live far away from here," she told Qin Zhong, "and in hot or frosty weather you'll find the trip too much. At such times you can remain here as long as you like and stay with your uncle Magic Jade. It's better for you two to study here at home than to join a pack of lazy young rascals."

Qin Zhong's father was pleased with the good reception by his rich relatives. He was very glad that his boy's education had now been readily solved without too much trouble. He saw that his son would be in the best hands at this family school. Of course he could not avoid paying a formal visit to the tutor and giving him the customary gift of money.

After the father and son paid their proper respects and presented their gift to the tutor, the uncle and nephew arrived at the school on a lucky day chosen by Magic Jade from the calendar. And because they were attending the family school together, Magic Jade and Qin Zhong became an inseparable pair. Within a couple of months Qin Zhong had become as intimate with everyone in the Honored Mansion as he might have been had he been a member of this big household.

8/ Phoenix Takes over the Household Management

Towards the end of the year news suddenly came from Yangzhou that Black Jade's father, Lin Ruhai, was ill and wished his daughter sent home for a visit. This increased the Lady Dowager's distress, but they had to get everything ready immediately for Black Jade's departure. Magic Jade was naturally very upset. However, he could not prevent the reunion of a father and a daughter at a time like this.

The Lady Dowager decided to send her granddaughter home under the escort of her cousin, Jia Lian. He was also to bring her back safely. A fine day was quickly chosen for the departure. Jia Lian and Black Jade took their leave and, accompanied by attendants, they set sail for Yangzhou.

Magic Jade was certainly sad at being deprived of the company of his favorite cousin for a time. Madam Phoenix, too, found it hard to bear the separation from her husband. She passed her lonely evenings as best she could with her maid, Patience, before retiring listlessly to bed.

One night, though tired from doing her embroidery, Phoenix's restless thoughts kept her awake long after Patience had fallen asleep. Her eyelids were drooping drowsily when, to her astonishment, Qin Keqing, her niece, came into her room. The niece had been seriously ill for a long time.

"How you enjoy your sleep, aunt!" Keqing said to her, smiling, "but I must set out on my last return journey today. We've been close to each other all these years, so I couldn't go without saying a last farewell to you. Besides, there's something I'd like to tell you which I could never entrust to anyone else."

"Just leave it to me," replied Phoenix, rather puzzled.

"You're such an exceptional woman, aunt. In the matter of intellect and energy you are the equal of any man or high-ranking official. You undoubtedly know the sayings that 'the moon waxes only to wane, water brims only to flow,' and 'the higher the climb the harder the fall'?"

She then explained that she was concerned for the future of the big household. "True, the Jia clan had endured, strong and powerful, for hundreds of years, but blossoming is likely to be followed by decay, and the day might come 'when the mighty tree falls, and the crowd of monkeys that it had sheltered in its branches would be scattered.' This means that in good times provision should be made for bad ones."

Keqing said that two things were particularly on her mind: the consolidation of the family school and the assurance of continuing the family sacrifices to the ancestors. She was worried that in times of emergency there would be no funds available for either of these two projects.

Quick to comprehend, Madam Phoenix became quite uneasy. "Your fears are well founded, but how can we prevent such a calamity?"

"I'd like to suggest that, while we're still rich and noble, we should invest in some farms and estates near our ancestral tombs so as to provide for the sacrifices. The family school should be moved to the same place. Then, even if the family property might be confiscated because of some crime, the estate for ancestral worship would be exempted. In such hard times, the young people could go there to study and farm. Don't forget the proverb, 'Even the grandest banquet must have an end.' Think for the future before it's too late. Because we're good friends let me give you some parting advice. Do remember it, aunt!" With that Keqing chanted:

After spring has gone, all flowers fade,
And each has to seek for his own way.

Later that night, Phoenix was awakened with a start. She heard the chime bar booming at the second gateway. Its heavy boom resounded four times. This was the signal that somebody in the family had died. It was followed by a servant announcing, "Madam Jia Rong of the East Mansion has passed away!"

Madam Phoenix broke into a cold sweat. She dressed quickly and hurried over to her aunt, Lady Wang. Needless to say, the sad news of the early death of the young and beautiful lady, who was so much loved by old and young, caused sobbing and lamenting everywhere in the household.

During that night Magic Jade was also aroused from his dreams by the news of the death. He had been feeling quite lonely after Black Jade's departure, and had even given up playing with his other companions. Each night he went to bed gloomily. The news of the death startled him and he jumped out of bed. At once he felt a stab of pain in his heart, and he coughed a mouthful of blood. The maids, in consternation, rushed to help him back into his bed. They asked him what was the matter and inquired as to whether they should send for a doctor or not.

"Don't be scared. It's nothing," he said. Magic Jade got up again and asked to be dressed so that he could go to the Peaceful Mansion and offer his condolences to Jia Zhen's family.

Aroma, his favorite maid, was quite concerned for him, but dared not try to stop him when he was in this mood. The Lady Dowager, however, advised him not to go, but Magic Jade would never listen to her advice. At last she allowed him to go in a closed carriage and in the care of many attendants.

Despite the late hour, Magic Jade found the entrance gate to the Peaceful Mansion wide open and brightly lit up. There was an excited coming and going of people with torches and lanterns in their hands. From the inner rooms he could hear loud cries of lamentation.

Magic Jade also gave free vent to his sorrow by the side of the bier. Then he greeted the relatives, who had come in a dense crowd.

Bathed in tears, Jia Zhen told the others, "Everyone in the family, old and young, distant kin or close friends, knows that my daughter-in-law was much superior to my son. Now that she has gone, my branch of the family is fated to die out." With that he broke down again.

The men present tried to console him: "Since she has departed this world, what's the use of weeping? Now the most important thing is to conduct the funeral service properly."

"What must be done?" Jia Zhen asked. "I'm ready to give everything possible for this."

After much consideration, it was finally decided that the body should remain in the house for forty-nine days, the highest mourning service accorded by ancient Chinese custom. One hundred and eight Buddhist monks and Taoist priests were invited to offer sacrifices and prayers in line with the religious rites for the salvation of the dear departed.

For forty-nine days the street outside the Peaceful Mansion was a sea of mourners in white sandwiched by officials in their colorful robes.

At the end of this time, Jia Zhen was fully satisfied with the arrangements, yet he was still troubled by his wife's illness and her inability to see to things. When there were visits and receptions taking place during this time, he missed her presence. He knew that if any breach of etiquette occurred while so many nobles were calling, it would leave him open to the mockery of all.

Magic Jade read his cousin's mind and asked him, "Why do you look so blue, since everything's settled satisfactorily?" When Jia Zhen told him the reason, Magic Jade said cheerfully, "That's easily settled. I'll recommend someone to take charge for you. Let her see to things during the rest of this month, and I'm sure everything will be in perfect order."

"Who do you mean?" asked Jia Zhen. Because there were other friends and relatives around, Magic Jade whispered the name into his ear.

"Excellent!" Jia Zhen said, overjoyed at this idea. "Let's see about it right away."

Seizing Magic Jade by the hand, he excused himself from the company and hurried to the reception room in his own apartment.

As luck would have it, this was not one of the major days on which prayers were offered by the monks and priests, and only a few ladies, close relatives, were there. These guests were being entertained by Lady Xing, Lady Wang, Madam Phoenix, and other ladies of the household when Jia Zhen's arrival was announced. The ladies immediately jumped up with alarm and rushed off to hide themselves in the inner room. Only Phoenix stood up with ease. Lady Xing, Lady Wang, and Phoenix remained in the reception room to greet him.

Jia Zhen was not in good physical shape these days and, being weighed down with grief, he limped as he came into the room. He was supported by a cane.

"You're not well," said Lady Xing. "You have been doing too much for days. You ought to get some rest."

With the support of his cane, Jia Zhen made an effort to kneel to greet and thank her. Lady Xing urged Magic Jade to support him, and she had a chair placed for him, but he would not take it.

Forcing a smile, Jia Zhen announced, "Your nephew has come to ask a favor of his aunts and cousin."

"What is it?" asked Lady Xing.

"You know, how it is, aunt," said Jia Zhen. "With my daughter-in-law gone and my wife ill in bed, everything is at sixes and sevens in the inner apartments. If my cousin Phoenix would agree to take charge here for a month, that would set my mind at rest."

"So that's it," Lady Xing smiled. "Phoenix is part of your Aunt Wang's establishment, so you'd better talk to her about it."

"She's inexperienced, you know," Lady Wang put in hastily. "What experience has she ever had of this sort of thing?"

"I can easily see what's in your mind, aunt," said Jia Zhen. "You're afraid we might overwork her. As for handling things badly, I'm sure that wouldn't be the case. Ever since her childhood Cousin Phoenix has known her own mind. Since she's been married and has had some experience at running things in the other mansion, she's gained skills in management. I've been thinking this over for days and there's no one as competent as she is. If you won't agree for our sake, at least do it for the one who's just died." His tears flowed again.

Lady Wang's concern was indeed that Phoenix might find the task too much for her. This might result in Phoenix making a fool of herself, as she had had no experience in managing large-scale funeral services. However, Jia Zhen's moving plea caused her to soften her attitude considerably. She eyed Phoenix thoughtfully, as though struggling to make up her mind.

Now Phoenix loved nothing more than showing off her administrative abilities. Although she ran the household competently, she had never been entrusted with such grand affairs as weddings or funerals, and she was afraid others were not fully convinced of her efficiency. She was indeed longing for a chance like this. Jia Zhen's request delighted her.

Seeing that his eagerness was overcoming Lady Wang's initial reluctance, Phoenix took the chance to put in a word. "Since my cousin is so earnest and pressing, won't you give your consent, madam?"

"Are you sure you can take on the job?" whispered Lady Wang.

"I don't see why not. Cousin Zhen has seen to all the important outside arrangements. It's just a question of keeping an eye on the domestic side. And in case of doubt, I can consult you."

As this was reasonable, Lady Wang made no further objection.

Jia Zhen thanked Phoenix with a low bow and immediately gave her full authority in writing. He told her to manage the servants and housekeeping funds freely and at her own disposal. He further suggested that she move over to the Peaceful Mansion during the period of her management. But Phoenix told him she was also needed in the other household, so she would prefer to come every day.

That very day Madam Phoenix began the management of the Peaceful Mansion. She set out to make sure that nothing in the big household would ever get lost. She also recognized that unless duties were assigned the servants may shirk their work and pass it to others. And she knew that heavy expenditures might lead to extravagance and faked receipts. Furthermore she recognized that if no distinction is made between one job and another, the rewards and hardships will be unfairly distributed. Finally, Phoenix recognized that these servants were so arrogant and undisciplined, that those with any pretensions might defy her, and those without wouldn't do their best.

The first thing Phoenix did was to make a list of the names of all the staff. And then, every morning at six thirty, she held a roll call. With this list in her hand and the head maid by her side, Madam Phoenix directed the man servants and maid servants one after another. She assigned them tasks for the day and demanded their punctuality. Among other things, she introduced a daily consultation hour from ten a.m. until eleven-thirty p.m., when all requests and needs were to be reported to her.

Phoenix also made a daily round of the entire household. She took stern measures against any violation or negligence. Once, when a woman servant was missing from the roll call, she punished her with twenty strokes and the deduction of a full month's wages. This established Madam Phoenix's absolute reputation among the household staff. The slovenliness that had formerly reigned in the Peaceful Mansion was now replaced by strict discipline.

The long weeks of mourning ceremonies passed to the great satisfaction of Jia Zhen. Madam Phoenix's power grew with each passing day because of her fine management.

9/ Grand View Garden

One day Jia Zheng's birthday was celebrated by a grand family banquet. At the height of the celebration, a doorkeeper rushed in suddenly to announce, "His Excellency, Chief Eunuch of the Six Palaces, has come with an Imperial message!"

Jia She, Jia Zheng, and the rest were taken completely by surprise, quite unable to figure out what this visit might mean. The banquet and the theatrical performance had to be stopped at once. Throwing open the central gate, they knelt down, as required, to receive the Imperial message.

The Chief Eunuch arrived on horseback, followed by a retinue of other eunuchs. Dismounting in front of the entrance to the main hall, he climbed the steps with a beaming smile and announced, "By special order of His Majesty, Jia Zheng is to present himself at once for an audience in the Palace."

This said, and without even taking a sip of tea, he remounted his horse and rode off.

Jia She and the others didn't know whether this command was a good or bad thing. Jia Zheng hurried to put on his court dress and rushed to the Palace, leaving the whole family in a state of great suspension. The Lady Dowager sent one messenger after another, at short intervals, to get information about him.

It was four hours before the stewards came back panting through the inner gate and crying, "Good news! Our master asks the old lady to go at once to the Palace with the other ladies to thank His Majesty's grace."

The Lady Dowager had been waiting anxiously in the corridor outside the great hall with Lady Xing, Lady Wang, Madam You, Phoenix, and the other young ladies of the household, as well as Aunt Xue. On hearing this news, they demanded more details from the chief steward of the Honored Mansion.

"Our eldest young lady has been appointed Chief Secretary to the Phoenix Palace, with the title of Worthy and Virtuous Consort," the chief steward said. "Now our master has gone to the East Palace and asks the old lady and the other ladies to go at once to offer thanks!"

This happy news freed the ladies from all their anxious doubts, and proud joy was visible on every face. They all quickly dressed properly to go to the Palace where they gave their thanks to the Emperor.

However, there was one person who did not share the unbounded joy among the members of the two mansions. This was Magic Jade. The reason for this was his general depression. After Black Jade's departure, Magic Jade lost his appetite. Later he found pleasure in the company of Qin Zhong. Unfortunately Qin Zhong had fallen seriously ill. So Magic Jade had become depressed and this lasted throughout these days. Even the great honor conferred on Yuanchun, his eldest sister, failed to raise his morale. His indifference made everyone in the household conclude that he was growing more and more eccentric.

Only one thing might cheer him up, and that would be the return of Black Jade. After her father, Lin Ruhai, breathed his last, she escorted her father's coffin back to Suzhou, his native town. In this she was helped by her cousin, Jia Lian. The two returned to the Honored Mansion near the end of the year.

The reunion of Magic Jade and his orphaned cousin was a mingling of joy and sorrow. After a storm of weeping, they two exchanged condolences and congratulations. Magic Jade found Black Jade now to be considerably more mature and far more beautiful and attractive than before. She had brought back with her many books and she distributed various graceful objects among her cousins and Magic Jade.

Madam Phoenix and her husband, Jia Lian, naturally had a great deal to tell each other on the first day of their happy reunion. Phoenix had just finished a long report of her seven weeks in charge of the Peaceful Mansion when the little maid, Patience, stuck her head in the door. When the maid saw that Jia Lian was with her mistress she stopped short and was about to disappear, but then they heard voices outside and Phoenix asked who was there.

Patience came in and said, "Madam Xue sent Sister Lotus over to ask me something. I've given her an answer and sent her back."

"Ah yes!" smiled Jia Lian, apparently pleased by the recollection. "When I went to call on Aunt Xue just now to tell her I was back, I ran into such a pretty young lady. It seems that she's the little maid they had that lawsuit about. Her name was something like Lotus. She's finally been given as a concubine to that idiot Xue Pan. Now that she's been powdered like a grown-up woman, she really does look most attractive."

"Well!" exclaimed Phoenix. "I should have thought you'd have seen enough of the world now that you're back from a trip to Suzhou and Hangzhou, but I see you're still the same greedy guts as ever. You know what Xue Pan is like. He keeps 'one eye on the dish and the other on the pan.' Look how he plagued his mother for a whole year just to get hold of Lotus. In the end Aunt Xue went to all the trouble of inviting guests in a proper style to a feast to make her his concubine. Yet, in less than a fortnight, he's already treating her like dirt!"

At this point a page from the inner gate reported that Jia Zheng was waiting for Jia Lian in the big library. At once Jia Lian buttoned up his clothes and went out.

Then Phoenix asked Patience, "What on earth did Aunt Xue just now send Lotus along for?"

"It wasn't Lotus," said Patience, giggling. "I had to make something up. You see, Madam, that wife of the Chief Steward is such a stupid woman." She drew closer and lowered her voice. "She wouldn't come earlier or later but had chosen this very moment, when the Master's just got home, to bring you the interest on that money you loaned her. It's lucky I met her in the hall or she'd have come in and blurted everything out. That would be too bad. We all know what our Master is like where money is concerned. He's ready to snatch money from a pan of burning oil; he'd start spending even more recklessly if he knew that you had private savings. Anyway, I took the money from her quickly and gave her a piece of my mind. That's why I had to make up a story in front of the Master."

Phoenix laughed. "So it was just one of your tricks."

Just then Jia Lian returned. Phoenix called for wine and dishes of food , and the husband and wife took their seats opposite to each other and began their drinking and eating.

Jia Lian told her what he had heard about the gracious nature of the Emperor. "Our present Emperor believes that the filial affection of a child for his parents is the most important thing in the world, and that the family feeling is the same everywhere, irrespective of social rank. So he requested permission of the Ex-Emperor and Ex-Empress to allow the families of court ladies to visit them at the Palace on the twelfth day of every month. All those court ladies with adequate accommodation at home for the reception of an Imperial retinue are allowed to ask for a Palace carriage to visit their families. In this way they can show their affection and enjoy a reunion with their dear ones.

"All of them," Jia Lian continued, "were so grateful for this decree, they leapt for joy. The father of the Imperial Lady of Zhou has already started building a separate court for her home visit; and the father of the Imperial Concubine Wu looking for a site outside the city too."

"If that's really true," said Phoenix, "then I'll get a chance to see great doings when Yuanchun comes for such a visit. I've often wished that I'd been born twenty or thirty years earlier so that the old folk wouldn't be despising me for having seen so little of the world."

"In the old days our Jia family was in charge of ocean-going ships and repairing the sea wall around Suzhou and Yangzhou. To prepare for that Imperial visit, we spent money just as if we were pouring out sea water," Jia Lian said proudly.

"Our Wang family did the same," put in Phoenix. "At that time my grandfather was in charge of all the foreign tribute, and whenever envoys came from abroad to pay homage, it was our family that entertained them. All the goods brought by foreign ships to Guangdong, Fujian, Yunnan, and Zhejiang passed through our hands."

At that point Lady Wang sent to inquire if Phoenix had finished her meal. Realizing that she was wanted elsewhere, Phoenix hastily ate half a bowl of rice and rinsed her mouth. She was starting to leave when some pages from the inner gate reported the arrival of Jia Rong and Jia Qiang. Jia Lian rinsed his mouth and Patience brought him a basin of water in which to wash his hands.

As soon as the two young men came in, he asked them what they wanted. Phoenix stayed to hear Jia Rong's reply.

"My father sent me to tell you, uncle, that the uncles have reached a decision," said Jia Rong. "We've measured the distance from the east wall through the garden of the East Mansion to the north, and it comes to over a quarter of a mile, just enough to build a separate residence for an Imperial visit. They've already authorized someone to work out the blueprint. It'll be ready tomorrow. Since you must be tired after your long journey, please don't bother to come over. If you've any proposals, you can make them the first thing tomorrow."

"Thank your father for me," said Jia Lian with a smile. "It's very kind of him to let me off tonight, and I'll do as he says and not go over until tomorrow. This is the best possible plan, the easiest and the simplest to carry out. Tell him, when you get back, that I quite agree. Anyway, when I come over tomorrow to pay my respects we can talk it over in detail."

Jia Rong promised to forward the message.

Jia Qiang now stepped forward to announce, "My uncle has given me the job of going to Suzhou with the chief steward's two sons. We're to hire instructors and buy girl actresses, musical instruments, and costumes there so that we can have our own theatricals for the visit. He told me to let you know."

Jia Lian looked the young man up and down and then asked, "Are you sure you're up to the job? This may not be a big one, but there should be additional benefits if you know the ropes." Jia Qiang laughed, "I'll have to learn as I go along."

Jia Rong, standing in the shadow, quietly plucked Phoenix's lapel. Taking the hint she said to her husband, "Don't worry. Your cousin knows best whom to send. Why should you be afraid Qiang isn't up to it? Is everyone born capable? Cousin Zhen is sending him as a supervisor, not to do all the bargaining and accounting himself. I think it's an excellent choice."

Jia Lian explained that he only wanted to offer some advice.

At this point Phoenix left, and Jia Rong slipped out after her to whisper, "If there's anything you want, aunt, make out a list and I'll give it to Jia Qiang to see to."

"Don't talk rubbish!" Phoenix snorted. "Do you think you can buy my favor with a few knickknacks? And anyway, I don't like all this whispering in corners."

Meanwhile Jia Qiang was making a somewhat similar proposal to Jia Lian. "If there's anything I can get for you while I'm away, uncle, I'll be glad to do you a service."

"Don't look so pleased," replied Jia Lian mockingly. "So this trick is the first thing you learn when you start handling a trade. If I need anything, of course I'll write." With this he saw them out.

Then several servants came to make reports. But Jia Lian felt so tired that he sent orders to the inner gate to admit no one else. All business he told them must wait until the next day.

Phoenix did not get to bed until the small hours of the night.

The next morning, after calling on Jia She and Jia Zheng, Jia Lian went to the Peaceful Mansion. With some old stewards, secretaries, and friends he inspected the grounds of both mansions, drew plans for the palaces for the Imperial visit and estimated the number of workmen required for the construction project.

Before long all the craftsmen were assembled, and endless loads of supplies were brought to the construction site: gold, silver, copper, and tin, as well as earth, timber, bricks, and tiles. First they pulled down the walls and pavilions of the Garden of Fragrance in the Peaceful Mansion so as to connect it with the large eastern court of the Honored Mansion. All the servants' quarters were also dismantled.

Artificial rockeries and lakes were constructed, pavilions made, and bamboos and flowers planted, according to the plan of the gardener.

The family's engagement in these important developments released Magic Jade from his father's periodical quizzes about the progress of his studies, and the boy was thus having an easy time. The only thing that worried him and spoiled his pleasure was Qin Zhong's illness, now going from bad to worse. It was impossible for Magic Jade to feel happy about anything else.

One morning, just as he had finished dressing and was thinking of going round to the Lady Dowager to ask if he might pay Qin Zhong another visit, he caught sight of a page dodging about behind the screen wall of the inner gate. The lad was obviously trying to catch his attention. Magic Jade hurried over to the page.

"What is it?"

"Young Master Qin. He's dying," the page said.

Magic Jade was stunned.

"He was clear-headed when I saw him only yesterday," Magic Jade cried. "How can he be dying so soon?"

"I don't know. That's what an old fellow from his home just told me."

Magic Jade went to tell the Lady Dowager. She then instructed some trustworthy men to accompany him when he went to see Qin Zhong. "You may call to show your friendship for your schoolmate," she told him. "But you must come back as soon as it is over. Don't stay too long."

Magic Jade hastily changed his clothes and drove off in a hurry. By the time he arrived, Qin Zhong had already lost consciousness several times and now had been lifted onto a trestle bed to die. Seeing this, Magic Jade burst out sobbing.

"Dear brother!" Magic Jade cried. "It's me, Magic Jade!"

He called a couple of times but Qin Zhong made no reply. Qin Zhong had, by now, breathed his last.

Magic Jade wept long and bitterly over Qin Zhong's death and it was some time before the servants could calm him down.

The final preparations for the reception of Yuanchun, the Imperial Consort, were eventually completed. The newly-built majestic garden for the imperial visit was well laid out and artistically designed according to the traditional Chinese art of gardening. It was filled with oriental pavilions, criss-crossed with flowers and plants, a delightful place for the pleasure seeking of Chinese nobles.

Now Jia Zheng received the information that His Majesty had consented to his eldest daughter's visiting her family. The date was fixed for the fifteenth of the first lunar month, the time of the Lantern Festival. The preparations for the visit threw the whole household into a condition of unrest. Every member was at work day and night. They hardly had time to celebrate the Lunar New Year.

Finally the Imperial Consort arrived to visit her family. She came with a long procession of attendants and eunuchs clearing the way.

All present, including the Lady Dowager, hastily fell to their knees by the side of the road. Yuanchun was helped by the Imperial ladies-in-waiting out of the sedan chair and then escorted to the apartment so that she could change from her royal dress into civilian clothes. After she had changed, she got into the chair again and was carried to the newly-built garden.

Yuanchun entered the garden and found it wreathed with the perfumed smoke of incense, splendid with flowers, brilliant with countless lanterns, and melodious with strains of music. Words fail to describe that scene of peaceful magnificence and noble refinement. The Imperial Consort sighed, "This is too extravagant!"

Now that the official part of the reception had come to an end, the Imperial Consort entered a side chamber and changed her clothes to become once more the simple daughter who could now visit with her parents and grandmother.

The private reception took place in the Lady Dowager's reception room. As Yuanchun stood there holding her grandmother's left hand and her mother's right, tears rolled down her cheeks. The women could do nothing but sob. Lady Xing, Phoenix, and Yuanchun's three younger sisters also stood beside them, weeping silently.

At last the Imperial Consort controlled her grief and forced a smile, as she tried to cheer them up. "Since you sent me away to that forbidden place, it hasn't been easy to get this chance to come home and see you all again," she said. "Instead of chatting and laughing, we're crying. Soon I'll have to leave you again, and there is no knowing when I can come back." At this she broke down again.

Lady Xing and the others did their best to console her, and the Lady Dowager asked her to take a seat. Then she exchanged courtesies with each in turn and more tears were shed. Next the stewards and attendants of both mansions paid their respects outside the door.

After the ladies of the family had spoken with feeling about their separation and all that had happened since, Jia Zheng came to the door to ask after the health of his daughter. She, in return, paid her respects to him. Then she inquired why Magic Jade had not come to greet her. The Lady Dowager explained that since he was a young man without official rank he dared not show up, unless specially summoned.

The Imperial Consort sent for Magic Jade at once and a young eunuch ushered him in to pay homage, according to palace etiquette. His sister asked Magic Jade to come closer. She then stroked his neck and commented with a smile, "How you have grown up!" But even as she spoke, her tears fell like rain.

Before Yuanchun entered the Palace to be an Imperial Consort, she had been brought up by the Lady Dowager. And after Magic Jade was born, she loved him more than any of her other brothers and she lavished great care on him. After she entered the Palace, she often wrote letters home reminding her parents to educate him well, for she knew that unless strictly disciplined he would not achieve much. Her loving concern for him had never ceased. This happy reunion between brother and sister was really a rare occasion.

Now Madam You and Phoenix stepped forward to announce, "The banquet is ready. We beg Your Highness to favor us with your presence." Yuanchun rose and told Magic Jade to lead the way.

Accompanied by all the rest, she walked into the garden, where the magnificent sights were lit up by lanterns. They strolled, mounting pavilions, crossing streams, climbing hills, and enjoying the view from different locations.

Yuanchun was greatly impressed by the unusual sights around this garden. But she advised them, "You mustn't be so extravagant next time. This is far too much!"

When they reached the main reception palace she asked them to take their seats. It was a grand banquet. At the same time Yuanchun asked for a writing brush and ink stone so that she could write down the names she selected for the spots she liked best. She named the pleasure grounds the "Grand View Garden." And she named some of the buildings in it the "Bamboo Cottage," "Happy Red Residence Hall," "Sweet Rice Village," and "Pear Fragrance Garden." The main pavilion became the "Grand View Pavilion."

After the banquet, theatrical performances were given to entertain the Imperial Consort. And rewards were given to the outstanding actors and actresses.

It was nearly three in the morning by the time everyone had expressed their thanks, and the eunuch in charge announced that it was time to leave. Yuanchun forced a smile though her eyes filled with tears again, and she clasped the hands of her grandmother and mother, unable to bring herself to let them go.

The Lady Dowager and the other women were sobbing too. Although Yuanchun could hardly bear to leave, she could not disobey the Imperial regulations. She had no other alternative but to reenter her royal sedan chair. The whole household did its best to console the Lady Dowager and Lady Wang as they helped them out of the Grand View Garden.

10/ Aroma Plays a Trick

Everybody in the two mansions was completely worn out after the Imperial Consort's visit to the Grand View Garden. It took a couple of days to remove and store all the decorations from the garden. Phoenix had the heaviest responsibilities; unlike the others, she did not have a moment's rest. She was always eager to shine, anxious to give no room for criticism. She tried to carry out her many tasks as if they were nothing. Magic Jade, on the other hand, was the one with the least to do and the one with the most free hours to relax.

One morning Aroma's mother came and asked the Lady Dowager for permission to take her daughter home for a New Year's party. She would be gone until evening. So Magic Jade was left to amuse himself with the other maids at dice or chess games.

He was feeling rather bored when a girl announced that a message had come from Jia Zhen, inviting him over to the Peaceful Mansion to watch some operas and to see their New Year's lantern show. While Magic Jade was changing his clothes before setting out, a gift of sweetened cream arrived from the Imperial Consort. Remembering how Aroma had enjoyed this delicacy the last time they had some, he asked the maids to keep it for her. After taking his leave of the Lady Dowager, Magic Jade went over to the other mansion.

He had no real interest in the operas. After lingering for some time there, he decided to go to Aroma's home instead.

Aroma's mother was enjoying tea and sweetmeats with her daughter and a few nieces when they heard shouts of "Brother Hua!" And Aroma's brother was taken aback when he hurried out and found the master and servant there. Helping Magic Jade to get off his horse, he called out from the yard, "Here's the young master!"

This came as a greater surprise to Aroma than to any of the rest of them. Running out to meet Magic Jade she caught his arm and asked, "Why did you come here?"

"I was rather bored," he told her with a laugh. "I've just come to see what you're doing."

Reassured, she said with anger, "So you're up to mischief again. Why should you come here?" She turned to Tealeaf, Magic Jade's servant. "Who else is with you?"

"Nobody," said Tealeaf with a grin, "nobody knows we're here."

By now Aroma's mother had come out to welcome the visitors. Aroma led Magic Jade into the house. He saw four or five girls inside, who lowered their heads and blushed when he entered. Afraid that the young master might feel cold, Aroma's mother and brother made him sit on the bed and served him fresh sweetmeats and some choice tea.

"Now don't you two rush about," said Aroma, "I know how to look after him. Don't give him anything he won't be able to eat."

Seeing that Magic Jade did not touch anything he liked, she smiled. "Since you've come, we can't let you go without tasting something of ours. You'll have to try something to show you've been our guest." She picked up a few pine nuts, blew off the skins, and handed them to him on her handkerchief.

He noticed that her eyes were slightly red and there were tear stains on her powdered cheeks. "Why have you been crying?" he whispered.

"Who's been crying?" she retorted cheerfully. "I've just been rubbing my eyes." Thus she glossed over the matter.

Aroma noted that Magic Jade was wearing his dark gown, the one embroidered with a pattern of golden dragons and lined with fox fur under a fringed, bluish-grey sable coat. "Surely you didn't get yourself dressed up just to come and see us," she said. "Did no one ask where you were going?"

"No, I changed clothes to go to Cousin Zhen's in order to watch some operas."

She nodded. "Well, after a short rest you'd better go back. This is no place for you."

"I wish you'd come home now," said Magic Jade. "I've got something nice for you when you get back."

"Hush! What will the others think if they hear you?" She reached out to take the magic jade from his neck and, turning to her cousins, said with a smile, "Just look! Here's the wonderful thing that you've heard so much about. You've always wanted to see this rare object. Now's your chance for a really good look. Here it is. You may look to your hearts' content. There's nothing so special about it, is there?"

After passing the jade around for their inspection, she fastened it on Magic Jade's neck again. Then she asked her brother to hire a clean cab to take him home.

Aroma's brother hurried out to hire a cab, and they saw him off. Aroma warned Tealeaf, "Keep this visit a secret, for you'll be in trouble if they find out about it." The young master and the servant went back to the Peaceful Mansion, entering through the back gate so as to keep the trip a secret.

During his absence, the maids in his apartments had amused themselves at chess, dice, and card games until the floor was covered with melon-seed skins. Nanny Li, with her cane, chose this moment to come and call on her young master to see how he was. She saw that Magic Jade was out, and that the uproar created during his absence by the maids was quite offensive. She scolded them severely.

The maids knew that Magic Jade did not mind so much about such matters. They also knew that Nanny Li had no more power over them since she had retired and left the house. So they continued with their fun and generally ignored her. Nanny Li then ate the cream that Magic Jade had specially set aside for Aroma, even though the maids advised her not to eat it.

Presently Magic Jade came home and sent someone to fetch Aroma. He saw Skybright lying motionless on her bed. "Is she ill?" he asked. "Or did she lose some game?"

"She was winning," answered one maid. "But Nanny Li came along and raised such a fuss that she lost. So she went to bed to sulk."

"You shouldn't take Nanny Li so seriously," Magic Jade said. "Just leave her alone."

At that moment Aroma came back. After asking where he had his meal and what time he reached home, she gave the girls greetings from her mother and cousins. After she changed out of her visiting clothes, Magic Jade made an apology to her because the greedy old woman had snapped up that cream that was specially kept for her.

Aroma laughed this off, saying: "Thank you for your kindness, but last time I took that cream it did not agree with me at all. It gave me a bad stomach and I vomited. It's fine that she's had it. Otherwise it would have spoiled. I'd much prefer a few roasted chestnuts before going to bed. Would you peel some for me, while I make your bed?"

Magic Jade picked out some roasted chestnuts and peeled them for her by the light of the lamp. Seeing that others were not around, he asked her with a smile, "Who was that girl in red this afternoon?"

"She was a cousin of mine."

Magic Jade heaved a couple of admiring sighs.

"What are you sighing for?" asked Aroma. "I know how your mind works. You think she isn't good enough to wear red."

"No, on the contrary. If a girl like that isn't good enough to wear red, who has a better right to do so? I found her charming. How nice it would be if we could have her come to live with us."

"Certainly not," said Aroma with a bitter smile, "Since I'm unlucky enough to be a slave here, does it mean that my relations ought to be slaves too? I guess you think every pretty girl you see wants to be a servant in your house?"

"Don't be so touchy," he retorted. "Living in our house doesn't have to make one a slave. Couldn't she be our relative?"

"But my folks are not grand enough for that," said Aroma.

Magic Jade fell silent and went on peeling the chestnuts.

Aroma laughed after a long silence. "Why don't you say anything? Have I offended you? Well, never mind. Tomorrow you can buy her for a few ounces of silver."

"I don't see what answer I can give you when you say things like that," Magic Jade grinned. "I only said what a nice girl she was. I think she's the right person to live in a big household like ours, much more than some of us country folk who were born here."

"She may not have your luck, but she's her parents' darling, the apple of their eyes. She's just turned seventeen and all her dowry is ready. She'll be married off next year."

The word "married" made Magic Jade utter an involuntary expression of regret.

Aroma observed, with a sigh, "You know, these last few years, since I came here, I haven't seen much of my cousins. Soon I'll be going home, but they'll all be gone."

Shocked by the implications of her remark, Magic Jade dropped the chestnuts. "What do you mean, going home?"

"Today I heard my mother discussing it with my brother. They told me to be patient for one more year and by then they'd have saved enough money to buy my freedom."

"Why should they do that?" Magic Jade was uneasy at these words.

"What a funny question! After all, I wasn't born a slave in your family. I have my own folk outside. There's no future for me here. Of course I want to rejoin them."

"You can't go if I won't let you," said Magic Jade.

"I never heard of such a thing!" retorted Aroma. "Even in the Palace hall, law is the lord of all. A bond is a bond. When a person's term of service is over, you have to let them go. No one can force a person to stay as a slave forever, so how can you?"

Magic Jade thought a bit. What she said was reasonable enough. Nevertheless he tried to put forward some other objections. "You'll find it difficult to get free without the permission of the Lady Dowager," he said.

"Why shouldn't she let me go? If I were somebody special or had so won the hearts of the old lady and Lady Wang that they couldn't do without me, they might give my people a few extra ounces of silver so as to keep me. But I'm quite an ordinary sort. There are plenty of girls better than me. When I came here as a child, I was with the old lady. Then I waited on little River Cloud for a couple of years, and now I've been serving you for quite a time. If my people come to redeem me, your family is bound to let me go. They may even be generous enough not to ask for any ransom money. If you say I look after you well, that's my job. There's nothing remarkable about that. There'll be plenty of other good ones to take my place when I'm gone. I'm not irreplaceable."

Every word Aroma said seemed sound enough to Magic Jade. Indeed, she had every reason to leave and none at all to stay. Yet in desperation he argued, "That may be so, but if I insist on keeping you, I'm sure Grandmother would speak to your mother about it, and pay her so much that she won't take you away."

"I'm sure my mother wouldn't refuse. Even if you didn't talk nicely to her or pay her a cent, so long as you made up your mind to keep me here against my will, she wouldn't dare to object. But your family has never thrown its weight about like that. This isn't like offering ten times the usual price for something you happen to like when the owner finds it worth his while to sell. If you kept me for no reason at all, it would do you no good and would break up my family. The old lady and Lady Wang would never be willing to do so."

Magic Jade remained thoughtful for a few minutes. "So this means you'll be leaving for sure?"

"Definitely."

"Who would believe that she's so heartless?" he wondered.

Finally he said with a sigh, "If I'd known that you'd be leaving in the end, I shouldn't have let you work for me in the

first place. Now I'll be left alone here, a poor forsaken ghost!"
And he retired sulkily to bed.

He didn't realize that Aroma had only been play-acting a
bit to test his feelings for her. Actually when Aroma went
home and heard her mother and brother talk of buying her
out, she had assured them that Magic Jade would never let
her go so long as he lived. She had no desire to be ransomed
and would rather die than leave her service.

After they said this, she wept until her mother and brother realized that there was no convincing her. They then decided to drop their intention. Magic Jade's unexpected visit
and the apparent intimacy between maid and master opened
their eyes to the true situation, leaving them much reassured.
In fact, this was something they had not even hoped for. So
they gave up all thought of buying her freedom. All that Aroma had just said about leaving and being ransomed was sheer
fiction.

Since early youth Aroma had always been aware that
Magic Jade's character was peculiar. He was no ordinary
youth and he had been more naughty and willful than other
boys. In addition, he had some queer eccentricities of his
own. Recently, even his parents were unable to control him,
as he had been much spoiled by his grandmother. Now he
had become so reckless and headstrong that he was losing
patience with all conventions.

She had long wanted to speak to him about this, but was
convinced he would not listen to her. Luckily, by throwing
dust in his eyes that evening, she was able to sound him out
and get him into the right mood for a good lecture. His silent
retreat to bed showed her how upset he was and how
wounded he had been.

As for the chestnuts, she had pretended to enjoy them in
order to make him forget the cream. She now gave the chestnuts to the other maids. Aroma went to Magic Jade's bedside
and gave him a cheerful shaking. She found his face wet with
tears. "What has wounded your heart?" she asked gently. "If
you really want me here, of course I won't go."

Magic Jade brightened at once.

"Just tell me what else I must do to keep you here," he said. "I really don't know how to convince you to stay."

"I know we're both fond of each other," she responded. "That's for sure. I've got two or three things to ask of you. If you agree to them, I'll take it that you really want me to stay. Even a knife at my throat could not make me leave you then."

Magic Jade's face lit up. "Well, what are your conditions? I agree to them all, dear sister, my kind sister. I'd agree to three hundred conditions, let alone three. All I beg you is to stay and watch over me until the day when I turn into a puff of smoke to be scattered by the wind. Then you'll no longer be able to watch over me, and I'll have to let you go wherever you please."

"My good gentleman, stop that!" Aroma tried to cover his mouth with her hands. "I just wanted to give you a warning, but there you go talking more wildly than ever."

"All right," agreed Magic Jade promptly, "I promise not to."

" This is the first fault you must correct," said Aroma.

"O.K. If I ever talk that way any more, you can pinch my lips. What else?"

"The second thing is this. Whether you like to read or not, in front of the old master and other people, stop making sarcastic remarks about it. At least try to pretend to like books, so as not to provoke your father and to give him a chance to speak well of you to his friends. After all, he thinks to himself that the men of his family have been scholars for generations, but his son has let him down—he doesn't care for books. No wonder your father gets so angry with you that he keeps punishing you."

"All right," Magic Jade laughed. "That was just wild talk when I was too young to know any better. I'll never say such silly things any more. What else?"

"Most important of all, stop playing about with girls, cosmetics, and powder. You must stop kissing the rouge on girls' lips on the sly and running after everything in red."

"I promise. What else is there? Tell me, quick!" demanded Magic Jade.

"That's all," Aroma said. "Just be a bit more careful about things in general instead of getting carried away by your whims and fancies. If you do all I ask, I promise never to leave you, not even if they send a big sedan chair with eight bearers to carry me away."

"If you stay here long enough, you'll have your sedan chair and eight bearers some day. I bet you take a handsome husband!" Magic Jade chuckled.

"I don't treasure that luck," smiled Aroma haughtily. "I'm not willing for such blessing. Even if I did go, I should take no pleasure in it."

At this point another maid appeared and said, "It's very late, it's time you were in bed. Just now the old lady sent around a nurse to ask, and I told her you were asleep."

Magic Jade washed and rinsed his mouth all over again, then undressed and settled down once more to sleep.

The next morning, after having breakfast, Magic Jade went off to see Black Jade.

11/ Black Jade, a Sentimental Girl

Black Jade was taking a nap. Her maids had all gone off about their own affairs. Not a sound could be heard from inside the room. As Magic Jade lifted the embroidered door curtain and entered, he found her asleep. He hurried over to rouse her:

"Dear cousin!" he called, shaking her gently. "How can you sleep just after a meal?"

His voice woke her. She opened her eyes and saw that it was Magic Jade. She said: "Why not go away and play for a bit? I'm terribly tired. I didn't get any sleep the other night. I'm still aching from head to foot."

"A few aches are nothing, but if you go on sleeping you'll fall ill. I'll stay to amuse you and keep you awake. Then you'll be all right," Magic Jade advised.

"I'm not sleepy," she said and closed her eyes. "All I want is a little rest. Can't you go and amuse yourself somewhere else for a while and come back later?"

"Where can I go?" He gave her another shake. "I'm so bored with everyone else."

Black Jade could not suppress her laugh. "All right, since you're here, you may stay. Go and sit down properly over there and we'll talk."

"I'd prefer to lie down," said Magic Jade. "O.K. Lie down then."

"There isn't a pillow. Why don't we share that pillow of yours?"

"What nonsense! Look at all those pillows in the next room. Why don't you get one of them for yourself?"

He went into the outer room, coming back to say, "I don't want any of them. Who knows what dirty old woman has been using them?"

Black Jade opened her eyes at this and sat up, laughing. "You really are the bane of my life. Here, take this." She pushed her pillow towards him and fetched herself another. Then they lay down facing each other.

Taking a back glance, Black Jade noticed that there was a blood stain, the size of a button, on his left cheek. She bent over him to examine it more closely and touched it lightly with her finger.

"Whose nails were they this time?" she asked.

Magic Jade lay back to avoid her scrutiny and grinned. "That's not a scratch. I've just been helping make rouge. A little of it must have splashed onto my face." He searched for a handkerchief with which to wipe it. Black Jade wiped it off with her own, clicking her tongue critically as she did so.

"So you're up to those tricks again? You might at least try to tell a tale. Even if Uncle doesn't see it, that's the sort of thing people love to gossip about. Some may tell on you in order to win favor; and if such stories reach his ears, it'll mean trouble for all of us."

Magic Jade was not listening attentively, however. He was enchanted by the fragrance that seemed to come from her sleeve. The fragrance seemed to melt the marrow of his bones. He caught hold of her sleeve to see what she had hidden inside.

"Perfume? At this season?" laughed Black Jade.

"I'm not wearing any in mid-winter."

"Well, where does it come from, then?" he asked.

"How do I know? It might have come from the wardrobe."

Magic Jade shook his head. "I doubt it. It's a very unusual scent. Not the kind you would get from a scent cake, a perfume ball, or sachet."

"Do I have a Buddhist arhat to give me some immortal scent?" demanded Black Jade. "Even if I had some rare recipe, I've no kind cousin or brother to make it up for me. I've only got the ordinary sort of perfume."

"Whenever I say one word, off you go like that," Magic Jade grinned. "Very well. I'll have to teach you a lesson. From now on I'll show you no mercy!"

He rose to his knees, blew on his hands, then stretched them out and started tickling her in the ribs and under her armpits. Black Jade had always been ticklish, and the mere sight of his surprise attack set her giggling so much that she nearly choked.

"Oh! Stop it!" she gasped. "Stop it, or I'll be angry."

"Will you say things like that any more?"

"No," she said, patting her hair into place. She laughed weakly, "I dare not. You say I have an unusual scent, have you got a warm scent?"

"A warm scent?" Magic Jade was puzzled.

She shook her head with a sigh. "How dense you are! You have your jade, and someone else has gold to match it. So don't you have a warm scent to match her cold scent?"

Magic Jade caught her meaning then and chuckled. "You were begging for mercy just now, but now here you go again, worse than ever." He again stretched out his fingers.

"Dear cousin, I promise not to tease," she cried hastily.

"All right, I'll forgive you if you let me smell your sleeve."

With that he covered his face with her sleeve and started sniffing as if he would never stop. She pulled away her arm.

"I really think you ought to go now."

"Couldn't go even if I wanted to. Let's lie down quietly and chat gently." He stretched out again while Black Jade lay down too, covering her face with a handkerchief.

Magic Jade feared that if she kept on sleeping like this, it would injure her health, so he tried another trick. "Why, yes! There's a big story that took place near Yangzhou. I wonder if you know about it." This statement was delivered with so straight a face and in such a serious tone of voice that Black Jade was quite taken in. Suppressing a laugh, Magic Jade started to make up a story.

"Near the city of Yangzhou there is a mountain called Mt. Dai, in the side of which is a cavern called the Cave of Lin."

"You're making this up," cried Black Jade, "I've never heard of such a hill."

"There are a great many mountains and streams in this world," said Magic Jade, "you could hardly come to know them all. Leave your comments until I finish my story."

"Go on, then," said Black Jade.

"In the Cave of Lin," Magic Jade went on, "lived a number of rat spirits. One year on the seventh day of the twelfth month, the Old Mouse ascended his throne to hold a council with his tribe. He announced, 'Tomorrow is the Eight-flavored Breakfast before New Year's Eve when all the men on earth will cook their delicious porridge. Here in our cave we have few fruits or nuts left; we should take this opportunity to go raiding theirs.'

"The Old Mouse issued orders: 'Who will go to steal rice?' One rat accepted the order and went off. 'Who will go to steal beans?' the Old Mouse asked. Another rat accepted the mission. One by one they went off until there were only sweet potatoes left to be stolen.

"The Old Mouse then issued another order. 'Who will go and steal sweet potatoes?' A very small, weak mouse volunteered, 'I'll go!' But seeing how small and weak she was, the Old Mouse and the rest of the tribe did not let her go, for fear she might be unequal to the task.

"But the little mouse insisted, 'Young and weak as I am, I have wonderful magic powers and great eloquence and resourcefulness. I swear to manage better than all the rest.'

"'How can you manage to do that?' asked the other mice. 'I'll not steal like them at all,' said the little mouse, 'but by giving my body a few shakes I'll change myself into a sweet potato and mix in a pile of others to escape detection.' 'It certainly sounds nice,' said the other mice, 'but how do you manage the transfiguration? Do show us first.' 'That's easy,' said the little mouse with a confident smile, 'just watch.' She gave her body a couple of shakes and changed into a lovely girl with a most charming face.

"The other rats all laughed. 'Oh no, you've made a mistake,' they cried. 'You've changed into a young lady, not a sweet potato!'

"'You're so ignorant!' retorted the little mouse, resuming her original form. 'You only know what sweet potatoes are, but don't know the daughter of Salt Commissioner Lin is really sweeter than any sweet potatoes'!"[2]

Black Jade immediately got up on her knees and pinned Magic Jade down. "You ill-tongued creature!" she cried, laughing. "I knew you were making fun of me."

She pinched Magic Jade until he begged for mercy. "Dear cousin, let me off. I won't do it again," he pleaded. "It was smelling that sweet perfume of yours that reminded me of this allusion."

"You make fun of me and then pretend it's but an allusion."

Just at that moment in walked Hairpin with a radiant smile. "Who's talking about allusions?" she asked. "I must hear this."

Black Jade hastily offered her a seat. "Can't you see? He mocks at me, and then pretends it's only an allusion."

"Oh, Cousin, really? I'm not surprised at all. He does know so many allusions. The only trouble is that he forgets them just when he needs them most."

"Amida Buddha!" cried Black Jade laughing outright. "After all you're my kind cousin. You've met your match now," she said to Magic Jade. "Now you're going to get as good as you give. We will see you paid in your own coin!"

At that moment the conversation was interrupted by a burst of angry shouting from Magic Jade's apartment. The three of them pricked up their ears.

"It's your nurse scolding Aroma," announced Black Jade. "There's nothing wrong with Aroma, yet your nurse is forever

---

[2]   This is an untranslatable pun. The "Yu" in Black Jade's Chinese name has the same sound as "Yu" meaning "potato."

finding fault with her. She really must be getting old and befuddled."

Magic Jade began to go towards the door to rush over to his apartment, but Hairpin stopped him. "Don't quarrel with your nurse. She's a silly old woman, but you should tolerate her."

"I know," said Magic Jade, and dashed off. He returned to his apartment to settle the dispute, and that night was peaceful.

The next day, with the arrival of cousin River Cloud, the Honored Mansion was afresh with new life. River Cloud was a granddaughter of the Lady Dowager. This pretty young lady had always been a welcome guest. Since her childhood she had been a good playmate for her cousin, Magic Jade.

Magic Jade happened to be with Hairpin when his child-hood playmate arrived. Accompanied by Hairpin, he went off to welcome her. He found her with the Lady Dowager. Black Jade and the other cousins were also all there. After they had greeted each other, Black Jade asked Magic Jade where he had been.

"With Cousin Hairpin," he answered.

"I see," said Black Jade sharply. "Thank goodness there is someone to keep you here, or you'd have flown away long ago."

"Are you the only one I'm allowed to play with or to amuse?" he answered with a smile. "I happen to drop in on her once and you make such an issue of it."

"Nonsense. What do I care if you go to see her or not?" Black Jade said. "I've never asked you to amuse me either. From now on maybe you can ignore me once and for all." With that she retired angrily to her room.

He ran after her. "Why lose your temper for no reason at all?" he pleaded. "Even if I said something wrong, you might at least sit there and chat with the others for a bit, instead of sulking alone."

"What I do is none of your business," she replied.

"Of course not, but I can't bear to see you spoiling your health."

"If I spoil my health and even die, that's my own affair. Nothing to do with you."

"Why talk about 'dying' or 'living' now in this joyful New Year?"

"I don't care. I will talk about death if I like. I'm going to die this minute. If you're afraid of death, I wish you long life. How about that?"

"If you carry on like this all the time I'm not afraid." Magic Jade said, smiling, "I wish I were dead. It would be a relief then."

"Exactly!" she retorted swiftly. "If you carry on like this, it would be better for me to die."

"I mean better for me to be dead. How you twist my words," he said.

As they were arguing, Precious Hairpin slipped in. "Cousin River Cloud is waiting for you," she said. Then she took him away.

More sulky than ever, Black Jade sat down by the window and shed tears of rage.

But in less time than it takes to drink a cup of tea, Magic Jade came back. The mere sight of him made her sob violently. He knew that it would be hard to pacify her and he was ready to coax her with all sorts of kind words. But before he could open his mouth she forestalled him:

"Why have you come back to bother me again? You've got a new playmate now, someone better than I am at reading and writing, and better at chatting and laughing with you, too. Someone who dragged you away for fear you might lose your temper. So why come back?"

Magic Jade stepped to her side and said softly, "Old friends are best friends and close relatives are kindest. You are too intelligent not to know that. Even dense as I am, I know it. You see, you're the daughter of my father's sister, while Hairpin's a cousin on my mother's side. Thus you're more closely related to me than she is. Besides, you came here first. We've eaten at the same table, shared the same bedroom, and grown up together, while she only recently arrived here. How could I be less close to you because of her presence?"

"Do I want you to be less close to her?" asked Black Jade. "What do you take me for? It's just that my feelings are hurt."

"And it's your feelings that concern me. Do you only know your own heart and not mine?"

Black Jade lowered her head and kept silent. After a little pause she said, "You blame other people for finding fault with you, without realizing how provoking you can be. Take today, for example. Why did you leave off your fox-fur cape when it's turned so cold?"

"I was wearing it until you got angry. Then I got so hot and bothered that I took it off," Magic Jade said with a laugh.

"Well," she sighed, "if you catch cold, then you'll be complaining about that!"

At this moment their conversation was interrupted by the arrival of River Cloud, who said with her funny-sounding lisp, "You two can be together every day. I come here so seldom, yet you both ignore me."

"What a funny pronunciation our little cousin has!" laughed Black Jade, trying to copy River Cloud's mode of speech.

"If you copy her long enough, you'll soon be talking the same way," Magic Jade teased. "You're always finding fault with others. You won't even overlook the tiniest defect in another's pronunciation. But I know someone you'd never dare to find fault with. If you do, you can be really proud of yourself."

"Who's that?" Black Jade asked promptly.

"Dare you pick fault with Cousin Hairpin? If so, you're really great."

"Oh her!" Black Jade said with a cold smile, "I wondered whom you meant. How could I ever presume to find fault with her?"

Magic Jade tried to cut her short and began talking about something else. But River Cloud rattled on. "Of course I'll never be a match for you in this lifetime. I just pray that you'll marry a *huthband* who talks like me. Amida Buddha! May I live to see that day!"

That set Magic Jade laughing, and River Cloud turned and ran out of the room.

Magic Jade called after her, "Mind you, don't fall! She can't catch up with you." He barred Black Jade's way at the door and urged with a chuckle, "Do let her off this time."

"Never! I'll get her if it's the last thing I do in my life," said Black Jade, trying in vain to push him aside.

Seeing Magic Jade blocking the doorway and Black Jade unable to get past, River Cloud stopped and called with a laugh, "Let me off, dear cousin, please. Just this once, OK?"

Hairpin, who had come up behind her, chimed in, "I advise you two to make up for Cousin Magic Jade's sake."

"Nothing doing!" cried Black Jade. "You two are hand in glove to pull my leg."

"Give it up. Who dares make fun of you?" Magic Jade tried to persuade her. "She wouldn't have teased you, if you hadn't teased her first."

The four of them were still in the thick of their domestic battle when they were invited to dinner in the Lady Dowager's room. Lady Wang, Phoenix, and the other cousins were already there. After dinner they chatted for a while before retiring. River Cloud went back to Black Jade's room, with Magic Jade escorting them. That night River Cloud shared a bed peacefully with Black Jade. It was after eleven o'clock when Aroma came to hurry Magic Jade to bed. She had to urge him to leave several times before he would return to his own room to sleep.

12/   Magic Jade's Enlightenment

Early the next morning Magic Jade put on his clothes and slippers and went to Black Jade's bedroom. He found his two cousins still in bed, fast asleep. The absence of the maids made it possible for him to observe them freely. Black Jade lay peacefully with closed eyes, wrapped in an apricot-red silk quilt, while River Cloud's dark hair had fallen beside the pillow, her quilt barely reached her armpits, and one white arm adorned with two gold bracelets lay exposed outside the bedding.

"She can't be still even when asleep," he sighed. "If there's a draught, she'll be complaining of a stiff neck!" He gently pulled up the bedding to cover her arm.

Black Jade sensed someone's presence and opened her eyes. Looking around, she found it was Magic Jade, and she asked: "What are you doing here so early?"

"Early? Get up and see if it's early."

"You'd better go outside a minute if you want us to get up."

So Magic Jade went into the outer room. The two cousins got up and dressed. He then rejoined them and sat by the dressing table, watching them wash themselves. After River Cloud finished washing, a maid began to take the basin away.

"Just a minute!" called Magic Jade. "I may as well wash here to save the trouble of going back to my room."

He went over and leaned down to wash his face, but declined the maid's offer of toilet soap, explaining, "There's plenty in here." Then he rinsed his mouth and cleaned his teeth. After that he turned to River Cloud. She had just finished doing her hair.

"Kind cousin, do my hair for me, please!" he begged.

"No, I can't," said River Cloud.

"Dear cousin, you did it before," he coaxed with a smile.
"But now I've forgotten how to."

"I'm not going out today, and I'm not going to wear a cap," Magic Jade persisted. "Just plait it up a bit."

He coaxed and wheedled her with endless terms of endearment until she finally gave in. Then River Cloud combed and dressed his hair.

At that point Aroma entered the room, but withdrew when she saw that Magic Jade had obviously finished his toilet. Aroma returned to his apartment to do her own hair and there Hairpin came to ask her where Magic Jade was.

"He's hardly ever at home nowadays." replied Aroma with an ironic smile, indicating the apartment next door, the one occupied by Black Jade and River Cloud.

Hairpin took the hint.

The maid went on with a sigh, "It's all right for cousins to enjoy each other's company, but still there's a limit. They shouldn't play about together day and night. Yet it's no use our talking, it's just a waste of breath."

Judging by what she said, Hairpin thought that this maid showed excellent sense. Hairpin sat down with her for a chat, asking her age and where she came from. She carefully sounded the maid out on various subjects and got a most favorable impression. But soon Magic Jade returned, and then Hairpin took her leave without even a word of greeting.

"You two seemed to be enjoying a nice chat," he said to Aroma. "Why did Cousin Hairpin leave when I came in?"

Aroma didn't answer until he repeated the question.

"Why ask me?" she then retorted. "How do I know what goes on between you two?"

Magic Jade saw that Aroma was not her usual self. "What makes you get so worked up?" he asked gently.

"Who am I to get worked up?" Aroma smiled sarcastically. "You'd better keep away from me. There are others who'll look after you, so don't bother me. I'll go back to wait on the old lady." She lay down and closed her eyes.

Magic Jade sat down beside her and tried to soothe her with kind words, but she kept her eyes shut and paid no attention to him.

Magic Jade finally sighed, "All right. If you're going to ignore me, I'll go to bed."

That whole day Magic Jade stayed indoors, not playing about with the girls of the house or the maids, but just reading or writing to while the time away.

After spending part of the New Year holiday with the Jias, it was time for River Cloud to go home. However, the Lady Dowager urged her to stay until after the birthday of Hairpin and the opera performance. So River Cloud agreed to stay on. She sent someone home to fetch two pieces of embroidery as a birthday gift for her cousin.

Since Hairpin's arrival, the Lady Dowager had been deeply impressed by her steady and amiable behavior. As this would be Hairpin's first birthday celebration in their house, the old lady asked Phoenix to come, and she gave Phoenix twenty ounces of silver from private savings for a birthday banquet and an opera celebration.

On the twenty-first a small stage was set up in the Lady Dowager's inner courtyard. A new troupe of young actresses had been invited to perform the operas. Tables were spread in the hall for a family banquet.

That morning, not seeing Black Jade around, Magic Jade went to look for her and found her curled up on her bed.

"Come on, time for breakfast," he said. "The show will soon begin. Tell me what opera you'd prefer to see and I'll know which one to choose."

"If you're so anxious to please me," said Black Jade coldly, "you ought to hire a troupe specially to put on all my favorite operas. It's a cheap sort of kindness to treat me at someone else's expense!"

"That's easy enough to do," said Magic Jade, "we'll hire the troupe next time and return the kindness by having their favorite operas performed."

He pulled her up from the bed and they went off hand in hand.

The opera performance lasted from morning till night. Exciting scenes from *Pilgrimage to the West* were followed by *The Drunken Monk* and *The General Feigns Madness*. The Lady Dowager enjoyed the comedies very much. After the entertainment she had two of the young artists brought to her. One of them had played the heroine; the other, the merry clown. The old lady rewarded each with some delicacies and extra money.

"When that young actress is made up, she's the living image of someone here," remarked Phoenix. "Have none of you noticed?"

Hairpin immediately knew to whom she was referring, but she just smiled. Magic Jade too nodded, but did not dare reply. Only River Cloud was tactless enough to blurt out, "Oh, I know! She looks just like Cousin Black Jade."

Magic Jade shot her a warning glance, but too late, for by now everyone had noticed the resemblance, and declared that it was most striking. Black Jade, of course, was angered by the remark. Soon after this the party broke up.

That evening, while undressing, River Cloud ordered her maid to pack her things.

"What's the hurry?" asked the maid. "We can start packing when it's time to leave."

"We're leaving tomorrow morning. Why should we stay here and put up with unwelcome looks?"

Magic Jade overheard this exchange and hurried in to take River Cloud by the hand.

"Dear Cousin, you've got me wrong," he said. "Black Jade is so sensitive that the others didn't name her for fear of upsetting her. How could she help being annoyed, the way you blurted it out? I shot you a warning glance because I didn't want you to hurt her feelings. It's ungrateful and unfair of you to be angry with me. If it had been anybody else but you, I wouldn't care how many people she offended."

River Cloud waved him away crossly.

"Don't try to get round me with your flattering talk. I'm not in the same class as your Cousin Black Jade. It's all right for other people to make fun of her, but I'm not even allowed to mention her. She's a grand young lady, I'm only a slave. How dare I offend her?"

"I was only thinking of you, yet now you put me in the wrong." Magic Jade was desperate. "If I meant any harm, may I turn into dust this instant and be trampled down by everyone!"

"Stop talking nonsense just after the New Year. Or go and keep up that kind of talk for the sensitive, easily upset person you were talking about. She knows how to manage you. Don't make me spit at you!" said River Cloud angrily as she ran off to the Lady Dowager's apartment to spend the night.

Magic Jade turned back, much dejected. He was longing for Black Jade's company, but he had scarcely set his foot in her room when she pushed him out and closed the door in his face. Perplexed, he called in a soft voice through the window:

"Dear cousin!"

Black Jade simply ignored him.

He hung his head there in depressed silence. The house maid knew it would be useless to reason with him at a time like this. So he was left standing there like a fool. As there was no sound for some time, Black Jade thought that he had gone to his room. She opened the door. Then, when she saw him still standing there, she hadn't the heart to shut him out again. He followed her into the room.

"There's always a reason for everything," he said. "If you explain, people don't feel so hurt. What's upset you suddenly?"

"A fine question to ask!" Black Jade gave a cold laugh. "I don't know. For you I'm but a poor figure, to be compared with a young actress in order to raise a laugh."

"But why are you angry with me? I didn't make the comparison. I didn't laugh at you either."

"I should hope not. But what you did was even worse than the others laughing and making comparisons."

Magic Jade did not know how to defend himself and so he remained silent.

"I wouldn't have minded so much if you hadn't made eyes at River Cloud," Black Jade went on. "Just what did you mean by that? That she'd reduce her status by kidding with me? She's the daughter of a noble house, I'm nobody. If she were to joke with me and I were to answer back, that would be degrading for her. Was that your idea? That was certainly kind on your part. Too bad she didn't appreciate your thoughtfulness, but flared up instead. Then you tried to excuse yourself at my expense, calling me 'narrow-minded and quick to take offense.' You were afraid she might offend me. But what is it to you if I get angry with her? Or if she offends me?"

Magic Jade then realized that she had overheard his conversation with River Cloud. He had tried to play the part of a mediator between them, but instead of getting a reward for his good intentions, was now blamed by both sides. This reminded him of the passage by the great Chinese philosopher Zhuang Zi:

> *The cunning waste their pains;*
> *The wise men vex their brains;*
> *But the fool seeks no gains,*
> *Enjoying the simple food, he wanders free*
> *Like a drifting boat with no ties on the sea.*

And again:

> *Mountain trees are the first to be felled,*
> *clear springs the first to be consumed.*

The more Magic Jade thought about the matter, the more depressed he grew.

If I can't even cope with just these two girls, what will it be like in the future, he reflected. At this point it seemed quite useless to attempt to justify himself, so he started back to his room.

Black Jade realized that he must be very downcast by what had happened between them, but this only made her angrier.

"Go off, then!" she cried. "And never come back! Don't speak to me any more!"

Magic Jade ignored her. He went straight to his own room, threw himself on the bed, and lay there staring at the ceiling. After a little while, he got up and went to the desk to work off his bad humor by writing a stanza depicting the trouble of life and Buddhist renunciation of the world:

Should you test me and I test you,
Should heart and mind be tested too,
Till there remains no more to test,
That rest would be of all the best.
When nothing can be called a test,
My feet will find a place to rest.

He was not completely satisfied with the verse because he feared others might not be able to read between the lines, so he wrote another poem, this one to the tune of *Parasitic Grass,* and then he read them both through again. Having done this, he felt more free and relieved and he lay down peacefully to sleep.

A little later Black Jade slipped into his room full of curiosity. Under the pretext of looking for Aroma, she was trying to find out how things were with Magic Jade. Aroma told her that Magic Jade was already asleep.

Black Jade was ready to leave when Aroma said with a smile, "Just a minute, miss. He wrote something you might like to look at."

She handed Black Jade the verses Magic Jade had written before he went to sleep. Black Jade was amused by their content but, at the same time, felt sorry for the boy.

"It's just a joke, nothing serious." she told Aroma.

Black Jade then took the verses back to her own room and shared them with River Cloud. The next day she showed it to Hairpin, as well. The second verse ran:

If there's no "I," neither is there "you,"
If she misunderstands you then why rue?
Freely I come and freely, too, I go,
Giving myself to neither joy nor woe,
Close kin or distant—it's the same to me.
What was the point of all my past toil?
Looking back now, it's worth nothing at all.

Having read this, Hairpin laughed. "So it's all my fault for reciting that song to him yesterday. There's nothing that so easily leads people astray as these Taoist teachings and paradoxes. If he really starts taking such nonsense seriously, I'll be the first to blame."

She tore up the verses and told the maids to burn them at once.

"You shouldn't have done that," Black Jade said with a smile. "I've some questions to ask him. Come with me, we'll cure him of this nonsense."

So the three girls went to his room.

Black Jade opened the attack by saying, "Let me put a question to you. 'Bao' means that which is most precious, and 'Yu'[3] that which is most solid. But in what way are you precious? In what way are you solid?"

Magic Jade could not answer.

The girls laughed: "Such a stupid fellow wants to go in for Buddhist Enlightenment!"

Black Jade continued, "The last two lines of your verse are all very well,

When nothing can be called a test
My feet can find a place to rest.

but it seems to me they still lack a little something. Let me add two more:

---

[3]   "Bao" and "Yu" are two of the words that Magic Jade used in his verse.

When there's no place for feet to rest,
That is the purest state and best."

"Yes, that shows your *real* understanding," put in Hairpin. "In the old days when the Sixth Master of the Buddhist Southern Sect went to Shaozhou in search of a teacher, he heard that the Fifth Master was in the monastery on Mt. Yellow Plums. So he took a job as a cook there. The Fifth Master was looking for a successor. He ordered each of his monks to compose a Sutra stanza. His senior disciple recited:

The body is a Bodhi tree,
The mind a mirror dear;
Often keep it polished clean,
Let no dust settle there.

"Well, the cook monk heard this as he was hulling rice in the kitchen and commented, 'It's not bad, but it's still not right.' Then he recited his own version:

The Bodhi tree is no tree,
The mind no mirror clear;
Since nothing is really there,
Where can any dust appear?

"Then the Buddhist sectarian resigned the leadership of his sect in favor of the cook monk. Your verse amounts to much the same thing. But Magic Jade, what about the Buddhist puzzle you set him just now? He hasn't answered it yet. How can you leave it at that?"

"Failure to answer promptly means defeat," said Black Jade. "You mustn't talk about Buddhist contemplation any more. You know even less about it than the two of us, yet you're striving for Buddhist contemplation."

Magic Jade had, in fact, thought that he had already attained Buddhist enlightenment, but now he had been floored by Black Jade and Hairpin. He thought to himself, they understand more about these things than I do, yet still they haven't attained full enlightenment. Why should I trouble myself over such matters?

After reaching this comfortable conclusion, he explained with a smile, "I wasn't striving for Buddhist contemplation. It was only for fun, the mood of a moment, that's all."

So the four of them made up.

13/ Black Jade Buries the Fallen Blossoms

After Yuanchun returned to the Palace from her visit to the Grand View Garden, she thought it would be a pity and waste if her father should lock up and close such charming pleasure grounds after her visit. And she thought that because the girls of the family were all poetically inclined, the garden would make a perfect setting for them if they were to move there. They would be surrounded by flowers and willows.

She also reflected on the fact that her brother, Magic Jade, was always in the company of the girls, and so if he alone were excluded, he would feel left out in the cold. This might distress the Lady Dowager and Lady Wang. She decided that she had better give directions for him to move into the garden, too.

Having reached this decision, she sent a eunuch to the Honored Mansion with orders that, "Precious Hairpin and the other young ladies are to live in the garden, which is not to be closed. Magic Jade is to move in as well and to continue his studies there."

Jia Zheng and his wife lost no time in sending servants to clean up the garden and furnish the various places with blinds and bed curtains to be used by Magic Jade and the young ladies of the family.

When he heard of these arrangements, Magic Jade was beside himself with joy. He was discussing the matter with his grandmother, demanding this, that, and the other. Then he asked Black Jade, who was also there, in which part of the garden she would like to live.

Black Jade had already been thinking this over and answered, "My choice would be the Bamboo Cottage. I love the bamboos and the winding, half-hidden balustrade. It's more quiet and peaceful than anywhere else."

"Just what I thought!" Magic Jade clapped his hands. "That's where I'd like you to stay. With me in the Happy Red Residence Hall, we'll be close together and both places are cozy and quiet."

At this point Jia Zheng sent a servant to report to the Lady Dowager that the twenty-second of the second month would be a lucky day for the group to move into the Grand View Garden. The rooms would be ready for them then.

It was finally settled that Hairpin would live in the All-spice Hall, Black Jade in the Bamboo Cottage, Yingchun in the Fine Splendor Pavilion, Tanchun in the Autumn Breeze Studio, Xichun in the Lotus Pavilion, Li Wan in the Sweet Rice Village, and Magic Jade in the Happy Red Residence Hall. Two old nurses and four maids were assigned to each apartment in addition to the occupant's own attendants. There were other servants also assigned there, whose sole duty was cleaning and sweeping.

On the twenty-second they all moved in. The silent and deserted garden came to life at once. The flowers and willows waved in the breeze.

Magic Jade found life in the garden all he could wish for. He asked nothing more than to spend every day with his sisters, cousins, and maids, reading, writing, playing the lute and playing chess, chanting poems and painting, watching the girls embroider their phoenix patterns, enjoying the flowers, guessing riddles, or playing finger games. In a word, he was happy.

However, after some time of this quiet life he became dissatisfied. His servant tried to think of some way to amuse him and decided that there was one thing that might appeal to his master—exicting stories. The servant went to a bookstore and bought his young master a pile of novels, old and new, tales about imperial concubines and queens as well as romantic play scripts.

Magic Jade had never read such books before. He believed that he had discovered a new world of treasures.

"Don't take them into the garden," the servant warned him. "If they were found there I'd be in real trouble."

But how could Magic Jade agree to this? After much hesitation, he picked out several volumes written in a more refined style to keep by his bed and read when no one was around. Then he left the cruder and more indecent ones hidden in his study outside the garden.

One day, about the middle of the third month, he was carrying a copy of *The Romance of West Chamber* as he strolled across a bridge after breakfast. There he sat down on a rock under a blossoming peach tree to read. He had just reached the line "red petals are falling in drifts" when a gust of wind suddenly rained a shower of petals down from the tree above. The petals covered his clothes, his books, and all the ground about him. He didn't want to shake them off for fear they might be trampled underfoot. Thus he caught as many as he could in the lap of his gown, carried them to the water's edge, and shook them into the brook. They floated and circled there for a while, then drifted down the river.

Going back to the bridge, he found the ground still carpeted with falling petals. As he hesitated, a voice from behind him said, "What are you doing here?"

He looked around and saw it was Black Jade. She was carrying a garden hoe, a gauze bag, and a broom in her hands.

"You've come at the right moment," said Magic Jade, smiling at her. "Here, sweep these petals up and throw them into the water for me. I've just thrown a lot of them in myself."

"It isn't a good idea to throw them in the water," said Black Jade, "the water here is clean, but once it flows out of these grounds people empty all sorts of dirt and filth into it. The flowers will be spoiled. I've a grave for flowers in the corner over there. I'm sweeping them up and putting them in the gauze bag so I can bury them. In due time they'll turn back into soil. Isn't that cleaner?"

Magic Jade was overjoyed with this idea.

"Just let me put this book somewhere and I'll help," he offered.

"What book's that?"

"Oh, nothing but the *Doctrine of the Mean* and *The Great Learning* compiled by Confucius," he said, hastily trying to conceal the volume.

"There you go trying to fool me again. You would have done much better to let me have a look at it."

"I don't mind showing you, dear cousin," Magic Jade replied, "but you mustn't tell anyone else. It's a real masterpiece. You won't even think of eating once you start reading it." He passed her the book.

Black Jade put down her gardening tools to read. The more she read, the more she liked it. In less time than it takes to eat a meal, she had read several chapters. The power of the words and the beauty of the language left a lingering fragrance in her mouth. After finishing the reading, she sat there entranced, going over some of the lines in her mind.

"Cousin, don't you think it's wonderful?" he asked.

She smiled and nodded.

Magic Jade laughed, and quoted:

"How can a man, always sick, for I'm too sentimental,
Not be charmed by your beauty which causes cities and
    kingdoms to fall?"[4]

Black Jade flushed to the tips of her ears. She raised her sulky brows, and her half-drooping lids flashed with anger as she pointed an accusing finger at him. "You really are insolent! You're taking advantage of me by using those immoral words and tunes to insult me." At the words "taking advantage of me" her eyes were filled with tears. "I'll tell uncle and aunt."

She turned to go. Magic Jade rushed after her and barred her way. "Do forgive me this once, dear cousin," he said. "If I really meant to insult you, I'll fall into the pond tomorrow and let the scabby-headed tortoise swallow me so that I'll

---

[4]   Lines from *The Romance of West Chamber*.

change into a turtle myself. When you become a noble lady of the first rank and go to your paradise in Heaven, I'll bear the stone tablet at your grave on my back for ever as punishment."

Black Jade burst out laughing at this comical oath, and wiped her eyes.

"You're so easy to scare, yet you still go on talking nonsense," she teased. "Why, you're nothing but a flowerless sprout."

Now it was Magic Jade's turn to laugh. "Just listen to you! I'll tell on you, too. You boast that you can 'memorize a passage with a single glance.' Why can't I learn ten lines at a glance?" Laughing, Magic Jade put the book away. "Never mind that. Let's get on with burying the flowers."

No sooner had they buried the fallen petals than Aroma appeared.

"So here you are," she said, "I've been looking all over for you. Your uncle is not well and all the young ladies have gone to inquire after his health. The old lady wants you to go too. Come quickly and change your clothes."

Magic Jade then got his book, took leave of Black Jade, and went back to his own room with Aroma.

In the evening, after supper, Black Jade decided to pay Magic Jade a visit. As she strolled over, she saw Precious Hairpin going to the Happy Red Residence Hall before her. And by the time she reached the Hall, the gate was closed and she was obliged to knock on it.

It so happened that Skybright was in a bad humor, having just had a quarrel with another maid, and at Hairpin's arrival she transferred her anger to the visitor. She grumbled in the courtyard, "She keeps coming here and sitting around for no reason at all, keeping us up till midnight."

This fresh knocking on the gate only incensed her further. "They've all gone to bed," Skybright shouted, not bothering to ask who it was, "come back tomorrow."

Black Jade knew the maid's ways and tricks they played on each other. Assuming that girl in the courtyard had failed to recognize her voice and taken her for another maid, she called out again more loudly, "It's me, open the gate!"

Skybright still failed to recognize Black Jade's voice. "I don't care who you are," she said crossly, "our Master's given orders that no one's to be admitted."

Rooted indignantly to the spot and tempted to really let fly at the maid, Black Jade reflected on the fact that although her uncle's house was a second home to her, she was still an outsider here. With both her parents dead, she had no one to turn to except this family. It would be foolish to start a real fuss.

As she thought this, tears ran down her cheeks. She was wondering whether or not to go back when the sound of talk and laughter inside reached her ears. Listening attentively, she noted the voices of Magic Jade and Hairpin. This upset her even more. She thought back then to the events of the morning. Magic Jade must be angry with me, thinking I told on him, she reflected. But I never did. A person should really investigate before flying into a temper like this. He can shut me out today, but won't we still see each other tomorrow?

The more she thought, the more distressed she became. Standing under the blossom by the corner of the wall, with the cold dew on the green moss and the chill wind on the path, she gave way to sobs.

As she was sobbing to herself, the courtyard gate creaked open and out came Hairpin escorted by Magic Jade, Aroma, and some of the other maids. Black Jade thought of stepping forward to question Magic Jade, but not wanting to embarrass him in public, stood in the shadows, instead, until Hairpin had left and Magic Jade had gone back in with the maids.

As the gate was closed, she turned and her eyes were still fixed on the closed gate. Meanwhile she shed a few silent tears. Realizing that it was pointless to remain standing there alone, she turned and went back to her room in low spirits. Then she began to take off her ornaments and prepared listlessly for bed.

Cuckoo and Snowswan knew their young mistress' ways. She would often sit in gloomy silence, frowning or sighing

over nothing. Or, for no obvious reason, she would give way
to long spells of weeping. At first they had tried to comfort
her, imagining that she missed her parents and home or that
someone had been unkind to her; but, as time went by, they
found this was her habit and they paid little attention to it
any more. So this night they ignored her and left her alone to
her misery, continuing to attend to their own affairs in the
outer room.

Black Jade leaned against her bed rail, clasping her knees.
Her eyes were brimming with tears. There she stayed motionless as a statue, not lying down until late in the evening.

The next day was the twenty-sixth day of the fourth
month, the Festival of Grain in Ear. It was the time-honored
custom on this day to offer all manner of gifts and a farewell
feast to the God of Flowers, for this festival was said to mark
the beginning of summer when all the blossoms withered and
the God of Flowers had to leave his throne. As this custom
was most faithfully observed by women, all the girls in the
Grand View Garden rose early that day. They decked themselves out in their summer dresses so beautifully that they put
the very flowers and birds to shame. This added the final
touch of brightness to a scene beyond description.

Hairpin, the three Jia girls, Phoenix, and the maids enjoyed themselves in the Grand View Garden. Only Black Jade
was absent from this grand occasion.

Black Jade had risen late after a sleepless night. When she
heard that the other girls were saying farewell to the God of
Flowers in the garden, she made haste to dress and join them
for fear of being laughed at for her lazy habits.

A smiling Magic Jade appeared in the gateway as she was
stepping down into the courtyard. "Dear cousin, did you tell
on me yesterday?" he greeted her laughingly. "You had me
worrying the whole night long."

Black Jade turned, ignoring him, to speak to Cuckoo
about something. Then she walked on.

Magic Jade attributed this cold behavior of hers to the
lines he had quoted at noon the previous day, having no idea
of the incident in the evening. He bowed and raised his

clasped hands in salute, but Black Jade simply ignored him, walking straight off to find the other girls.

He was puzzled. Surely what happened yesterday can't account for this. he thought to himself. And I came back too late in the evening to see her again, so how else can I have offended her? With this reflection, he decided to follow her.

Meanwhile Black Jade had disappeared, and Magic Jade knew she was trying to avoid him. He decided to wait a couple of days until her anger had calmed down. Then, lowering his head, he noticed that the ground was carpeted with a bright profusion of the fallen petals of balsam and pomegranate trees.

"She's too angry to gather up the blossoms," he sighed. "I'll take these over and try to speak to her tomorrow."

He gathered up the fallen flowers in the skirt of his gown and made his way to a small hill across a stream and through plantations of trees and flowers towards the mound where Black Jade had buried the peach blossoms. Just before rounding the hill by the flowers' grave he heard the sound of sobs from the other side. Someone was lamenting and weeping there in a heart-rending manner.

Some maid's been badly treated and come here to cry, he thought to himself. He wondered who it might be. He halted to listen. And this is what he heard:

As blossoms fade and fly across the blue sky,
Who pities the faded red, the scent that has broken?
Softly the gossamer floats over spring pavilions,
Gently the willow fluff wafts to the embroidered screen.

A girl in her chamber mourns the passing of spring,
No relief from full sorrow her poor heart knows;
Rake in hand she steps through her embroidered curtain,
Hating to tread on the petals as she comes and goes.

Willow-floss and elm-pods, fresh and luxuriant,
Care not if peach and plum blossom drift away;
Next year the peach and plum will bloom again,

But who will stay in her lovely chamber that day?

This spring the scented nest is newly-built,
Yet the swallow on the beam is heartless all;
Next year, though again he may peck the buds,
From the beam of an empty room his nest will fall.

For three hundred and sixty days every year
The cutting wind and biting frost close them round.
How long can pretty flowers remain fresh and fair?
Once fallen off, their trace is nowhere to be found.

Easy to see their bloom, hard to find their fall;
The gravedigger's heart is overwhelmed with pain.
With a rake in hand, she sheds secret tears,
Falling on the bare twigs with blood stains.

The cuckoo sings no more when twilight unfolds,
Her rake brought back, the lodge is locked and still;
A dim lamp lights the wall as she has her first dream,
Cold rain pelts the window and her quilt remains chill.

What makes her heart so full of grief and sorrow?
She loves spring, yet is partly vexed by spring;
For suddenly it comes and suddenly it goes;
So silent its arrival, so soundless its parting!

Last night from the yard floated a sad song—
Was it the soul of blossoms or the soul of birds?
But neither flowers nor birds would stay long,
For blossoms are so shy, birds have no words.

How I wish I could fly with wings this day
With the flowers towards earth's furthest bound!
And yet at the earth's furthest bound
Where can a fragrant burial mound be found?

Better shroud the fair petals in a silk bag

With clean soil for their romantic attire;
For pure you came and pure you shall go,
Not sinking into some foul ditch or mire.

Now you are dead and I have come to bury you;
None has divined the day when I shall die;
Men laugh at my folly in burying fallen flowers,
But who will come to bury me when dead I lie?

When spring closes and flowers begin to fall,
Rosy cheeks must then lose color and fade;
Once spring is gone and youth has fled,
Who cares for the fallen petals or the dead maid?[5]

All this was chanted in a low voice, half-choked with sobs. As the words were recited, they only inflamed the grief of the reciter, Black Jade. However, she did not know Magic Jade, listening to the sad tune, was also overwhelmed with grief.

Black Jade held Magic Jade to blame for Skybright's refusal to open the gate for her. As today happened to be the occasion for feasting the God of Flowers, her pent-up resentment merged with her grief at the transience of spring. And as she buried the fallen petals, she could not help weeping over her own fate and thus composed the lament.

Magic Jade listened from the slope. At first he just nodded and sighed sympathetically, but then she came to the last few lines:

Men laugh at my folly in burying fallen flowers,
But who will bury me when dead I lie?...
The day when spring is gone and beauty fades
Who will care for the fallen petals or dead maid?

---

[5]   Quoted from Yang Xianyi and Gladys Yang's English version with some variations.

At this point he flung himself on the ground in a fit of weeping, scattering his load of fallen flowers all over the ground.

Black Jade, giving way to her own grief, now heard the weeping on the slope. She thought to herself, everyone laughs at me for being foolish. Is there someone else equally foolish? Then, looking up, she saw it was Magic Jade.

"So that's who it is," she snorted. "That heartless, wretched..."

But the moment the word "wretched" escaped her, she covered her mouth and moved quickly away with a long sigh.

By the time Magic Jade recovered sufficiently to look up, she had gone, obviously to avoid him. Getting up listlessly, he dusted off his clothes and walked down the hill to make his way back to the Happy Red Residence Hall.

Near there he caught sight of Black Jade walking ahead. He overtook her. "Do stop!" he begged, "I know you won't look at me, but let me just say one word. After that we can part company for good."

Black Jade glanced around and would have ignored him, but was curious to hear this "one word," thinking there must be something in it. She came to a halt.

"Out with it," she said.

Magic Jade smiled. "Would you listen if I said two words?" he asked.

At once she walked away. Magic Jade, close behind her, sighed. "Why are things between us so different now from in the past?" Against her will, she stopped once more and turned her head.

"What do you mean by 'now' and 'the past'?" Magic Jade asked, heaving another sigh.

"Oh, wasn't I your playmate when you first came?" he demanded. "Anything that was mine became yours if it pleased you. If I knew you fancied a favorite dish of mine, I put it away in a clean place till you came. We ate at the same table and slept on the same bed. I took care that the maids did nothing to upset you, for I thought cousins growing up together as good friends should be kinder to each other than to anyone else. I never expected you to have grown so proud that now you have no use for me, while you're so fond of outsiders like Hairpin and Phoenix.

"You ignore me or cut me off for three or four days at a time. I've no brothers or sisters of my own—only two by a different mother, as you well know. So I'm an only child like you, and I thought that would make for an affinity between us. But apparently it was no use my hoping for that. There's nobody to whom I can say how unhappy I am." With that, he broke down again.

This appeal and his obvious wretchedness melted her heart. Sympathetic tears stole down her own cheeks, and she hung her head saying nothing.

This encouraged Magic Jade to go on.

"I know my own faults now. But however bad I may be, I'd never dare do anything to hurt you. If I do something the least bit wrong, you can warn me, scold me, or even strike me, and I won't mind. But when you just ignore me and I can't tell why, I'm at my wits' end and don't know what to do. If I die now I can only become a 'ghost hounded to death,' and even the prayers of the best bonzes and Taoists will not be able to save my soul. I can only be born again if you'll tell me what's wrong."

By now Black Jade's resentment over the previous evening's gate incident had been completely forgotten.

"Well, in that case, why did you tell your maids not to open the gate for me when I called last night?" she asked.

"I honestly don't know what you are referring to," he said in surprise. "If I really did such a thing, may I die on the spot!"

"Hush! Don't talk about death at this time of the morning. It's not lucky to say things like that. Did you or didn't you tell them to keep me out? There's no need to swear."

"I honestly know nothing about your call. Hairpin did drop in for a chat, but she didn't stay long and went away."

Black Jade thought this statement over. "Yes," she said more cheerfully, "it must have been the maids being lazy. Certainly they can answer the door rudely, sometimes."

"That's it, for sure. I'll find out who it was when I get back and give her a dressing-down."

"Those maids of yours deserve one, although it's not really for me to say so. It doesn't matter their offending me, but just think what trouble there'll be if next time they offend your precious Hairpin."

She compressed her lips into a smile, and Magic Jade didn't know whether to grind his teeth or laugh.

At this point the maids came to summon them to a meal, and the two reconciled cousins went together to Lady Wang's apartment.

14/ A Lovelorn Girl Falls Deeper in Love

As the Dragon Boat Festival was near at hand, the Lady Dowager decided to visit a Taoist temple outside of town. Her purpose was to effect a change of her monotonous life at home. During the visit, Zhang, the Chief Priest, suggested to the grandmother a plan for the marriage of Magic Jade. But after the priest opened the subject to Magic Jade, he began to sulk and he declared that he would never visit the temple again.

Then, learning that Black Jade had a slight sunstroke, he became so worried that he would not touch a bit of his food. He kept going to her quarters to find out how she was. Once, as he entered her room, she asked, "Why don't you go to the temple and enjoy the shows with the others? What's the point of staying at home?"

Her question annoyed him. He was, of course, trying to avoid the temple because of Priest Zhang's recent attempt at matchmaking. Her seeming indifference to this fact made him even more irritated. He thought to himself, I could forgive others for misunderstanding me, but now even she is making fun of me. His resentment increased a hundredfold. He would not have flared up had it been anyone else, but Black Jade's words were a different matter. His face clouded over.

"All right, all right," he said sullenly, "after all, we've known each other for many years in vain."

"Yes, it's quite true," she replied. "Unlike certain other persons, there is nothing at all about me which suits you," she laughed sarcastically.

He moved close to her, deeply irritated, and said, "You do realize, don't you, that you've deliberately spoken a cold-hearted curse regarding my death."

Black Jade did not understand what he was driving at.

"I swore an oath to you yesterday, and today you provoke me. If Heaven and Earth destroyed me, what good would it be for you?" Magic Jade went on.

Now Black Jade remembered their previous conversation and realized that she was wrong to have spoken as she did. She felt both ashamed and a little frantic.

"If I wish you harm, may Heaven and Earth destroy me too," she sobbed. "I don't see why you have gotten so worked up. I know, when Zhang the Taoist spoke of your marriage yesterday, you were afraid he might prevent the match of your choice. And now you're working your temper off on me."

Magic Jade had developed a fascination with girls since early childhood. And having been intimate with Black Jade, he found that their hearts were one. Now that he had read some forbidden books, he had come to feel that none of the other girls of fine beauty and breeding he knew could possibly be compared with Black Jade. He had long since set his heart on her, but could not admit it. So, whether happy or angry, he used every means to sound her out and see if this feeling for her was reciprocated.

And Black Jade felt the same about him, but disguised her real feelings to test him in return. Thus each concealed his or her real sentiments to sound the other out. As the proverb says so well, 'When false meets false, the truth will come out.' So inevitably, in the process of testing each other, they kept quarreling over trifles.

Take the present instance. Magic Jade was reflecting on the fact that he could forgive others for misunderstanding him, but Black Jade ought to know that she was the only one he cared for. Instead of sharing his trouble, she only provoked him with silly talk. It should be obvious to her that she was always in his heart, but she seemed to have no place for him in her's. However, to tell Black Jade this was beyond him.

As for Black Jade, she was thinking to herself that she knew he had a place for her in his heart, and that he certainly couldn't take that vicious talk about gold matching jade very seriously. Instead, he was probably thinking of her in a serious manner. Even if she raised the subject, he should be taking it calmly so as to show that it meant nothing to him, that the only one he really cared for was her. Why should he get so worked up at the mention of gold and jade? This only showed that he was thinking about them all the time. Perhaps he was afraid that she suspected this when she mentioned them, and so he put on a show of being worked up—just to fool her.

Magic Jade told himself that nothing else mattered as long as she was happy, that, if necessary, he'd die for her at that very instant. Whether she knew it or not, she could at least feel that in his heart she was close to him, not distant.

And Black Jade told herself that he should not mind her, but just be his own self. Since they had been so close to each other, his formality now just meant that he would not let her be close to him anymore, but that he wanted her to keep her distance.

So their mutual concern for each other resulted in their estrangement. But it is hard to describe in detail all their secret thoughts. Let us now just record the outward appearances.

Those words "the nice match of your choice" infuriated Magic Jade. Too choked with rage to speak, he tore the magic jade from his neck and dashed it on the floor.

"You rubbish thing!" he cried, gritting his teeth. "I'll smash you to pieces and put an end to this once and for all."

The jade was too hard to break, however, and so no damage was done. Magic Jade looked around for something to smash it with.

Black Jade weeped before such a scene. "Why smash a dumb object?" she sobbed. "Better destroy me instead."

The sound of their quarreling brought Cuckoo and Snowswan hurrying in to stop the battle. Seeing that Magic

Jade was trying to smash his stone, they tried to snatch it away from him, but failed. This quarrel was more serious than usual, and they had to send for Aroma. She came back with them as fast as she could and eventually managed to rescue the jade stone.

Magic Jade smiled bitterly. "I can smash what's mine, can't I? What business is it of yours?"

Aroma had never before seen him so livid with rage, his eyes and brows wild and contorted. "Because you have a disagreement with your cousin, there is no reason to smash this up," she said, taking his hand gently, "suppose you broke it, just think how bad she'd feel."

This touched Black Jade's heart, yet it only hurt her more to think that Magic Jade had less consideration for her than he did for Aroma. She sobbed bitterly. So much emotion was too much for her weak stomach. Suddenly she threw up the herbal medicine she had taken shortly before. Cuckoo quickly held out a handkerchief to receive the vomit. Soon the handkerchief was soaked through. Meanwhile Snowswan massaged Black Jade's back.

"No matter how angry you are, miss, do think more of your health!" Cuckoo said. "You were feeling a little better after the medicine; it's this tiff with the young master that's made you retch. If you really fall ill, how upset he will be."

This touched Magic Jade's heart, yet it also struck him as proof that Black Jade had less consideration for him than she did for Cuckoo. But now Black Jade's cheeks were flushed and swollen. Weeping and choking, her face streaked with tears and sweat, she looked fearfully frail. The sight filled him with regret.

I should never have argued with her and got her into this state, he thought regretfully. I can't even suffer instead of her. Then he, too, couldn't help shedding tears.

Aroma, forcing a smile, said to Magic Jade, "You shouldn't quarrel with Black Jade, if only for the sake of this pretty cord she made for your jade."

At this Black Jade forgot her nausea and rushed over to snatch the jade, seizing a pair of scissors to cut off the cord.

Before Aroma and Cuckoo could stop her, she had cut it into several pieces.

"It's a waste of my effort," she sobbed. "He doesn't care for it. He can get someone else to make him a better one."

Aroma hastily took the jade from her.

"Why do that?" she protested. "It's my fault. I should have held my tongue."

"Go ahead and cut it up," said Magic Jade. "I'll not wear it anyway, so it doesn't matter."

Preoccupied with the quarrel, the four of them had failed to notice that several old nurses had bustled off without their knowing it to inform the Lady Dowager and Lady Wang about the quarrel, for they didn't want to be held responsible if any serious trouble would come of it. Their hurried and earnest report so alarmed the old lady and Lady Wang that both came to the garden to see what terrible thing had happened.

When the Lady Dowager and Lady Wang entered the room and found both Magic Jade and Black Jade quiet, neither of them willing to admit that anything was the matter, they vented their anger on their two chief maids. "Why don't you look after them properly?" they scolded. "Can't you do something when they start quarreling?"

The two maids had to listen meekly to a dressing-down, and peace was only restored when the old lady took Magic Jade away.

The next day, the third of the month, was Xue Pan's birthday, and the whole Jia family was invited to a feast and theatricals. Magic Jade had not seen Black Jade since he offended her, and he was feeling too remorseful and depressed to enjoy any show. He found an excuse not to attend the theatricals on the pretext of illness.

Black Jade was not seriously ill. She was simply suffering from the heat. When she heard of Magic Jade's refusal to go she thought to herself, he usually enjoys drinking and watching operas. If he's staying away today, either because he is still angry about yesterday's tiff or because he knows I'm not going. I should never have cut that cord off his jade. I'm sure he won't wear it again now unless I make him another. Indeed, she regretted the quarrel very much.

The Lady Dowager had hoped that they would stop sulking and make up while watching operas together. When both refused to go, she became upset. "What sins have I committed in a past life to be plagued with two such troublesome children?" the old lady grumbled. "Not a day goes by without something to worry about. How true the proverb is that 'Enemies and lovers are destined to meet!' Once I've closed my eyes and breathed my last, they can quarrel and storm as much as they like. What the eye doesn't see the heart doesn't grieve for. But I'm not ready for my last gasp just yet." With that she also wept.

When the word of this reached Magic Jade and Black Jade, neither of whom had heard that proverb before, they felt as if a great light had dawned. With lowered heads, they pondered its meaning and could not hold back their own tears. True, they were still apart, one shedding tears to the breeze in the Bamboo Cottage, the other sighing to the moon in the Happy Red Residence Hall. So the lines:

Though each was in a different place,
Their hearts in love beat as one.

Aroma advised Magic Jade, "It's entirely your fault. The day after tomorrow, the fifth of the month, is the Dragon Boat Festival. If you two go on looking daggers at each other that will make the old lady even angrier. Then there will be no peace for anyone. Do get over your temper tantrum and apologize. Let bygones be bygones. Wouldn't that be better for both of you?"

Black Jade also regretted her quarrel with Magic Jade, but could think of no pretext to go to him and make it up. So she spent all day and night in a state of unrelieved depression, feeling as if a part of her was lost.

Cuckoo, who guessed how she felt, tried to reason with her. "As a matter of fact, you were too hasty the other day, miss," she said. "We should know Magic Jade's temper even if no one else does. After all, it's not the first time there's been a quarrel over that jade."

"Why do you side with the others and blame me," snapped Black Jade. "In what way was I hasty?"

"Why did you cut off the cord for no reason at all?" answered Cuckoo. "That put you more in the wrong than Magic Jade. I know how devoted he is to you, miss. All this comes of your being easily offended and of the way you twist his words."

Before Black Jade could retort they heard someone calling at the courtyard gate.

"It's Magic Jade's voice," Cuckoo said, "He must be coming to apologize."

"Don't let him in."

"That wouldn't be right, miss. It's so hot. You're going to keep him standing outside in the blazing sun. Do you want him to get sunstroke?"

She went and opened the gate, ushering Magic Jade in with a smile. "I thought our young master would never cross this threshold of ours again," she remarked. "But here you are."

"You've made a mountain out of a molehill," he chuckled. "Why shouldn't I come? Even if I were dead, my ghost would be round here a hundred times a day. Tell me, is my cousin better?"

"In her health, yes, but not in her feelings," Cuckoo replied.

"I know what the trouble is with her," said Magic Jade.

He went in and found Black Jade in a fresh fit of weeping on her bed, because his arrival had touched her so much.

Walking up to her bedside he asked, "Are you feeling a little better?"

When she simply wiped her tears without responding, he sat down on the edge of the bed.

"I know you're not really angry with me," he said, "but if I stayed away, others might think we'd quarreled again. That would give them a chance to be peacemakers between us, as if the two of us were alienated from each other. So beat me or scold me as much as you like, but for pity's sake don't ignore me, dear cousin, sweet cousin!"

Black Jade had been determined to ignore him, but his words of endearment proved that she was dearer to him than anyone else, and so she could not keep her silence any more.

"You needn't flatter me," she sobbed. "I shall never dare be close to you again. Behave as if I'd gone"

"Where would you go?" Magic Jade laughed.

"Home."

"I'd go with you."

"What if I should die?"

"I'd become a monk."

At this Black Jade's face darkened. "What a silly thing to say! Why talk such nonsense? Think of all the sisters and girl cousins you have. Do you have so many lives that you can become a monk every time one of them dies? Wait and see what the others say when I tell them about what you just said."

Magic Jade realized at once that he had spoken without due consideration. Flushing red, he hung his head without a word, thankful that no one else was in the room.

Black Jade, too angry to speak, fixed him with furious eyes until his cheeks were burning. Then, clenching her teeth, she stabbed with one finger at his forehead. "You," she said. But this exclamation ended in a sigh as she took out her handkerchief and wiped away her tears.

Magic Jade's heart was very full and he was ashamed of speaking so foolishly. When she struck him and then sighed and wept without a word, he too was reduced to tears. He started to wipe them away with his sleeve, having forgotten to bring a handkerchief. Black Jade noticed through her own tears that he was wearing a new lilac-blue summer gown. She turned and took a silk handkerchief from her pillow, tossed it to him in silence, and then covered her face again.

Magic Jade picked up the handkerchief and wiped his tears away, then stepped forward to clasp her hand.

"You're breaking my heart with your tears," he declared. "Come, let's go and see the old lady."

"Take your hands off me!" She pulled away. "You're not a child any more, yet you still carry on in this shameless way. Can't you behave yourself?"

She was interrupted by the cry "Bravo!" This gave both of them a start. Turning around, they saw Phoenix sweeping in with beaming smiles.

"Grandmother has been grumbling away something awful," she informed them. "She insisted I come to see if you'd made it up. I told her, 'No need, they'll be friends again in less than three days.' But she scolded me for being too lazy. Well, here I am. Am I right to say so? I can't see what you two have to quarrel about. Come along with me, quick, to your grandmother to set the old lady's mind at rest." Phoenix caught hold of Black Jade meaning to lead her away.

Black Jade turned to call her maids, but not one was there.

"What do you want them for?" asked Phoenix. "I'll look after you." With that she pulled her out of the room. And Magic Jade followed them to the Lady Dowager's quarters.

"I said 'don't worry, they'll make it up themselves,'" announced Phoenix to the Lady Dowager, cheerfully. "But you wouldn't believe me, and insisted I go along as a peacemaker. I found they'd already asked each other's forgiveness, and were clinging together like an eagle sinking its talons into a hawk. They didn't need any peacemaker at all."

This set the whole room laughing.

Black Jade said nothing, but took a seat by her grandmother. To make conversation Magic Jade said to Hairpin, who was also there, "I would have to be out of sorts on your brother's birthday. That's why I haven't sent any present over, or even gone to offer my congratulations. If he doesn't know I'm unwell, he may think I was merely making excuses. If you can spare a moment, next time you see him, do explain to him, will you, cousin?"

"You're making a fuss about nothing," said Hairpin. "We wouldn't dare put you to any trouble even if you wished to go, much less so when you're unwell. As cousins you're always seeing so much of each other, I can't see any reason to behave like strangers."

"So long as you understand, then that's all right," he added. "But why aren't you watching the operas, cousin?"

"I can't stand the heat," said Hairpin, "I did watch a couple of acts, but it was so hot that I couldn't stay any longer. Since none of the guests left, I had to pretend not to feel well in order to slip away."

This sounded to Magic Jade like a reflection on him. In his embarrassment he said with a sheepish smile, "No wonder they compare you to Lady Yang,[6] you're both plump and sensitive to the heat."

Hairpin was so annoyed by this remark that she could have flown into a temper, but restrained herself. She reddened and laughed sarcastically. "If I'm so like Lady Yang," she retorted, "it's too bad I've got no brother or cousin to become another Prime Minister."

At this moment one of the young maids jokingly accused Hairpin of having hidden a fan she was looking for.

"You must have hidden it, miss," she said playfully, "come on, miss, please give it back to me."

"Behave yourself!" cried Hairpin sharply, pointing at her angrily. "Have I ever played such tricks with anyone else? You should ask the other young ladies who are always pulling your leg."

This rebuff scared the maid and she quickly went away.

Magic Jade realized that he had once again given offense by his thoughtless words. As this time he had done so in front of a lot of people, he was surely more embarrassed than he had been earlier with Black Jade. He turned away and tried to mutter a few words to someone else in order to smooth over his embarrassment.

---

[6]   Lady Yang, the favorite of the Brilliant Emperor of the Tang Dynasty, was said to be rather plump. Her brother became the prime minister through nepotism. Corrupt and lawless, he was put to death by the Imperial Guards during the Tang General An Lushan's rebellion.

But Magic Jade's scoffing remark gave Black Jade some secret satisfaction. She would have joined in had it not been for Hairpin's retort about the fan. Now she decided to change the topic of conversation. "What were the two operas you saw, cousin?" she asked.

Hairpin had observed the self-satisfied smile on Black Jade's face and knew quite well that Magic Jade's remark must have pleased her. Thus Hairpin answered with a smile. "The opera I saw was *Li Kuei Abuses Song Jiang and Then Apologizes.*"[7]

Magic Jade laughed. "Why, cousin," he cried, "surely you're well versed enough in ancient and modern Chinese literature to know the proper title of that opera. Why do you have to describe it in this way? It's called *A Sincere and Serious Apology.*"

"*A Sincere and Serious Apology*, is it?" retorted Hairpin. "You two are so well versed in ancient and modern literature, you must know all about 'A sincere and serious apology'—that's something quite beyond me."

Her words touched Magic Jade and Black Jade in a sensitive spot, and they immediately blushed.

When Hairpin saw Magic Jade so out of countenance, she simply smiled and let the matter drop. None of the others present had understood what they were talking about, so the others just kept silent.

Shortly after this, when Hairpin and Phoenix had left the room, Black Jade turned with a smile to Magic Jade. "Now you've come up against someone with a sharper tongue than mine. Not everyone's as simple and tongue-tied as I am, or so easy to tease."

---

[7]   Li Kuei was a peasant rebel, Song Jiang the leader of the outlaws in the classic Chinese novel, *Outlaws of the Marsh.*

15/ Magic Jade Bares His Heart

It was the day of the Dragon Boat Festival. At midday Lady Wang gave a family feast to celebrate the occasion. She invited Aunt Xue and her daughter, Hairpin, to join the banquet.

Magic Jade noticed that Hairpin was cold shouldering him. Obviously this was because of what had happened the day before. Seeing that Magic Jade was in such low spirits, Lady Wang ignored him deliberately. Black Jade, for her part, assumed that his dejection was the outcome of having offended Hairpin, and that displeased her too.

Now Black Jade preferred to be left alone rather than to congregate with other cousins. The reason for this she said was that, "Getting together is often followed by parting. The more pleasure people find in parties, the more lonely and unhappy they must feel when the parties break up. So better not get together in the first place. The same is true of flowers; they give people much pleasure when in bloom, but it's so heart-rending to see them fade away. It would be better if they never blossomed at all." Thus she grieved over what others enjoyed.

Magic Jade, on the other hand, wished that the parties would never break up, and the flowers never fade away. When at last a party ended and the flowers withered away, he found it extremely sad and heartbreaking, but it couldn't be helped.

So, though Black Jade didn't care when the guests parted in low spirits that day, Magic Jade went back to his room feeling so gloomy that he could do nothing but sigh.

About noon the next day, while Lady Wang, Hairpin, Black Jade, and the girls were gathering in the Lady

Dowager's room, one of the maids came in to announce the arrival of River Cloud.

Shortly afterwards, River Cloud appeared in the courtyard, attended by a group of maids and nurses. Hairpin, Black Jade, and the rest hurried out to the foot of the steps to greet her. As the cousins had not seen each other for a month, they naturally had a most affectionate reunion. After these greetings River Cloud went in to pay her respects to the Lady Dowager and others.

"When you've finished your tea and rested a bit," said the Lady Dowager to River Cloud, "then you can go and see your married cousins. After that, you can take a stroll and amuse yourself in the garden with the girls. It's nice and cool there."

River Cloud thanked her grandmother. After a little rest, she went off, accompanied by her nurses and maids, to call on Madam Phoenix. They chatted for a little while and then she went into Grand View Garden. There she turned to dismiss her escort.

"You needn't stay with me any longer," she said, "you can go off now and visit your friends and relatives. I'll just keep Fishy with me here." The others thanked her and went off, leaving River Cloud alone with Kingfisher.

By now they had reached the rose trellis.

"Look, what's that thing glittering like gold?" exclaimed River Cloud. "Has someone dropped a trinket here?"

Kingfisher quickly picked up the object and closed her fingers around it.

"I can't let you see this treasure, miss," she teased. "I wonder where it comes from. How very odd. I've never seen anyone here with such a thing."

"Let me have a look."

Kingfisher held out her hand. "There you are."

River Cloud saw it was a splendid gold unicorn, even bigger and handsomer than the one she wore. As she took it and held it on her palm, a strange fancy crossed her mind. Just at that moment they were joined by Magic Jade.

"What are you doing here in the sun?" he asked. "Why don't you go and see Aroma?"

"We're on our way there," replied River Cloud, hiding the unicorn. "Let's go together."

They went on to the Happy Red Residence Hall. Aroma made haste to greet River Cloud and invite her inside to sit down, asking what she had been doing since last they met.

"You should have come earlier," remarked Magic Jade. "I've got something nice for you." He searched his pocket, and then said, "Aiya!" Turning to Aroma he asked, "Did you put that thing away?"

"What thing?" Aroma asked.

"That unicorn present I got the other day."

"You've been carrying it on you all the time, why ask me?"

"Oh, I've lost it!" He clapped his hands. "But where can I find it now?"

River Cloud laughed. "It's lucky it's just a toy. Yet see what a state you're in!" With that she unclenched her fingers. "Look, is this it?"

Magic Jade was overjoyed to see that she had it. He reached out eagerly for it, laughing. "Fancy your finding it!" he said. "How did you come to pick it up?"

"It's lucky it was only this." River Cloud smiled. "Will you let it go at that if you lose your official seal later on?"

"Losing an official seal is nothing," he grinned. "But I deserve death for losing this."

Then River Cloud unwrapped her handkerchief and took out a ring for Aroma. Aroma was greatly touched and loud in her thanks.

"Actually, I was given one of those you sent your cousins," said Aroma. "And now you've brought me one yourself —a sure sign that you hadn't forgotten me. It's not the rings I value, but the thought behind it."

"Who gave you one?" asked River Cloud.

"Miss Hairpin," Aroma answered.

"I thought it might be Black Jade. So it was Hairpin." River Cloud sighed. "At home every day I often think that of all my cousins, Hairpin is the best. What a pity we aren't sisters! If we were, it wouldn't be so bad being an orphan." Her eyes brimmed with tears.

"All right, all right," cried Magic Jade. "No more of this."

"What's wrong?" demanded River Cloud. "I know what's on your mind. You're afraid your Black Jade may hear and be angry with me for praising Hairpin. Right?"

Aroma giggled. "The older you grow the more outspoken you get."

"I always say it's hard to talk with you girls, and I am once again right," Magic Jade chuckled.

"Don't make me sick, dear cousin, speaking like that," said River Cloud. "You say what you like to us. It's only with your cousin Black Jade that you are careful in the choice of words."

At this point a servant came to announce: "Mr. Jia of Prosperity Street has called. The master wants the young master to receive him."

Knowing that this visitor was Jia Yucun, Magic Jade was most reluctant to go, but Aroma lost no time in fetching his formal clothes so that he could receive the guest.

As Magic Jade pulled on his boots he grumbled, "Surely it's enough for my father to keep him company. Why must he see me each time?"

Cooling herself with a fan, River Cloud replied with a smile, "I'm sure you're good at entertaining guests. That's why my uncle sent for you."

"It's not my father's idea," Magic Jade said. "It's that fellow who asks for me each time he visits us."

"'When the host is cultured and hospitable, guests frequent his house,' quoted River Cloud. "There must be something about you that has impressed him, otherwise he wouldn't want to see you."

"I make no claim to being cultured and hospitable," scoffed Magic Jade, "thanks all the same. I'm the most vulgar sort of person, and I'm not willing to mix with such people."

"You haven't changed a bit," sighed River Cloud. "But you're growing up now. Even if you don't want to study and sit for the civil exams, you should at least try to associate with officials and learn something about the world and administration. That will help you to manage your own affairs in the future, and you might make some decent friends. You'll certainly get nowhere if you spend all your time with us girls."

Magic Jade found such talk unpleasant to his ears. "You'd better go and call on some of your other cousins, young lady," he retorted. "People with worldly wisdom like yours will become polluted here!"

"Don't say such things to him, miss," Aroma cut in hurriedly. "Last time Miss Hairpin gave him the same advice he just snorted and walked away without any regard for her feelings. He just said 'Hai!' and marched off in the middle of what she was saying. She flushed crimson and hardly knew whether to go on or not. Thank goodness it was Miss Hairpin and not Black Jade—she'd have made a terrible scene, weeping and sobbing. But there you are. It's true that nobody can help admiring Miss Hairpin. She just blushed and went away. I felt very bad. She must have been very offended, but later she behaved as if nothing had happened. She's really good natured and broad minded. He's the one, believe it or not, who seems to have fallen out with her."

"If you sulked and ignored Black Jade like that," Aroma said, turning to Magic Jade, "how many apologies would you have to make her?"

"If Black Jade ever talked such stupid nonsense," said Magic Jade, "I'd have fallen out with her long ago."

Aroma and River Cloud nodded and laughed.

"So stupid nonsense is the name for that," Aroma said.

Black Jade knew that River Cloud had arrived, and that Magic Jade would lose no time in telling her about his newly-acquired gold unicorn. That set her thinking. In most of the romances Magic Jade had recently been reading, a young scholar and a beautiful girl came together and fell in love thanks to a pair of lovebirds, a male and female phoenix, jade rings or gold pendants, silk handkerchiefs, embroidered belts, and so forth. So Magic Jade's possession of a gold unicorn much like River Cloud's might lead to a romance between them.

So she slipped over to see what was happening and how the two of them were behaving. She then shaped her own actions accordingly. Imagine her surprise when, as she was about to enter, she heard River Cloud speaking of worldly affairs, and heard Magic Jade answer, "Black Jade would never talk such stupid nonsense. I'd have fallen out with her if she ever did." Mingled emotions of happiness, surprise, sorrow, and regret assailed Black Jade.

Black Jade was happy to know she had not misjudged him, for he had now proved to be as understanding as she had always thought he was. Surprised that he had been so open as to praise her in front of other people, she knew his warm affection for her would be sure to be misunderstood. She thus became somewhat distressed because their mutual understanding ought to make a perfect match between the two lovers.

Why, she wondered, did there have to be all this talk of the gold and jade? Why did there have to be a Hairpin with her gold necklace? Black Jade felt grieved because her parents had died, and, although Magic Jade's preference was clear, there was no one to propose the match for her. Besides, she had recently been suffering from dizzy spells. The doctor had warned that these might end in consumption, as she was so weak and frail. Dear as she and Magic Jade were to each other, she might not have long to live. So, she thought, even if I'm your true love, I'm afraid that I won't last long. You can do nothing to change my ill fate. These thoughts sent tears coursing down her cheeks. Instead of entering the room, she turned away.

Magic Jade hurried out after changing his clothes. He saw Black Jade walking slowly ahead, apparently wiping away her tears. He overtook her.

"Where are you going, cousin?" he asked with a smile. "What, crying again? Who's offended you this time?"

Black Jade turned and seeing it was Magic Jade, said, "I'm quite all right." She forced a smile. "I wasn't crying."

"Don't tell such fibs. Just look, your eyes are still wet."

He couldn't help raising his hand to wipe away her tears. At once she recoiled a few steps. "Are you crazy? There you go it again! Can't you keep your hands to yourself?."

"I did it without thinking," he laughed. "My feelings got the better of me. But really I don't care much about anything."

"Then no one will care about you. But what about the gold necklace and unicorn you'll have to leave behind?"

This remark irritated Magic Jade. "How can you talk like that?" he asked. "Are you trying to put a curse on me, or to make me angry?"

Remembering what had happened three days before, Black Jade regretted her thoughtlessness and hastened to make amends. "Don't get so excited," she begged. "It's really not serious. Why take to heart a slip of the tongue? You see, the veins on your forehead are all swollen with anger, and your face is all covered with sweat."

So saying, she too stepped forward and wiped his perspiring face. Magic Jade fixed his eyes on her. After a while he said gently, "Don't worry."

Hearing this, Black Jade gazed at him for some moments. and then said at last, "Why shouldn't I worry? I don't really understand. What do you mean?"

"Don't you really understand?" he sighed. "Could it be that since I've known you all my feelings for you have been wrong? If I can't even enter into your feelings, no wonder you're angry with me all the time."

"I really don't understand what you mean by telling me not to worry."

"Dear cousin, don't tease," Magic Jade nodded and sighed. "If you really don't understand, all my devotion's been wasted and even your feeling for me has been thrown away. You ruin your health by worrying so much. If you'd take things less to heart, your illness wouldn't be getting worse every day."

These words struck Black Jade like a thunderbolt. As she turned them over in her mind, they seemed closer to her innermost thoughts than if they had been wrung from her own heart. There were a thousand things she longed to say, yet she couldn't utter a word. She just stared at him in silence.

As Magic Jade was in a similar state, he also stared at her. They stood transfixed for some time, and then Black Jade gave a choking cough as tears rolled down her cheeks. She was turning to go when Magic Jade caught hold of her.

"Dear cousin, stop for a moment," he said. "Just let me say one word."

She dried her tears with one hand, pushing him away with the other.

"What more is there to say?" she asked. "I understand." She hurried off without one look, while he just stood there in a trance.

Magic Jade in his haste to go and meet the visitor had forgotten his fan, and Aroma ran after him with it. She, however, stopped when she caught sight of Black Jade talking with him. As soon as Black Jade left, the maid walked up. Magic Jade was still standing there as if rooted to the ground.

"You forgot your fan," Aroma said." Luckily I noticed it. Here it is."

Too preoccupied to even recognize her, Magic Jade seized Aroma's hands. "Dear cousin, 1 never ventured before to bare my heart to you," he declared. "Now that I've plucked up my courage to tell you, I'll die content. I was making myself ill for your sake, but I dared not tell anyone, and I hid my feelings. I can't forget you even in my dreams."

Aroma listened to this declaration in consternation and embarrassment. Shaking him, she asked, "What sort of talk is this? Are you bewitched? You'd better hurry up."

As soon as Magic Jade came to himself and saw the person he was speaking to was Aroma, his face turned a deep red in embarrassment. He snatched the fan and ran off without another word.

16/ Lovebird Rejects the Marriage Offer

One day Phoenix was asked to see Lady Xing. Not knowing the specific nature of this call, she hurriedly went off in her carriage to the East Mansion.

Lady Xing dismissed the other maids and then told Phoenix, her daughter-in-law, privately, "The Elder Master, Jia She, has given me a difficult task. I hardly know how to go about it, so I'd like to consult with you first. He's taken a fancy to the old lady's maid, Lovebird, and wants to make her his concubine. He's told me to go and ask the old lady for her. As I see it, there's nothing unusual in such a request, but I'm afraid the old lady may not agree. What would you advise me to do?"

"I don't think it's worth asking her," Phoenix replied. "Why run your head against a brick wall? The old lady can't even eat without Lovebird around, how could she part with her? Besides, I've often heard the old lady say that the Elder Master shouldn't be taking concubines, one after another, at his advanced age. Please don't be annoyed, madam, but I haven't the courage to approach her about this. As far as I can see, it would be useless and just cause unpleasantness. The Elder Master's behavior is rather unbecoming for a gentleman getting on in years. You should talk him out of it. This sort of thing is all right for a younger man, but not for a man of his age with a flock of younger brothers, nephews, children, and grandchildren. Doesn't it look bad, his fooling around like this?"

"Other noble families often have three or four concubines, so why shouldn't we?" retorted Lady Xing with a cold smile. "I doubt if I can talk him out of it. Even if Lovebird is the old lady's favorite maid, when her eldest son, a grey-bearded official, wants that maid for his concubine, his mother can hardly refuse him. I invited you over simply to ask your opinion, but at once you gave all sorts of reasons against it. Did you think I'd send you on this errand? I'll go myself, of course. You blame me for not dissuading him, but surely you know your father-in-law better than that. He'd ignore my advice and fly into a temper."

Phoenix knew that her mother-in-law was a weak and silly woman. To save herself trouble, she would always humor her husband, finding pleasure in getting property and money to enlarge her private savings. Not one of her children or servants did she trust, nor would she listen to their advice. It would be useless to reason with her now, seeing that she was so stubborn.

So, with a pleasant smile, Phoenix replied, "You're quite right, madam. What can I know, young as I am? After all, she's his mother and would surely never refuse him the rarest treasure, not to say a maid. Whom else would she give the maid to if not the Elder Master? I was silly to take what she said in private so seriously. As she's in high spirits today, it seems to me now's the time to make this request. Would you like me to go first to coax her into a good humor? Then, when you come, I'll make an excuse to leave and take everyone else there in the room with me, so that you can broach the subject. If she agrees, so much the better. If she doesn't, no harm will be done as no one else will know about it."

Thus, hearing what she wanted to hear, Lady Xing's good humor returned. She told Phoenix, "My idea was not to approach the old lady first, for if she refused that would be the end of the matter. I was thinking of telling Lovebird first in private. She may be a little shy, but when I've explained it all to her, she naturally won't say anything against it, and that means it's settled. Then I'll go and ask the old lady, and she'll find it difficult to refuse, even though she doesn't want to part with the girl."

"After all, you know best, madam," Phoenix smiled. "This is bound to work well. Every girl, even Lovebird, wants to improve her position and get on in the world."

"That's exactly what I think," agreed Lady Xing. "Surely Lovebird will agree. I'm sure any one of the senior maids in responsible positions would jump at a chance like this. All right, you go first. But don't breathe a word of this to anyone else. I'll come over after supper."

Meanwhile Phoenix was thinking that since Lovebird was a girl of character, she might refuse. If she went to Lovebird first and agreed, then all would be well and good. But if she refused, then Phoenix's mother-in-law would become suspicious and conclude that she had encouraged Lovebird to hold out. It would be better if the two of them went to see Lovebird together. Then, whether Lovebird agreed or not, no suspicion could fall on her.

So Phoenix said cordially, "As I was coming over just now, my aunt asked me to deliver two baskets of quails. I told the kitchen to have them deep-fried and sent over for your supper. And as I came through your main gate, I saw some pages carrying off your carriage for repairs. They said it was cracking up. Why don't you come back with me in mine? Then we can go together."

Lady Xing called for her maids to change her clothes, and, supported by her shrewd daughter-in-law, the two of them got into the carriage.

Then Phoenix said, "If I accompany you to the old lady's place, madam, she may ask what I've come for, and that would be awkward. Suppose you go first, and I'll join you as soon as I've put on my everyday clothes."

Lady Xing thought this reasonable, and went on first to call on the Lady Dowager. After chatting with her for a while, she departed on the pretext of going to see Lady Wang. Instead, she slipped out through the back door to Lovebird's bedroom. The girl was sitting there doing some needlework. She rose to her feet as Lady Xing entered.

Lady Xing asked with a smile, "What are you making? Let me have a look. I'm sure you're doing finer embroidery than ever." So saying, she entered the room, inspected the embroidery and praised it as nicely done. Then, putting the embroidery down, she examined Lovebird with her eyes carefully from head to foot.

The maid was wearing a light purple silk tunic, none too new, a black-satin sleeveless jacket with silk borders, and a pale green skirt. She had a wasp-like waist, slender shoulders, an oval face, glossy black hair and a finely arched nose, while her cheeks were slightly freckled. This close inspection embarrassed and puzzled the maid.

"What brings you here at this hour, madam?" Lovebird asked with a smile.

Lady Xing made a sign to her attendants to leave the room, then sat down and took the maid by the hand. "I've come specially to congratulate you," she announced.

This gave Lovebird some inkling of what her visit was about. She blushed and lowered her head without a word.

"You see, the Elder Master has no one reliable to wait on him," Lady Xing continued, "He could buy a girl, of course, but those one gets through brokers aren't clean. So he's been trying to choose one in our household. After looking for the past six months, he's decided that of all the girls here you're the best—pretty, well-behaved, dependable, and sweet-tempered. So he wants to ask the old lady to let him have you for his concubine.

"Your position will be quite different from that of a girl bought from outside, for as soon as you enter our house we'll go through the ceremonies and give you the rank of a secondary wife, treated with all respect and honor. Besides, you're a girl with a will of your own. As the proverb says, 'True gold will find its price.' Now that the Elder Master has picked you, you'll be able to realize your highest ambitions, and this will shut the mouths of those who dislike you. So come along with me to tell the old lady about it."

Lovebird simply hung her head and took her hand away. Lady Xing assumed that she did so from shyness.

"What's there to be so shy about?" asked Lady Xing, seeing how embarrassed she was. "You won't have to say a word. Just come with me."

But Lovebird still hung her head and did not move.

"Don't tell me you're unwilling!" cried Lady Xing. "You're a very silly girl if that's the case, turning down the chance to be a mistress and choosing to remain a maid instead. If you let slip this chance to better yourself, you're going to regret it. Then it'll be too late."

Still Lovebird simply hung her head and said nothing.

"I suppose you're too shy to say 'yes' yourself and would prefer to leave it to your parents," Lady Xing smiled. "Quite right and proper too. I'll speak to them and get them to speak to you. You can be frank with them."

With that she left, and went off to Phoenix's apartment.

Phoenix had long since changed back into her ordinary clothes, and because no one else was in the room but Patience she disclosed this news to her.

Patience shook her head. "I don't see this working out," she said. "From the way Lovebird's spoken when we were chatting on our own, she's not likely to agree. We'll have to wait and see."

"Lady Xing is sure to come here to discuss it," said Phoenix. "If Lovebird's willing, all right; if not, she'll be feeling put out. It would be embarrassing for her to find you and the others here. Tell the rest to go and deep-fry some quails and prepare a few other dishes to go with them. Then you can go off and amuse yourself somewhere else until you think she'll have gone."

Patience passed on the instructions to the other servants, and then went off to enjoy herself in the garden.

Meanwhile Lovebird had guessed that Lady Xing would be going to discuss this business with Phoenix, and that other people were sure to soon come to sound her out. Thinking it wisest to stay away from trouble, she went to tell Amber, another maid, to give an excuse for her.

"If the old lady should ask for me, tell her I'm not feeling well, that I did not have any breakfast, and that I've gone for a stroll in the garden but will be back again shortly."

Amber agreed to do this. Then Lovebird went off to wander about in the garden. There she came across Patience quite unexpectedly.

Seeing that there were no other people around, Patience cried teasingly: "Here comes the new concubine!"

Lovebird blushed bright red. "So that's it!" she exclaimed. "You're all hand in glove against me. Wait till I go and have this out with your mistress."

Patience could see that Lovebird was really angry, and regretted her foolish mockery. Drawing Lovebird over to sit on a rock under a maple tree, she told Lovebird frankly all that Phoenix had told her just a few minutes before.

Still blushing, Lovebird answered bitterly, "You and I, at least, are still good friends. From the time we were small all of us maids worked together and we never had any secrets from each other. But now that we've grown up, we've gone our different ways. But you and I haven't changed a bit. I don't hold back anything from you. So I am telling you this now, but mind you don't tell Madam Phoenix. It's not just a question of not wanting to be the Elder Master's concubine. Even if Lady Xing had died and he sent matchmakers and witnesses as required to make me his proper wife, I wouldn't agree to it."

Before Patience could reply they heard laughter behind the rocks.

"For shame!" someone cried. "Such talk's enough to set one's teeth on edge."

Startled, they jumped to their feet to see who it was. It was Aroma, who appeared laughingly from behind the rockery.

"What's up?" she asked. "Let me share the secret, too."

The three of them sat down again and Patience retold the whole story.

"Since you're unwilling to be his concubine," said Patience, "I'll tell you an easy way to refuse him."

"What's that?" asked Lovebird.

"Simply tell the old lady you've already given yourself to Master Lian," Patience giggled. "The father can hardly take what belongs to his son."

Lovebird spat in disgust. "What rubbish! Your mistress was making such wild suggestions the other day. How can you repeat the same nonsense today?"

"If you don't want either of them," teased Aroma, "get the old lady to tell the Elder Master you're promised to Magic Jade, the Young Master. Then he'll have to give up."

Frantic with rage and embarrassment, Lovebird cursed, "You two rotten nuts, you won't come to a good end! I turn to you in trouble, thinking you'll have the decency to help me, but instead you take turns making fun of me. You think your own future is assured and you'll both end up as secondary wives. I'm not sure. In this world, things don't always turn out the way you want. So don't start counting your chickens before they're hatched."

Seeing how frantic she was, the two others did their best to calm her down with their smiles.

"Don't take it so much to heart, dear sister!" they cried. "We've been like real sisters since we were small and were only having a joke among ourselves. But, seriously, tell us your plan, so that we can stop worrying about you."

"Pah! As long as the old lady lives, I'll not leave her house. If she passes away, he'll have to observe three years' mourning, so he can't take a concubine the moment his mother dies. And in those three years anything might happen. I'll just have to wait and see. If worst comes to worst, I can shave off my hair and become a nun, or I can kill myself. I don't care if I never get married. An unmarried life is much simpler."

"What a shameless slut!" laughed Patience. "The wild way she runs on!"

"Things have gone too far for shame," Lovebird retorted. "If you don't believe me, wait and see."

Just then they saw Lovebird's sister-in-law approaching.

Aroma said, "As they can't get in touch with your parents now, they must have had a word with your sister-in-law."

"That whore!" swore Patience. "She's a regular camel dealer. She won't let this chance slip by to flatter them."

By now her sister-in-law had come up to Lovebird. "I've been looking for you everywhere," she said smiling, "so this is where you've run off to. Come with me. I want to have a word with you."

Patience and Aroma asked the sister-in-law to sit down.

"No, thank you. Don't stir," said the woman. "I just want to have a word with our Lovebird."

"What's the hurry?" they asked, pretending not to know anything. "We're guessing riddles and making bets. We must hear her answer to this one before she goes."

"What is it?" demanded Lovebird of her sister-in-law. "Out with it."

"Come with me," the other insisted. "I'll tell you over there. It's good news for you, anyway."

"You mean what Lady Xing told you?"

"If you already know about it," the sister-in-law replied, "why keep putting me off? Come on, and I'll give you the details. It's simply the most wonderful piece of good fortune."

Lovebird sprang up and spat in her face. Pointing an accusing finger at her sister-in-law, she swore, "Shut your foul mouth and clear off, if you know what's good for you. What's all this talk of 'good news' and 'good fortune'? You've always envied those families who start throwing their weight about once their daughters are concubines, as if every one of them was a concubine too. You can't wait to push me into that fiery pit."

Lovebird wept and stormed while Patience and Aroma tried to calm her down.

That evening Lovebird passed a sleepless night. The next day her brother came and asked the Lady Dowager's permission to take her home for the day. The old lady agreed and told her to go. This was not what Lovebird wanted, but she complied reluctantly in order not to arouse the old lady's suspicions. Her brother tried to tell her what Jia She had promised and what dignity she would have as his secondary wife. However, Lovebird refused the offer categorically. Unable to change her mind, he had to go back and report this to Jia She.

Jia She flew into a rage. "Tell your wife to tell her this from me," he fumed. "Tell her these are my own words. She must think me too old for her. I dare say that she has set her heart on one of the young masters, most likely Magic Jade, or possibly my son. If that's her idea, tell her to forget it and the sooner the better. For if she refuses me, who else will dare take her later? That's the first thing.

"The second is this: no matter whom she marries, she'll still be within my reach unless she dies or remains single all her life."

After a good many "Yes, sirs," Lovebird's brother withdrew and returned home. When he got back, without waiting to get his wife to pass on the message, he told Lovebird himself. The news reduced her to a state of speechless anger.

After some time she said, "Well, even if I agree, you'll still have to take me back to report this to the old lady."

Her brother and his wife were overjoyed by this apparent change of heart. Her sister-in-law at once took her to the Lady Dowager, who happened to be chatting with Lady Wang, Aunt Xue, Phoenix, Hairpin, and the other girls, as well as a few of the chief stewards' wives, all of whom were doing their best to amuse the old lady.

Delighted by this opportunity, Lovebird drew her sister-in-law forward and threw herself on her knees before her mistress. Sobbing, she told the old lady what Lady Xing had said to her, what her sister-in-law had told her in the garden, and how her brother had threatened her earlier that day.

"Because I wouldn't agree, the Elder Master says I've set my heart on Magic Jade. He swears I'll never escape him, not even if I marry someone outside, no, not even if I go to the ends of the earth—he'll have his revenge in the end. Well, I've made my mind up. Everybody here can bear witness. I will never marry so long as I live, neither Magic Jade with his precious jade, nor someone born with silver or gold, not even a Heavenly King or Emperor!

"If Your Ladyship tries to force me, I'll kill myself rather than marry anyone. If I'm lucky, I shall die before you do, madam. Otherwise I mean to serve you till the end of your life. Then, rather than go back to my parents or to my broth-er, I will commit suicide or shave my head and become a nun. If you think I'm not in earnest and this is just empty talk, just trying to get myself out of a corner, may Heaven, Earth, all the gods, and the Sun and Moon be my witnesses. May I choke with thick boils in my throat if I lie!" she stated with great solemnity.

She had hidden a pair of scissors up her sleeve before en-tering the room, and, while taking this oath, she let down her hair with her left hand and started cutting it with the scissors in her right. Maids and serving women hurried over to stop her. She had cut off one lock already, but luckily, her hair was so thick that it was difficult to cut much more. The maids lost no time in dressing it again for her.

Now the Lady Dowager was trembling with rage. "The only girl left I can trust, and they want to get her away from me," she said in a shaking voice. Her eye fell on Lady Wang, who was sitting beside her, and she cried, "So you're all de-ceiving me, putting on a show of being dutiful but plotting against me in secret. Now you're trying to get Lovebird away from me, so you might get me under your thumbs."

Lady Wang had risen to her feet but didn't venture a word in self-defense. And Aunt Xue being her sister, could not try to shift the blame from her. After listening for a while outside the window, Tanchun entered the room with a smile.

"What has this to do with Mother, Grandma?" she asked her grandmother. "Just think. How could a younger sister-in-law know that her elder brother-in-law was going to get a concubine?"

The old lady at once chuckled. "I'm losing my wits with age," she exclaimed. "Don't laugh at me, Mrs. Xue. This el-der sister of yours is a very good sister-in-law, not like my el-der son's wife, who's so afraid of her husband she only makes a show of compliance to me. Yes, I was wrong to blame your sister."

Madam Xue murmured agreement, then added, "I won-der if you're not, perhaps, rather partial to the wife of your younger son, madam?"

"No, I'm not partial," the old lady declared.

Just then a maid came in to announce, "Lady Xing is here, madam."

Lady Wang hurried out to greet her. She had come for the news, not knowing that the Lady Dowager knew all about her proposal to Lovebird. As she stepped into the courtyard, she was quietly informed of this by one of the serving women, but it was too late to retreat now that her arrival had been announced and her sister-in-law, Lady Wang, had come out to meet her. She had no choice but to go in and pay her respects to the Lady Dowager.

The old lady received her without a word, and she was thus covered with shame and regret. Phoenix had already left on the pretext of some business, while Lovebird had retired to her room to sulk alone. Now Aunt Xue, Lady Wang, and the others withdrew, one by one, to spare Lady Xing's embarrassment. She herself dared not leave, however.

When they were alone, the Lady Dowager at last broke the silence. "I hear you've been doing some matchmaking for your husband," she said. "Quite a model of wifely submission and virtue, aren't you? Only you're carrying this a bit too far. You have children and grandchildren now, yet you're still afraid of him. They tell me that you simply let him carry on just as he pleases."

Blushes covering her face, Lady Xing replied, "I have tried several times to dissuade him, but without success. You know how it is, madam. I had no choice."

"Would you commit murder, too, if he insisted? Have some sense. Lovebird is the only maid left who's not just a child and knows something of my ways of seeing things done. It's not just that I rely on her, she saves your sister-in-law and daughter-in-law trouble too. As long as I've someone like her, I don't have to worry about running short of anything, even if my daughter-in-law or my grandsons' wives forget to keep me supplied, and that keeps me in good temper. But who would you give me to replace her if she left now? Even if you managed to produce a girl of her size made of pearls but unable to talk as nicely as Lovebird does, she would be of no use to me.

"I was just on the point of sending someone around to tell your husband that I've money here for him if he wants to buy someone, but it's impossible for him to have this girl of mine! If she can be left to wait on me for a few years, that'll be the same as him waiting on me day and night himself, like a dutiful son should. It's a good thing that you've come. I'm sure you'll be able to take this message back to him."

When Lady Xing went back and gave her husband the briefest report of what the Lady Dowager had said, Jia She realized that he could do nothing more about Lovebird. He simply had to put up with his mortification. After this, on the pretext of being ill, he stopped making daily calls on his mother. In fact, he was afraid to face her. Instead, he sent his wife and son to pay their respects every day.

Meanwhile, he sent his men to scout around the slave market for likely girls. Finally a pretty girl of seventeen was purchased for the sum of five hundred ounces of silver. She was taken into his house and became his concubine.

17/ Artful Cuckoo Tests Magic Jade's Feelings

One day, Magic Jade went to call on Black Jade. She was taking an afternoon nap. Cuckoo chanced to be sitting outside the verandah doing some needlework. Not wishing to disturb Black Jade, Magic Jade went over to talk with Cuckoo.

"How was your mistress last night?" he asked. "Is her cough any better?"

"Yes, a bit better," answered Cuckoo.

Seeing that she was wearing a thin padded-silk tunic with black dots under a lined blue-silk sleeveless jacket, he reached out his hand to feel her clothes.

"You shouldn't sit in the wind so lightly dressed," he said. "It's much too thin for this time of the year. If you get sick in this early spring weather, it will be bad."

"Don't touch me when we talk to each other," said Cuckoo sharply. "Keep your hands to yourself. You're growing up now and should let people respect you, but you keep provoking those wretches to gossip behind your back. You're so careless. You still carry on like a little boy. Well, that won't do. Our young lady has warned us time and again not to joke with you. Haven't you noticed how she's been avoiding you recently?"

Cuckoo then got up and took her needlework inside.

The effect of this rebuff on Magic Jade's feelings was like being doused with a bucket of icy water. He sank down in a daze on a rock and shed tears, not really knowing what he had done. For quite a while he sat there brooding, but couldn't decide what to do.

Just then Snowswan passed with some ginseng tonic. She was on her way back from Lady Wang's quarters. Turning her head towards the rock below the peach tree she noticed Magic Jade there lost in thought, his face propped in his hands. Going over, she crouched down beside him. "What are you doing here?" she asked.

"Why do you come up to me like this?" countered Magic Jade, as soon as he saw it was Snowswan. "You're a girl, aren't you? To prevent gossip Black Jade asked you to ignore me, but here you've come to talk to me. If we're seen together, there'll only be more gossip. Hurry up and go home."

Snowswan assumed that his bitter remarks came from his being wrongly accused by Black Jade. So the maid left him and entered the Bamboo Cottage. As Black Jade was still asleep, she gave Cuckoo the ginseng tonic.

"Who's been upsetting Magic Jade?" asked Snowswan. "He's sitting out there alone, crying."

"Out where?" asked Cuckoo sharply.

"Under the peach blossoms behind a pavilion."

At once Cuckoo laid down her needlework.

"Be ready if Black Jade calls," Cuckoo told Snowswan. "If she asks for me, tell her I'll be back in a minute." So saying, Cuckoo left the Bamboo Cottage to look for Magic Jade. When she came up to him, she tried to calm him with a smile.

"That was only a little casual remark I made," she said, "and it was for the good of us all. Why take offense and rush over here to sit crying in the wind? Are you trying to scare me by risking your health like this?"

"I didn't take offense," he smiled. "I thought what you said was quite reasonable. But if everyone feels the way you do, before long nobody will speak to me at all. That's what upset me."

Cuckoo sat down beside him.

"Just a moment ago we were talking face to face, but you wouldn't stay," he pointed out. "Why are you sitting right beside me now?"

"Perhaps you've forgotten," she answered, "but a few days ago you and your cousin had just started talking about bird's-nest tonic when somebody came in and interrupted. I've come to ask what more you meant to say that day."

"Oh, nothing much really," said Magic Jade. "I simply think that since Black Jade is taking that tonic she has to keep up. I dropped a hint to the old lady, and I suspect she must have told Phoenix. That was what I started explaining. I understand an ounce of bird's nest is being sent over to you every day now, so that's all right."

"So it was you who told her about it," said Cuckoo, "That was very kind of you. We've been wondering what made the old lady suddenly start sending an ounce of bird's nest every day. So that's the reason."

"If she takes it regularly every day," he said, "after a couple of years she should be getting much better."

"Well, she can have some every day here, but could she afford to continue the cure when she goes home next year?" asked Cuckoo deliberately.

Magic Jade gave a start. "When who goes home? What home?" he demanded.

"Your cousin's home, back in Suzhou!"

"Nonsense!" Magic Jade chuckled. "Suzhou may be her native town, but she came here because when my Aunt Lin died there was no one to look after her. So we brought her here. Who could she go back to next year? Are you kidding?"

"What a poor opinion you have of other people!" Cuckoo snorted. "Yours may be a big, wealthy family, but do other families have only a father and mother with no relatives? Our young lady was brought here while she was still a child, because the old lady had a tender feeling for her and didn't think her uncles could take the place of her parents. So the old lady intended to keep her here for only a few years. As soon as she's old enough to be married, she'll have to go back to the Lin family.

"How can a daughter of the Lins stay all her life with you in your Jia family? The Lins may be too poor to afford a square meal, but for generations they've been a family of scholars and officials. They'd never sink so low as to hand over responsibility for their own girl to relatives. That would be quite a disgrace. So next spring or next autumn at the latest, even if your family doesn't send her back, the Lins are sure to come to fetch her.

"The other evening our young lady told me to ask you for all the little gifts and souvenirs she's given you since you were children. She means to return all yours to you as well."

To Magic Jade these words were like a thunderclap exploding overhead. Cuckoo waited for him to answer, but he couldn't say a word. Just then Skybright came up.

"So here you are!" Skybright cried. "The old lady wants you."

Cuckoo answered with a smile, "He's been asking about Miss Lin's health, and I keep telling him how she is, but he won't believe me. You'd better take him away." With that she returned to her room.

Skybright noticed Magic Jade's distracted look, the hectic flush on his cheeks and the sweat on his forehead. She at once led him by the hand to the Happy Red Residence Hall.

Aroma was naturally alarmed to see Magic Jade come back in such a state. She thought he must have gotten overheated and then caught a chill in the wind. A fever is nothing really serious, but his eyes were fixed and staring, saliva was trickling from the corners of his lips, and he seemed to have lost all consciousness of what he was doing. When they brought him a pillow he lay down. When they pulled him by the hand he sat up again. When they handed him a cup of tea he drank it, but he did all these things with mechanical movements. His condition threw them all into a panic, yet no one dared to report this to the old lady. Instead, they sent for his old nurse.

Magic Jade's old nurse came in presently, and examined him carefully. She asked him a few questions, but he made no reply. Then she felt his pulse and pinched his upper lip so hard that her fingers left deep imprints—yet he felt no pain. At that she gave a great cry of despair, and, taking him in her arms, started weeping and wailing.

"It's all up with him now," she wailed. "A lifetime of care has gone for nothing!"

Aroma had asked the nurse to have a look at him because she respected her age and experience. Now her words sounded convincing. They all started sobbing.

Skybright then told Aroma what had just happened, and without a moment's hesitation Aroma dashed off to the Bamboo Cottage. There she found Cuckoo giving Black Jade her medicine. Blind to everything else, Aroma flew at her.

"What have you been saying to our Magic Jade?" she demanded. "Just go and see the state he's in!"

Black Jade was taken aback by Aroma's furious, tear-stained face, and by this behavior which was so unlike her.

"What's the matter?" she asked.

Making an effort to calm herself, Aroma sobbed, "I don't know what your Cuckoo's been telling him. He's more dead than alive. Even Nanny Li says there's no hope, and she is weeping and wailing there. He may be dead by now for all I know."

Nanny Li was such an experienced old nurse that Black Jade could not but believe her gloomy predictions. With a cry she threw up all the medicine she had just taken, and was racked by such dry coughing that her stomach burned and it seemed her lungs would burst. Red in the face, hair in disorder, eyes swollen, limp in every limb, she choked for breath and could not lift her head. Cuckoo made haste to massage her back while she lay gasping on her pillow.

"Stop that!" cried Black Jade at last, pushing her away. "You'd far better get a rope and strangle me."

"I didn't say anything," the maid protested with tears. "Just a few words in fun; he must have taken them seriously."

"You should know how seriously the silly boy always takes teasing," retorted Aroma.

"Whatever you said, go and clear up the misunderstanding, and do it quickly," urged Black Jade. "That may bring him back to his senses."

Cuckoo then jumped up and hurried with Aroma to the Happy Red Residence Hall, where the old lady and Lady Wang had already arrived. At the sight of Cuckoo the old lady's eyes flashed angrily.

"You wicked creature!" she stormed. "What did you say to him?"

"Nothing really, madam. Nothing but a few words for fun."

At the sight of Cuckoo, Magic Jade cried out and burst into tears. The sudden change in his behavior was a relief for everybody present. The Lady Dowager caught Cuckoo's arm, thinking she had offended Magic Jade and urged him to beat her. But Magic Jade seized hold of Cuckoo and would not let go.

"If you go," he shouted, "you must take me with you!"

No one could make head or tail of this until Cuckoo, when questioned, explained her joking threat of Black Jade's going back to Suzhou.

"Is that all?" exclaimed the Lady Dowager, the tears running down her cheeks. "So it was all because of a joke." She condemned Cuckoo, "You're such a sensible girl normally, how could you tease him like that when you know how readily he believes things?"

At this point it was announced that a servant named Lin and his wife had come to see how the young master was doing.

"Show them in," said the old lady. "It's thoughtful of them."

But at the sound of the name Lin, Magic Jade grew frantic again. "No, no!" he shouted wildly from his bed. "The Lins have come to fetch her. Drive them away!"

"Yes, send them away!" his grandmother reassured Magic Jade, "They are not from the Lin family. All those Lins are dead. Nobody will ever come to fetch Black Jade. Don't you worry."

"Never mind who they are," stormed Magic Jade tearfully. "I don't want any Lins here except Cousin Lin."

"There are no Lins here," repeated the old lady. "They've all been driven away."

She then ordered the attendants. "From now on don't let anyone named Lin into the garden. And never mention the name Lin again. Mind you all do as I say. Is that clear, children?"

Suppressing their smiles, all the servants echoed "yes, madam," in chorus.

Magic Jade's eye now fell on a golden boat with an engine, a toy from the West, which was lying on his cabinet.

"Isn't that the boat coming to fetch them?" he shouted, pointing at it. "It's docked over there."

The Lady Dowager ordered its instant removal, but when Magic Jade reached out for it Aroma gave it to him. He tucked it under his bedding.

"Now they won't be able to sail away," he laughed. Then, seizing and holding onto Cuckoo tightly, he refused to let her go.

At this point the arrival of Doctor Wang was announced, and the old lady ordered him to be brought straight in.

After taking Magic Jade's hand to feel his pulse, the doctor rose and declared, "The trouble with our honorable brother is that some sharp distress had clouded his mind. It is only a temporary blockage, however, not so serious."

"Just tell us if he's in danger or not," urged the Lady Dowager.

Doctor Wang bowed. "He is in no danger, no."

When the prescribed medicine had been taken by Magic Jade, he did calm down a little. However, he still refused to let go of Cuckoo.

"If she leaves here, they'll go back to Suzhou!" he cried.

The Lady Dowager and Lady Wang could do nothing but let Cuckoo stay with him. Instead, they sent Amber to look after Black Jade. During the rest of the day Black Jade's other maid, Snowswan, was sent over from time to time to ask for news about Magic Jade's condition.

That evening Magic Jade remained calm. The Lady Dowager, Lady Wang, and the other visitors returned to their own apartments, but throughout the night they continued to send messengers to inquire after him.

And the next day, after more of Doctor Wang's medicine, Magic Jade gradually improved. His mind was clear now, but because he did not want to let Cuckoo go away, he pretended that it was still affected.

As for her, she was very regretful about the mischief she had done, and she served him day and night without a word of complaint.

River Cloud happened to be in the Jia's home during this period. She came every day to see Magic Jade. As soon as he seemed normal, she tried to amuse him by imitating his crazy behavior during the illness. Her mimicry was so amusing that Magic Jade had to laugh into his pillow. Having no idea of what he had been like, he could hardly believe what they told him about his behavior.

When no one else was around but Cuckoo, he took Cuckoo's hand in his own. "Why did you scare me like that?" he asked.

"I only did it for fun," she replied. "But you took it too seriously."

"It was no joke," said Magic Jade. "It sounded so convincing."

"Well, I made the whole thing up. There's really no one left in the Lin family except for some very distant relatives who no longer live in Suzhou and are scattered in different provinces. Even if one of them asked for Black Jade, the old lady would never let her go."

"I wouldn't, even if she did," he said firmly.

"You wouldn't?" Cuckoo laughed. "That's just talk, I'm afraid. You're growing up now and are already engaged. In a couple of years you'll get married, and then you won't have time for anyone else."

"Who's engaged?" asked Magic Jade in dismay. "To whom?"

"Before the New Year I heard the old lady say she wanted to engage you to a girl of the Xue family."

He burst out laughing.

"People may call me crazy, but you're even crazier. That was just a joke. That girl's already engaged to the son of Academician Mei. If I were engaged to her, would I be in this state? Didn't you plead with me and say I was mad when I swore that oath and wanted to smash that silly jade? Now you've come to provoke me again just as I'm getting better."

Through clenched teeth he added, "I only wish I could die this very minute and tear out my heart to show you." Tears were running down his cheeks as he spoke.

Cuckoo hastily put her hand to his mouth, then wiped away his tears. "You needn't worry," she urged. "I was putting you to the test because I was worried."

"You worried? Why?" he asked in surprise.

"You know, I don't belong to the Lin family. Like Aroma and Lovebird, I was given to Miss Lin. And she couldn't have been kinder to me. She treats me ten times better than she does the maids she brought from Suzhou. We've become inseparable. I'm worried now because if she leaves I shall have to go with her; but my whole family's here. If I don't go, it would seem like a betrayal after what we've been to each other all these years. If I did go, it would mean leaving my family behind. That's why I made up the story. It was to test you. How was I to know you'd take it so hard and make such an uproar?"

"So that's what's worrying you," Magic Jade chuckled. "What a silly girl you are! Well, set your heart at rest. Let me just put it in a nutshell for you. If we live, we'll live together; and if we die, we'll turn into ashes and smoke together. What do you say to that?"

Cuckoo was turning this over in her mind when the arrival of Jia Huan and Jia Lan were announced. They had called to ask after Magic Jade.

"Thank them for coming," Magic Jade said, "but tell them I've just gone to bed and they needn't take the trouble to come in."

The woman who brought the message said "yes, sir," and went out.

"Since you're better you should let me go back to see my own patient," said Cuckoo.

"Sure," he replied. "I meant to send you yesterday, but then I forgot. Go along, I'm completely well again."

Cuckoo began to gather up her bedding and to get her toilet set together. Then she took her leave of everyone in the Happy Red Residence Hall and went back to the Bamboo Cottage.

The news of Magic Jade's disorder had made Black Jade suffer a relapse, and was the occasion for fits of weeping. Now she asked why Cuckoo had returned and, learning that he was better, she was a little relieved.

That night, when all was quiet and Cuckoo had undressed and climbed into bed, she whispered to Black Jade: "Magic Jade's heart is really true to you. Fancy his falling ill like that when he heard we were leaving!"

Black Jade made no answer.

Presently Cuckoo went on, half to herself, "Much better to stay where we are. You couldn't ask for a better family than this. It's the hardest thing in the world to find people who've grown up together and know each other's character and ways."

"Aren't you tired after the last few days?" scoffed Black Jade. "Why don't you sleep instead of talking such nonsense?"

"It isn't nonsense. I was thinking entirely of your happiness. I've worried about you all these years because you have no father, mother, or brothers to care for you. The important thing is to settle the main affair in your life in good time, while the old lady's still clear-headed and healthy."

"The girl's crazy!" exclaimed Black Jade. "A few days away, and you've suddenly changed into a different person. Tomorrow I'll ask the old lady to take you back. I no longer dare keep you here."

"I really meant well," Cuckoo replied, smiling. "I just wanted you to look out for yourself, and not to do anything wrong. What good will it do if you report me to the old lady and get me into trouble?" With that Cuckoo closed her eyes.

Although Black Jade had spoken so sharply, this talk had actually been disturbing. After Cuckoo went to bed she wept all night, not dozing off until daybreak.

18/ Jia Lian Secretly Marries Second Sister You

Jia Jing, father of Jia Zhen and nominal head of the Peaceful Mansion branch of the family, was living in retirement in a Taoist monastery outside the city. He was looking for the secret of immortality by taking elixirs.

One day the startling news of Jia Jing's sudden death came. Madam You was most upset by this news. As her husband, Jia Zhen; their son, Jia Rong; and her brother, Jia Lian, were all away from home, there was no man to take charge of things of this kind.

She immediately sent a steward to the Taoist temple to have all the priests there locked up until her husband came back to question them. Then she hastily sent for doctors to see what had been the cause of the sudden death of her father-in-law. As Jia Jing had passed away, it was no use for the doctors to feel his pulse. They knew that he had died of excessive heat as a result of taking too many Taoist drugs.

Seeing that the weather was too hot for the funeral to be delayed, Madam You decided to hold the funeral service as soon as possible. Because Phoenix of the Honored Mansion was ill and Magic Jade knew nothing of practical affairs, the work outside was entrusted to a few second-rank stewards. Madam You, being unable to return home, invited her stepmother, old Mrs. You, to come and take care of things in the Peaceful Mansion. Mrs. You brought her two unmarried daughters with her.

As soon as the news of his father's death reached him, Jia Zhen asked for leave, and with his son, Jia Rong, they set out to attend to the funeral. It was nighttime when they came to the outskirts of the capital. They reached the Taoist temple well after two in the morning. Madam You and the others came to meet them.

Jia Zhen and his son changed into mourning gowns, according to the Chinese rites, and prostrated themselves before the coffin. Then, since Jia Zhen had to give instructions to the servants, his attention to business necessitated a reduction in his participation in the mourning process. He sent Jia Rong home to arrange for the transportation of the coffin there.

Jia Rong was glad to receive this order. He rode home swiftly and gave hasty instructions for the closing of mourning services. Then he went to greet his step-grandmother and two aunts.

"Sorry to have put you to so much trouble, Grandma," he said, "and my two aunts as well. My father and I are most grateful. When this business is over, we'll take the whole family, young and old, to your place to bow before you in grateful thanks."

"Bless the boy, what eloquence!" said the old lady, nodding appreciatively, "For our own relative, though, it's the least we could do. And how is your father? When did you get the message and hurry back?"

"We've only just got back," he told her. "Father sent me on to see how you are, and to beg you to stay till everything is over." As he said this, he winked at his second aunt.

Gritting her teeth and smiling, Second Sister You scolded softly: "You glib-tongued ape! Are you keeping us here to be your father's secondary wives?"

"Don't worry madam," said Jia Rong to old Mrs. You. "My father has your interests much at heart. He's been looking for years now for a couple of well-born, handsome young gentlemen from rich and noble families to be husbands for my two aunts. Luckily he's found one at last—someone he met the other day on the journey home."

Old Mrs. You was only too ready to believe him. "What family is he from?" she asked promptly.

At this, Second Sister put down her needlework to chase and strike Jia Rong. "Don't believe a word of this rascal, mother," she cried.

"Just say what you want to say, but don't use dirty words!" put in Third Sister.

Just then, someone came in to announce, "We've made everything ready. Please go and have a look, Master Rong, and report to the Master that it's all ready."

Off went Jia Rong, a smile all over his face. He hurried back to the temple to report to his father that all was ready at home.

Five o'clock in the morning of the fourth day was fixed as the hour to have the coffin taken into the city, and all relatives and friends were informed. Jia Zhen and Jia Rong, duty bound to keep vigil by the coffin and mourn, nevertheless seized the chance to fool around with the two You sisters once the guests were gone.

Jia Lian had long heard of Madam You's lovely stepsisters and longed to have the chance to meet them. Now, with Jia Jing's coffin in the house, he saw Second Sister and Third Sister every day and so he was able to be on familiar terms with them.

The mere sight of the two beautiful girls aroused Jia Lian's burning lust. Whenever he had the chance, he would make eyes at them. Third Sister treated him coolly. However, Second Sister appeared very interested in him, but since there were so many people about, he could not make any advances. Fear of arousing Jia Zhen's jealousy also kept him from acting too rashly. The two of them could only flirt silently.

After the funeral, however, there were few people left in Jia Zhen's house. The main quarters were occupied by old Mrs. You and her two daughters, attended by a few of the maids and serving women who did the rough work. All the senior maids and concubines had gone to the temple. As for the female servants who lived outside, they simply kept watch at night and minded the gate in the daytime, and would not go inside unless they had business there. So Jia Lian was eager to make good use of this chance. He spent the nights in the temple too, on the pretext of keeping Jia Zhen company, but he often slipped back to the Peaceful Mansion to continue his interest in seducing Second Sister.

One day when Jia Lian and Jia Rong were chatting idly, Jia Lian mentioned Second Sister You, praising her for her good looks and modest behavior, her ladylike ways and gentle speech, as if she were a model of excellence admired and loved by all.

Jia Rong could read his uncle's mind very easily. "If you love her so much, uncle, I'll act as your go-between to make her your secondary wife. How about that?"

"Is that a joke," beamed Jia Lian, "or are you in earnest?"

"I'm quite serious," Jia Rong replied.

"It's certainly a nice proposal. I'm only afraid your Aunt Phoenix wouldn't agree. Besides, your Grandmother might not be willing. I heard that your Second Aunt is already engaged to someone."

"None of those things is really a problem," said Jia Rong. "I have been told that old Mrs. You promised her second daughter to the Zhang family who managed the Imperial Farm, before the child was born. Since that time the Zhangs have been ruined by a lawsuit. Old Mrs. You often complains that she'd like to break off the engagement, and my father also wants to find Second Aunt a different husband. As soon as they've picked a suitable family, all they need do is send someone to find the Zhangs, pay them a dozen or so taels of silver, and have a deed written to break off the betrothal. If a gentleman like you, uncle, wants her as a secondary wife, I guarantee both her mother and my father will be willing. The only problem is my Aunt Phoenix."

At this Jia Lian was too overjoyed to say anything and could only grin foolishly.

After a little reflection Jia Rong continued, "If you have the nerve to do as I say, uncle, I'm pretty sure it will be all right. That simply means spending a little extra money."

"If you have any idea, dear boy," said Jia Lian eagerly, "just tell me what it is."

"Don't let out a word about this when you go home. Wait till I've told my father and settled it with my grandmother. Then we'll buy a house and the furnishings for it somewhere near the back of our mansion, and we'll install a couple of our servants and their wives there. That done, we'll choose a lucky day and you can get married on the sly. We'll forbid the servants to breathe a word of it. As Aunt Phoenix lives far away inside the big mansion, how can she possibly know anything about it? Then you'll have two homes, uncle. After a year or so, if word does get out, at the most you'll get reprimanded by your father. But you can say that, as my aunt had no son, you arranged this in secret outside, in the hope of having descendants. When Aunt Phoenix sees that the rice is already cooked, she'll have to put up with it. And if you then ask the old lady to put in a word for you the whole thing will blow over."

Jia Lian was so charmed by Second Sister's beauty that he felt Jia Rong's plan was foolproof. At the time he entirely forgot that he was in mourning and how improper it was to have a concubine outside when he had a strict father and jealous wife at home.

Jia Lian thanked his nephew, saying, "Dear boy, if you can really fix this up I'll buy you two of the prettiest girls as a present."

By now they had reached the Peaceful Mansion and Jia Rong said, "Uncle, while you go in to get the silver from my grandmother and give it to the steward, I'll go on ahead to call on the old lady."

Jia Lian nodded with a smile, "Don't tell the old lady that I've come with you."

"All right," Jia Rong whispered into his ear, "If you see Second Aunt today, don't act too rashly. If there's any trouble now, it will make things more difficult later on."

"Don't talk rot," chuckled Jia Lian. "Go on. I'll wait for you here."

Then Jia Rong went to pay his respects to the Lady Dowager.

When Jia Lian entered the Peaceful Mansion, some of the stewards stepped forward with other servants to welcome him. They then followed him to the hall. Jia Lian asked them a few questions briefly for formality's sake, then dismissed them and went in alone. As he and Jia Zhen were intimate cousins, who kept no secrets from each other, they felt free to come and go in each other's apartments without announcement.

Jia Lian went straight to the main apartment. The old woman on duty in the corridor lifted the door curtain as soon as she saw him; and, on entering the room, he saw Second Sister sewing with two maids on the couch. There was no sign of old Mrs. You and Third Sister. Jia Lian went forward to greet Second Sister, who asked him to take a seat.

He sat down with his back to the east partition and, after an exchange of formalities, asked, "Where are your mother and Third Sister? Why aren't they here?"

"They just went to the back for something; they'll be here soon," she told him.

Because the maids had gone to make tea and there was no one else present, Jia Lian kept darting smiling glances at Second Sister, who lowered her head to hide a smile but did not respond. He dared make no further passes.

Suddenly the door curtain behind them swished and in came old Mrs. You and Third Sister with two young maids.

Jia Lian said to them, "I wanted to come to visit you and to see both the young ladies. It's good of you to have come here, madam, but I'm sorry to be putting our two cousins to such inconvenience, too."

"What way is that for close relatives to talk!" she smiled. "We've made ourselves at home here. To be frank, since my husband died we've found it hard to make ends meet, and we've only just managed, thanks to my son-in-law's help. To look after the house for him in his time of trouble is the least we can do in return. How can you talk of putting us to inconvenience!"

Now they heard Jia Rong's voice outside in the court-yard, and a few moments later he appeared. He greeted his grandmother and two aunts before turning with a smile to Jia Lian.

"Just now your father was asking about you, uncle," Jia Rong said. "I told him you'd be coming presently. He told me to ask you to hurry up, if I met you."

As Jia Lian rose to leave, he heard Jia Rong tell old Mrs. You, "You know, the other day I was telling you that Father has found a husband for Second Aunt. He has much the same features and build as Uncle Lian. Does that please you?" As he said this he pointed slyly at Jia Lian and motioned with his lips at Second Sister.

She was too embarrassed to say anything, but her sister scolded: "What a devilish monkey you are! Have you got nothing else to talk about? Just wait, I'm going to pull out that tongue of yours!" Third Sister said this half angrily and half in jest.

Jia Rong had slipped out, laughing, and now Jia Lian took his leave with a smile.

It was evening by the time Jia Rong got back to the temple and reported to his father, "The old lady's much better now that she has stopped taking medicine." He then took this chance to describe how Jia Lian had told him on the road of his wish to make Second Sister You his secondary wife and to set up house outside so that Phoenix would know nothing about the secret marriage arrangement.

"This is because he's worried at having no son," Jia Rong explained. "Uncle begged me time and again to propose this to you, father." He, of course, omitted to mention that he, himself, was the author of this plan.

Jia Zhen thought it over. "Actually, it would be just as well," he said finally. "But we don't know whether your Second Aunt would be willing or not. Go and talk it over tomorrow first with your old granny. Get her to make sure your Second Aunt agrees before we make any decision."

After giving his son some more instructions, he went to tell his wife about the matter. Madam You could see at once that it was improper and did her best to dissuade him. But, as Jia Zhen had already made up his mind and she was in the habit of falling in with his wishes, and as Second Sister was only her stepsister, she had to let them go ahead with this scheme.

Jia Rong went back to the city early the next morning and told his grandmother about his father's proposal. He also added a good deal of his own. "They'll take you in to live in comfort in your old age, madam," he assured her. "And later they'll see to Third Aunt's marriage too."

His eloquence painted such a rosy picture that naturally old Mrs. You could hardly fail to agree. Besides, she depended on Jia Zhen for her livelihood and it was he who was sponsoring the marriage. She would not have to provide any dowry. Furthermore, Jia Lian was a young gentleman from a noble family, ten times better than the wretched Zhang family. So she agreed to go straight away to discuss it with her second daughter.

Second Sister was a coquettish young lady. She had already had an affair with Jia Zhen, and it was her constant regret that her betrothal to Zhang Hua prevented her from making a better marriage. So, because Jia Lian had taken a fancy to her and her brother-in-law had proposed the match, she was more than willing. She nodded in agreement, and this was at once reported back to Jia Rong, who went back to inform his father.

The next day they sent men to invite Jia Lian to the temple. When Jia Zhen told him that old Mrs. You had agreed to this proposal, he was so overjoyed that he could not thank Jia Zhen and Jia Rong enough. They made plans to send stewards to find a house, to have trinkets made, and to have the bride's trousseau prepared, as well as the bed, curtains and other furnishings for the bridal chamber.

Within a few days everything was ready. The house they bought was in Flower Twig Lane, about half a mile behind Peaceful and Honored Street. It had more than twenty rooms. They also bought two young maids. In addition, Jia Zhen installed his own servant there to wait on Second Sister after she moved in. He then sent for Zhang Hua and his father. Finally he ordered them to write a deed canceling the engagement for good.

When Jia Lian saw that all preparations were ready, he chose the third of the next month, an auspicious day, for the wedding. Jia Lian, Jia Zhen, and Jia Rong had a consultation, and soon had everything arranged.

On the second of the month, old Mrs. You and Third Sister were escorted first to the new house. Old Mrs. You saw at a glance that it was not as grand as Jia Rong had claimed. Still, as it appeared quite respectable, she and her daughter were both satisfied.

The next day at dawn, when Second Sister was brought out in a plain sedan chair without bridal trimmings, she was carried over to her new home. The bride was helped into the bridal chamber where, that night, she and Jia Lian enjoyed the transports of love.

Now the more Jia Lian saw of Second Sister, the more he loved her. He did his best to please her in every way possible. He ordered his servants to call her "Mrs. Lian."

Whenever he went home he merely claimed to have been detained by business in the East Mansion; and Phoenix, knowing how close he and Jia Zhen were, thought it natural for them to talk things over together and never suspected the truth. As for the domestics, they never interfered in affairs of this kind.

Everything seemed to be working out very smoothly.

19/ The Death of Third Sister You

Third Sister You was a strange young lady. She was good looking and romantic, and she liked to dress in a striking manner. Adopting every conceivable kind of seductive attitude to infatuate men, she amused herself by keeping them on a string, unable either to approach her or to stay away.

Her mother and sister tried in vain to dissuade her from this behavior. But she would retort, "How silly you are, sister. Why let those rascals ruin girls like us? Why act so helpless? In the case of Jia Lian, that wife of his is a real terror. As long as this secret marriage is kept from her, we're all right. If she comes to hear of it one day, she won't take it lying down and there's sure to be a big row. Who knows which of you will survive? How can this be the right place for you to stay the rest of your life?"

Her mother and sister realized now it was no use trying to persuade her, and gave up.

When Jia Lian came to the house he spent all his time in Second Sister's room. However, he was beginning to regret this set-up because he had to keep it such a secret from Phoenix. Yet Second Sister was so loving and so devoted to him that he kept returning to her. As for her wifely submissiveness, she was ten times better than Phoenix. And in terms of her looks, voice and behavior, she was at least five times better than Phoenix. That's why he stuck to her. They were of one heart and one mind. He swore they would live and die together. Phoenix and Patience were completely forgotten.

When they shared the same pillow and quilt, Second Sister often urged him, "Why not talk it over with your cousin Zhen, and choose some man you know to marry my sister? She can't stay here like this indefinitely. Sooner or later there's bound to be trouble."

"I did mention this to him the other day," said Jia Lian, "but he can't bear the idea of giving her up. So what can I do about it?"

"Don't worry," said Second Sister, "we'll try to talk her around first thing tomorrow. If we can persuade her, we'll let her go on making rows until he has no choice but to marry her off."

"That's an excellent idea," agreed Jia Lian.

The next day Second Sister prepared a dinner party and Jia Lian stayed indoors. At noon, they invited Third Sister and her mother over and made them take the seats of honor. Third Sister had a good idea of what this meeting was for. When they began to serve wine and before her sister had a chance to break the ice, she said tearfully. "You must have invited me today, sister, to talk over something important. I'm no fool. There's no need to repeat the same story time and again. But marriage is something serious; it's for life, not a children's game!"

"That's no problem," said Jia Lian, "you can make your own free choice. We'll take care of the whole dowry. Your mother needn't worry about that either."

"Anyway, sister knows who I mean," said Third Sister, "I don't have to name him."

"Who is it?" Jia Lian asked Second Sister. But she could not for the moment think who it might be.

"Don't just think about the present, sister," said Third Sister, "just think back five years and you'll remember."

As they were talking, one of Jia Lian's trusted pages, Joker, came in to report, "The old master wants you to go over at once, sir. I told him you'd gone to see your uncle. Then I came straight to fetch you."

"Did my wife ask about me yesterday?" demanded Jia Lian hastily.

"I told Madam Phoenix that you were at the family temple with Lord Jia Zhen making plans for the hundredth day sacrifice, so you might not be able to get back home."

Jia Lian promptly called for his horse and rode off, accompanied by another page, leaving Joker behind to attend to other things. Second Sister ordered two dishes for Joker and made him drink a large cup of wine while she asked him a few questions.

As they were chatting, the other page came back to report, "The old master has something important to attend to. He can't come back today. He asked me to tell you to go to bed early, madam." This said, he went off with Joker.

Second Sister ordered the gate to be closed and they turned in early, but she spent most of the night questioning her sister.

It was not until the afternoon of the next day that Jia Lian arrived.

"Why are you in such a hurry to come when you've some important business?" Second Sister asked him. "Be sure not to delay your journey for my sake."

"It's not all that important," he told her. "Only I've got to make a long business trip, starting early next month, and I'll not be back for half a month."

"Well, just go with an easy mind. You needn't worry about anything here. My sister's not the kind of girl that keeps changing her mind. She has surely chosen her man. I think you will have to fall in with her wishes."

"Who is he?" demanded Jia Lian promptly.

"It's a long story," smiled Second Sister. "Five years ago, when it was our grandmother's birthday, my mother took us there to join in the birthday party. They'd invited a troupe of amateur actors. Among them was a certain Liu Xianglian, who used to play the young scholar's role in operas. She took such fancy to him and even declared that he was the only man she's ready to marry. Last year he was said to have got into some sort of trouble and had run away. We haven't the faintest idea whether he has come back or not."

"So that's who it is!" said Jia Lian. "She's made a good choice. You may not know about him, though. Young Liu is a pretty handsome young man, but he's quite a cold fish. He has few real friends. Magic Jade is the person with whom he gets on best. Last year he beat up that fool Xue Pan and then ran away. I suppose he was rather embarrassed and didn't want to meet any of us, and we don't know where he has gone. Someone did tell me that he's returned, but it may be just a rumor. You know, Liu is such a rolling stone, who knows how many years he may stay away. Won't it be a waste of time for Third Sister to put off marrying for so long?"

"Well, when my sister says she's going to do something, she really does it," said Second Sister, "you'd better let her have her own way."

At this point Third Sister came in to join the conversation. "Believe me, brother-in-law, I'm not one of those who say one thing and mean another; I really mean what I say. If Mr. Liu turns up, I'll marry him. From now on I'll spend all my time praying, fasting and looking after my mother, while I wait for him to come and marry me. I'll do this even if I have to wait a hundred years. If he never comes, I'll quit the world and become a nun," Drawing a jade pin from her hair she broke it in two, exclaiming, "If I've said a single word that isn't true, may I end up like this pin!"

This said, she went straight back to her room.

Jia Lian could see that he had no choice but to accede to her wishes. After a brief discussion about domestic affairs with Second Sister, he went home for further consultation with Phoenix about the preparations for his journey. Then he sent to ask Tealeaf whether Young Liu had come back or not.

"I really don't know," said Tealeaf, "probably not. Otherwise I would have heard."

He also asked information from his neighbors, and confirmed that Liu had not come back. So Jia Lian passed this information on to Second Sister.

As the time for his departure approached, he announced that he was leaving two days early. Actually he spent two nights in Second Sister's place, starting his journey secretly from there. He found Third Sister quite a changed person, but Second Sister was so careful and competent in the management of her house, he realized that there would be no need to worry about them while he was away.

He left the city early in the morning and took the road to Pinganzhou. After three days of travel, he met a caravan of packhorses. They were led by two horsemen who, to his astonishment, turned out to be Xue Pan and Liu Xianglian. After exchanging the usual greetings, the three of them went into an inn to sit down and chat.

Jia Lian said, "After the two of you fell out, we were anxious to patch things up between you, but Young Liu disappeared without a trace. How come you're together today?"

"You've never heard such a strange story as I have to tell," smiled Xue Pan. "I and my assistants bought some goods and started back to the capital this spring. All went well until the other day when we reached Pinganzhou, where a band of robbers took away all our things. Then, along came Brother Liu in the nick of time to drive the robbers away. He got all our stuff back for us, and saved our lives. He refused to let me thank him, and we have become sworn brothers. We've been traveling together ever since. At the next crossroads, he's leaving me and going off sixty or seventy miles south to visit an aunt of his. I'll go to the capital first to settle my own affairs, then find a house for him and a nice wife, so that we can settle down there as friends."

"I see," said Jia Lian, "I'm certainly glad to hear that. It's a pity we had all that worry for nothing."

Then he continued, "Since you mentioned just now you're trying to find Liu a nice wife, let me say that I've got the very bride for him, a splendid match for Brother Liu." Jia Lian went on to explain how he had married Second Sister You and wanted to find a husband for her younger sister. Only he didn't say that Liu was Third Sister's own choice.

He then told Xue Pan, "Don't say anything about this to the others when you get home. I'm waiting until we have a son, then of course they'll get to know about it."

Xue Pan was glad to learn about the marriage to Second Sister You. "You should have done that long ago. My cousin Phoenix is to blame for giving you no son at all!"

"There you're talking nonsense again," put in Xianglian, with a smile. "You'd better keep your mouth shut."

"Well, we must fix up this match." Xue Pan said, changing the topic.

"I have been wanting to marry an extremely beautiful girl," said Xianglian. "But since this proposal comes from my honorable elder brothers, why should I insist on that? I'll leave it to you to arrange the marriage."

"Words don't carry conviction," Jia Lian rejoined. "But once you see her, you'll come to know that this sister-in-law of mine is a beauty beyond compare."

Xianglian was overjoyed by this assurance. "In that case," he said, "after I've visited my aunt, I'll come to the capital in less than a month, and we can settle everything then. How about that?"

"We're both men of our words," replied Jia Lian. "But you are such a rolling stone, always on the move, how can I trust your word? If you drift away now and don't come back, will it mean her whole lifetime is wasted? I think you ought to give me some sort of pledge."

"A true gentleman never goes back on his word," replied Xianglian. "I'm always hard up and on the way home like this, where can I get a betrothal gift?"

"I've something suitable here," Xue Pan cut in. "Just take it, Second Brother."

"You don't have to offer any gold or jewelry," said Jia Lian. "Just give me something you carry about with you so I can take back with me as a token, not something valuable."

"Very well, then," agreed Xianglian. "The only thing I have with me is a pair of swords for self-defense. I've got another sword in my traveling bag. It's a family heirloom. You can take it back as my pledge. However much of a wanderer I am, under any other circumstances I'd never give up these swords."

After that, they drank a few more cups of wine, then mounted their horses, took leave of each other, and went on their different ways.

One day after Jia Lian reached Pinganzhou, he paid a call on the governor to settle his official business. Then he started back home the next day. As soon as he got there, he went to see Second Sister You.

After the routine exchange of greetings, he told the sisters about his encounter with Liu Xianglian. He took out the pair of swords and passed them to Third Sister. She looked at the dragon and serpent designs on the sheath, which were studded with bright pearls and jewels, then drew out the two swords. One was engraved with the word "duck," the other with the word "drake." Overjoyed, she hastily took them to her chamber and hung them on the wall over her bed. Every day she feasted her eyes on them, happy that her future marriage was assured.

Liu Xianglian did not come to the capital till the eighth month. He called first on Aunt Xue. Full of gratitude for the good turn Xianglian had done to save her son's life, Aunt Xue let bygones be bygones. Both she and her son, Xue Pan, expressed their thanks most gratefully. So did Xianglian.

The next day he called on Magic Jade. Xianglian told her all that had happened on the road.

"Congratulations!" cried Magic Jade. "You're lucky to find such a pretty girl. She's really a charming girl, just the right match for you!"

"Since she's so pretty she ought to have a lot of suitors," said Xianglian. "Why should your cousin single me out? Besides, I've never been his close friend, he certainly has no special concern for me. In our brief meeting on the road he kept pressing me to agree to this engagement. Why is the girl's family in such a hurry? I can't help feeling rather dubious about the whole thing. Now I really regret having given him my swords as a pledge. That's why I came to you to find out just what's behind all this."

"You're intelligent enough," answered Magic Jade. "Once you've given your pledge to marry her, how can you start having second thoughts? You always said you wanted a charming girl, now you have got one. Isn't that good enough? Why these suspicions?"

"Just now you told me you knew nothing about her sister's secret marriage," said Xianglian. "How do you know that she's so beautiful?"

"Well, she's one of the two daughters of Madam You's stepmother." said Magic Jade. "I saw them many times during the month when we were living in the same household, so of course I know. She and her sister are really a pair of rare beauties."

Xianglian stamped his foot impatiently. "That's no good," he said. "It won't do. The only things clean in your East Mansion are the two stone lions at the gate!"

Magic Jade blushed, and Xianglian, realizing that he had gone a bit too far, made haste to bow apologetically. "I deserve death for talking such nonsense. Anyhow do tell me something about her character."

"Since you know so much, why ask me? I may not be clean myself either." said Magic Jade wryly.

"I forgot your kindness just now," said Xianglian with a smile. "Anyway don't take it to heart."

At that point Xianglian took his leave with a bow and left. He made up his mind to ask for his pledge back. This decision reached, he went to find Jia Lian.

Jia Lian was in his new house. When he heard that Xianglian had come, he was overjoyed and hurried out to welcome him. Then Jia Lian took him into the inner room and introduced him to old Mrs. You. To Jia Lian's surprise, Xianglian merely bowed and addressed her as "aunt," referring to himself as "Your humble nephew."

Then, while they were sipping tea Xianglian came straight to the point. "During my journey home, I was over hasty, not knowing that my aunt, in April, had already chosen another girl to be my fiancee. It wouldn't be right for me to accept your proposal and refuse my aunt's. If I'd given you the usual gifts of gold and silk, I wouldn't venture to ask to have them back; but the swords I gave you were left me by my grandfather, so I must beg you to return them."

Jia Lian was quite put out when he heard this. "A pledge is a pledge after all," he argued. "And a pledge is given to stop a man from going back on his word. How can you cancel an engagement so freely? It's entirely impossible!"

"In that case," replied Xianglian, "I'm willing to accept any penalty, but on this matter I definitely cannot obey your order."

Jia Lian was about to argue further when Xianglian stood up. "Could you come out for a while and talk about it somewhere else?" he asked. "It's not so convenient here."

Third Sister had overheard this conversation from her room. She was highly distraught by what she heard. Obviously Xianglian must have heard some gossip in the Jia mansions that led him to believe her a shameless unchaste woman, unworthy to be his wife. If she let the two men go out now to have further discussion, she was sure the outcome would be further damage to her reputation. So, as soon as she heard Jia Lian agreeing to his proposal, she took down the swords from the wall, concealed the "duck" behind her back, and went out to intercept them.

"There's no need for you to go out to discuss this any more," she told them as she entered the room. "Here's your pledge back!"

With her tears falling like rain, she passed sword to Xianglian with her left hand, and with the other blade in her right, she cut her own throat.

All present were horrified and tried in vain to revive her. Old Mrs. You, sobbing hysterically, cursed Xianglian, while Jia Lian seized hold of him, calling servants to tie him up and take him to court.

Second Sister then dried her tears to urge her husband, "He didn't force her to do it, she herself committed suicide. So what's the good of taking him to court? That would only cause a worse scandal. Why not let him go to save further trouble?"

At this point Jia Lian didn't know what else to do. He let go of Xianglian and told him to get out quickly.

However, Xianglian did not move, but instead burst into tears. "I never knew she was so chaste, with such a noble heart! It wasn't my luck to have her as my wife!" he exclaimed.

Prostrating himself over her corpse he gave way to a storm of weeping. And when a coffin was brought and her body laid in it, he clasped it and lamented bitterly before he finally left them.

Once outside the gate, he did not know where to go. Blinded by his tears and sunk in gloom as he recalled what had just happened. "She was so lovely and chaste," he reflected, torn by remorse. Then he looked up and suddenly saw a lame Taoist priest sitting in a tumble-down temple. Xianglian rose to his feet, turned to the priest, and bowed to the ground.

"Where are we, holy master?" he asked the priest. "May I know your immortal name?"

The priest chuckled, "I myself don't know where we are or who I am. I'm simply stopping here for a moment to relax."

At this Xianglian shuddered with cold, as if the marrow of his bones had frozen. He drew the companionless "drake" sword from his waist and cut off his hair with one stroke. At this, all of his worldly sorrows seemed to disappear. He went away with the Taoist priest, and was never seen again.

20/ Jealous Phoenix's Decoy

Soon after the death of Third Sister You, Jia Lian began again to go on official business trips to Pinganzhou. The stewards and servants in the mansion now came to know of the secret marriage of Jia Lian and Second Sister You. Madam Phoenix was the only one who was still kept in the dark.

However, as the Chinese proverb goes, "Truth can never be kept in the dark." As soon as Phoenix found out, she became livid with jealousy. She immediately began to make secret plans. She ordered the workmen to fix up three rooms on the eastern wing, decorating and furnishing them just like her own. On the fourteenth of the month, she took Patience and other maids on a secret trip. But before setting out, she disclosed her true purpose to them.

She ordered them to dress in mourning. Then they set off, Joker leading the way, to the house where Second Sister You lived. Joker knocked at the gate, which was opened by a maid. Joker announced with a grin, "Tell the Second Mistress that Madam Phoenix is here, and do it quickly!"

Scared out of her wits, the maid flew in to report this visitor. Second Sister You was taken aback, but since Phoenix had come, she had no choice but to receive her with the expected courtesies. Adjusting her dress, Second Sister You went out to meet Phoenix as she got down from her carriage. Phoenix was dressed in half mourning.

Second Sister You stepped forward with a smile to greet her, addressing her as "elder sister."

"I wasn't expecting the honor of your visit today," Second Sister You apologized. "Forgive me, elder sister, otherwise I should have come out to meet you."

Smiling, Phoenix returned her greeting and hand in hand they entered the house. Phoenix took the seat of honor.

Second Sister then knelt to pay her respects. "Your sister is still very young," she said. "Since I first came here, I've left all decisions to my mother and my step-sister. Now that I've had the honor to meet you, I'd like to ask for your advice and instructions. I'm willing to wait on you with all my service."

Phoenix returned the courtesy with a smile. "I'm as young and inexperienced as you are, sister," she answered.

"As a matter of fact, I'd advised my husband to take another wife," she continued, "because if he were to have a son, he would be a support for me in my old age. Who would have thought that my husband would take me to be some sort of a jealous woman who cannot tolerate a rival. The fact that he has done this on the sly is really a great injustice. To whom can I voice my complaint? That's why I've come to call on you in person. I do hope you'll understand how much I take this to heart.

"If you will agree to move into our house, we can live together as sisters with one mind. Let's tell Second Master to pay careful attention to his business and to look after his health. Is there anything more important than that? How can I set my mind at ease if we live in separate houses like this? Besides, once outsiders know about it, it would spoil both our reputations.

"What's far more important is our Second Master's reputation. The gossip about us is not so serious. I'm not as hard to get along with as they say. Would I have come to you today if I were such a terrible person? I've even offered him our maid Patience as a chamber wife, you know.

"I've come today to beg you to move in and live with me. If you won't agree to come back with me, I'd be willing to move out here to live with you and wait on you like a younger sister. All I beg of you is to put in a few good words for me to Second Master, so that he'll allow me somewhere to stay."

With that Phoenix started sobbing and weeping, which moved Second Sister You to tears as well. Since Second Sister was a kindhearted woman, she took Phoenix to be a good lady. Second Sister had longed to live with Jia Lian like a respectable married couple, and so she was naturally more than willing to agree.

"Since I've met you today, elder sister," she said, "I'll leave all the arrangements to you."

Then, after the servants carried Second Sister's things to the eastern rooms, Phoenix led her through the back gate of the Grand View Garden to settle down, as planned.

"Our family rules are strict," Phoenix now told her, confidentially. "So far the old lady knows nothing about this sort of thing. So you'd better not call on the old lady and the other ladies just yet. You can stay in the garden for a couple of days until I've found some way to break the news to them, and then it will be no problem to meet them."

"All right, I leave everything to you, elder sister," said Second Sister.

By this time nine out of ten of the people in the mansion had heard the news. They flocked over to see this newcomer. All were impressed by her beauty and charm.

"Don't let a word out," Phoenix warned them all. "If this comes to the ears of the old lady and other ladies, I'll kill you!" Then she dismissed Second Sister's maid, assigning some of her own maids to wait on her. Phoenix also ordered the other women in the garden to keep an eye on Second Sister.

"If she disappears or runs away, you'll have to answer for it!" Phoenix threatened them. After that she went off to make other secret arrangements.

Everyone in the household was amazed to see how kind-hearted Phoenix had become. As for Second Sister, she was quite satisfied to settle down in this nice place. All the girls in the garden treated her well. She felt assured about her future in the bosom of so delightful a family.

However, happy events do not last long. After three days, the new maid assigned to her started showing signs of insubordination.

"There's no more hair oil left," Second Sister told her. "Go ask Madam Phoenix for some."

"How can you be so inconsiderate, madam?" retorted the maid. "Madam Phoenix has to look after the old lady every day, as well as the mistresses of both mansions and all the young ladies. Not a day goes by but she has ten or twenty important matters to attend to, besides dozens of minor ones. How can you bother her with trifles like this? My advice to you is to be a bit more patient. Yours isn't a proper marriage. She's treating you well only because she's so exceptionally kind and generous. A less tolerant person might kick you out. And then what could you do? You'd really be stranded."

This response made Second Sister hang her head in silence. She saw she would just have to put up with such inconveniences. And things went from bad to worse. The maid stopped fetching her meals, or served them earlier or later than usual, bringing nothing but left-overs. When Second Sister tried to complain, the maid glared at her and lifted her voice to scream at her. For fear others might think that she didn't know her place, Second Sister put up with this behavior as best she could. Every week or so when she happened to see Phoenix, the latter was all smiles and sweetness, always addressing her as "my dear sister."

"If any servants are careless and you can't control them, just let me know and I'll have them beaten," promised Phoenix. Then she scolded the maids and matrons, "I know the way you bully the kind ones and fear those who are hard on you. Once you're behind my back, you're not afraid of anyone. But take care! If I hear one word of complaint from the second mistress, I'll have your lives for it!"

Second Sister was taken in by all this show of kindness. With her taking my side like this, I'd better not make any fuss, she thought to herself. Some servants have no sense, and that's only natural. If I report them and get them into trouble, I'm the one people will blame. So she said nothing about the maid's behavior.

Phoenix, meanwhile, had sent some servants to make detailed inquiries into the background of Second Sister You. It was ascertained that she had been engaged formally to a young man, now nineteen, a gambler, and a wastrel. Without telling him, his father had accepted ten ounces of silver from old Mrs. You to break off the engagement. The young man's name was Zhang Hua.

After Phoenix learned these particulars, she gave Brightie, the servant, a packet of twenty ounces of silver and told him to find Zhang Hua and have the man secretly move in with the servant so that Zhang Hua could bring a suit against Jia Lian. This indictment was to be based on the fact that Jia Lian's secret marriage was against Imperial decree, was unknown to his parents, and took place during a period of state and family mourning. The indictment also relied on the fact that, through his wealth and power, Jia Lian had forced Zhang Hua to break off his engagement, and that he took the second wife without the permission of his first.

Zhang Hua agreed to the arrangement, wrote out his indictment, and took it to the Court of Censors.

Phoenix secretly sent her man to find out when this summons was to be issued. She then sent another servant to bribe the judge with three hundred ounces of silver so that the judge would make a display of severity in order to scare the accuser.

The judge realized what was expected of him, accepted the bribe and the next day announced in a court hearing that Zhang Hua was a scoundrel who had brought these trumped-up charges against innocent people because he was in debt to the Jias and could not pay them back.

Because Jia Lian was not at home, Jia Rong was summoned to face the court. At the time he was handling some of Jia Lian's business affairs. The person who brought him word of the charges against his uncle urged him to think of a way out of the mess. Jia Rong at once went to report the matter to his father, Jia Zhen.

Immediately Jia Zhen sealed two hundred ounces of silver in a packet to be sent to the judge, and ordered a servant to go and answer the charge. Then, as the two of them were discussing their next step, Phoenix arrived from the West Mansion. This was a most unpleasant surprise. Both father and son attempted to take French leave, but it was too late—Phoenix had already entered.

"A fine head of the family you are!" she cried. "A fine thing you got your younger brother to do!"

Jia Rong hastily stepped forward to greet her. She seized him by the hand and marched him towards the interior of the mansion.

"Try to entertain your aunt well," said Jia Zhen, "order a good meal for her." He then called for his horse and quickly departed.

Phoenix walked into the main sitting room. Madam You came out to greet her.

"What's the matter?" Madam You asked, seeing how furious she looked. "Why this hurry?"

Phoenix spat in her face. "Couldn't you find husbands for the girls of your You family? Why did you have to smuggle them into the Jia family?

"Even if you want to pawn off your sisters," she continued, "there's a proper procedure for marriage, and it should be announced in a decent way. Have you taken leave of your senses? How could you send her over during a time of state and family mourning? And now that someone's brought a charge against us, even people in the law courts know what a jealous shrew I am! They have summoned me to stand trial. And I shall be divorced.

"What wrong have I done you since I've come to this house that you should treat me like this? Or did the old lady or Aunt Wang suggest that you trap me like this so as to get me out of the way? Let's face the court together and clear this up. You can give me a bill of divorce then if you want to, and I'll leave right away!"

She began to cry and caught hold of Madam You, insisting on going to court. Jia Rong knelt down in desperation and kowtowed, begging his aunt not to be too angry.

"You heartless wretch!" Phoenix said. "You fear nothing in heaven or on earth, playing such dirty tricks all the time and doing such shameless, lawless things to ruin our family.

Even your ancestors' spirit will never want you when you die. Don't you dare tell me what I ought to do!"

She began to raise her hand to strike him.

Jia Rong redoubled the frequency of his kowtows. "Don't be angry, aunt!" he cried. "Try to remember the good things as well as the bad. I may be very wicked, but surely in a thousand days there must have been one when I was good enough. But there is no need to punish me. I will slap myself instead." He raised his hands and slapped himself on both cheeks.

All present begged him to stop.

Phoenix threw herself on Madam You's bosom, weeping and wailing in a fine display of dramatic grief. "I wouldn't mind your finding another wife for your brother-in-law," she sobbed. "But why make him break the law and keep his parents in the dark? Why give me a bad name?

"Actually I've fetched your sister here myself, but didn't venture to report it to Their Ladyships for fear they'd be angry. Yesterday I was desperate when I found out that our family was being sued. Even if I appeared in court to answer the charge myself, your Jia family would be disgraced. So I'm afraid I had to take five hundred ounces of Lady Wang's silver on the sly to bribe the court. And my servant is still locked up by the police."

All this was said amid fits of weeping and cursing. She even made a dramatic attempt to dash her brains against the wall and kill herself, Madam You, reduced to almost a piece of dough, her clothes covered with tears, could only shout at Jia Rong.

"You degenerate!" she scolded. "A fine mess you and your father have made of things. I warned you against doing this."

Phoenix took Madam You's hand in both her hands, drawing her face close to her own. "Were you crazy?" Phoenix demanded. "Was your mouth so stuffed with something that you couldn't let me know? If you had told me about it at the time, I wouldn't be in such a fix. Things wouldn't have gone so far as to be taken to court. You're so short of talents and eloquence. All you care about is getting a name for your virtue." She spat a couple of times in succession.

"I did try to stop them," sobbed Madam You, tearfully. "If you don't believe me, ask the servants. I don't blame you for being angry, sister, but I simply couldn't help it."

The concubines and maids kneeling fearfully round them now pleaded with Phoenix. "You're so wise and understanding, madam, even if our mistress did wrong you've gotten even with her now. Usually, in front of us slaves, you're both on the best of terms. So please leave her some face."

They brought Phoenix some tea, but she smashed the cup on the floor. However, after some time, she stopped crying and smoothed her hair.

Then she ordered Jia Rong, "Go and fetch your father here! I want to ask him why, with still a fortnight to go before the mourning for his uncle was over, he let his nephew take a wife. I've never heard of such a thing! I must learn the reason from him so that I can teach it to the younger generation."

Still on his knees, Jia Rong kowtowed and said, "This had nothing to do with my parents. It was I who put my uncle up to it. I don't know what came over me. I must have been out of my mind. You're so intelligent you must know the saying: 'If your arm is broken, hide it in your sleeve.' You've got a very foolish nephew, and he has done something very silly. There's nothing for it. Please do your best to settle this." He went on kowtowing as if he would never stop.

His miserable behavior soon melted Phoenix. But she could not change her tune too suddenly when there were so many pairs of eyes watching her. She did not answer him, but merely raised him up with a sigh. Wiping her eyes, she apologized to Madam You, "I'm too young and inexperienced. When I heard someone had sued us, I was scared out of my wits. You must forgive me. Please ask Cousin Zhen to lose no time in settling this lawsuit."

"Don't worry," Madam You and Jia Rong assured her all at once.

"And, Uncle won't be involved at all," added Jia Rong. "You said just now you'd spent five hundred ounces on this case, aunt. Of course we'll try to get that sum and send it over to make it up to you. How can we allow you to lose money over us? But one thing, aunt, do cover up for us and don't let Grandma and Lady Wang get to know anything about this!"

Phoenix looked sarcastically at Madam You. "First you stab me in the back, and now you ask me to hush it up for you. I may be a fool, but I'm not at all that foolish. If you were worried because he had no heir, don't you think I would share in that concern myself? I take your sister in as my own, and then, like a slap in the face or a bolt from the blue, comes this suit against us brought by Zhang Hua.

"All I could do was to get the servants to find out who this Zhang Hua was and why he had such nerve. The servants told me, 'The new mistress was engaged to him. Now he's desperate. A man so desperately poor is up to anything. He's in the right too.' My husband is away so I had no one to consult with. I could only try to patch things up with money. Yet the more I gave him, the more I was at his mercy, and the more he blackmailed me. That's why I was in a panic, so desperate that I came looking for you!"

Jig Rong had sense enough to understand what she was driving at. He said with a smile, "Well, I have another plan. Since I caused the trouble, it's up to me to fix it. I'll go and sound Zhang Hua out. If he insists on having her back, I'll persuade my second aunt to leave here and marry him. If he wants money, we'll have to give him some more."

"That's all very well," said Phoenix hastily, "I certainly don't want her to leave us. What would people think of us if we let her go? No, I think we must keep her, even if it means giving him more money. We'll have to give him some more."

Jia Rong knew quite well that Phoenix said one thing and meant another. However, he had to agree now with whatever she said.

"The problem outside is easy to handle," Phoenix continued. "In the long run it's here at home that we're going to have the trouble. You must come back with me to report this to Grandma and Lady Wang."

This threw Madam You into another panic. She begged Phoenix to make up some story for her.

"If you can't talk your way out of this, why did you do it in the first place?" asked Phoenix sarcastically. "I'll take your sister to kowtow to Grandmother and the ladies, and I shall tell them that I have taken a fancy to your sister since I met her, and I have found her to be charming. As we're also relatives, I am willing to let her be Jia Lian's second wife, particularly because I haven't been able to give birth to a son. Once the mourning is over she can live with my husband. Do you think that will do?"

Madam You and Jia Rong responded with smiles. Madam You then ordered her maids to help Phoenix wash her face and comb her hair. A table was spread and she shared the dinner with Phoenix. Before long Phoenix rose to go.

When she arrived home, she went to the garden and told Second Sister You what had happened, trying to explain how worried she had been and telling her what would have to be done to keep them all out of trouble.

Full of gratitude, Second Sister went off with Phoenix to face the old lady.

The Lady Dowager was chatting and laughing with the girls from the garden. At the sight of the pretty young lady Phoenix brought in, the old lady stopped what she was doing and looked with searching eyes. "Whose child is this?" she asked. "So charming."

Phoenix stepped forward and said with a smile, "Take a good look, Grandma, isn't she sweet?"

Pulling Second Sister forward, she told her, "This is grandmother-in-law. Hurry up and kowtow to her." Second Sister lost no time in paying her respects.

Now the Lady Dowager looked her up and down while she stood there with her head lowered.

"Grandma," said Phoenix laughing, "just tell me, is she prettier than I am?"

The old lady put on her spectacles. "Bring the child closer," she told Lovebird, "let me look at her skin."

Amid suppressed laughter, Second Sister was pushed forward and subjected to a careful scrutiny. Then the old lady made Lovebird hold out Second Sister's hands for inspection. In the end the old lady took off her glasses. "Perfect!" she pronounced. "She's even prettier than you."

Smiling, Phoenix promptly knelt down to give a detailed rendition of the story she made up in Madam You's room.

"That's quite all right," the old lady agreed. "I'm glad you're so broad-minded and tolerant. But she mustn't live with Jia Lian until next year."

Phoenix kowtowed, then got up and requested that two maids be sent to present Second Sister to Lady Xing and Lady Wang, and tell them this was the old lady's decision. So, from now on, Second Sister could come in the open, and it was possible to move her from the Grand View Garden into the apartment in the West Wing that Phoenix had prepared for her.

21/ Phoenix Kills Second Sister You with a Borrowed Knife

Now Phoenix sent a messenger in secret to urge Zhang Hua to insist on claiming his fiancee, promising that she would come to him with a generous dowry. In addition, she said, he would be given money to set up house. Thus Zhang Hua brought a new suit. Phoenix sent a messenger to take a note to the judge, and the court's verdict was: "Zhang Hua's debt to the Jia family must be repaid in full by a specific date. As for his betrothed, he can marry her when he has the means."

Zhang Hua's father was summoned to court to hear this verdict. Since Phoenix had sent a servant to explain the whole arrangement, he was delighted to get both the money and the girl. He went to the Jia mansion to claim Second Sister.

Phoenix now reported this to the Lady Dowager with a great show of alarm. "Cousin Zhen's wife is to blame for all this mess," Phoenix complained. "Obviously the earlier engagement was never really canceled. That's why the Zhangs have sued us and the court has passed a judgment against us."

The old lady at once sent for Madam You to rebuke her for carelessness. "Since your sister was promised to the Zhang family before she was born, and they never broke the engagement properly, now they've brought this charge against us," she scolded.

"But they took the money," protested Madam You. "How can they still claim her?"

Phoenix put in. "According to Zhang Hua's testimony, he never saw any money, and no one contacted him. It's lucky Second Master isn't at home and they haven't been formally married. Still, as she's already here, how can we send her back? Wouldn't that make us lose face?"

"My mother really did give them ten ounces of silver to cancel the engagement," said Second Sister. "Now, in desperation because he's so awfully poor, he denies it. My sister really did nothing wrong."

"That shows how troublesome such rascals are to deal with," said the old lady. "Well, I will leave it to you to sort it out."

Phoenix had to comply. When she returned home, she sent for Jia Rong. He knew what she was aiming at. It would be a disgrace if Second Sister were to be reclaimed by Zhang Hua, so he reported this to Jia Zhen and secretly sent Zhang Hua this message: "Since you've got so much money out of them, why must you have the girl back? If you insist, the gentlemen may get angry and find a way to kill you where no proper place can be found for your grave. Now that you have enough money, you can easily go home and find a nice bride. If you do, we'll help you with the traveling expenses."

Zhang Hua thought this a good idea and discussed it with his father. The sum of the money he had received amounted to some one hundred taels. The next day at dawn, the father and son started home.

After Jia Rong had made sure of their departure, he told the old lady and Phoenix, "Zhang Hua and his father have run away for fear of being punished for bringing a false charge. The court knows of this but has decided to let the matter drop. The whole trouble is over!"

Phoenix considered the matter carefully. She realized that if she made Zhang Hua reclaim Second Sister, when Jia Lian returned he was sure to offer more money to get her back, and Zhang Hua was bound to agree. So she decided she had better keep Second Sister here with her until she was able to work out some other plan. The only thing she didn't know was where Zhang Hua had gone, and whether or not he'd spread this story and come back later to reopen the case. If he did that it would be her downfall. Oh, she thought to herself,

I should never have put a weapon like this into another's hands. She bitterly regretted what she had done.

But then Phoenix hit on another plan. She quietly ordered Brightie to send men to find Zhang Hua and kill him. In this way the root of the trouble would be removed and her reputation assured.

Brightie, however, went home and thought over her instructions. He mused that since the man's gone and the matter's dropped there was no reason to do anything so drastic. He realized that it's a serious crime to take someone's life, surely no children's game. Thus he decided to try to fool Phoenix into thinking that the job was done.

He lay low outside for a few days, then returned to report that Zhang Hua had been knocked down and killed at dawn by a highwayman who wanted the money he carried with him. His father had been scared to death in a nearby inn. Both of their bodies were then and there buried.

Phoenix did not believe him. "If I find out you've been lying, I'll knock out your teeth!" she threatened. But she did nothing, and soon let the matter drop.

From that time on Phoenix and Second Sister were on the best of terms. They were even much more intimate than blood sisters.

When Jia Lian came home, after completing his business, he went straight to the new house. But it was locked and deserted. An old caretaker there told him all that had happened. Jia Lian stamped his foot in anger, then went to report on his mission to his parents. To his great joy, Jia She, his father, praised his competence and rewarded him with a hundred ounces of silver as well as a new concubine. This seventeen-year old maid's name was Autumn.

Jia Lian was overjoyed. He expressed his thanks and left in high spirits with his concubine. Having paid his respects to Lady Dowager and other members of the family, he went home somewhat sheepishly to see Phoenix. To his surprise, his wife seemed to have become a different person. She came out with Second Sister to welcome him, all smiles. Jia Lian then told both of them about his father's reward. Phoenix immediately sent two serving women to fetch Autumn by carriage.

To Phoenix's sorrow, before she had gotten rid of one thorn in her side, here, out of the blue, was another! However, she had to swallow her pride and hide her anger by showing a smiling face. She ordered a "welcome home" dinner for her husband, and presented Autumn to the old lady and Lady Wang. Jia Lian was extremely amazed at the sudden change that had come over Phoenix.

Outwardly, Phoenix treated Second Sister well, but inwardly she plotted to destroy her. When the two of them were alone she told Second Sister, "You have such a bad name, sister, even the old lady and the mistresses have heard about it. They blame me. They ask me 'Why not get rid of her and choose someone better?' Talk like that makes me furious. If this goes on, how are we to hold up our heads in front of these slaves? I seem to have landed myself in a foul mess."

Having said this a couple of times, she pretended to fall ill with anger, and refused to eat or drink. All the maids and servants, with the exception of Patience, kept gossiping about Second Sister and making sarcastic remarks with hidden allusions.

Autumn was a gift from the family senior, Jia She, and so this seventeen-year-old concubine considered herself far above Second Sister in importance. Not even Phoenix or Patience impressed her greatly. Actually Phoenix was secretly satisfied with this attitude. And after she began to pretend illness, Phoenix stopped eating meals with Second Sister. She just ordered the servants to take food to Second Sister's room every day. The rice and dishes were always of the worst.

Patience took pity on Second Sister, and sometimes Patience would get some better dishes for Second Sister out of her own pocket money, or she would take her for a stroll in the garden, getting special soups made for her in the kitchen there. No one dared report this to Phoenix. However, once Autumn found this out, she immediately talked about it to Phoenix.

"Patience is spoiling your reputation, madam," Autumn told her. "The good dishes we have here are wasted on her. She won't eat them. Instead she secretly gets food from Patience in the garden!"

Phoenix swore at Patience, "Other people's cats catch mice for them, but mine just eat the chickens!" Patience didn't dare to talk back, and after that had to keep a distance from Second Sister. Secretly, she developed an extreme hatred for Autumn.

All the girls in the garden were privately worried about Second Sister, but none ventured to speak out openly. Whenever they talked with Second Sister, she would shed tears, but she never breathed a word of complaint against Phoenix.

When Jia Lian came home and observed his chief wife's pretended kindness to Second Sister, he did not give the matter a second thought. Besides, he had long had desires for his father's pretty concubines and maids. Since Autumn was his father's gift, Jia Lian could not tear himself apart from her. By and by his affection for Second Sister lessened and Autumn was the one he became particularly attached to.

Though Phoenix hated Autumn, she was happy to use her to get rid of Second Sister. Phoenix thus adopted the tactics of "killing people with a borrowed knife" and "watching the tigers fight from a mountain top." When they were alone, she would often whisper to Autumn: "Now Second Sister's the second mistress, your master's favorite. Even I have to give way to her to a certain extent, yet you keep provoking her. You're simply looking for trouble."

Incited by such talk, Autumn was so furious that she cursed Second Sister in a torrent of abuses every day. "The mistress is too softhearted," she would say. "I haven't got that kind of tolerance. I'm not going to put up with that bitch. I'll make sure she gets to know me!" Phoenix pretended to be too scared to say anything in response.

Second Sister, sitting in her own room and hearing these remarks through the wall, could only shed secret tears. She became too upset to eat anything. However, Second Sister dared not tell Jia Lian the whole story. And, when the Lady

Dowager asked why her eyes were so red and swollen, she was too timid to say anything.

Now it was the time for Autumn to begin playing her tricks in front of the Ladyships. She whispered to the old lady and Lady Wang, "Second Sister keeps making a fuss, moaning and wailing all day long for no reason at all. And she curses madam and me behind our backs."

"Imagine that!" exclaimed the old lady. "What a low creature!"

Gradually Second Sister fell out of the old lady's favor. Naturally the others bullied her too. Second Sister was thus in a real fix. She could neither go to her death nor go on living as a decent lady. Patience was the only one who tried to comfort her behind Phoenix's back.

After suffering in silence for a month, Second Sister fell ill and lost her appetite. Too listless to move, she grew thinner and paler with each passing day.

When Jia Lian happened to come to see her, she told him with tears, "I'll never get over this illness. I've been with you for half a year and I'm with child. But I don't know whether it will be a boy or a girl. If Heaven has pity and the child is born, well and good. Otherwise, I'll not be able to save myself, let alone the child."

"Don't worry," Jia Lian reassured her, in tears himself. "I'll get a good doctor for you."

He at once sent for Doctor Hu, who prescribed medicine for Second Sister and then took his leave. Jia Lian ordered his servants to prepare the medicine for the patient.

In the middle of the night, Second Sister had such a pain in her stomach that she miscarried. The fetus proved to be a male child. She bled so much that she fainted. Beside himself with worry, Jia Lian sent for another doctor, and also sent some men to fetch Doctor Hu. The incompetent doctor got word of this, packed up his things, and ran away.

Phoenix, pretending a great deal of anxiety, exclaimed, "Let me fall ill if only Sister You can recover, conceive again, and give birth to a boy. Then I'll gladly fast and chant Buddhist sutras for the rest of my life."

Jia Lian and the others, seeing this, could not but praise her noble mindedness and unselfishness.

While Jia Lian stayed with Autumn, Phoenix prepared soup and broth for Second Sister. Phoenix also sent out men to consult fortunetellers. They returned with the report that the trouble was caused by a woman born under the sign of the rabbit, and that this was what had likely brought misfortune to the patient. A rapid investigation revealed that Autumn was the only person in the household born under that sign.

Autumn's jealousy had already been aroused by the care Jia Lian lavished on Second Sister. Now she was told that she was to blame for Second Sister's illness, and Phoenix advised her to move out for a few months for the sake of Second Sister.

Autumn wept and stormed. "It's all rubbish anyway. I kept as clear of her as well water and river water. How could my horoscope bring her ill luck? Who can't give birth to a child? Give me a year or so and I'll have one myself. At least in my case there'll be no doubt who its father is!"

Hearing this, the servants wanted to laugh but suppressed it. Just then Lady Xing called.

Autumn told her, "The Second Master and Second Mistress want to throw me out. I've nowhere to go. Please take pity on me, madam!"

Lady Xing scolded Phoenix and then cursed Jia Lian: "You ungrateful cur! She was given you by your father and you want to get rid of her. Have you no respect for your father at all?" Lady Xing left in a temper.

Now Autumn felt more on top than ever. She went to abuse Second Sister under her window, making Second Sister feel more wretched than ever.

Jia Lian spent that night with Autumn.

Left to herself, Second Sister despaired over the fact that she was so ill and getting worse every day. She decided there was no hope for recovery. Since she had miscarried and thus didn't have a child to worry about, why should she go on putting up with such insults? Death seemed to her to be the only decent way out of her misery.

She rose with difficulty from her bed, opened one of her treasure boxes, and took out a piece of gold of fair size. Weeping and cursing at her fate, she put the gold in her mouth and, after several desperate attempts, succeeded in swallowing it. Then she hastily dressed herself and put on her jewels. She lay down on the bed and breathed her last.

The next morning, as soon as the maids opened the door of the bedroom, they found the dead woman lying there, well dressed and decorated. They ran out terrified and shouted for Patience to come.

She wept bitterly when she saw this sad scene. Soon the tragic news spread through the whole mansion. Jia Lian hurried in, clung to the corpse, and wept without end.

Phoenix, seeing that her plot had worked out so well, put on a great show of hypocritical sobbing, "Oh, dear sister," she wailed, "why have you left me in such a way? Is that your return for my deep love?"

After a simple funeral paid for with her own savings, Second Sister You was laid to rest in a little grave outside the city walls, a grave beside that of Third Sister You.

22/ A House Search in the Grand View Garden

One day Lady Xing took a stroll in the Grand View Garden. She had just reached the gate when Sister Silly, one of the Lady Dowager's maids, came along chuckling to herself over some colorful object she held in her hands. As the maid's head was lowered, she bumped into Lady Xing. She looked up and halted.

"Well, now, Silly," said Lady Xing, "you seem very pleased with yourself. What marvelous thing have you got there? Let me have a look."

Sister Silly had just turned fourteen, and was one of the maids chosen to do rough jobs for the old lady. Whenever she was free she would go and play in the garden. That day, while she was trying to catch crickets there, she saw behind the rock a colorfully embroidered pouch. The design embroidered on it was not one of the usual kind, such as birds and flowers, but was a design of two naked human figures locked in embrace. On the other side of the pouch were some Chinese characters. Sister Silly was too innocent to realize that this was pornography.

"Yes, this really is strange, madam. Just take a look!" She handed the pouch to Lady Xing.

A mere glance at it was enough to give Lady Xing a start. She clutched it tightly. "Where did you find it?"

"Behind a rock when I was catching crickets."

"Mind you don't tell anybody!" ordered Lady Xing. "This is something very bad. If you weren't such a fool, they would give you a beating just for touching it. But you mustn't mention it to anyone else."

Sister Silly turned pale with fright.

"I won't, madam!" she promised, then kowtowing several times she went off quite bewildered.

Lady Xing looked around and saw some girls in the distance. She stuffed the pouch into her sleeve to conceal it from them, at the same time wondering where it could have come from. Then she went to tell Lady Wang about it.

Lady Wang, in turn, went directly to Phoenix's apartment. With tears in her eyes, she produced an embroidered pouch from her sleeve and said, "Look at this!"

Phoenix took the pouch and looked at the indecent embroidery on it. Greatly surprised, she exclaimed, "Where did you find this, madam?"

Tears streaming down her cheeks, Lady Wang's voice trembled, "Where did I get it from? I've been in the dark all this time. I'd no idea you were just as careless as I am. Fancy leaving a thing like this on a rock in the garden openly, in broad daylight too! Luckily your mother-in-law found the maid with it. How could you be so thoughtless as to leave this lying around?"

"What makes you think it's mine, madam?" asked Phoenix, changing color.

"Whose could it be?" Lady Wang sobbed. "Just think, you're the only young couple in our household. It must be that worthless playboy of a husband of yours who picked it up somewhere. As intimate as you are, you would keep playthings of this kind in your bedroom. Don't try to deny it."

Red in the face with shame and irritation, Phoenix knelt down beside the bed. "Of course, your reasoning is logical, madam," she said tearfully, "I dare not contradict you. Still, do think more carefully, madam. In the first place, this pouch was made by a craftsman outside. However young and flirty I may be, I wouldn't want such trash.

"In the second place, this isn't the sort of thing I'd carry around with me. Even if I had one, I'd keep it indoors. In the third place, of all the ladies of our house I'm the only young married woman, but there are plenty of servants' wives younger than me. Fourthly, I'm not the only visitor to the garden. Lady Xing of the other house often takes other young concubines there. They're all more likely than me to have such things.

"In the fifth place, with so many maids in the garden, can we guarantee that they all behave properly? This pouch not only isn't mine, I can assure you that my maid Patience has never had such a thing either. Please reconsider the matter carefully, madam."

This line of argument made good sense to Lady Wang. "Get up," she said with a sigh. "I should have known that a girl of good family like you couldn't be so frivolous. I just challenged you because I was so angry."

"Don't be angry, madam," said Phoenix. "If this gets out, it may come to the old lady's ears. We must calm down and look into this matter on the quiet so as to get the bottom of it. And even if we fail to find the culprit, we mustn't let outsiders know about it." Phoenix then called Patience to pass on orders to the wives of the stewards, who were told to go into the garden and keep an eye on things there.

"I suppose the maids who wait on the young mistresses are a bit more spoiled," said Lady Wang.

"The others aren't so bad," said Mrs. Huang, one of the steward's wives. "But do you know Skybright in Magic Jade's place, madam? She's prettier than the others and has a ready tongue, and she makes herself up every day to look like the classic Chinese beauty, Xishi. She's constantly showing off and putting on airs. A single word can offend her, and when she hurls abuse up fly her eyebrows. She's quite a bitch!"

This reminded Lady Wang of an almost forgotten incident. She turned to Phoenix, "Last time we went for a stroll in the garden with the old lady, I noticed a girl with a willowy waist, sloping shoulders, and eyes and eyebrows rather like Black Jade's. I didn't like the wild look of her at all. I wonder if this is the same girl? She seems to fit this description of Skybright."

"Skybright is certainly the best looking among the maids," Phoenix replied. "And she does act and talk a bit too freely. Your description sounds like her, but I don't know whether that was her or not."

"It's easy enough to make sure," said the steward's wife. "We can call her now and see."

"She's just the sort of girl I've always disliked," said Phoenix. "Oh dear! When a thing like this happens I worry about what if Magic Jade were to be corrupted by a little bitch like that!"

Lady Wang told her own maid to go to the garden. "Just give them this message: I want Aroma and Musk to stay to look after Magic Jade. But that clever Skybright is to come here at once. Don't tell her why I want her."

The maid went off to the Happy Red Residence Hall.

Skybright happened to be ill that day and had just gotten up from a nap, feeling out of sorts. She, however, had no choice but to obey the order.

When Skybright entered Phoenix's room with her hair disheveled and her costume rumpled, like a sick beauty just aroused from sleep, Lady Wang immediately recognized her as the girl she had seen in the garden. Being genuinely outraged at her behavior in the garden and already prejudiced, Lady Wang was too outspoken to conceal her feelings.

She smiled sarcastically. "What a beauty!" she sneered. "Whom are you trying to charm, going about like this? Do you think I know nothing of your goings-on. I'll let you off now, but soon I'll have you skinned alive. Is Magic Jade any better today?"

Skybright realized that someone must have been running her down, but did not venture to express her resentment. Quickly recovering from her surprise, she was intelligent enough not to give a truthful answer. "I seldom go into Magic Jade's rooms or spend much time with him," Skybright lied. "So I can't say how he is, madam." She knelt down.

"You deserve a slap on your mouth," said Lady Wang angrily. "Are you dead? What are you paid for?"

"I used to serve the old lady," answered Skybright. "Then she said there were too few older maids in the garden so I was to go and keep watch at night in the outer rooms, just to keep an eye on the place. Magic Jade's meals and all the personal service are looked after by the older servants, or by Aroma and Musk. Whenever I've free time I still do some sewing for the old lady, so I've never paid much attention to Magic Jade's affairs. But if you wish, madam, I'll be more attentive from now on."

"Amida Buddha! Don't trouble yourself!" exclaimed Lady Wang, quite taken in by this. "The less you have to do with Magic Jade, the better."

She turned and told Mrs. Huang, "When you people go into the garden, I want you to keep a good watch on her for a few days. Don't let her sleep in Magic Jade's room. We'll deal with her after I've talked with the old lady. You get out of here!" she shouted at Skybright. "The sight of such a bitch offends my eyes! Who let you dress in those garish reds and greens?"

Skybright withdrew quickly, and once out of the door, covered her face with her handkerchief and wept all the way back to the garden.

Knowing that Mrs. Huang often told tales to Lady Xing to incite her to make trouble, Phoenix could do nothing to defend Skybright, even if she had good reasons for doing so. She just lowered her head and assented.

"You must look after your health, madam," urged Mrs. Huang. "Just leave trifling matters like this to your slaves. It should be very easy to find the culprit. This evening after the garden gates are locked and no news can get in or out, we'll take them by surprise and have a thorough search made of all the maids' rooms. When we find more articles of that sort we'll know whose this pouch is."

"That's a good idea," approved Lady Wang. "We'll never get anywhere unless we do something like that. What do you think?" she asked Phoenix.

"Of course you're right, madam," Phoenix had to agree. "That's the way to do it."

So, after supper when the old lady had gone to bed, Mrs. Huang accompanied Phoenix to the garden. They ordered all the gates to be locked and then began their search in the rooms of the servants on night duty. But they discovered nothing more incriminating than some leftover candles and a jar or two of lamp oil.

Then they went to the Happy Red Residence Hall and had the courtyard gate locked. Magic Jade was feeling rather unhappy because Skybright was not well. When he saw the women marching into the maids' rooms, he asked Phoenix what they were trying to do.

"Something important is missing," she told him. "As people are accusing each other and we think one of the maids may have stolen it, we're making a general search to clear up suspicion." Phoenix then sat down to sip tea, while Mrs. Huang and the others continued the search.

Aroma had already guessed from what had happened to Skybright that something must be missing. Now she was the first to step forward and open her cases and boxes for inspection. Finding nothing out of the ordinary, the women went on to search the other maids' cases, one by one. When they came to Skybright's case they asked: "Whose is this? Why doesn't anyone open it for us?"

Aroma was about to do so when Skybright rushed in, her hair loosely knotted. She flung the lid back and raised the case bottom upwards in both hands to empty all its contents on the floor.

Mrs. Huang blushed with embarrassment. "Don't get angry with me, miss," she said, "I'm carrying this search out on Lady Wang's orders. There's no need to carry on like this."

At this Skybright's wrath blazed. She pointed at the old woman's face. "You say you are here on Lady Wang's orders. Well, I'm here on the old lady's orders. Anyway, I know all the women who work at Lady Wang's and I never saw a self-important, meddlesome old busybody like *you* there before!"

Phoenix was secretly delighted to see Mrs. Huang getting the rough side of Skybright's sharp tongue, but because the woman was her mother-in-law's favorite, she had to pretend that she was shocked. She shouted at Skybright to be silent.

Mrs. Huang looked angry and flustered and seemed on the point of retorting, but Phoenix stopped her. "All right,

Mrs. Huang, that will do. You don't have to put yourself on the same level by arguing with the girl. You get on with your search."

Though she was furious inwardly, Mrs. Huang had to swallow her anger. Having found nothing of importance, she then asked Phoenix if they might go elsewhere.

"You'd better make a careful search," warned Phoenix. "If you fail to find anything, what are we going to say to Lady Wang?"

"We've been through everything carefully," one of the stewardesses assured her. "There's nothing here of any importance."

Phoenix smiled. "In that case we can go to another house."

As they went out, Phoenix said to Mrs. Huang, "I think we should confine the search to our own family. We mustn't search Miss Hairpin's quarters."

"Of course not. How can we search our relatives?"

"Exactly."

By now they had reached the Bamboo Cottage where Black Jade was already in bed. When visitors were announced, she began to get up, but Phoenix came in and made her lie down again. "Go back to sleep," Phoenix said, "we'll be going in a moment."

She chatted with Black Jade while Mrs. Huang took the others to the maids' quarters and searched their cases and baskets one by one. Nothing really important was found so they went on to Tanchun's place.

Apparently Tanchun had been informed of their coming, and she knew there must be some reason for this indignity. She had already ordered her maids to open all the doors and light candles so as to be ready for the search.

"Well, what do you want?" she asked when Phoenix and Mrs. Huang arrived.

"Something's missing, and we don't know who took it," Phoenix told her. "We are making a general search to clear suspicion so that no one may put the blame on these girls."

Tanchun laughed scornfully. "Naturally, all my maids are thieves and I'm the head of their robber band," she said. "So search my cases first. They've given me all their stolen goods for safe keeping." She then ordered her maids to open up all her cases for Phoenix's inspection.

"I'm simply carrying out Lady Wang's orders," said Phoenix with an uncomfortable smile. "There's no point in getting offended with me, cousin." Phoenix turned to the servants and asked them to close the cases at once.

"I'll let you search my things, but not my maids," Tanchun insisted. "If that doesn't satisfy you, go and report to Lady Wang that I won't obey her orders, and I'll accept any punishment she thinks fit. Just you wait, though. The day will come when you're raided too. Now I realize why big families like ours can't be destroyed in a day. We must start killing each other first before our family can be completely destroyed." By this point she was shedding tears.

Phoenix looked in silence at the stewardesses. Taking the hint, one of them said, "As all these girls' things are here, madam, we'd better go elsewhere and leave Miss Tanchun to rest." Phoenix got up to take her leave.

But Tanchun cried, "Mind you make a thorough search. I won't have you coming here again tomorrow!"

"Since all your maids' things are all here, there's no need to search," replied Phoenix with a smile.

Tanchun laughed coldly.

"How smart you are! You've opened everything of mine, yet still pretend you haven't searched the place. Will you accuse me later of putting a fence around my maids and refusing to let you search? Let's get this clear now. If you want to search again, just go ahead."

Phoenix knew how hard Tanchun was to deal with and therefore answered soothingly, "We've made a thorough search, even including your things."

"Are you all satisfied?" Tanchun challenged the others.

"We've searched enough," reassured the other women, forcing smiles.

Mrs. Huang had heard that Tanchun was hard to deal with, but she refused to believe that a concubine's daughter could have her own way like this. As a confidential serving woman of Lady Xing and the special delegate of Lady Wang, she was sure of her authority. Going up to Tanchun, she took hold of a lapel of her gown and turned it back, a grin all over her face. "There!" she answered. "Now I've searched our young lady, and there's nothing on her either!"

"Come along, old woman!" interposed Phoenix, "Stop this fooling!" But even as she was speaking, Phoenix heard Tanchun give Mrs. Huang a resounding box on the ears.

"Who do you think you are?" Tanchun was in a towering rage, pointing a finger at her. "How dare you touch me? Today you've gone a bit too far. I didn't condemn you for coming in to raid our place, but you've no right to take liberties with me."

While she fastened up the buttons of her gown with her left hand, she drew Phoenix back with her right. "Will you search me please? But spare me the disgrace of being searched by a slave," Tanchun cried angrily.

Phoenix and Patience tried to pacify Tanchun and they scolded Mrs. Huang. "Be off with you now, and not another word." By their united efforts Phoenix and Patience finally managed to smooth things over for both sides and the search party went on its way to Xichun's place.

Being younger and more inexperienced than the other cousins, Xichun was much more frightened by this sudden night search. Phoenix tried her best to calm her. However, the searchers discovered a big package of thirty to forty gold and silver ingots in one maid's case. So, instead of evidence of immoral conduct, they had found stolen goods. There was also a set of jade ornaments for a man's belt and a bundle containing a man's sandals and socks. Even Phoenix turned pale at this discovery.

"Where did these come from?" she asked the unhappy maid.

The maid knelt down and tearfully confessed the truth. "They were given to my brother by Lord Zhen," she faltered.

"Since our parents are down south, he lives with our uncle. And because my uncle and aunt are fond of drinking and gambling and might sell these things for the money, my brother made a secret arrangement with one of the old women to bring them to me for safe keeping."

Phoenix smiled. "If what you say is true, it's forgivable. If you're lying and these are stolen goods, don't expect to get off alive!"

The frightened maid knelt before her and sobbed, "I dare not lie to you, madam. You can check with Mr. and Mrs. Zhen. If they say my brother wasn't given these things, I'll not complain if you beat us both to death."

"Of course I'll check. But even if these were gifts you still did wrong. Who gave you permission to bring them here in secret? I'll let you off this once if you tell me who brought these things in secretly. But you mustn't ever do this again."

The searchers took their leave of Xichun and went on to Yingchun's place.

Yingchun was already asleep. They knocked for some time before the gate was opened. Phoenix gave orders not to disturb the young lady and went with the others to the maids' quarters. As Chess was Mrs. Huang's granddaughter, Phoenix was curious as to whether or not she would show any favoritism toward this girl. Phoenix, therefore, paid special attention to this search.

Mrs. Huang started with the other girls' cases and, finding nothing exceptional, went on to open Chess's case. After a little search she declared there was nothing there. She then started to close it.

"Wait!" cried one of the stewardesses. "What's this?"

The stewardess reached in to pick out a man's silk socks and slippers, as well as a small bundle. When they opened this, they found inside a love knot and a letter. These were handed over to Phoenix for inspection. Phoenix saw that the letter was red with a double-happiness design. It was written to Chess by her lover.

This letter amused Phoenix. But, as Mrs. Huang knew nothing of the romantic story of her granddaughter, the sight of the slippers and socks had made her quite uneasy. When Phoenix started laughing at what was written on the red paper Mrs. Huang said, "I suppose this is some account and you're amused by their poor writing, madam?"

"Quite. This account takes some working out. As you are Chess's maternal grandmother, let me read this letter to you."

Everybody present was shocked to learn the contents. It had never occurred to Mrs. Huang, so intent had she been on exposing others, that her own granddaughter would be found out. She was quite overwhelmed by shame and vexation.

"Well, what have you to say to that?" asked the stewardesses. "How should we deal with her in your opinion?"

Mrs. Huang wished she could sink into the ground, and Phoenix laughed with satisfaction. "This is just as well," Phoenix said to the stewardesses, "The girl has picked out a fine young man for her husband. This at least has saved her granny the trouble of choosing one for her!"

The others chuckled and made some caustic comments. Unable to vent her anger on anyone else, Mrs. Huang slapped her own face.

Phoenix was somewhat surprised to find that Chess showed no sign of shame or fear. She only stood there silent, her head lowered. It was too late to question the girl, but for fear she might commit suicide that night, Phoenix asked two matrons to keep an eye on her. Then she took the uncovered evidence back to her own place and retired.

During the night, however, Phoenix had to get up several times because of illness and she lost a good deal of blood. The next morning she kept to her bed, feeling weak and dizzy. A doctor was called. Thus judgment on Chess's affair was put off for the time being.

23/ Skybright Dies in the Flower of Her Youth

When the Mid-Autumn Festival was over and Phoenix had somewhat recovered, the interrupted house search in the Grand View Garden was resumed. Lady Wang dismissed Chess, Yingchun's maid, from the house. In order to make a clean sweep, she decided to turn out Skybright as well.

The news that Skybright, the most lovable of his waiting maids, was being dismissed hit Magic Jade like a bolt of lightning. As soon as he heard that his mother was coming to check the matter out, he dashed from school to the Happy Red Residence Hall. It was packed with people. His mother, Lady Wang, sitting there with a face like thunder, ignored him.

Having touched no food for four or five days, Skybright was wasting away. She was dragged from her bed, her hair disheveled. Two women carried her to Lady Wang.

"Throw out the clothes she used to wear," ordered Lady Wang. "She can take them away with her. Leave the rest of her clothes for better maids!" Thus Skybright had to leave the house crying bitter tears.

Lady Wang then had the whole house searched and dismissed the other two pretty maids, as well as some attractive actresses in the garden who she thought might corrupt Magic Jade.

Knowing that there was no saving the situation, Magic Jade returned to his room where he found Aroma weeping, too. Distressed by the loss of his favorite maid, he threw himself on the bed with loud sobs.

Aroma knew that Skybright's dismissal was the only thing that really mattered to him. She tried to cheer him up. "It's no use crying," she said. "Get up and listen to me. Skybright will be better off where she is going. Back at home she will at least be able to have a few days of peace and quiet. If you really can't bear to be without her, you have only to wait until your mother's anger has cooled down a bit and then go and ask the old lady to have Skybright brought back again. That shouldn't be too difficult. Lady Wang did this in a fit of anger because she was taken in by some gossip."

"How is it my mother knows all the faults of the other girls," Magic Jade asked, "but not yours or Musk's?"

Thus touched in a raw spot, Aroma was at a loss for an answer and just lowered her head for a while. Then she laughed in embarrassment, "Yes, that's strange," she said. "Maybe she has other things on her mind and won't send us away until she's dealt with them."

"You're the girl of perfect virtue," he retorted. "But Skybright is like you. She was transferred here as a child from the old lady's quarters. She may be better looking, but what does that matter? Though she's outspoken and has a sharp tongue she's never done you any harm. I suppose it's her good looks that were her undoing." He then burst into tears again.

Thinking Magic Jade suspected her of telling tales, Aroma did not want to pursue the topic any further. "Only Heaven knows the truth," she sighed. "We can't find out now who did this, so it's no use crying. Take it easy till the old lady's in a good mood, then you can tell her about it and ask her to have Skybright brought back."

"Don't raise any false hopes," he snorted. "If I wait till my mother calms down it'll be too late, because Skybright's illness won't wait. Sending her away at this moment," he went on more bitterly, "seriously ill as she is and with all that resentment bottled up inside her, is like throwing a delicate orchid, just coming into bloom, into a pigsty. Besides, she has no parents. She only has an elder cousin, who's a drunkard. How can she stand it there? How can you talk of waiting for a few days? Who knows whether I'll ever see her again?

"But let's talk about practical matters," Magic Jade continued. "We must secretly send her things to her without letting the others know anything about it. We might send her some cash from our savings to help cure her illness. We owe her that for old times' sake."

"How heartless and stingy you must think us to be!" Aroma exclaimed. "We don't need a reminder from you. I've already sorted out all her clothes and things and put them aside. In the daytime there are too many busybodies around, all eager to make trouble. But as soon as it gets dark, we'll quietly get an old woman to take them over. I've saved a bit of cash too. I'll give her that."

That evening, they sent an old woman on this errand. After settling his maids down, Magic Jade slipped out of the back gate alone and begged the old woman to take him to see Skybright. At first she refused, saying that if it was found out and it was reported to the mistress she'd lose her job. But, after he pleaded at length and promised her a tip, she finally agreed to take him to Skybright.

At the age of ten, Skybright had been sold to the Chief Steward Lai Da as a slave girl for his wife. Mrs. Lai often took Skybright with her when she worked in the Honored Mansion. It was in this way that she first came to the attention of the Lady Dowager. The old lady took a great fancy to the beautiful, intelligent little girl. So Lai Da's wife gave Skybright to her as a present. Skybright was later given as a maidservant to her beloved grandson.

Several years later Lai Da gave one of the bond maids to Skybright's cousin as his wife. And this wife happened to be a good-looking, amorous woman. She dressed smartly and attracted quite a few suitors. By and by, she had some affairs with some of the men in the Mansion.

Now when Skybright was kicked out of the Mansion, she had to stay with this couple. As her cousin was away at the time and his wife had gone out after supper to visit her friends, Skybright was left lying alone in the outer room. Magic Jade told the old woman to keep watch in the courtyard, then lifted the door curtain, and went in. There was Skybright on the bed, covered with a coarse mat. Not knowing what to do, he approached her with tears in his eyes and gently took her hand, softly calling her name.

Skybright had caught a chill. The reproaches from her relatives only made her illness worse. After coughing for most of the day, she had just dozed off when Magic Jade arrived. But hearing her name called, she opened her eyes with an effort. When she saw who it was, she was so overwhelmed with a mixture of pleasure, grief, and pain that she promptly burst out sobbing. Grasping his hand with all her might, she managed at last to gasp, between fits of coughing, "I never thought I'd see you again."

Magic Jade could only sob, as well.

"Merciful Buddha!" cried Skybright. "You've come just in time. Please pour me half a cup of tea. I've been parched for some time, but when I call, no one comes."

"Where is the tea?" he asked, wiping his eyes.

"On the stove."

Magic Jade picked up the pot and poured out half a bowl. The dark red brew was unlike any tea he had seen before.

Skybright, leaning on her pillow, urged, "Pass it over, quick, so I can take a sip. You can't expect them to have the kind of tea we're used to here." She gulped it all down as if it were sweet dew.

Shedding tears, he asked, "Have you got anything to tell me while nobody's around?"

"What is there to say?" she sobbed. "I know I'll live a few more days at most. But I can't die content. I may be a bit better looking than the others, but I've never tried to make up to you. Why will they insist that I am some sort of vampire? It's so unfair. Now I've got this bad name for nothing, and I'm dying. How could I guess there'd be this sudden scandal and I'd have nowhere to plead my innocence?" She burst into tears again.

Magic Jade took her hand. On her wrists, thin as sticks, were four silver bracelets. "Better take these off," he advised. "You can wear them when you're better." He took them off for her and put them under the pillow.

Then she reached down inside the bedding and managed, after a great deal of effort, to take off her old, red jacket. She held it out to him. Because of her weakness, the effort in doing this left her so breathless she could not speak; but Magic Jade understood what she wanted. He removed his outer garment, took off his shirt and laid it over her. Then he put on the red jacket. While he was fastening his belt again, he noticed that she was staring at him, trying to say something.

"Help me up," she finally said with great difficulty.

But even with Magic Jade's support, it took a great deal of effort for her to sit fully upright. Once she was sitting, she stretched one of her arms out and tried to put the shirt on herself. Magic Jade draped it over her shoulders and eased each of her arms in turn into the sleeves. Then he gently laid her down again. Skybright cried, "You may go now! It's so dirty here. You should take good care of yourself. That's most important! Today you've come to see me. I'll die content for having known my reputation is undeserved."

Magic Jade tried to cheer Skybright up and then he returned to the garden. Luckily he was able to slip back in unobserved.

Home again, Magic Jade simply told Aroma that he had been with Aunt Xue. When he was preparing his bed, she had to ask him how they should sleep that night.

"Anyway you like," was his answer.

During the last couple of years, because Aroma was in Lady Wang's favor, she had begun to stand on her dignity. She had broken off her intimacy with Magic Jade, even in private or at night, behaving more distantly than when they were young.

Magic Jade often woke up in the night, and as he was timid, he would always call for someone. Skybright was a light sleeper and soft footed. So she had been given the job of pouring him tea and attending to him at night, and for this reason she had slept on a bed near his. Since Skybright was gone, Aroma had to take this job as in the old days.

That evening Magic Jade was lost in thought. It must have been four o'clock before he finally fell asleep. Just as he was dropping off, Skybright walked into the room, looking her usual self. She said to him with a smile, "Take good care of yourself. I must leave you now." With that she turned and vanished.

Magic Jade called to her, which woke Aroma.

"Skybright is dead," he told her.

"What a thing to say!" Aroma replied. "How can you know? Don't let other people hear you talk such nonsense."

Magic Jade insisted that he was right and could hardly wait till dawn so that he could send someone to find out. He was so anxious to know the news of Skybright that he asked two younger maids, "Did Sister Aroma send anyone to see Sister Skybright?"

"She sent Mrs. Song," one girl told him.

"What did she say after she came back?"

"She said Sister Skybright was crying all night. First thing this morning, she closed her eyes and stopped calling because she'd fainted away and could do nothing but gasp for breath."

"Whom was she calling all night?" he asked hastily.

"Her mother."

Magic Jade wiped his tears.

"Who else?"

"Nobody else."

"You silly thing, you can't have heard her clearly."

The other girl was much smarter. She stepped forward and told Magic Jade, "She really is silly. I not only heard Mrs. Song clearly. I went over on the sly to see Skybright myself."

"Why did you do that?"

"Because I remembered how good Sister Skybright always was to us—not like other people. If we could not find any other way to help her, we should at least go to see her to repay her former kindness. That's why, at the risk of a beating, I slipped over to her cousin's place to see her. She was clear in her head right up to the time of her death. She only held my hand and opened her eyes wide when she saw me.

"'Where is Magic Jade?' she asked me. I told her where you'd gone. She sighed, 'I won't be able to see him then.' 'Why can't you hold out?' I asked. 'Then he can see you once more.' She smiled and told me, 'You don't understand. I'm not really dying. I'm going to heaven to be a flower goddess. I have to leave at half past two to take up the job, and Magic Jade will come at a quarter to three, so we'll miss each other by only a quarter of an hour!' When I got back and looked carefully at the clock. It was true, she died at half past two!"

Magic Jade, far from being surprised, felt his grief turn into pleasure. He pointed at the hibiscus. "This flower needs a girl like her to care for it," he observed. "I always thought that someone with her talents was bound to be given something to do in the world."

The thought that they would never meet again filled Magic Jade with grief and longing. Though he didn't see her at the end, he decided that now he should go and place a sacrifice at her shrine, for the sake of their friendship the last half dozen years.

Thus he went straight back to change his clothes and, on the pretext of going to see Black Jade, he went out of the garden alone and to the house where he had last visited Skybright, assuming her coffin would be there.

However, as soon as Skybright breathed her last, her cousin and his wife lost no time in having her body coffined and taken to the burying ground outside the town. They kept her clothes and trinkets, which were worth some three or four hundred ounces of silver, for future use. Then they locked up the place and went to attend her funeral.

Finding no one there, Magic Jade stood outside the door for a while. As there was nothing more he could do, he had to return to the garden.

24/ The Secret Trouble of Black Jade

Now, after Magic Jade was told by his father to go back to the family school, the Happy Red Residence Hall became quiet and Aroma had more time for her embroidery. One day, as she was embroidering a betel-nut bag, she began to think about her future. What was to become of her? What sort of life would she lead as Magic Jade's concubine? She knew how to handle him, so that was no problem. But what if he were to marry someone like Phoenix? Was she fated to become another Second Sister You?

Judging from Lady the Dowager and Lady Wang's attitude and the hints dropped by Phoenix, Black Jade seemed to have the best chance to become Magic Jade's wife. Flushing at this thought, her heart beat faster and her aim with the needle became more and more random. Finally she pushed her embroidery aside and went to Black Jade's place to sound her out.

Black Jade was reading a book. When Aroma came in, she moved over a little and offered her a seat.

"I hope you're feeling better these days, miss," greeted Aroma.

"Not really," replied Black Jade. "Anyway, I don't feel as weak as before. What have you been doing?"

"Since Master Magic Jade went back to school, we've had very little to do. So I dropped in here for a chat."

At this point Cuckoo came in with tea.

Aroma thanked her with a smile. "I heard the other day that you'd been gossiping behind our backs!"

"Don't believe that," Cuckoo laughed. "I only said that with Magic Jade away at school and with Miss Precious Hairpin gone, you must be feeling quite bored."

"Yes," said Aroma, "I only think about the tragic death of Second Sister You. She was a woman like Phoenix, but just a little different in status. Why should Phoenix be so cruel? It spoils our reputation inside and outside, as well."

Black Jade sensed that there was something more behind this. Aroma had never before gossiped in such a way behind people's backs. "Well, it's hard to say," she answered. "Incidents of this kind are inevitable in a big household with wives and concubines. No doubt there will always be rivalry between the east wind and the west wind. If the east wind doesn't prevail over the west wind, then the west wind is bound to prevail over the east wind."

"A concubine should know her place. How dare she take advantage of the wife?" said Aroma.

Just then an old woman's voice was heard in the courtyard, "Is this Miss Lin's house?"

Snowswan went out and saw that she was one of Aunt Xue's servants. "What do you want?" Snowswan asked.

"Our young lady sent me here to bring something to Miss Lin," replied the woman.

"Wait here just a minute," Snowswan said and then went in to report this. Black Jade told her to show the woman in.

The woman came in, curtseyed to Black Jade, and then screwed up her face to stare at her.

Embarrassed by her scrutiny, Black Jade asked, "What did Miss Hairpin tell you to bring me?"

"A jar of lichees preserved in honey," replied the old woman. She gave the jar to Snowswan, took another look at Black Jade, then turned to Aroma and said with a smile, "No wonder our Madam says that Miss Black Jade and your Master Magic Jade would make a nice pair. She really looks like an angel."

To put a stop to such foolish talk, Aroma hastily put in, "You must be tired out, aunty. Take a rest and have some tea."

"Oh no," the woman chuckled. "And I have two more jars of lichees from Miss Hairpin to deliver to Master Magic Jade." She took her leave and started to waddle away.

Though Black Jade was annoyed by her rough manners, she had tried to graciously receive the messenger sent by Hairpin. When the woman was outside, she called to her, "Thank Miss Hairpin for me."

The old woman was still mumbling, "Such a nice-looking young lady—only Magic Jade could match her!" Black Jade could only pretend not to have heard.

Aroma remarked with a smile, "When people grow old they often talk foolishly, one really doesn't know whether to be angry or amused."

After chatting a little while longer Aroma left.

That evening, when Black Jade went into the inner room to undress for the night, the sight of the jar of lichees reminded her of the old woman's remarks. She felt a pang of longing in her heart. Dusk was falling, and in the stillness a thousand gloomy thoughts seemed to seize her mind.

I'm in such poor health, she thought to herself, and I've reached the age for marriage. Judging by Magic Jade's feelings for me, he isn't interested in anyone else. But my grandmother and aunt haven't mentioned a word about it. If only my parents were still alive, or had fixed this match in advance!

Then it occurred to her that if they had lived, they might have married her to someone else, one who couldn't possibly compare with Magic Jade. In the present circumstances there might still be a chance for a match with Magic Jade. Her heart was on tenterhooks, her secret fears and hopes went up and down. With a sigh and a few tears, she lay down in her clothes, listless and depressed.

She was lying there in a daze when a young maid approached to report that Mr. Jia Yucun had come to see her.

"He was my tutor in the past," said Black Jade, "but I'm not a boy, why should he want to see me?"

"I think he's here to offer congratulations," said the girl. "Some people have come to take you to Nanjing."

That same moment in walked Phoenix, Lady Xing, Lady Wang, and Precious Hairpin. "We've come to congratulate you and to see you off," they said cheerfully.

"What do you mean?" asked Black Jade in alarm.

"Come on now," teased Phoenix. "Don't try to pretend you haven't heard the news. Your father has been promoted to become the Grain Commissioner of Hebei Province and has taken another wife, a perfect match. He asked Mr. Jia, as a go-between, to arrange for you to marry a relative of your stepmother's, a widower himself, I believe. They've sent to fetch you back, and maybe the wedding will take place as soon as you get home."

"This can't be true!" Black Jade protested. "Cousin Phoenix, you must be pulling my leg."

She saw Lady Xing wink at Lady Wang. Then Lady Xing said, "She still doesn't believe it. Let's go."

With tears in her eyes Black Jade begged, "Dear aunts, please wait!"

But, smiling coldly, they all departed.

Black Jade sobbed bitterly until, through her tears, she saw the Lady Dowager standing before her. Thinking to herself, if I beg my grandmother she may save me. She's the only one who can.

She fell on her knees and hugged the old lady's feet. "Save me, grandmum!" she begged. "I'd rather die than go south. You know, she's my stepmother, not my own mother. Do let me stay with you!"

But, with a look of indifference, the old lady said, "This has nothing to do with me."

"What does that mean, madam?" Black Jade sobbed.

"It's no use. All girls must get married sooner or later. You ought to know that, child, you can't stay here forever, can you?"

"I'd rather be a bond maid here, earning my keep. Please, please speak up for me, madam!"

The old lady still remained silent.

Black Jade hugged her again and sobbed, "Oh Grannie! You've always been so kind to me, so fond of me, how can you leave me in the lurch in a time of need. Though I'm only your granddaughter on the maternal side, my mother was your own daughter, your own flesh and blood! Won't you protect me for her sake at least?"

With these words she flung herself frantically upon the Lady Dowager, burying her head in her lap and sobbing violently.

"Lovebird," ordered the old lady, "take her out and calm her down. She's wearing me out, making such a scene."

Now Black Jade realized that appealing for help was useless. Suicide seemed to be the only way out. She stood up and started to go outside. She grieved bitterly that she had no mother of her own, for no matter how her grandmother, aunts and cousin had seemed good to her in the past, their concern for her now appeared to be nothing more than a sham. Suddenly she thought, why haven't I seen Magic Jade today? He might have some way out for me.

Just then Magic Jade stood in front of her. "My warmest congratulations, coz!" he said, all smiles.

This made Black Jade even more frantic. Her last maidenly reserve vanished. She seized him by the arm. "Fine!" she cried. "Now I know how heartless you really are, Magic Jade!"

"In what way am I heartless?" he asked. "Since you're engaged to someone else, we must go our separate ways."

Feeling more desperate and helpless, she gripped his arm. "My good cousin, to whom do you want me to go?" she sobbed.

"If you don't want to go," he said, "then just stay here. You were promised to me. That's why you came to live here. Haven't you realized this from how I've always treated you?"

Suddenly it all became clear. She was really engaged to Magic Jade, after all. Of course she was. In an instant her sorrow turned to joy. "My mind is made up even if I die!" she cried. "Tell me honestly, do you want me to leave or to stay?"

"I've told you, stay here with me," he said. "If you still don't trust me, I'll show you my heart."

With these words he took out a small knife and plunged it into his chest so that blood came rushing out. In terror, she thrust one hand over his heart.

"How can you do that?" she asked. "You'd better kill me first!"

"Don't be afraid," he said, "I'm going to show you my heart." He groped around with his hand in the gaping wound, while Black Jade pressed him to her tightly and wept bitterly.

Then Magic Jade exclaimed, "I'm done for! Now I've lost my heart. I must die!" He turned his eyes upward and fell heavily to the ground.

As Black Jade started screaming, she heard Cuckoo calling her. "Miss! Miss! Have you had a nightmare? Wake up! Come along now, you must get undressed and go to sleep properly."

Black Jade turned over and realized it was all a dream. She could still feel her throat choking. Her heart was pounding wildly. Her pillow was drenched and she felt icy cold.

Mother and father died long ago she thought to herself. Magic Jade and I have definitely never been engaged. What ever could have made me have such a dream?

The scenes of her dream passed before her eyes once more. She was all alone in the wide world. She wondered what would become of her if Magic Jade were really to die. She burst out weeping again until soon she was bathed in sweat. Tossing and turning, she couldn't get a wink of sleep.

There was a rustling outside like the sound of wind or rain. She sat up with effort, wrapping the bedding around herself, but a cold draught through the window cracks made her shiver. So once more she lay down. By now she was wide awake. She started coughing, waking up Cuckoo.

"Still not asleep, miss?" Cuckoo asked. "There, you're coughing again. You must have caught a cold. Please go back to sleep. Don't let your thoughts wander."

"I really want to sleep, but I can't," said Black Jade. "You should go back to sleep." Talking set her coughing again.

Cuckoo was too upset by Black Jade's fit of coughing to sleep any longer. She hastily got up to fetch the spittoon.

Later, when she went to empty it in the courtyard, she was shocked to find some specks of blood in the phlegm.

"My goodness" she exclaimed. "How awful!"

"What's the matter?" called Black Jade from the inner room.

"Oh nothing, miss." Cuckoo said, trying her best to cover up the slip of tongue. Her voice was choked. Tears came streaming down her cheeks.

Black Jade's suspicions were aroused by the sweet, salty taste in her throat, and now they were confirmed by Cuckoo's exclamation of dismay as well as by the catch in her voice. When Cuckoo returned, she was wiping her eyes with a handkerchief.

"Why are you crying so early in the morning?" Black Jade asked.

"Who's crying?" Cuckoo replied, forcing a smile. "When I got up my eyes felt itchy. You're so delicate, miss. I don't think you should worry so much. Health is everything. As the saying goes, 'As long as the green hills remain, we'll never be short of firewood.' Besides, everyone here, from Their Ladyships on down, is ever so fond of you."

The mere mention of these ladies reminded Black Jade of her nightmare. Her heart missed a beat. All turned dark before her eyes, and the color drained from her face. Cuckoo hastily held up the spittoon for her while Snowswan patted her back. After a long while she coughed another mouthful of dark red blood.

Her two maids turned pale with fright. As they stood there gasping, she fell back in a faint. Aware of her critical condition, Cuckoo signaled to Snowswan to go for help.

As soon as Tanchun and River Cloud learned the news, they came to the Bamboo Cottage to visit Black Jade. Their arrival upset Black Jade, reminding her of her nightmare. What can I expect of them, when even my grandmother cold shouldered me, she wondered.

But instead of showing what was in her mind, she made Cuckoo help her to sit up and offered them seats.

Cuckoo, standing on the other side of Black Jade, secretly pointed to the spittoon. Being so young and outspoken, River Cloud picked it up to have a look. What she saw horrified her. "Is this yours, cousin?" she exclaimed. "How awful!"

Black Jade had been too dazed to look carefully at the contents of her spittoon. But now River Cloud's question re-awakened her suspicions. Her heart sank as she turned to look.

To cover up River Cloud's tactlessness, Tanchun hastily put in, "This is nothing out of the usual—it's just that you've got some inflammation in your lungs, and have brought up a drop or two of blood. But River Cloud is so silly, she always makes a fuss about the least little thing."

River Cloud blushed and wished she had never opened her mouth.

Seeing how listless and tired Black Jade seemed, Tanchun got up and said, "You must rest well, to build up your strength, cousin. We'll call again later on."

"Thank you both for your concern," replied Black Jade.

Just as Tanchun turned to leave, somebody outside started shouting, "You good-for-nothing little bitch! Who are you to come and fool around in our garden?"

At this Black Jade pointed outside. Showing the whites of her eyes she exclaimed, "I can't stay here any longer!" She was sure that this abuse was aimed at her, and no one else. She wondered who had sent this old woman to insult her. It was too much to bear. With a heart-rending cry, she passed out.

"What's come over you, miss?" wailed Cuckoo. "Wake up, quick!"

Tanchun called out in an effort to rouse her, and after a while Black Jade came round. She still could not speak, but just kept pointing out of the window.

Tanchun caught her meaning and opened the door. Outside was an old woman with a stick chasing a dirty little girl.

"You people are getting too out of hand now!" Tanchun shouted at the woman. "Is this the place for you to shout? Get out of here, quick!"

"Yes, miss." The old woman made off, the small girl running after her.

Going back inside Tanchun found that Black Jade was opening her eyes slowly.

"Did you take offense at what the old woman said?" Tanchun asked with a smile.

Black Jade just shook her head feebly.

"She was shouting at her granddaughter. Don't bother about them. If you'll just have a good rest, take your medicine, and look on the bright side of things, I'm sure you'll get well enough for us all to start the poetry club again. Wouldn't that be nice?"

"You want me to cheer up," sobbed Black Jade. "But how can I? I'm afraid I will never pull through."

"That's no way to talk," said Tanchun. "Who doesn't feel ill or have trouble from time to time? How can you think in that way? Now just have a good rest while we go to see the old lady. We'll come and see you again later."

"Dear cousin!" cried Black Jade in tears. "When you see the old lady, please give her my respects and tell her I'm a bit unwell, but it's nothing serious. She's not to worry."

"I know. Just have a good rest and get better."

After Tanchun and River Cloud departed, Cuckoo helped her young mistress to lie down again. After a little rest, Black Jade was feeling slightly better. She heard a low voice outside asking, "Is Sister Cuckoo at home?"

Snowswan hurried out and saw it was Aroma.

"Come in, sister," she whispered.

"How is your young lady?" Aroma asked.

As they entered, Snowswan described what had happened just a little while earlier and the night before. This frightened Aroma.

"When we got the news," Aroma said. "Master Magic Jade was so alarmed, he told me to come and see how she is."

As they whispered, Cuckoo lifted the door curtain of the inner room and beckoned Aroma over.

"Is she asleep?" asked Aroma, tiptoeing towards her.

Cuckoo nodded, then frowned, "Have you only just heard about it?"

"How is this going to end?" Aroma asked, without expecting an answer. "I was nearly scared to death last night by Master Magic Jade, too."

"What happened?" asked Cuckoo.

"He was all right when he went to bed in the evening," Aroma told her. "But in the middle of the night he suddenly yelled that he had a pain in his heart, and talked wildly about someone cutting it out. He kept up this wild excitement for some time. Not until about dawn did he become quiet. Wouldn't you call that a real fright?"

Just then they heard Black Jade coughing behind her bed curtains. Cuckoo hurriedly took her the spittoon. Black Jade opened her eyes feebly, "Who were you talking to?"

"Sister Aroma has come to see you, miss."

By now Aroma had come over to the bed. Black Jade told Cuckoo to help her sit up, then indicating the edge of the bed, invited Aroma to be seated.

Aroma sat on the bed and smiled in her best manner, "You'd better lie down, miss."

"I'm all right," said Black Jade. "Don't make a fuss over nothing. Who was that you mentioned just now, with a pain in the heart during the night?"

"Oh, that wasn't real," replied Aroma. "That was just a nightmare Master Magic Jade had."

Black Jade was both touched and distressed, knowing that Aroma had said this for fear she might be anxious.

"Did you hear him talk in his nightmare?"

"Oh, he didn't say anything," lied Aroma.

Black Jade nodded. After a while she sighed. "Don't tell Master Magic Jade that I'm ill. It would affect his studies and thus worry his father."

"Of course, miss. You'd better rest now."

Black Jade nodded and asked Cuckoo to lower her to her pillow. Aroma stayed a little while longer to say a few more encouraging words. Then she took her leave and went back to the Happy Red Residence Hall. She simply told Magic Jade that Black Jade was a bit under the weather, nothing serious at all.

After leaving the Bamboo Cottage, Tanchun and River Cloud went to call on the Lady Dowager. On the way Tanchun warned her young cousin, "When you see the old lady, mind you don't talk in that wild way you did just now!"

"I won't," River Cloud nodded with a smile. "I was careless because I was scared out of my wits."

When they arrived, Tanchun's report that Black Jade was unwell worried the old lady.

"Oh dear! Those precious two are always falling ill," she said. "Now that Black Jade's growing up, she should pay more attention to her poor health. The child thinks a bit too much."

As no one ventured any comment, she ordered Lovebird, "Go and tell them that after the doctor has seen Magic Jade tomorrow, the doctor should go to visit Black Jade too."

Lovebird nodded and withdrew to pass on these instructions to the serving women. They, in turn, went off to relay the message.

25/ Magic Jade's Wedding in the Making

Magic Jade finally recovered from his illness. He returned to the family school as usual. One day, after he came back from school, he paid his respects to his father, Jia Zheng, and then he visited his grandmother. As soon as he entered the room, he heard the laughter of Lady Wang, Phoenix, and Tanchun.

At the sight of him the maid, who lifted the door curtain, whispered, "Your aunt is here."

Magic Jade hurried in to greet Aunt Xue, then paid his evening respects to the old lady. He asked the others, "Where is Cousin Hairpin?"

"She didn't come," answered Aunt Xue with a smile. "She's doing needlework at home."

Magic Jade was disappointed, but he couldn't leave at once. The table was set for dinner as they chatted.

Then, as they drank, the Lady Dowager remarked, "Just now, aunt, you mentioned Hairpin. Not everyone can have Hairpin's sweet disposition. She's so broadminded and sweet-tempered, really a girl in a hundred!"

"Well, it's no use," said Aunt Xue, "no matter how good she is, she's only a girl."

At the end of the meal, Magic Jade was the first to take his leave.

Aunt Xue asked about Black Jade's illness. "She is a good child, only a bit too sensitive," said the old lady, "that's spoiled her health. As far as intelligence goes, she's a match for Hairpin, but she lacks your daughter's easy way with people. Hairpin is so considerate and generous."

After a little more idle talk, Aunt Xue took her leave.

Let's return now to Jia Zheng. Pleased by the results of Magic Jade's lessons, he went out to chat with one of his secretaries, Mr. Wang, who was a good chess player.

"We have noticed that Master Magic Jade has made great progress in learning," Mr. Wang remarked.

"Progress? No," said Jia Zheng, "he's only making a start. He has a long way to go yet."

"I would venture to make a proposal, sir," said Mr. Wang.

"What's it?"

With a flattering smile, Mr. Wang went on, "Some acquaintances of mine, the family of Lord Zhang, the former Governor of Nanshao, have a daughter. She is said to be a beautiful and virtuous young lady, who is not yet engaged. Lord Zhang is most particular in choosing his son-in-law, stating that he must come from a rich and noble family and that he must be an outstanding young gentleman. After two months here, I can see that your young master's disposition and scholarship show him to be a man of great promise. And your family, sir, is, of course, most favorable. If I propose the match, I'm sure they will agree at once."

"Yes," replied Jia Zheng, "Magic Jade has reached the right age, and the old lady often speaks of this. But I know very little about this Lord Zhang."

"I know the family Mr. Wang means," put in another secretary. "The Zhangs are related to the Elder Master. You can ask him about them, sir."

Jia Zheng thus knew that they were relatives of Lady Xing. After sitting for a while, he went in to pass on this proposal to his wife and to get her to make inquiries of Lady Xing.

The next day, when Lady Xing came over to pay her respects, Lady Wang told her mother-in-law of this proposal about the Zhang family.

"Though we are relatives from way back, in the last few years we've been out of touch," said Lady Xing, "I really don't know what that girl is like. I only have heard that she's an only child and very much spoiled. Mr. Zhang is rather reluctant to marry her off, for fear her husband will be too strict with her. They want a son-in-law who will live with them and help to manage the household."

"That would never do." cried the old lady, not waiting for her to finish. "Our Magic Jade needs people to look after him. How can he manage someone else's household?"

"Quite so, madam," agreed Lady Xing.

Then the old lady turned to Lady Wang. "When you go back, tell your husband from me that this match is out of the question."

Lady Wang promised to do so. Phoenix put in, smiling, "I hope you'll excuse me for speaking out of turn. But why look for a wife for Magic Jade when there's a 'predestined match here before our very eyes?'"

The old lady, chuckling, asked what she meant.

"One 'magic jade' and one 'gold locket'—how could you forget that, madam?" replied Phoenix.

"Why didn't you make this proposal yesterday when your aunt was here?" countered the old lady, laughing.

"In the presence of elders and betters, it would hardly have been right for me to speak up," replied Phoenix. "Besides, Aunt Xue had come to see you, so how could I bring that up? The proper way to do it is for Mother and Aunt Wang to go over and ask Aunt Xue for Precious Hairpin's hand."

Lady Dowager, Lady Xing and Lady Wang all laughed.

Now, after attending the Prince's birthday celebration, Magic Jade returned to report this visit and to display the jade gift given him by the Prince. When it had been admired by all, the old lady ordered the maids to put it away so that he would not lose it.

"Mind you keep your own jade well," she warned Magic Jade. "Don't mix it with the piece from the Prince."

Taking the jade from his neck, he rejoined, "This is mine. How could I lose it? It's impossible to mix them up. And there's something else I'd like to tell you, madam. The other night when I went to bed and hung my jade on the curtain, it started glowing, making the whole bed curtain red!"

"You're talking nonsense again," she said, "the valance of the canopy is red, so naturally when it catches the light the curtain seems red too."

"No, the light had been put out by that time. The whole room was pitch dark, yet I saw it clearly."

Lady Xing and Lady Wang exchanged meaningful smiles.

"It's a lucky sign anyway," Phoenix assured him.

"A lucky sign? What do you mean?" asked Magic Jade.

"You wouldn't understand," replied his grandmother, "you've had an exciting day, so go and take a rest now. Don't stay here telling tall stories."

Magic Jade hung around for a while before going back to the garden. But as soon as he had gone, the old lady turned to Lady Wang. "Well, when you went to see Aunt Xue did you bring up that business?" she asked.

"We told Aunt Xue, and she was only too willing," replied Lady Wang. "However, she says she must consult Xue Pan first, as the eldest in the family. He is still away from home at this time."

"Quite right too," agreed the old lady. "We'd better not make it public. We need to wait until they have talked it over and come to a decision."

After Magic Jade returned to his quarters, he told Aroma, "Just now my grandmother and Cousin Phoenix were talking so cryptically, I'd no idea what was going on."

Aroma thought for a while, then smiled. "I can't figure it out either," she said. "Was Black Jade there at the time when they were talking?"

"Of course not! You know she has just recently been up and about from her sick bed. How could she go there?"

Aroma now realized from Magic Jade's remarks that his marriage was under consideration. She pretended to be ignorant of this, for fear that his senseless notions would make him burst out in a flood of foolish talk. She was also concerned about his marriage, and she lay awake that night thinking. She decided that the next day she would to go to see if Cuckoo knew anything about the latest developments that might shed light on the matter.

The next morning Magic Jade dressed and set off for school. As he was going out, he saw Jia Rong hurrying towards him.

At the sight of Magic Jade, Jia Rong saluted his uncle. "Congratulations, uncle!"

"What's up?" Magic Jade asked.

Just then they heard shouting outside.

"Have you no manners?" they heard someone shout. "How dare you make such a row here?"

Another voice answered, "Your old master has been promoted! How can you stop us from announcing the good tidings? Other families would be only too happy to hear us!"

Magic Jade then realized, with delight, that they were announcing his father's promotion to the post of vice minister. He immediately hurried toward the school. But Jia Rong caught up with him, saying, "Are you pleased, uncle? Once your marriage is fixed, that'll be double happiness for you!"

Magic Jade flushed and spat. "Clear off, you silly fool!"

When Magic Jade arrived at the school, his tutor, beaming, asked him, "What brings you here today?"

"I've come to see you, sir, before going to my father," said Magic Jade respectfully.

"You don't have to study today. You may have a holiday."

Magic Jade was thus happy to leave his tutor and go home. Passing through the inner gate, he saw that the maids and matrons were all smiles.

Magic Jade entered his grandmother's room and his face lit up when he saw Black Jade sitting on his grandmother's left, River Cloud on her right. All the ladies of the house had assembled there except for Precious Hairpin and Yingchun. Beside himself with joy, he offered congratulations to his grandmother and to their Ladyships. Then he greeted his cousins one by one.

"Are you getting better now, cousin?" he asked Black Jade.

"Thank you, much better now," she answered with a smile. "I heard you were not very well either. Are you all right now?"

"Oh yes," he answered. "One night I suddenly had a pain in my heart, but these few days I've been well enough to go back to school. That's why I've had no time to visit you."

While he was still speaking, Black Jade turned away to talk to Tanchun. Phoenix, who was standing near them, smiled.

"You two are behaving like guests, not like two inseparable lovers," she teased. "All these civilities! Well, as the saying goes, 'you show each other respect as to a guest.'"[8]

The others laughed, while Black Jade blushed so much that she didn't know whether to respond or not. After some hesitation she blurted out, "Who'd expect you to understand." This seemed to amuse everyone even more.

After a moment's reflection, Phoenix realized that her joke had been in rather poor taste. As she was about to change the topic, Magic Jade suddenly turned to Black Jade and said, "Cousin Black Jade, you never saw anyone as ill-mannered as Jia Rong..." He broke off without finishing the sentence.

This provoked a fresh burst of puzzled laughter.

"What is all this about?" some asked. Black Jade was also in the dark. She smiled shyly.

Magic Jade hedged, "Just now I heard that some operas are to be presented. When will that be?"

All looked at him, still laughing.

"If you heard that outside," said Phoenix wittily, "you should come and tell us, not ask us about it."

"Well, I'll go and find out," Magic Jade said promptly, then slipped away.

The old lady asked Phoenix, "Who's talked of presenting operas?"

---

[8]   Meng Kuang and Liang Hung of the Eastern Han Dynasty (25-220 A.D.) were a loving couple. They were described as showing each other respect as guests.

"Uncle Wang. General Wang said that the day after tomorrow is a lucky day. He'll send over a new company of actresses to congratulate you, madam, as well as the master and mistress." She added with a twinkle. "It'll not only be a lucky day, but a happy occasion too. That day..." She winked at Black Jade, who smiled back.

"Why, of course!" exclaimed Lady Wang. "It's our niece's birthday."

The old lady thought for a second and then said, "It shows I'm growing old, I get so muddle-headed. It's lucky I have Phoenix as my right hand. All right then. If Magic Jade's uncle wants to offer congratulations, Black Jade's uncle's family can celebrate her birthday too. What could be better?"

This made everyone present laugh.

26/ Black Jade Rejects All Nourishment

One day Cuckoo went out and found Snowswan all alone. Cuckoo came up to her and said, "What's on your mind? Tell me, please."

Snowswan gave a start, then said, "Hush up! Today I heard something very strange. If I tell you, you must promise not to say anything about it."

Then Snowswan whispered, "Did you know, sister, that Magic Jade is engaged?"

"Who says that?" Cuckoo demanded. "Surely not!"

"It's true. Almost everyone knows, except we're kept in the dark."

"Where did you get that information?"

"From a maid," replied Snowstorm. "She says the girl's father is a prefect. She is nice looking too. Her family is quite wealthy. I asked the maid, 'Is it settled?' And she said, 'Sure. A certain Mr. Wang was the go-between. He is related to the East Mansion. So without too much effort, they accepted right away.'"

Cuckoo cocked her head, thinking this extremely strange. "Why has nobody in the house ever mentioned it?" she pressed.

"Well, it was the old lady's idea. She was afraid that if Magic Jade knew anything about it, he would be disturbed from his studies."

Snowswan pointed at the room where Black Jade stayed and went on, "That's why I didn't tell her a word about it. Since you asked me about it today, I couldn't hide it from you any more."

At this point they heard a loud squawk from the parrot overhead. "The young lady's back! Serve tea! Quick."

Startled, they turned to look, and seeing no one there they scolded the bird. Then, going back inside, they discovered Black Jade out of breath and just about to sit down on a chair. Cuckoo asked, rather awkwardly, if she wanted something to drink.

Black Jade went back to her bed and sank down, her face to the wall. She told them to let down the bed curtain. The two maids did so and went out, each wondering whether Black Jade had overheard them or not, but neither daring to ask.

Now Black Jade had been brooding anxiously, and had eavesdropped on the conversation between the two maids. Though she did not hear everything, she caught the main point and was plunged into a raging sea of despair. The news bore out the details of the ominous dream she had so recently had. Frustration and grief overwhelmed her. There was only one way of escape, she thought. She must die. She must not live to see this terrible thing taking place.

Black Jade also reflected bitterly on the fact that she had no parents to turn to. She decided she would let her health run down, and in half a year or so leave this sea of troubles. Having reached this conclusion, she closed her eyes and pretended to be asleep.

The next morning Black Jade rose early without waking either of the maids. She sat up alone, lost in thought.

When Cuckoo woke and saw her already up she said in surprise, "You're up very early, miss."

"I know I am," said Black Jade, "I went to bed early, that's why I woke early this morning."

Cuckoo got up quickly and roused Snowswan to help Black Jade with her toilet.

Black Jade sat staring into the mirror. Tears began to stream down her face, and soon her silk handkerchief was soaked through. Sitting there, she asked Cuckoo to light some of the Tibetan incense because she wanted to sit at the desk and do some writing.

"You woke up so early, miss. If you start writing now you'll exhaust yourself," Cuckoo said.

"Don't worry," Black Jade answered. "The sooner I finish the better. I only want to keep myself occupied so as not to be too upset. Later on, when you see my handwriting, it'll be like seeing me again." As she said this, tears began to pour down her cheeks.

Cuckoo could not cheer Black Jade up and soon could not hold back her own tears.

Since Black Jade had made up her mind to ruin her health, she lost her appetite little by little and began to waste away. Magic Jade visited her after school whenever he could. Although she longed to tell him why she was ill, now that they were no longer children she could hardly tease him playfully, as she had before, to express her pent-up feelings. He also wanted to bare his heart to console her, yet he feared this might offend her and make her illness worse. So, when they met, they could only express their concern in the most superficial way. Truly, theirs was a case of "Devotion leading to alienation."

For a month Black Jade ate less and less. Eventually her appetite had been reduced so much that she could not even swallow a mouthful of congee. Every fragment of conversation she overheard during the day seemed, to her, to be connected in some way with Magic Jade's marriage. Every servant she saw from the Happy Red Residence Hall seemed to be involved with his wedding. She refused to take her medicine. Her only wish was to be left alone so that she could die as quickly as possible.

Her grandmother and other aunts came to visit her in turns, while she was still strong enough to say a few words, but in the last few days of the month she hardly said a word. Sometimes she seemed unconscious, sometimes she had moments of mental clarity.

Wondering what had caused this illness, her grandmother questioned her maids more than once. But they dared not tell her the truth. The day finally came when Black Jade would eat nothing at all. Cuckoo saw that all hope was gone. She stood by Black Jade's bedside weeping for awhile, and then went outside and whispered to Snowswan, "Go in and look after her carefully while I go to tell the mistresses. She's never been as bad as this before."

After this, Cuckoo left and Snowswan went in to take care of Black Jade, who was now in a coma. Too young to have seen anything like this before, Snowswan thought her young mistress must be dying and she was torn between grief and alarm. If only Cuckoo would hurry up and come back, she thought to herself. At that very moment she heard footsteps outside the window. It must be Cuckoo, she concluded with relief.

Snowswan heard the swish of the outer door curtain, and in came not Cuckoo but Scribe, sent by Tanchun to inquire how Black Jade was. Seeing Snowswan, Scribe asked, "How is Black Jade?"

Snowswan nodded for her to come in and Scribe entered the inner room. She noticed that Cuckoo was not there, and when Scribe looked at Black Jade and saw how feebly she was breathing, a look of terror came over her face.

"Where is Sister Cuckoo?" Scribe asked.

"Gone to tell their Ladyships," replied Snowswan.

Under the impression that Black Jade was unconscious and knowing that Cuckoo was away, Snowswan took Scribe's hand and asked her in a low voice, "You told me the other day that some Mr. Wang proposed a match for Magic Jade. Was that true?"

"Of course it was," answered Scribe.

"When was the engagement fixed?"

"How could it be fixed? I heard about it from a young maid. Later I went to Madam Phoenix's place and overheard her talking about it with Sister Patience. She said, 'This is just a pretext for those literary gentlemen to please the old master.' The Lady Dowager has someone else in mind for Magic Jade, someone from right in our garden. Phoenix said the Lady Dowager wants Magic Jade to marry one of his cousins. Since her mind is quite made up, any other proposals are a waste of time and effort."

Snowswan was beside herself now. "Then our mistress is dying for nothing!" she exclaimed.

Just then Cuckoo lifted the door curtain and stepped in. "What's all this?" she exclaimed softly. "If you want to gossip, gossip outside instead of here. You might as well drive her to her death!"

"This is so strange," cried Scribe, "I simply can't believe it!"

The three of them were interrupted by a sudden cough from Black Jade. Cuckoo hurried to the bedside, while Snowswan and Scribe stood in silence. Cuckoo bent down and whispered to Black Jade, who was lying with her face to the wall, "Would you like some drinking water, miss?"

"Yes," was the faint reply.

Snowswan at once poured half a cup of boiled water, which Cuckoo took from her. Scribe stepped forward too, but Cuckoo shook her head to make her keep quiet. They stood there until Black Jade coughed again.

"Would you like the water now, miss?"

There was another faint "yes" and Black Jade seemed to be wanting to lift her head, but this effort was quite beyond her. Cuckoo sat on the bed beside her, cup in hand. First she made sure that the water was neither too hot nor too cold, then held it to Black Jade's lips, supporting her head as she sipped. Cuckoo was about to remove the cup when she saw that Black Jade wanted some more. Cuckoo then held the cup there while she took another sip.

After this, Black Jade shook her head to show that it was enough, took a deep breath, and lay down once more. Then, following a pause, she half opened her eyes and asked, "Was that Scribe I heard talking just now?"

"Yes, miss," replied Cuckoo.

Scribe was still in the room and came over to greet her. Black Jade opened her eyes to glance at her and nodded.

After another pause, Black Jade said, "When you go back, give my regards to your miss." Scribe took this to mean that Black Jade wanted to be left in peace, and left the room quietly.

Now Black Jade, though so gravely ill, had been clear in her mind. She had caught fragments of the conversation between Scribe and Snowswan, but she lay as if unconscious, owing partly to weakness. From what she overheard she realized that the match proposed remained only a proposal. Then she heard Scribe repeat Phoenix's words that the Lady Dowager intended to marry Magic Jade to one of his cousins in the garden. Who could that be but herself? At this realization, her despair gave way to joy and her mind became clearer too. That was why she decided to drink some water and even spoke to Scribe.

Just then the old lady arrived with Lady Wang and Phoenix. They hurried over after hearing Cuckoo's report. Since Black Jade's suspicions were now gone, she no longer wanted to die. Weak and short of energy as she was, she was able to answer their inquiries briefly.

Seeing this Phoenix called Cuckoo over. "What do you mean by frightening us like that?" she demanded. "Your young lady's not in such a bad way after all."

"Honestly, madam," replied Cuckoo, "only a little while ago she was really in a bad way. That's why I came over to see you. I would never have dared to bother you otherwise. She does seem a lot better now. It's most strange."

"You shouldn't take what she says so seriously, my dear," the Lady Dowager said to Phoenix, smiling. "What does she know anyway? When something's wrong, it shows good sense to report it. I like a girl who's not too lazy to use her tongue and feet."

The ladies stayed for a while, then believing Black Jade to be out of danger they returned to their own apartments.

After this, Black Jade's condition continued to improve. Snowswan and Cuckoo secretly gave prayers of thanks to Buddha.

"Thank God she's better now," said Snowswan to Cuckoo. "How strange her illness! How strange her recovery!"

"Her illness wasn't strange," replied Cuckoo, "but her sudden recovery is. I think Magic Jade and Black Jade must be destined to be married after all. As the sayings go, 'The way to happiness is full of twists and turns.' and 'Marriage arranged by fate can never be broken.' So it seems human wishes are in line with the will of Heaven, and the two of them are fated to marry!"

The two maids exchanged a secret smile at this romantic theory, and Snowswan said again, "Well, thank goodness she's better anyway. We must never gossip any more. Even if Magic Jade marries some other girl and I see the wedding with my own eyes. I won't breathe a word about it."

"That's right," agreed Cuckoo, smiling.

Theirs was not the only secret discussion on this topic. Black Jade's strange illness and stranger recovery gave rise to a great deal of whispering and speculation in the household. This soon reached the ears of Phoenix. Lady Xing and Lady Wang found it puzzling. The Lady Dowager was the only one who had a some inkling what was at the bottom of it all.

One day Phoenix and the ladies were chatting with the old lady in her room. The topic of Black Jade's illness came up again.

"I was just going to tell you something," said the old lady. "Magic Jade and Black Jade have been together ever since they were small, and this has never troubled me, as I have always thought of them as children. But recently I have noticed how frequently their illnesses come and go. Surely they have grown up now. So I don't think it's proper to leave them together all the time. What do you say?"

Taken aback, Lady Wang could only answer, "Black Jade is a bright and intelligent girl. As for Magic Jade, he's such a stupid muddle-head, he may get himself talked about sometimes. On the face of it, though, they're both of them still children. If we remove either one of them from the garden, won't it be too obvious? Don't you think it would be better to lose no time in arranging their wedding?"

The old lady frowned.

"Black Jade is over-sensitive," she said. "It's the reason why I don't want to marry her to Magic Jade. Besides, she's so delicate, I doubt whether she would live long enough. I'm sure Precious Hairpin is the more suitable choice."

"Of course we all agree with you there, madam," said Lady Wang. "But we must find a husband for Black Jade, too. If she's really set her heart on Magic Jade, it may make things difficult to handle if she were to discover that Magic Jade was engaged to Hairpin."

"But we can't marry her off before Magic Jade," objected the old lady. "Who ever heard of arranging a marriage for someone else's child before one's own? And especially since she's two years younger than he is. Still, there's something in what you say. We'll just have to see to it that there's no talk about Magic Jade's engagement."

Phoenix turned at once to the maids. "Did you hear that?" she said. "Mind you don't gossip about Master Magic Jade's engagement. If I catch anyone of you gossiping about it, I'll show you no mercy!"

"Phoenix dear," said the old lady, "since that illness of yours you've stopped paying much attention to what goes on in the garden. I want you to keep your eyes open, and not just in regard to this. You have sharper eyes than the rest of us, so you should take the trouble to keep the two of them under strict control. And you seem to be the one they respect most."

Phoenix promised to do her best, and after a little further talk the ladies left to go their separate ways.

27/ The Cunning Trick of Phoenix

The crab apple trees in the Happy Red Residence Hall had withered, and no one bothered to water them. One day Magic Jade took a look at them. He saw buds on the branches. The next day the buds suddenly burst out into bloom with lovely flowers. This caused such a stir that people came to see the blossoms, which had bloomed strangely out of season.

When Black Jade heard the news, she came with Cuckoo to join the fun. She greeted the old lady and the other cousins. Only Phoenix was absent, for she was ill at home.

"Why are these withered plants blossoming right now?" Black Jade asked. "There must be some reason."

"In my foolish opinion, they have flowered specially to tell us of some happy event that is about to take place in Magic Jade's life," put in one of the girls.

Elated by this talk of a happy event for Magic Jade, Black Jade said gaily, "There was once a family of farmers. They had a red-bud tree that withered when the three brothers split up the property. That moved the brothers to live together. Then the tree blossomed again. So you see, plants follow closely the fortunes of people to whom they are attached. Cousin Magic Jade is devoting himself to his studies. This pleases Uncle Jia Zheng. It also pleases the crab apple trees. That's why they're flowering."

The old lady and Lady Wang were both delighted with this explanation. "Black Jade has made a wonderful comparison. It's most interesting," they said to each other, "this is surely a good omen."

The old lady told the servants to have the kitchen to prepare a family feast to celebrate the blossoming of the flowers.

That year two things happened at the same time. One was a happy event: Magic Jade's father was appointed Grain Commissioner of Jiangxi Province. Relatives and friends came to offer congratulations. The other was an unhappy event: Magic Jade lost his jade and became very distraught. The old lady got someone to tell Magic Jade's fortune. The fortuneteller said, "He must marry a bride with gold in her stars to help turn back his bad luck."

Since Jia Zheng would soon leave for his new post, the old lady asked him to join her for a family consultation about Magic Jade's trouble. After some consideration, they agreed there should be some kind of happy event to ward off evil. This should be his marriage to Precious Hairpin. The marriage would turn his ill luck around, and her gold necklace might bring back his magic jade. They also decided to keep this marriage a secret.

The servants were ordered not to breathe a word about it. Jia Zheng left the arrangements for Magic Jade's wedding to his mother, wife, and Phoenix.

Aroma happened to overhear the conversation between the old lady and Jia Zheng. She thought that this would be just the match for Magic Jade. If Precious Hairpin comes into the household her load would be ever so much lighter. But, she knew, Magic Jade had set his heart on Black Jade. Heaven only knew how wildly he might carry on.

Aroma further wondered what could be done. The old lady and Lady Wang had no idea of the secret feelings Magic Jade and Black Jade had for each other. If they were to tell him now that he was to marry not Black Jade but Precious Hairpin, then far from curing his madness, it might speed up his death. Unless she explained this to them, she might ruin three lives.

Aroma's mind was made up. She slipped out and quietly, asking Lady Wang to go with her to the back room. Once there, Aroma threw herself on her knees and burst into tears.

Lady Wang pulled her up and asked, "What's come over you? Who has done you wrong? Get up and tell me."

"You have decided to marry Precious Hairpin to Magic Jade," Aroma said, "and of course nothing could be better. All I'm wondering, madam, is this: which of the two, Miss Hairpin or Miss Black Jade, do you think Magic Jade prefers?"

"As he and Black Jade were together as children," Lady Wang replied, "he's slightly closer to Black Jade."

"More than slightly," replied Aroma. She then went on to give Lady Wang a detailed account of how things had always stood between Magic Jade and Black Jade. "These are all things that you would have seen for yourself, madam," she added. "With the exception of his outburst during the summer, I have not mentioned a word to anyone until now."

Holding Aroma's hand Lady Wang said, "I did have some inkling from what I saw. What you have said simply bears out my own observations. But since you heard the Master's words, Magic Jade must have heard them also. Tell me, how did Magic Jade react?"

"As things are at present, madam, Magic Jade smiles if someone talks to him. Otherwise he just goes to sleep. He heard nothing."

"In that case, get back to your work," said Lady Wang. "I won't mention it to the old lady now, as there are too many people there. I'll wait for a chance to tell the old lady later on, and then we shall see."

She rejoined the Lady Dowager, who was discussing Magic Jade's marriage with Phoenix.

"What did Aroma want?" the old lady asked. "She looked so secretive."

Lady Wang took this opening as a chance to give the old lady a detailed account of Magic Jade's feeling for Black Jade. For a while the old lady said nothing. Lady Wang and Phoenix kept silent also.

"Nothing else really matters," the old lady sighed at last. "We needn't worry about Black Jade. But if Magic Jade really feels this way about her, it's going to be difficult."

"Not too difficult," said Phoenix after some thought, "I've an idea, but don't know whether Aunt Xue will agree to it or not."

"If you have a plan, tell the old lady then," said Lady Wang.

"To my mind," said Phoenix, "the only thing to do is to tell a white lie, and then use a piece of discreet substitution."

"Substitution? What do you mean?" asked the old lady.

"Never mind whether Magic Jade is in his right mind or not," said Phoenix, "we must all drum it into his head that on the master's orders he is to marry Black Jade, and see how he takes it. If he doesn't care either way, we needn't trick him. If he's pleased, we'll have to follow an intricate plan."

Phoenix went over to whisper something into Lady Wong's ear. Lady Wang nodded and smiled at this. "That should work," she said.

"Tell me what you two are plotting," urged the old lady.

In order not to give away the secret, Phoenix whispered in her ear also. As she anticipated, the old lady did not understand at first, and Phoenix, smiling, had to explain more fully.

"That's all right," agreed the old lady. "Rather hard on Precious Hairpin, though. And if word gets out, what about Black Jade?"

"We'll just tell Magic Jade and forbid any mention of this outside. Then how could she hear?"

At this point a maid announced Jia Lian's return. Not wanting the old lady to question him, Lady Wang cast Phoenix a meaningful glance to go out to meet him, signaling to him to go with her to Lady Wang's place. By the time they were joined by Lady Wang, Phoenix's eyes were red from weeping.

After he had paid his respects to Lady Wang, Jia Lian described his trip to Ten Mile Village to help arrange for General Wang's funeral. Lady Wang was naturally so upset by this account that Phoenix had to cheer her up.

"Please have a rest now, madam," she urged. "This evening we'll come back to discuss the Magic Jade business."

Going home with Jia Lian, Lady Wang told him what had happened, and asked him to send servants to prepare the bridal chambers.

Several days later and after breakfast, accompanied by Cuckoo, Black Jade set off to call on her grandmother and also to dispel her pent-up sorrow. They had not gone far from the Bamboo Cottage when she found that she had forgotten to bring a handkerchief with her. She told Cuckoo to go back for one then catch up with her. She walked on slowly.

She had passed the bridge and reached the rocks behind which she and Magic Jade had buried the peach blossom, when she suddenly heard sobbing. She stopped to listen, but could not tell who was lamenting there or hear what the person was saying. Very puzzled, she strolled over and found that the one crying was an under-maid.

When Black Jade appeared, the maid dared not go on crying, but stood up and wiped her eyes.

"Why are you weeping here? What's come over you?" Black Jade asked.

"Oh Miss Lin!" replied the maid, amid fresh tears. "Judge for yourself. I made a slip of the tongue, but sister had no call to slap me."

Black Jade could not make head or tail of this.

"Which sister do you mean?" she asked.

"A maid in the old lady's apartment."

Knowing from this that she worked for the old lady, Black Jade asked again, "Why did she slap you? What did you say wrong?"

"Why? Just because of the marriage of our young Master Magic Jade to Miss Precious Hairpin."

Black Jade felt thunderstruck. Her heart beat wildly. Composing herself a little she said, "Come with me."

The maid accompanied her to the quiet spot where she had buried the peach blossom. Then Black Jade asked, "Why should she slap you because Master Magic Jade is marrying Miss Precious Hairpin?"

"The old lady and Lady Wang have settled it with Madam Phoenix. Because His Lordship's going to leave so soon, they're hurriedly fixing it up with Aunt Xue to have Miss Precious Hairpin brought over before he goes. They want this wedding to turn Magic Jade's luck around and then," she beamed at Black Jade. "after his wedding, they'll fix up a match for you, miss."

At this, Black Jade felt as if her heart were filled with a mixture of oil, soy, sugar, and vinegar—so sweet, bitter, painful, and sharp that she could not put her sensations into words. After a pause, in a trembling voice she said, "Don't talk such nonsense. If they heard, they'd give you another slapping. Be off with you now."

Black Jade turned to go back to the Bamboo Cottage. But there seemed to be a millstone around her neck and her legs were limp, her steps as faltering as if treading on cotton wool. It seemed a long way to the bridge, she was walking so slowly and so shakily. When at last she reached the bridge, she started back along the dyke quite unaware of where she was going.

When Cuckoo brought her handkerchief, she saw Black Jade's white face, her eyes fixed in a vacant stare, wandering unsteadily this way and that. In shocked surprise, Cuckoo ran over. "Why are you going back, miss?" she asked gently. "Where do you want to go?"

Hearing her as if in a dream, Black Jade answered without thinking, "To ask Magic Jade what this means."

Cuckoo could not tell what was going on, and could only try to guide her on her way to see Magic Jade. When Black Jade reached his door, her mind seemed to clear. Turning to the maid who was supporting her, she asked, "Why have you come?"

"To bring your handkerchief," was the smiling answer. "Just now I saw you by the bridge, but when I asked you where you were going, you took no notice."

"I thought you'd come to see Master Magic Jade," Black Jade laughed. "Why else should you come this way?"

Cuckoo saw that her wits were wandering, and knew that she must have heard something from someone. Cuckoo could only nod and smile. However, she was trying to imagine what sort of an encounter this was going to be between the young master who had already lost his wits and her young mistress who was now herself a little touched. What if they said something improper? But for all this, she had to do as she was told and help her young mistress inside.

Lifting the door curtain herself instead of waiting for Cuckoo to do so, Black Jade stepped in. The clack of the door curtain alerted Aroma, who came out from the inner room.

"Please come in and take a seat, miss," Aroma invited Black Jade.

"Is Master Magic Jade in?" Black Jade asked with a smile.

Aroma was about to answer when Cuckoo signaled to her from behind Black Jade and, pointing at her young mistress, waved her hand warningly. Aroma was too puzzled to say any more.

Black Jade, disregarding her, went on into the inner room where Magic Jade was sitting. Instead of rising to offer her a seat, he simply stared at her with a foolish grin. Black Jade sat down and gazed back at him with a smile. They exchanged neither greetings nor civilities, just simpered at each other without a word.

"Magic Jade," said Black Jade finally. "Why are you ill?"

"Because of Miss Lin," he answered with a smirk.

Aroma and Cuckoo turned pale with fright and at once tried to steer the conversation in a different direction. But the other two ignored them, still smiling foolishly. It then dawned on Aroma that Black Jade was now deranged in the same way as Magic Jade.

Aroma whispered to Cuckoo, "Your young lady's just over her illness. I'll get Sister Ripple to help you take her back to rest." She turned to tell Ripple. "Go with Sister Cuckoo to see Miss Lin back. Mind you don't say anything foolish."

Ripple smiled, and without a word came over to help Cuckoo. The two of them began to help Black Jade to her feet. Black Jade stood up, unsupported, still staring fixedly at Magic Jade. She smiled and nodded her head.

"Come on, miss!" urged Cuckoo. "It's time to go home and rest."

"Of course!" exclaimed Black Jade. "It's time!"

Black Jade turned to go. Still smiling and refusing any support from the maids, she strode out at twice her normal speed. Ripple and Cuckoo hurried after her. Black Jade kept on walking, in quite the wrong direction. Cuckoo hurried up to her and took her by the hand.

"This is the way, miss," Cuckoo said.

Still smiling, Black Jade allowed herself be led. She followed Cuckoo towards the Bamboo Cottage. When they were not far from there, Cuckoo exclaimed, "Buddha be praised! Home at last!"

She had no sooner uttered these words when she saw Black Jade stumble forwards onto the ground, and give a loud cry. A stream of blood came gushing from her mouth. The two maids picked her up and carried her inside. Then Ripple left Cuckoo and Snowswan to attend to her.

After a while, Black Jade regained consciousness and saw that her maids were crying. She asked them the reason.

In relief Cuckoo answered, "You seemed unwell just now, and we didn't know what to do. We cried for fright."

"Oh, I'm not going to die as easily as all that," retorted Black Jade, panting as she spoke.

When Black Jade learned that Magic Jade and Precious Hairpin were to be married, she was so enraged that she lost her senses. After she spat out the blood, her mind gradually became clearer. At first she could remember nothing at all, and then when she saw Cuckoo crying, the little maid's words slowly came back to her. This time she did not feel grieved, but just longed to die quickly and finally settle her debt with fate.

Ripple, however, had gone back panic-stricken to report the incident to the old lady. Her fearful description of what she had seen made the old lady exclaim in horror and send at once for Lady Wang and Phoenix to communicate this bad news.

"I ordered all the maids to keep it a secret," said Phoenix. "Who could have betrayed us? This makes things even more difficult."

The three of them went to the Bamboo Cottage and found Black Jade there, deathly pale. She seemed barely conscious and her breathing was quite weak. Presently Black Jade had another fit of coughing. Her maid brought over the spittoon and, to the consternation of all present, her sputum was streaked with blood.

Black Jade's eyelids fluttered as she saw the old lady by her side. "Grandma," she gasped, "your love for me has been wasted."

Her heart aching, the old lady said, "Don't be afraid, dear child. You must rest well."

Black Jade smiled faintly, closing her eyes again as a maid came in to report the doctor's arrival to Phoenix. Now the ladies withdrew, and Doctor Wang was led in by Jia Lian to take the patient's pulse.

"She will be all right," he observed. "Pent-up anger has drained her liver of blood, resulting in a nervous disorder. Some medicine to regulate the blood will set her right again." This said, he went out with Jia Lian to write out his prescription and fetch medicine.

The Lady Dowager had seen that Black Jade's state was critical. After leaving her, the old lady said to Phoenix. "It's not that I want to put a jinx on her but it doesn't look to me, I'm afraid, like the child will recover. You must prepare afterlife things to counter her bad luck. If she gets over this illness, that'll be a great weight off our minds. And if it comes to the worst, you won't be caught unprepared at the last minute. We've that other business to attend to these days."

After Phoenix silently agreed, the old lady questioned Cuckoo as to who had told Black Jade the news. But Cuckoo did not know.

Dubiously, the old lady went on, "It's natural for young people who've played together as children to be partial to each other; but now that they're big enough to know the facts of life they should keep at a distance. That's how a girl should behave if she wants me to love her. To get other ideas into her head is most improper, and all my love for her will be thrown away. I'm quite upset by what you've been telling me."

Phoenix put in, "Don't worry about Cousin Lin, madam. Jia Lian will take the doctor to see her every day. It's the other business that matters. Why not ask Aunt Xue over for a consultation this evening? Then we can settle everything tonight."

"You're right," the old lady and Lady Wang agreed. "But it's too late today. We'll go over tomorrow after breakfast."

The next day, Phoenix arrived after breakfast and went in to sound out Magic Jade. "Congratulations, Cousin Magic Jade," she greeted him gaily. "The master has chosen a lucky day for your wedding. Doesn't that make you happy?"

Magic Jade just grinned at her and nodded faintly.

"Your bride will be Cousin Lin. Are you glad?"

He burst out laughing, and this left her unclear about his mental state.

"The master says you can marry her if you're better, not if you go on acting like a fool," Phoenix warned.

"If anyone's a fool, it's you, not me!" he retorted seriously. Then he stood up and announced, "I'm going to see Cousin Lin to reassure her."

Phoenix promptly barred his way.

"Black Jade knows it already," Phoenix said, "as she's to marry you, she'll naturally feel too shy to see you."

"Will she see me after the wedding?" he asked.

Amused and disturbed by this question, Phoenix thought to herself, Aroma was right. At the mention of Black Jade, though he still talks like an idiot, he seems to understand what's going on. If he really comes to his senses and finds out that it isn't Black Jade, and that we've played a trick on him, then the fat will be in the fire.

Suppressing a smile Phoenix said, "If you're better she'll see you, but not if you act crazily."

"I've given her my heart," Magic Jade said. "When she comes, she's bound to bring it and put it back in my breast."

As this was madman's talk, Phoenix came out of Magic Jade's room and joined the old lady, who had been both amused and upset by their conversation that she could hear through the walls.

"I heard," said the old lady, "we can ignore him for now and leave Aroma to calm him down. Let's go."

That evening Aunt Xue came over. Having paid her respects to the old lady, she called on Lady Wang.

"Just now in the old lady's place," said Aunt Xue, "Magic Jade came out to pay his respects. He looked all right, simply a little thinner. Why do you speak as if it were so serious?"

"Actually it's nothing much," replied Phoenix. "But the old lady is worried. The master is going to a provincial post and may not be back for some years. Her hope is to have Magic Jade's wedding while the master is still here. First, to set his father's mind at rest, and second, in the hope that Cousin Precious Hairpin's golden necklace will bring Magic Jade good luck and overcome the evil influences so that he recovers."

Aunt Xue wanted the match but feared Hairpin might feel herself wronged. "That's all right," she said, "but we must think it out more carefully."

At this point Lovebird arrived, sent by the old lady to find out what they had decided. Though she realized that this was treating Precious Hairpin shabbily, Aunt Xue could hardly refuse as they were pressing so hard. She consented with a show of readiness. Lovebird went back to report this to the old lady, who was happy to learn about it. The old lady then sent Lovebird back to urge Aunt Xue to explain the situation to Precious Hairpin so that she would not feel unfairly treated. Aunt Xue agreed to this.

Having decided that Phoenix and her husband should act as go-betweens, the others left. Then Lady Wang and her sister sat up half the night talking.

The next day Jia Lian called on Aunt Xue.

"Tomorrow is a very auspicious day," he said, "so I've come to propose that we exchange gifts tomorrow. We only hope you won't be too critical about the arrangements, aunt." He handed her the Chinese lunar calendar on which was written the auspicious date of the wedding, and, after she said a few polite words of acceptance and nodded her consent, he hurried back to report this to the Lady Dowager. Lady Wang told Phoenix to take all the gifts to the old lady for inspection, and to ask Aroma to let Magic Jade know as well.

"Why go to all this bother?" Magic Jade chuckled. "We send things to Black Jade, then they send them back here again—our own folks doing the same thing back and forth!"

The Lady Dowager and Lady Wang remarked cheerfully after hearing Magic Jade's comment, "We say he's weak in the head, but today he's talking sense."

Phoenix then instructed the servants, "Don't take the gifts through the main gate, but use the old side gate in the garden. I'll be coming over presently. That gate is a good distance from the Bamboo Cottage. If people from other households notice you, warn them not to mention this to anyone else there."

The stewards went off to carry out the orders.

In the happy belief that he was to marry Black Jade, Magic Jade's health improved, though he still talked foolishly.

28/ Black Jade Dies of a Broken Heart

Although she took the medicine, Black Jade continued meanwhile to grow more ill with each passing day. Cuckoo and her other maids did their utmost to raise her spirits.

"Things have come to such a pass, miss, we must speak out," they said. "We know what's eating your heart out. But nothing unforeseen can possibly happen. If you don't believe us, just think of Magic Jade's health. He's so ill, how could he get married? Don't listen to silly rumors, miss, but rest quietly until you're better."

Black Jade smiled faintly without a word, then started coughing again and brought up more and more blood. Her maids saw her feebly struggling for breath, and nothing they could say would save her. They remained at her bedside weeping.

Each day Cuckoo and other maids went over three or four times to tell the old lady. But, as Lovebird had noticed that Black Jade had recently lost favor in her grandmother's eyes, she often neglected to pass on their messages. As the old lady was occupied with preparations for the approaching wedding, when she had no news of Black Jade she asked no questions.

Not one relative or servant now came to see Black Jade, and none even sent inquires. When she opened her eyes, there was nobody but Cuckoo and Snowswan in the room. Black Jade began to feel her end drawing near, and struggled to say a few words to Cuckoo. "Sister, you're the only one close to me. Over the years you have become a sister to me." Here she had to stop for breath.

Cuckoo felt pangs of pain, was reduced to tears, and could say nothing.

After a long silence, Black Jade panted, searching for breath between words, "Sister Cuckoo, I'm so uncomfortable lying down like this. Please help me up and sit next to me."

Cuckoo and Snowswan felt they could no longer deny her request. They propped her up on both sides with soft pillows, while Cuckoo sat by her on the bed to give further support. Though Black Jade was so weak that she felt the bed beneath her to be painfully hard, she struggled with all her remaining strength to stick it out. She told Snowswan to come closer.

"My poems..." Her voice failed, and she fought for breath again. Snowswan guessed that she wanted the manuscripts she had been going through a few days ago. She found them and gave them to her. Black Jade nodded, then glanced up at the case on a shelf. But this time the maid could not read her mind and stood there at a loss.

Black Jade stared at her now with feverish impatience. She began to cough again and brought up another mouthful of blood. Snowswan went to fetch some water, and Black Jade rinsed her mouth and spat into the spittoon. Cuckoo wiped Black Jade's lips with a handkerchief. Taking it, Black Jade pointed at the case, gasping for breath again so that she could not speak. Her eyes had closed.

"Better lie down, miss," urged Cuckoo.

When Black Jade shook her head, Cuckoo thought that she must want a handkerchief and told Snowswan to fetch a white silk one from the case. But at the sight of it, Black Jade put it aside.

"The one with the writing on..." she said, with a supreme effort. Cuckoo finally realized that she meant the handkerchief Magic Jade had sent her, on which she had written her own poems. She asked Snowswan to get it out and passed it to Black Jade.

"You must lie down and rest, miss!" Cuckoo begged her. "Why tire yourself out? You can look at it when you're better."

But, not even glancing at the poems, Black Jade tried with all her might to tear up the handkerchief. However, her trembling fingers lacked the strength.

Cuckoo knew that Magic Jade was the source of all this bitterness but dared not mention his name, begging instead, "There's no sense in working yourself up again!"

Black Jade nodded faintly and stuffed the handkerchief up her sleeve. Then she closed her eyes again and sat there breathing hard.

"Make a fire in the brazier," she murmured presently.

Thinking she was feeling cold, Cuckoo urged, "You'd better lie down, miss, and put on another cover. Charcoal fumes might be bad for you."

Because Black Jade shook her head, Snowswan had to light the brazier and put it on its stand on the floor. Black Jade made a sign with her hand, indicating that she wanted it moved up onto the bed. Snowswan had to do as she requested.

Black Jade bent forward, supported by Cuckoo's two hands. She pulled out the handkerchief, looked at the fire and nodded, then dropped the handkerchief on it. This shocked Cuckoo, who wanted to snatch it off but could not let go of her mistress. By now the handkerchief was burning. Then Black Jade dropped her manuscripts on the fire. Not caring whether she burned her hands or not, Snowswan snatched the manuscripts from the fire, threw them on the ground and trampled on them. It was too late. They had burned beyond recognition. Only a few charred fragments remained.

Black Jade closed her eyes and sank back, nearly knocking over Cuckoo. Her heart beating wildly, Cuckoo hastily asked Snowswan to help lay Black Jade down. It was too late at night to ask for help. Yet what if they called no one and their young mistress died during the night with only herself and some other junior maids around? The two of them passed a restless night.

Morning came at last, and Black Jade seemed a little more comfortable. But after breakfast she had a sudden relapse, coughing and vomiting again.

Cuckoo could see that Black Jade had reached a crisis. She left Snowswan and the others to handle the situation while she hurried over to report this to the old lady. However she found the Lady Dowager's place quiet and deserted, except for a few old nurses and some young maids doing odd jobs and left there to watch the house. When she asked where the old lady was, they gave evasive answers.

By now Cuckoo had more or less guessed the truth. How heartless and cruel these people are, she thought to herself, remembering that not a soul had called on Black Jade during the last few days. The more she thought it over, the more bitter she felt. In her indignation, she turned and left abruptly.

I'd like to see what Magic Jade looks like today, she fumed to herself. I wonder how he will manage to brazen it out in front of me. Just think that he is now openly doing this sort of thing. It shows that all men's hearts are as cold as ice. It really makes you gnash your teeth.

Brooding over the matter, she soon reached the Happy Red Residence Hall. The gate was closed and all inside was quiet. It occurred to her then that if he was getting married, he must have new bridal chambers. She wondered where they might be.

She was looking around when a page boy came flying along. She called to him to stop. The page walked over, grinning broadly. "What brings you here, sister?" he asked.

"I heard Master Magic Jade is getting married today so I came to watch the fun, but apparently the wedding's not here. When exactly is it to be?"

"I'll tell you in strict confidence, sister," he whispered. "But don't let Snowswan know about it. Our orders are not even to let you know. The wedding will take place this evening. Of course it won't be here. Well, is there anything you want me to do?"

"No, nothing, off you go."

The page boy darted off.

Cuckoo remained lost in thought until she remembered Black Jade. Was she still alive?

"Magic Jade!" she swore through clenched teeth, her eyes swimming with tears. "If she dies tomorrow, you'll get out of seeing her. But when you are happily married, and have your heart's desire, how are you going to face me?"

She walked on in tears towards the Bamboo Cottage. There she saw two young maids at the gate looking out nervously for her.

At sight of her one cried, "Here comes Sister Cuckoo!"

With a sinking heart she signaled to them to keep quiet. Hurrying to Black Jade's bedside, she found her red in the face, the internal heat from her liver having risen upwards to inflame her cheeks. This was a dangerous symptom, and Cuckoo called Black Jade's old wet nurse to come and take a look. One glance was enough to reduce this old woman to tears.

The nurse's helpless reaction threw Cuckoo into a tizzy until she thought of someone else to turn to. She sent a young maid quickly in search of her. It was Li Wan. As a widow, it was out of the question for her to attend Magic Jade's wedding.

Li Wan was correcting a poem for Jia Lan when a young maid burst in. "Madam!" she cried. "It looks as if Miss Black Jade is dying! Everyone over there is in tears."

Li Wan was horrified. Without a word she hurried out. On the way she reflected tearfully on the fact that the poor girl was fated to die so young and to be buried so far from home. She thought to herself that she hadn't wanted to visit Black Jade because of Phoenix's underhanded plan to fob off a different bride on Magic Jade. So, she said to herself, I've let my cousin down. How tragic that is.

Now, reaching the gate of the Bamboo Cottage, Li Wan was unnerved not to hear a sound inside. Perhaps she's already dead and they've finished lamenting her, she thought as she hurried inside. She wondered if they had the clothes, bedding, and shroud ready.

At the sight of her, a young maid by the door of the inner room announced, "Here's Madam Zhu."

Cuckoo hastily came out as Li Wan walked in. "How is she?" Li Wan asked urgently.

Cuckoo, choked with sobs, could only point at Black Jade.

The maid's grief distressed Li Wan even more. Asking no more questions she went over to look at the dying girl, who was already past speaking. She called her softly twice. Black Jade opened her eyes slowly and seemed to recognize her. She was still breathing faintly, but her eyelids and lips could only make a trembling suggestion of a movement. She couldn't utter a word or shed a tear drop.

Turning away, Li Wan noted that Cuckoo had vanished. She asked Snowswan where she was. "In the outer room," was the answer.

Li Wan hurried out and found Cuckoo lying on the empty bed there, her face yellowish pale, tears flowing so fast from her closed eyes that a big patch of the silk-bordered, flowered mattress was all wet.

"Silly girl!" scolded Li Wan. "This is no time for weeping. Hurry up and get Miss Lin's grave clothes ready. How long will you wait to dress her? Are you going to expose an unmarried girl to start out naked for the other world?"

At this, Cuckoo broke down and sobbed bitterly. Li Wan, though also weeping, was impatient. Wiping her own eyes, she patted the maid on the shoulder. "Good child, your crying is driving me mad! Prepare her things quickly before it's too late."

Li Wan was startled just then by the arrival of Patience. Bursting in on this scene Patience stood rooted to the spot, speechless.

"Why aren't you over there now?" asked Li Wan. "What brings you here?" At this point Steward Lin's wife also joined them.

Patience said, "Our mistress was worried and sent me to have a look. But as you're here, madam, I'll tell her that she need only attend to affairs over there."

Li Wan nodded.

"I'll go in to see Miss Black Jade too," added Patience, already in tears as she entered the inner room.

"You've come in the nick of time," Li Wan told Mrs. Lin. "Go out quickly and get some steward to prepare Black Jade's funeral details. When everything's ready he's to report to me. There's no need to go over there."

"Yes, madam," replied Lin's wife, but made no move to go.

"Well? Is there something else?" asked Li Wan.

"Mrs. Jia Lian and the old lady," replied the steward's wife, "have decided that they need Cuckoo to help out there."

Before Li Wan could answer, Cuckoo put in, "Please don't wait for me, Mrs. Lin. When she's dead, of course we'll leave her. They needn't be in such a hurry." Embarrassed by her own outburst, she went on more mildly, "Besides, since I'm nursing an invalid here, I'm not clean. Black Jade is still breathing and wants me from time to time."

Li Wan helped her out by explaining, "It's true. The affinity between Black Jade and Cuckoo must have been predestined. I can see that they can't be separated for a second."

Mrs. Lin was somewhat offended by Cuckoo's reply, but only said, "It's quite all right for Cuckoo to talk like that. But what am I to say to the old lady? And could I repeat this to Madam Phoenix?"

At these words, Patience came out wiping her eyes. "Repeat what to Madam Phoenix?" she wanted to know.

Mrs. Lin explained the situation, and Patience lowered her head to think it over. "In that case," she suggested, "let Snowswan go instead."

Patience had told Snowswan to come out. She hastily smoothed her hair and, on Patience's instructions, changed into colorful clothes, then went off with Mrs. Lin.

That evening Black Jade recovered consciousness and feebly opened her eyes. She seemed to want something to drink. Since only Li Wan and Cuckoo were present, Cuckoo brought her a bowl of pear juice and dried longan syrup and gave her two or three sips with a small silver spoon. Black

Jade closed her eyes to rest for a while. Li Wan thought that the end would not come to Black Jade for a few hours. She returned briefly to Sweet Rice Village to see to her own affairs.

Black Jade then opened her eyes again. Seeing no one in the room but Cuckoo, her old wet nurse and a few other maids, she clutched Cuckoo's hand and said with a great effort, "I'm finished. You have served me for several years. I had hoped that the two of us could always stay together. But now..." She broke off, panting for breath, and closed her eyes in exhaustion.

After a long pause, Black Jade continued again, "Sister! I have no dear ones here. My body is pure. Promise me you'll ask them to bury me at home."

She closed her eyes again and was silent. Her grip tightened still more on Cuckoo's hand as she panted silently, breathing out more than she breathed in at her last gasp.

This caused Cuckoo great alarm, and she sent at once for Li Wan. Tanchun happened to arrive at that moment.

"Look at Miss Lin, miss!" whispered Cuckoo, her tears falling like rain. Tanchun came over and felt Black Jade's hand. It was already cold, and her eyes were glazed and lifeless. Tanchun and Cuckoo wept as they asked for water to be brought and for Black Jade to be washed. Then Li Wan hurried in. The three of them looked at each other, but were too shocked to say a word.

They were washing Black Jade when she raised a sudden cry, "Magic Jade, Magic Jade! How could you..."

Those were her last words. She broke out in a cold sweat. Cuckoo and the others, holding her as she sweated, felt her body grow colder and colder. Finally Black Jade's eyes turned up.

Her sweet soul had gone with the wind.
Her sorrow but a dream, drifting into the night!

29/ Precious Hairpin Goes through Her Wedding Ceremony

It was in the very same hour when Magic Jade and Precious Hairpin were married that Black Jade breathed her last. Now, though the loss of his jade had caused Magic Jade's mental disorder, the news that he was to marry Black Jade seemed to him a most wonderful thing. He could hardly wait to go through with his wedding and see Black Jade again. Beside himself with joy, he behaved quite differently from when he had gone mad, although he still sometimes talked nonsense.

Magic Jade, seated in Lady Wang's room, was pressing Aroma to help him into his wedding clothes. He was also watching busy Phoenix and Madam You as he longed for the auspicious hour to arrive.

"Black Jade is only coming from the garden," he said to Aroma. "Why should it take her so long?"

Suppressing a smile, Aroma answered, "She has to wait for the appointed hour."

A big sedan chair now entered the courtyard and the family musicians went out to meet the bride, while twelve pairs of maids filed in two rows holding palace lanterns—a brand new and distinctive sight. The bride was invited to step out of the bridal sedan chair, and Magic Jade saw a maid with a red sash help her out. The bride's face was veiled according to ancient Chinese customs. Another maid assisting the bride was Snowswan.

Why is Snowswan helping her and not Cuckoo, he wondered. Then he told himself that this must be because Black Jade brought Snowswan with her from her home town when she first arrived at the Honored Mansion. Cuckoo, however, was one of our household and so naturally she needn't have brought her. Reasoning in this way, he could almost see tne face of Black Jade beneath the veil.

The Master of Ceremonies announced the wedding procedures. Bride and bridegroom knelt down before Heaven and Earth, then invited the old lady to come out and receive four bows from each of them. After that, they bowed to Jia Zheng and Lady Wang. Next they ascended into the hall and paid their respects to each other before being ushered into the bridal chamber. Here they were made to sit on the bridal bed in accordance with the old rule of Jinling.

Jia Zheng had never really believed that this wedding would cure Magic Jade, but he had to go along with his mother's decision. Today, however, he was pleased because Magic Jade looked as if he had really recovered.

After the bride sat down on the bridal bed, she had to be unveiled. To be on the safe side, Phoenix had earlier asked the old lady and Lady Wang there to keep an eye on things.

Magic Jade at this point foolishly stepped over to the bride. "Are you better, dear cousin?" he asked. "It's quite a long time since I last saw you. Why keep your face covered with that silly thing?"

But, as he was ready to take off the veil, the old lady broke out in a cold sweat. Magic Jade hesitated, thinking to himself that Black Jade was very sensitive and so he mustn't offend her. He waited until he felt he could wait no longer, then stepped forward and removed the veil. The bridesmaid took it away, and at the same time Snowswan withdrew and Oriole came in to wait on her young mistress.

Magic Jade looked at his bride and could not believe his eyes. The bride appeared to be Precious Hairpin. He held the lamp up to her face to get a better look and rubbed his eyes. There was no doubt about it. It was Precious Hairpin!

Magic Jade was stupefied by the discovery and the fact that Snowswan had disappeared and Oriole had taken her place. At a loss, he thought he must be dreaming. He stood there in a daze until one of the maids took the lamp from his hand and made him sit down. Staring vacantly, he uttered not a word.

The old lady, afraid he had lost his senses again, took charge of him herself, while Phoenix and Madam You led Precious Hairpin to the inner room to rest. At that moment Hairpin could do nothing but remain silent, lowering her head.

Soon Magic Jade calmed down sufficiently to notice the presence of his grandmother and mother. "Where am I?" he whispered to Aroma. "Is this a dream?"

"This is your wedding day," she answered. "Don't let the Master hear you talking such nonsense. He's just outside."

"Who's that beautiful lady sitting there?" he asked, pointing inside.

Aroma put a hand to her mouth to hide her laughter. "That's your bride," she answered, "the new Mrs. Magic Jade."

The other maids also turned away, unable to contain their laughter.

"Don't be so silly," he said. "What do you mean, Mrs. Magic Jade? Who is Mrs. Magic Jade?"

"Miss Precious Hairpin."

"Then where is Black Jade?"

"The Master decided you should marry Miss Hairpin, so why ask in that foolish way about Miss Black Jade?"

"But I saw her just a moment ago," Magic Jade said, "and Snowswan, too. How can you say they're not here? What game are you all playing?"

Phoenix stepped forward to whisper, "Miss Hairpin is sitting in the inner room; don't talk foolishly. If you offend her the old lady won't like it."

This bewildered Magic Jade still more. Already deranged, after the mysterious goings-on of that night he knew even less what to think. Ignoring all else, he just clamored to go and find Cousin Black Jade.

The old lady and the other ladies tried to pacify him, but he would not listen to reason. And, as Precious Hairpin was inside, they could not speak out plainly. Indeed, they knew that explanations were useless now, since his wits were wandering again. They lit benzoin incense to calm him and made him lie down. No one made a sound and, after a little while, he fell into a deep sleep.

As for Jia Zheng, being outside, he had no knowledge of these happenings. In fact he felt relieved by what he had seen. As the next day was the auspicious day for him to start his journey, he too rested for a while before receiving the congratulations of those who had come to bid him farewell.

The next morning Jia Zheng bowed farewell in the ancestral temple, then went to take leave of his mother. The younger male relatives and his old friends accompanied him three miles beyond the capital, then bade him farewell.

Magic Jade returned to his room after seeing his father, more dizzy, confused, and listless than before. Without eating his meal he drifted off to sleep. Doctors were called in to examine him but their remedies proved ineffective. Magic Jade could not even recognize those around him, although he looked normal enough when he was helped to sit up. And this state of affairs continued for several days.

The ninth day after the wedding now came. According to tradition, a newly-married couple should visit the bride's family on that day. If Magic Jade and his wife did not do this, Aunt Xue might well feel slighted. But if they went for this visit with Magic Jade in his present state, whatever would people say?

Knowing that his illness was caused by his attachment to Black Jade, the old lady would have liked to make a clean breast of it and tell Aunt Xue about how they had tricked Magic Jade into the marriage. But she feared that this would cause offense and ill-feeling. So she had to ask the servants to support him in the visit to the bride's family and attendant ceremonies.

Precious Hairpin now knew the full truth, and in her own mind blamed her mother for making such a foolish decision. Yet now that things had gone this far, she could say nothing. Aunt Xue herself, when she saw Magic Jade's pitiful condition, began to regret having ever made the decision to have her daughter marry him. Thus she could only bring herself to play a perfunctory part in the ceremonies.

When the couple returned home, Magic Jade's condition seemed to grow worse. The next day he could not even sit up, and he began to waste away day by day until he could not even take medicine or water. In panic, Aunt Xue and the others searched everywhere for good doctors, but not one was able to diagnose his illness.

One day when Magic Jade was left alone with Aroma, he called her over to his side and taking her by the hand said tearfully, "Tell me, how Cousin Hairpin came to be here? I remember my father choosing Cousin Black Jade to marry me, so how did she get driven out by Cousin Hairpin? Why should she force her way in here? And what news have you got of Black Jade? Is she crying her heart out?"

Aroma did not dare tell him the truth, but only said, "Black Jade is ill."

"I must go and see her," insisted Magic Jade.

He tried to get up, but after going several days without food and drink he was too weak to move.

"I know I'm going to die," he said. "There's something on my mind, something very important. I beg you to pass it on to the old lady. If I'm going to die, Cousin Black Jade will be sobbing herself to death, too. If we die apart, that'll make more trouble for you. So why not turn out a spare room and move the two of us there? You can nurse us both together while we're still living, and when we're dead you can lay us together. Please do this for me, for friendship's sake."

Aroma found this plea disturbing, comical, and touching. At that moment Precious Hairpin happened to be passing with Oriole. She also heard every word of it.

"Why talk in that unlucky way instead of resting well so as to recover?" Precious Hairpin asked, as she entered the room. "You've always been the old lady's favorite, and now she's over eighty. Though she's not expecting you to win her honors, if you turn out well that will please her, and the pains she's taken over you won't be wasted. As for your mother, surely she's given her heart's blood to bring you up, and if you die young, just think how she will suffer. As for me, I may be ill-fated, but you don't need to make a widow of me.

Because of the three of us, even if you want to die Heaven won't allow it! After four or five days of proper rest and care, your illness will pass, your strength will be restored and you will be yourself again."

This silenced Magic Jade for some minutes. Finally he gave a silly laugh and said, "After not talking with me for so long, here you are lecturing me. You are wasting your breath."

"Let me tell you the truth," Hairpin continued. "While you were in a coma for two days, Cousin Black Jade died."

Magic Jade sat up abruptly. "It can't be true!"

"Of course it is," said Hairpin. "I wouldn't say such a fearful thing if it wasn't."

Magic Jade burst out sobbing and fell back on his pillows. All before him was pitch dark. Soon he passed out.

Precious Hairpin knew that his breakdown was due to his longing for Black Jade, the loss of his jade being only secondary. She wanted to take the opportunity of breaking the news to him of Black Jade's death in the hope of cutting off his attachment once and for all, so as to end his torment and bring him to his senses. She thought that this was the way he might be cured.

The old lady and Lady Wang, not knowing Hairpin's real motive, blamed her for lack of caution. However, when Magic Jade came to, they felt relieved and at once sent for Doctor Bi from the outer study to examine him.

"Strange!" observed the physician after feeling his pulse. "His pulse is now steady and there is no sign of melancholia. We'll give him a restorative tomorrow. There's hope for a cure." Then the doctor left and the others retreated, their minds more at ease.

After a long while Magic Jade began to behave normally again. He insisted on going to the Bamboo Cottage. They had to send for a bamboo chair and help him onto it. Then they set off, with the old lady and Lady Wang leading the way.

As soon as Magic Jade arrived at the Bamboo Cottage, he began to think back to his visits there before he was ill. The cottage remained, but its young mistress was gone forever. Magic Jade gave way to a storm of grief. How close they had been, yet today they were parted by death. He felt his heart would break.

Alarmed by his frenzied agony, all tried hard to comfort him, but he was already beside himself with weeping. All they could do was help him lie down and rest. Precious Hairpin and the others who had come with him also mourned bitterly.

Magic Jade insisted on seeing Cuckoo to ask her what Black Jade's last words had been. Cuckoo had a deep grudge against him, but his present misery softened her heart and, in the presence of the old lady and Lady Wang, she dared take no liberties. So Cuckoo reported in detail how her young mistress had fallen ill again, how she had burned his handkerchief and her love poems, and what her last words had been.

Magic Jade wailed until he was hoarse and breathless. Tanchun seized this chance to repeat Black Jade's dying request to have her coffin taken back to the south, reducing the old lady and Lady Wang to tears once more. It was Phoenix with her persuasive tongue who succeeded in consoling them a little and in urging them to return home. When Magic Jade refused, his grandmother had to force him to go back to his room.

Knowing that Magic Jade's grief must run its course, Precious Hairpin made some cutting remarks instead of trying to console him. Magic Jade swallowed back his tears in order not to stir up her jealousy. That night passed peacefully.

The next morning, when others came to see how he was, they found him very weak but less distracted. They nursed him devotedly till he slowly recovered.

30/ Imperial Guards Raid the Peaceful Mansion

One day not long after Jia Zheng was recalled to the capital for demotion, he was entertaining his guests in the hall when in burst the chief steward. "The Chief of the Imperial Guards and several of his officers are here to see you, sir," the steward announced.

Since Jia Zheng had no dealings with the Chief, he could not understand why he should have come uninvited. He was thinking this over when Jia Lian urged, "Better go at once, uncle, before they all come in."

Jia Lian and others hastily prepared to meet the Chief of Imperial Guards. The Chief, smiling, said not a word as he walked straight into the hall. Behind him were five or six of his officers, only a few of whom the guests recognized. None of these answered their greetings.

Forcing a smile, Jia Zheng was about to make conversation when a flustered servant announced the arrival of the Prince. Before Jia Zheng could hasten to meet him, the Prince had entered.

The Chief of Imperial Guards stepped forward at once to salute the Prince, then said to his officers, "Since His Highness has arrived, you gentlemen can take runners to guard the front and back gates."

The officers assented and went out.

Knowing that this order spelt trouble, Jia Zheng fell on his knees to welcome the Prince, who helped him to his feet with a smile.

"We wouldn't presume to intrude without special reason," said the Prince. "We have come to announce an Imperial Decree to Lord Jia She."

After hearing this, Jia Zheng, Jia She, and their households became livid and trembled with fear. Meanwhile runners swarmed in to guard all the doors, so that no one, not master or servant, could stir from the place.

The Prince proclaimed slowly, "His Majesty has ordered me to bring the Chief of the Imperial Guards to search Jia She's property."

At this Jia She and the rest prostrated themselves on the ground.

The Prince continued, "Hear the Imperial Decree: Jia She intrigued with provincial officials and abused his power to bully the weak, showing himself unworthy of our favor and discrediting his ancestors good name. His hereditary rank is hereby abolished."

The Chief of Imperial Guards thundered, "Arrest Jia She! Keep guard over the others." Then he told his men to dispatch officers and runners to search the different apartments and draw up an inventory of what they found. Everyone in the household exchanged alarmed glances, while the runners gleefully rubbed their hands and began to ransack the place.

We will turn now to the ladies' feast that was taking place in the Lady Dowager's quarters. The fun was at its height when one of Lady Xing's maids came rushing in crying, "Ladies! We're done for! A whole lot of robbers have come, all in boots and official caps. They're opening cases, overturning crates, and ransacking the whole place!"

The old lady and the others had not recovered from this shock before Patience, her hair hanging loose, dashed in. "We're ruined," she wailed. "I was having lunch when some prince came to raid our house. I nearly died of fright. Before I could go in to fetch any valuables, a band of men drove me out. You'd better make haste to get together the clothes and things you need."

Lady Xing and Lady Wang were beside themselves with fright, not knowing what to do. Phoenix, who had listened wide-eyed, collapsed in a faint. The old lady was crying with terror, unable to utter a word.

Jia Lian feared that the news of Jia She's arrest by the Imperial Guards might make the old lady and Lady Xing die of fright. Thus, when he came to see them, he withheld it for the time being and went back to his own quarters without giving them the news.

Once over the threshold, he saw that all their cases and wardrobes had been opened and rifled. He stood speechless in consternation, shedding tears, till he heard his name being called and had to go out. Jia Zheng was there with two officers drawing up an inventory. Separate lists were made of all the furnishings and the mansions conferred on the Duke of Rongguo. The title deeds of houses and land and the bonds of the family slaves were taken to be sealed up.

Jia Lian, listening at one side, was puzzled not to hear his own property listed.

The Prince said, "Among the property confiscated are some IOU's that are definitely usurious. Whose are they? Your Lordship must tell the truth."

Jia Zheng knelt down and kowtowed. "I'm guilty of never having managed the household affairs, and that is the truth," he said, "I know nothing about such transactions. Your Highness will have to ask my nephew Jia Lian."

Jia Lian hastily stepped forward and knelt to report, "Since those documents were found in my humble house, how can I deny knowledge of them? I only beg Your Highness to be lenient to my uncle, who knew nothing about this."

The Prince said, "As your father has already been found guilty, your cases can be dealt with together. Very well then, let a guard be kept over Jia Lian. The rest of the household can return to their different quarters. Lord Jia Zheng, you must wait prudently for a further decree. We'll go now to report to His Majesty, leaving officers and runners here to keep watch."

By now Jia Zheng felt slightly calmer, although he was still dazed.

Jia Lan suggested, "Grandfather, won't you go in to see the old lady first? Then we can send for news of the East Mansion."

Jia Zheng entered his mother's room, where one and all were in tears. Lady Wang, Magic Jade, and others had gathered silently around the old lady, tears streaming down their cheeks. Lady Xing was shaken by sobs. At his arrival they all expressed relief.

"The master has come back safely," they told the old lady. "Don't worry any more, madam."

The Lady Dowager, gasping, feebly opened her eyes and quavered, "My son, I never thought to see you again." She then burst out weeping and all the others joined in. Jia Zheng, fearing these transports of grief might be too much for his mother, held back his tears.

"Set your heart at rest, madam," he urged. "It is a serious matter, but his Gracious Majesty and the Prince have shown us the kindest consideration. The Elder Master has been taken into custody for the time being. But once the matter is cleared up, the Emperor will show more clemency. And our property is not being confiscated."

Jia She's arrest greatly distressed the old lady, and Jia Zheng had to do his best to comfort her.

Jia Zheng was now on tenterhooks, waiting for the Emperor's next decree. A servant outside announced a messenger from the court. He went out at once and saw that it was the Prince of Baijing's chamberlain.

"Good news, sir," were the chamberlain's first words.

Jia Zheng thanked him and offered him a seat. "What instructions has His Highness for me?" he asked.

"You are to retain your post in the Ministry of Works. Regarding the family property, only Jia She's share is to be confiscated. The rest will be restored to you and you are enjoined to work well. As for those promissory notes, our master has been ordered to examine them. All those that are at usurious, illegal rates of interest are to be confiscated, according to regulations. Those on which the standard rates are charged are to be returned to you, together with your title deeds. Jia Lian is dismissed from his post, but will be released without further punishment."

Jia Zheng rose to kowtow his thanks to the Emperor, then bowed his thanks to the Prince.

Jia Lian came back a short time later. And Jia Zheng now reproached him with tears in his eyes. "Of course you could hardly keep a check on your father," Jia Zheng said, "but who is responsible for this usury? Such conduct is most unbefitting a family like ours. Now that those notes of yours have been confiscated, the financial loss is of secondary importance. But think of the damage to our reputation!"

Jia Lian fell on his knees to reply, "In running the household I never try to act with selfish interests. All our income and expenditures were entered in the accounts by the Chief Steward, and you can check on him by asking him, sir. In the last few years, our expenditure has exceeded our income; and I haven't made good the difference. There are certain deficits in the accounts. If you ask the mistress, sir, she will confirm this. As for those loans, I myself have no idea where the money came from. We'll have to find out from the stewards."

"From what you've just said," Jia Zheng replied, "you don't even know what is going on in your own apartments, to say nothing about family affairs. Well, I won't cross-examine you now. You got off lightly, but shouldn't you now go to find out about the cases of your father and Cousin Jia Zhen?"

Wronged as he felt, Jia Lian assented with tears and went away.

Heaving sigh after sigh, Jia Zheng thought to himself that as far as he could see, none of his sons or nephews amounted to anything. Merciful Heaven, he wondered, why should the Jia family be ruined like this? Though His Gracious Majesty had shown extraordinary compassion by restoring his property, he didn't know how he, alone, could meet the two households' expenses.

The next morning Jia Zheng went to court to express his gratitude for the Imperial favor. Then he called on both princes to offer his thanks and to beg them to intervene on behalf of his brother and nephew. After they had agreed to do this, he went to enlist the help of other colleagues.

Since all the estates of the Peaceful Mansion had been confiscated and all its bond servants registered and taken away, the Lady Dowager had to send carriages to fetch Madam You and her daughter-in-law. Alas for the Peaceful Mansion, once so grand. All that remained of it was these two ladies and the concubines.

As for the expenses incurred by Jia She, Jia Zhen, and Jia Rong, who were now in prison, the accountants office was quite unable to meet them. Phoenix had no property left; Jia Lian was heavily in debt; while Jia Zheng had no gift for family affairs. All he could do was send stewards in secret to raise a few thousand ounces of silver by the sale of certain country estates, thus defraying the prison expenses.

To return to the old lady.

Lady Wang had just brought Magic Jade and Precious Hairpin to pay their evening respects. The old lady's grief set the three of them crying, as well. The saddest of all was Precious Hairpin as she reflected on the fact that her brother, Xue Pan, was imprisoned and she didn't know whether his death sentence would be commuted or not. And though her parents-in-law were not in trouble, the Jia family was declining, while Magic Jade was still deranged and showed no sign of improvement. Anxiety over her future made her weep more bitterly than the old lady or Lady Wang. Her grief even affected Magic Jade.

He mused that his grandmother couldn't be at peace in her old age, and all the girls had scattered like clouds before the wind. After Black Jade's death he'd felt gloomy, yet, with Precious Hairpin at his side, he couldn't often cry. The sight of her now so overcome with grief was more than he could bear. He broke down and sobbed.

At this, all the maids who had their own cares started sobbing, too. The wailing in the room grew louder and louder until the women servants keeping watch outside hurried off in alarm to report this to the master.

Jia Zheng was sitting gloomily in his study when this message was announced. He hurried over frantically and, while still at a distance, heard the whole household crying. This convinced him that the old lady must be dying. Running in distractedly, he was relieved to see her sitting there sobbing.

"When the old lady is upset, the rest of you should comfort her," he chided the others. "Why are you all weeping too?"

They hastily dried their tears and stared blankly at him. Jia Zheng stepped forward to console his mother, then once more briefly reprimanded the rest.

Some days later Jia Zheng was thinking things over in his study when one of his men rushed in. "Master, you are wanted at once at court for questioning," the servant said.

With some trepidation, Jia Zheng listened to the edict.

The Prince of Baijing proclaimed the edict: "Jia She is to be shown leniency and sent to the frontier to expiate his crime. Jia Zhen deserves harsh punishment, but in view of his descent from a meritorious minister we will forbear from inflicting punishment and in our clemency will revoke his hereditary title and send him to serve at the coast to expiate his crime. Jia Rong, being young and not involved, is to be released. Since Jia Zheng has undeniably worked diligently and prudently for many years outside the capital, his reprehensible mismanagement of his household is condoned."

Jia Zheng, moved to tears of gratitude, kowtowed repeatedly while listening to this edict. He hurried home to reassure his mother. He hastened to the old lady's side to explain to her all the details of his pardon. Although this set her mind at rest, she could not help grieving over the loss of the two hereditary titles and the banishment of Jia She and Jia Zhen to such distant regions. As for Lady Xing and Madam You, this news reduced them to tears.

The old lady's heart ached for them. She asked Jia Zheng, "Can't your elder brother and Jia Zhen come home now that they've been sentenced? And as Jia Rong is not involved, shouldn't he be released as well?"

"According to the rules, elder brother can't come home," he told her. "But I've asked people to put in a good word so that he and Jia Zhen can come back to get their luggage, and the ministry has agreed to this. I expect Jia Rong will return with his grand uncle and father. Please don't worry, madam. I shall see to this."

"These years I've grown so old and useless that I haven't checked up on our family affairs," she said. "Do you know how much is left in our West Mansion's treasury? And how much land in our eastern estates? You must give them a few thousand ounces of silver for their journeys."

This put Jia Zheng in a dilemma. He answered, "I must tell you that yesterday I looked into the matter. Our treasury is empty. Not only is all the silver gone but we have debts outside, too. We've already used up next year's rent from our eastern estates, so we can't raise any sums there for the time being. We'll just have to sell those clothes and trinkets which, thanks to Imperial favor, weren't confiscated so as to cover the traveling expenses of elder brother and Jia Zhen. As to what to live on ourselves, we can worry about that later."

At this news the old lady kept shedding tears. "Is our family reduced to this?" she exclaimed. "Do you mean to say we won't be able to manage even for a couple of years?"

"If we'd kept those two hereditary stipends," Jia Zheng said in tears, "we could still maneuver outside. But whom can we turn to now to help us?"

The old lady was distraught when Jia She, Jia Zhen, and Jia Rong came in together to pay their respects to her. At the sight of them she clasped Jia She with one hand, Jia Zhen with the other, and sobbed. Her grief made them blush for shame and fall to their knees.

"We are degenerates who have discredited the honors accorded to our ancestors, and brought you grief, madam," they said tearfully.

All those present seeing this gave way to weeping. Jia Zheng had to say a few words to cheer them up.

After Jia She and Jia Zhen had withdrawn with Jia Zheng, they deplored their past excesses and spoke with tears of their grief at parting. For, though their banishment was less harsh than service in the army, the exiles might never again see their families.

The old lady made Lady Xing, Lady Wang, Lovebird, and the others open up their cases and take out all the things she had stored away since coming here as a bride. Then she summoned Jia She, Jia Zheng, and Jia Zhen to divide the belongings.

Impressed by the old lady's sound judgment and fair treatment, Jia Zheng and the rest knelt down and said, with tears, "You are so advanced in years, and your son and grandsons have failed in their duty to you. Your goodness to us makes us doubly ashamed."

"Stop talking nonsense," she answered. "Our household is not too large now, so we can manage with just a few servants. Tell the stewards to summon them all. The maids should be reassigned, too, and some of them married off, some given their freedom. As for our other estates, let Jia Lian investigate to see which should be sold and which kept. We must stop putting on an empty show."

Jia Zheng had no head for family affairs and readily agreed to all her proposals. He reflected that the old lady was certainly a good manager.

"I haven't much else," she continued. "What there is can be spent on my funeral, and anything left over can go to my maids."

31/ The Death of the Lady Dowager and Phoenix

The Lady Dowager was now ill, and her illness grew worse with each passing day. No medicine proved effective, and she developed a bad case of diarrhea. Worried because she was not likely to recover, Jia Zheng sent to ask leave from his post. He and his wife attended the Lady Dowager day and night.

One day they saw an old woman peeping through the door. Lady Wang asked a maid to see who she was. It turned out that she was one of the serving women who had accompanied Yingchun to the Sun family.

"What brings you here?" Lady Wang asked.

"My young lady's dying, Madam. The day before yesterday they had a row and she cried all night long. Yesterday she was choking, her throat blocked up with phlegm, yet they wouldn't get a doctor. Today she's worse!"

"The old lady's ill," said Lady Wang. "Don't kick up such a noise."

Since the Lady Dowager was lying there quietly, she had overheard the conversation. "Is Yingchun dying?" the old lady asked.

"No, madam," said Lady Wang, "these women are all making a fuss about nothing. She says Yingchun hasn't been well the last couple of days and may take some time to recover. They want us to get her a doctor."

"My doctor's a good one," said the Lady Dowager. "Have him fetched at once."

Lady Wang asked the maid to send the woman to report this to Lady Xing.

Just as the serving woman reached Lady Xing's apartments, word came that Yingchun was dead. Her mother wept. In Jia She's absence, she had to send Jia Lian to the Sun family to find out the situation. As the old lady was at death's door the others could not leave her, but had to let the Sun family arrange the funeral in a perfunctory fashion.

The Lady Dowager, failing from day to day, longed to see her granddaughters and nieces one more time.

Jia Zheng quietly drew Jia Lian aside and whispered some instructions. Jia Lian assented softly. He then went out to summon the stewards. "The old lady's sinking fast," he said, "you're to send at once to make the necessary preparations."

Then Jia Lian went back to the old lady's place and whispered to Jia Zheng that all the preparations had been made. Jia Zheng nodded.

At this point the doctor was announced. Jia Lian invited the doctor in to feel the old lady's pulse. After some time he withdrew and quietly said to Jia Lian, "The old lady's pulse is very weak. Be prepared."

Jia Lian understood and told Lady Wang, who signaled to Lovebird and, when she came over, sent her off to make ready the garments in which to lay out the old lady. At this point the Lady Dowager opened her eyes and asked for some tea.

Forced to humor her, they brought it quickly. She took two sips, then said, "I want to sit up."

The maid gently propped her up, and they saw that she did look better. But her face was flushed, a sign, as Jia Zheng knew, that the end was near. He lost no time in offering her some ginseng broth, but already her jaws were locked and her eyes closed.

Lady Wang and Precious Hairpin stepped forward and gently propped her up, while Lady Xing and Phoenix changed her clothes. Now they heard a rattling in her throat, and a smile overspread her face as she breathed her last—at the age of eighty-three. The women hastily laid her on the bier.

Jia Zheng and the other men knelt down in the outer room. Lady Xing and the ladies knelt inside, and together they lamented the death of the Lady Dowager. The family and the domestics lost no time in putting on mourning.

Jia Zheng reported his mother's death, and the Ministry of Rites reported it to the Emperor. In view of the Jia family's past achievements and the fact that the old lady was the Imperial Consort's grandmother, His Majesty bestowed on Jia Zheng one thousand ounces of silver and ordered the Ministry of Rites to take charge of the sacrifice.

The stewards spread word of the old lady's death. Though the Jia family had declined the silver, when their relatives and friends saw the favor shown them by the Emperor, they all came to offer their condolences.

Lovebird wept so bitterly that she fainted away. They raised her up and massaged her until she came around. After the bout of weeping, Lovebird thought of how she had been with the old lady all her life and had found no other place for herself. She didn't think much of the elder mistress or her husband, the elder master, who was presently away from home. She was particularly concerned because the second master was the one who had let things slide. She thought to herself that all the servants would now be at the mercy of these people she thought so little of. They'll be able to decide whether to make us concubines or to marry us off to some servants, she concluded. She decided that she couldn't stand that. Better die and be done with it!

This train of thought enabled an evil spirit to take possession of her and standing up, weeping, she opened her dressing case to take out the lock of hair that she had cut off when she swore never to leave the old lady's service. Tucking it inside her tunic, she undid her sash and looped it over the beam. She made haste to close the door, moved over a footstool and stood on it. Then she tied the sash into a noose, slipped it round her throat, and kicked the stool away. Thus, alas, she strangled to death, and her sweet spirit took flight.

Everyone in the house praised the honorable death of Lovebird. All shed tears for this devoted maid of the old lady. And because Lovebird had died for the Lady Dowager, Jia

Zheng called for incense, lighted three sticks, and bowed before her coffin.

"Since she immolated herself she can't be treated as a bond maid," he said. "All you youngsters should pay homage to her."

Magic Jade was only too glad to comply. He came over and kowtowed respectfully. Precious Hairpin went up to the coffin and poured a libation of wine over it, tears flowing down her cheeks. After that she bowed several times with clasped hands and wept bitterly. Jia Zheng approved of their conduct.

They agreed to leave Phoenix and Xichun in charge of the house while the rest joined the funeral procession. Then, while Jia Zheng and others were participating in the funeral procession, a gang of robbers broke into the house and ransacked the old lady's rooms. The next day Jia Rong made an urgent report to Jia Zheng. He was at a loss as to what to do.

Lady Xing and Lady Wang also heard the bad news. They were scared out of their wits. They could do nothing but shed tears over this sudden robbery. Jia Lian was even more worried, since he had to pay back the debts and routine expenses. Finally he made up a report of all the things that were missing and sent some of his men to the courts with the report.

After the death of the Lady Dowager, Phoenix's own illness went from bad to worse with each passing day. Jia Lian had, by now, lost his affection for her and showed almost no concern for her health. Patience tried to comfort her mistress, but Lady Xing and Lady Wang, who had returned several days earlier, merely sent servants to ask after her health, instead of coming themselves. This added to Phoenix's wretchedness. And when Jia Lian came home, he never seemed to have any kind word for her. Phoenix's sole wish, by now, was to die and be done with it.

As Patience was massaging Phoenix's back, Jia Lian came in. After a cursory glance at the bed, he entered the inner room without a word and plumped himself down, glowering.

Then he called for Patience. "Isn't your mistress taking her medicine?" he asked.

"What if she isn't?"

"How should I know?" he retorted. "Bring me the key to the chest."

As he was in a bad temper, she did not venture to question him but went out and whispered something to Phoenix. Patience then brought in a chest and put it before Jia Lian. She turned to go.

"What the devil's your hurry?" Jia Lian demanded. "Who's going to give me the key?"

Suppressing her annoyance Patience opened the casket. "What do you want taken out?" she asked.

"What is there?"

"Say plainly what you want," she cried angrily. "Then we can die content!"

"What is there to say? You were the ones who brought all the trouble on us. Now we're four or five thousand taels short for the old lady's funeral, and the master told me to raise some money from the title deeds of the family land—but what is there left? All I can do is sell the things the old lady left me. Are you against that?"

Patience was sulkily taking things out of the chest when a young maid darted in to fetch her.

Ignoring Jia Lian, Patience hurried out to discover Phoenix clawing the air with both hands. Restraining her, Patience wept and cried for help.

Jia Lian came out to have a look and stamped his foot. "Now this!" he groaned. "I'm finished!"

Phoenix was now so delirious that her maids set up a great wailing. Then Lady Wang arrived, alerted by one of the maids, and was relieved to find Phoenix had quieted somewhat.

At this point a maid came in to report, "The master wants you, madam." So, after giving Patience a few instructions, Lady Wang departed.

Phoenix had come to her senses by now. She told Patience that she seemed to have seen ghosts. Phoenix had been physically sick and mentally worn out by pangs of her guilty conscience and the depressing feeling she had of losing face. She finally died a few days after the funeral procession for the Lady Dowager.

Phoenix died an embittered woman at an early age, in her thirties. Alas, once the heart and soul of the household, she was tortured by terrible dreams in her last days.

Jia Lian didn't know how to cope with the situation. He told one of the stewards to see to the funeral. Having little money at hand, he was hard put to pay for the funeral. The thought of Phoenix's help in the past increased his wretchedness.

Patience appreciated his anxiety. "Don't ruin your health by worrying too much," she urged him.

"To hell with my health!" he exploded. "I haven't even the money for daily expenses. What's to be done?"

"Don't worry, Second Master. If you're short of money, I still have some things that luckily weren't confiscated. Take them, sir, to go on with."

Jia Lian was most relieved. "That's splendid," he answered with a smile. "It'll save me the trouble of borrowing here and there. I'll pay you back when I'm in funds again."

"All I have was given me by the mistress," said Patience. "So why talk about paying me back? I just want this funeral to be properly managed."

Feeling immensely grateful, Jia Lian raised money by selling these things that belonged to Patience, and thereafter he consulted her on all matters.

32/ Magic Jade Renounces the World

Soon after the funeral of Phoenix, Magic Jade, exhausted by the mental shocks of recent weeks, broke down and went completely out of his senses. He did not say anything, but just grinned foolishly all day long. Lady Wang was at the end of her resources. When she saw her son so deranged, she was anxious to send for a doctor.

Several days later, Magic Jade began to eat nothing at all. As he now lost consciousness, everyone in the house wondered what to do. They reported to his father, Jia Zheng, "The doctor said medicine would do him no good this time. Magic Jade is obviously approaching his end. You'd better prepare for his last breath!"

With a sigh of grief, Jia Zheng asked Jia Lian to take care of everything for his ill-fated son. But as Jia Lian was short of funds, he found it hard to deal with the situation.

Shortly thereafter, one of the gatekeepers came rushing in to report, "Second Master! That old wandering monk is outside again. He wants to sell a piece of jade that he has in his hand. He said it is the lost jade that once belonged to Master Magic Jade. He wants ten thousand ounces of silver for a reward."

In the meantime a tumult of voices could be heard outside, shouting, "Imprudent monk! Intruder! Stop him!"

Jia Lian went to see about the situation. The monk, by now, had entered the gate. Jia Lian was going to have his men chase the stranger away, when the monk began to yell, "Come, pay up! Pay up the money for a human life!"

Jia Lian grabbed the monk's arm and protested, "There are ladies inside. How can you rush in so wildly?"

"Any delay and it will be too late for me to save him," the monk shouted in reply.

At this, Jia Lian ordered, "Stop crying! Everyone get inside! A monk is coming!"

Lady Wang and the others were sobbing too bitterly to pay any attention. They turned and saw the monk, and although terrified, they had no time to hide as the monk marched straight to Magic Jade's bed.

"Patrons," cried the monk, "I've brought the jade." Then, holding it up, he added, "Hurry up and bring out the silver. Then I'll save him."

Panic-stricken, Lady Wang could not tell whether it was genuine jade or not. "If you can save his life, you'll get the money," she promised.

"Hand it over then!" the monk insisted.

"Don't worry, We can raise that much money," Lady Wang assured him.

The monk roared with laughter. Holding the jade, he bent over the bed and cried, "Magic Jade, Magic Jade. Your magic jade is back again."

Lady Wang and the rest saw Magic Jade open his eyes. Aroma cried out for joy, "He's cured!"

"Where is it?" Magic Jade asked.

The monk placed it in Magic Jade's hand. The young man grasped it tightly, then slowly held it up to examine it attentively. "Ah," Magic Jade exclaimed. "How long we've been separated."

All those present invoked Buddha in great joy.

Jia Lian went with the monk to report the matter to Jia Zheng. Overjoyed, Jia Zheng bowed his thanks to the monk, who bowed in return and then sat down, which made Jia Zheng realize that he would not leave until he received his reward.

Jia Zheng asked, "Where is your monastery, and what is your religious name? Where did you find this jade? How is it that the sight of it restored my son to life?"

"That I don't know," answered the monk with a smile. "All I want is ten thousand ounces of silver."

The monk looked so big and rude that Jia Zheng dared not offend him and simply replied, "You shall have it."

"If you have it, hurry up and bring it over," the monk said. "I must be going."

"Please wait a little while I go inside to find the silver."

"Go on then. Don't stay too long."

Never did Jia Zheng expect that when he came out the monk could have disappeared.

Magic Jade made a rapid recovery after his long spell of unconsciousness. Everyone was happy to see the favorable turn of events. Jia Zheng was now relieved of worry about his son Magic Jade. Peace and order were restored to the house.

Now Jia Zheng did not like to leave the old lady's coffin in the temple for long. So he consulted with Jia Lian and they decided to escort it back to the south for burial. At the same time the coffin of Black Jade was also taken to her native town of Yangzhou.

This was the year for the state examination. Jia Zheng asked his son to get ready for the exam. It goes without saying that Precious Hairpin and Aroma always encouraged him to study hard for the coming examination. However, after his recovery Magic Jade showed himself completely changed in character. He was silent and often lost in meditation. He buried himself in his books, avoided conversation and company. He paid no more attention to his feminine environment.

One day, the monk came back to visit Magic Jade.

"That crazy monk is back again," shouted some people outside the gate. "He is asking for his ten thousand ounces of silver." The shouting from outside set the whole house in an uproar.

"Where is my dear master?" Magic Jade asked.

To everyone's surprise he went out alone to meet the crazy monk. Then, without a word, he raced back to his own compound, snatched up the jade from his bed, and dashed out again. He ran into Aroma, who started with fright.

"The mistress said it was very good of you to entertain the monk," Aroma informed him, "and she means to give him some silver."

"Go straight and tell her there's no need to raise any money," Magic Jade replied. "I'll return him the jade, instead."

"Nothing doing!" Aroma caught him by the arm. "This jade is your life. If he takes it away, your illness will come back!"

"Not any more," said Magic Jade, wrenching himself free. "Now that I'm in my right mind again, what do I need the jade for?" He then headed for the gate where the monk was waiting.

Aroma ran frantically after him, calling. "Come back! I've something to tell you."

Magic Jade cried over his shoulder, "There's nothing we need to talk about."

Aroma continued to chase after him shouting, and finally overtook him. She clung to his belt desperately, and prevented him from going any further.

Her frantic cries of "Help! He wants to give up his jade!" attracted Cuckoo and the other maids. By exerting their joint strength they held him fast.

"Don't make a fuss about a jade stone!" he sighed. "What would you do if I went away myself?" At that they burst into uncontrollable sobbing.

They were still locked together when Lady Wang and Precious Hairpin hurried over. "Magic Jade," wailed his mother. "You've gone crazy again."

Magic Jade saw that he had no chance of escape now, so he gave up the struggle. With a sheepish smile he said, "Why all this fuss? Why upset yourself for no reason at all? I thought it unreasonable of the monk to insist on ten thousand taels, not one tael less. So that annoyed me and I came back meaning to return the jade to him, saying that it was not a real one anyway and we didn't want it. If he saw that we didn't value it, he'd be willing to accept whatever we offered."

"I thought you really meant to give it back," said Lady Wang. "All right then, but why didn't you tell Aroma and the others clearly? Why make them raise such an uproar?"

Hairpin put in, "If that's the case, well and good. If you really give the jade back, that monk is so odd that he might cause fresh trouble for our family and that would never do. As for the reward, you can raise it by selling my jewels."

"Yes," agreed Lady Wang. "Let's do that."

Magic Jade made no objection as Hairpin stepped forward to take the jade from his hand. "There's no need for you to go out," she said, "Lady Wang and I will give him the money."

"I don't mind not giving him the jade," Magic Jade replied, "but I must see him once more."

Aroma and Cuckoo were holding him. Precious Hairpin told them to let him go.

Then Aroma released Magic Jade, who said with a smile, "You people think more of the jade than you do of me. Now that you're not stopping me, suppose I go off with the monk and leave you the jade."

In renewed alarm, Aroma wanted to seize him again, but in the presence of Lady Wang and Precious Hairpin she could not take such liberties. Magic Jade soon slipped away.

Lady Wang and Precious Hairpin, because they were worried, sent word to the servants outside to wait on Magic Jade and to hear what the monk had to say.

A maid returned and informed Lady Wang, "Master Magic Jade is really rather crazy. He's gone out and begged the monk to take him with him."

Lady Wang expressed horror at this, and then asked what the monk had replied.

"He said he wants the jade, not its owner," the girl said.

"Doesn't he want the money then?" asked Precious Hairpin.

"I didn't hear anything about that, madam," the maid replied. "Later the monk and Magic Jade were overheard laughing and chatting together about many things, but the pages couldn't understand a word of their jargon." On Lady Wang's orders the maid immediately brought in one of the pages.

"Though you didn't understand the talk between the monk and Magic Jade, can you repeat it to me?" asked Lady Wang.

"All we caught were phrases like 'Blue Ridge Peak,' and 'cutting off mortal entanglements,'" was the answer.

Lady Wang couldn't make head or tail of this jabbering, but Precious Hairpin's eyes widened in alarm.

They were about to send the servant to fetch Magic Jade back, when in he came grinning and saying to himself, "Fine, fine!"

"What is all this crazy talk you had with the monk?" his mother asked.

"I'm in earnest," protested Magic Jade. "Yet you call me crazy. That monk and I knew each other long before, and he simply wished to see me. He never really wanted a reward but was just doing a good deed. After he'd explained that, he vanished. Isn't that fine? Well, my master told me, 'Whatever happens is predestined by Providence!'"

"Come back to your senses and take your head out of the clouds!" said Precious Hairpin impatiently. "Your father and mother love you so much, why not study hard to achieve something great?"

"Don't you know that what I have in my mind will advance us all? As the saying goes, 'When one son renounces the world, seven of his ancestors will go to paradise.'"

Lady Wang felt her heart torn when she heard these words. And she broke into violent sobbing.

"I was only kidding." said Magic Jade, smiling, trying to reassure her.

But Magic Jade was not joking. From then on he had shut himself off from the company of his friends and girls, and he devoted himself to studying the Chinese classics and his beloved philosophy in preparation for the coming state exam. It goes without saying that Lady Wang was pleased to know how hard Magic Jade was studying.

A few days later, the time for the examination arrived.

"This is your first examination," Lady Wang warned Magic Jade and Jia Lan. "Today you're going to be entirely on your own, so you'll have to take care of yourselves. Come out as soon as you've finished your compositions to find our family servants. Then come straight home to set the minds of your mothers and wife at rest." She was moved to grief as she spoke.

Jia Lan had assented to each word, whereas Magic Jade had said nothing. But when his mother finished he came over to kneel before her, shedding tears, "I can never repay the mother who gave birth to me. But I shall do as well as I can in the exam to obtain a degree and make you happy, mother. Then I'll have done my duty as a son. That will atone for all my past faults."

These words upset Lady Wang even more. But she merely replied, "Of course, it's good for you now."

"Even if the old lady can't see me," he said, "she'll know and be pleased. So it's all the same whether she sees me or not. We're separated in form only, not in spirit."

This exchange, besides striking her as inauspicious, made Li Wan afraid that Magic Jade was losing his mind again. She made haste to say, "Madam, why grieve on such a happy occasion? Especially as Brother Magic Jade has recently been so sensible and dutiful, studying hard as well. When he and his nephew have taken the exam and written some good compositions, they'll come straight back home. Then we can wait for news of their success."

Magic Jade turned to bow to her, saying, "Don't worry, sister-in-law. We're both going to pass. Later on, your Jia Lan is going to do so well that you'll be honored as a noble lady."

She chuckled, "I only hope it works out as you say, so that it won't have been in vain." She broke off there, afraid to upset Lady Wang.

"If you have a good son to continue our ancestors line," rejoined Magic Jade, "even though my brother hasn't lived to see it, it means he has done his duty."

Li Wan simply nodded, reluctant to say any more as it was growing late.

Precious Hairpin was almost dismayed. For not only Magic Jade's words but everything said by Lady Wang and Li Wan struck her as ill-omened. Still, trying not to take it seriously, she held back her tears and kept silent.

And now Magic Jade walked over to make her a deep bow. All present, though mystified by his strange behavior, did not want to laugh. They were even more amazed when Precious Hairpin wept.

Magic Jade told her, "I'm going now, cousin. Take good care of mother and wait for my good news."

"It's time you were off." she answered. "There's no need to talk like this."

"So you're hurrying me? I know it's time to be off." He turned to look around and noticed two people missing. "Send word for me to Xichun and Cuckoo," he added. "Well, all I want to say is that I'll be seeing them again."

He sounded half rational, half crazy, but the others attributed this to the fact that he had never left home before and was affected by what his mother had said. They thought it best to speed him on his way.

"People are waiting outside," they reminded him. "If you delay any longer you'll be late."

Magic Jade threw back his head and laughed. "I'm going now. No more ado! This is the end of everything!"

The others answered cheerfully, "Good-bye! Have a nice trip."

Only Lady Wang and Precious Hairpin behaved as if this were a separation for life. Their tears coursed down, and they nearly burst out sobbing. Laughing like a maniac, Magic Jade went out. Truly:

Taking the only approach to fame and wealth,
He breaks through the first door of his cage.

The day for the end of the state examination soon came, and Lady Wang looked forward to the return of Magic Jade and Jia Lan. By afternoon, when there was still no sign of them, Precious Hairpin and she sent servants to make inquiries. But the servants did not come back. Having no news, others were sent, and when these men also did not return both of the women became quite distraught.

Then, that evening, Jia Lan returned.

"Where is your Uncle Magic Jade?" he was asked.

Without stopping to pay his respects he sobbed, "Uncle Magic Jade has disappeared!"

Dumbfounded, Lady Wang collapsed. Luckily the maids were at hand to carry her to her bed and revive her, but at once she started wailing. Precious Hairpin remained speechless, dazed.

Dissolved in tears, Aroma reproached Jia Lan, "Stupid creature! You were with him, how could you lose him?"

"In the hostel we ate and slept in the same place," he told them. "And in the examination grounds our cells weren't too far apart, so we kept in close touch. This morning, Uncle Magic Jade finished his papers first and waited for me so we could hand them in together. Then we came out together. But in the crowd at the Entrance Gate he suddenly disappeared. The servants who'd come to meet us asked me where he was, but he was nowhere to be found. I sent the servants to search in different directions, while I took some men to search all the cells. But he wasn't there. That's why I'm back so late."

Lady Wang was crying too hard to be able to speak, Precious Hairpin had a fair idea of the truth of the matter, while Aroma was sobbing as if she would never stop. So without waiting for orders, Jia Qiang went out with others to search in different directions.

The banquet that had been prepared to welcome the candidates back went untouched. The Honored Mansion was half deserted and plunged into gloom.

Forgetting his own exhaustion, Jia Lan wanted again to join the search for Magic Jade, but Lady Wang restrained him. "Child, your uncle has disappeared," she said, "we can't have you getting lost too. Go and rest now, there's a good boy."

Still, Jia Lan insisted on going until Madam You and the rest managed to dissuade him.

Xichun was the only one to really grasp the truth. But she could not reveal it. Instead, she asked Precious Hairpin, "Did Cousin Magic Jade take his jade with him?"

"Of course, he always wore it." was the answer, to which Xichun made no reply.

The servants came back from time to time to report that they had searched high and low without finding a trace of Magic Jade. This went on for several days, with Lady Wang too grief-stricken to eat. She was at death's door. Day and night, high and low alike were waiting for word of Magic Jade.

One day near the time of dawn, servants from the outer apartments came to the inner gate to announce good tidings, "Such good news, madam," they cried.

Jumping to the wrong conclusion, Lady Wang stood up elatedly to ask, "Where did they find him? Bring him in at once."

"He's come in seventh among the successful candidates."

"But where is he?" she asked. When there was no answer, she sat down again.

"Who came in seventh?" asked Xichun.

"Magic Jade!" they told her.

Then another shout went up outside, "Master Jia Lan has passed too," was the report. The maids hurried out and came back with the announcement that Jia Lan's name was the hundred-and-thirtieth on the list.

Li Wan was naturally overjoyed, but while Magic Jade was missing she dared not show it. Lady Wang, too, was pleased that Jia Lan had passed but thought to herself if only Magic Jade were to come back how happy we all would be.

Precious Hairpin, the only one still overcome with grief, had to hold back her tears.

All who offered congratulations said, "Since Magic Jade was fated to pass, he's bound to turn up. Besides, now as a successful candidate, he's too well known to remain lost."

However, Xichun commented. "How could a grown man like him get lost? I suspect he's seen through the ways of the world and taken monastic vows. In that case it will be difficult to find him."

This set Lady Wang and the others weeping again.

When Jia Lian heard that his father was mortally ill, he sped to his place of exile. They wept on meeting again, and gradually Jia She recovered. When Jia Lian was informed of the recent happenings at home, he told his father about them and then started back home immediately. On the way he received news of a general amnesty granted by the Emperor. Now Jia Lian's return brought both joy and sorrow. The Imperial envoys instructed him, "Come tomorrow to the Imperial Treasury to receive your bounty. The Peaceful Mansion is yours to live in again."

Jia Zheng was on his way back from burying his mother in her southern homeland when he received a letter telling him of the latest events at home. The news that his child had passed the examination with honor filled his heart with joy. At the same time his joy was dimmed by his anxiety over Magic Jade's sudden mysterious disappearance.

Jia Zheng further learned that, as soon as His Majesty learned that the seventh successful candidate on the list was a brother of his former Imperial consort, Yuanchun, he was so moved that he poured out his Imperial favor over the Jia clan once more. Thanks to this amnesty, the exiled Jia She and Jia Zhen were permitted to return home from banishment. Their confiscated property was to be restored to them. In addition, the Emperor gave orders that an official search was to be made for the seventh successful candidate on the list. Jia Zheng heard all this cheerful news with tears of mingled joy and sorrow.

He arrived by river boat one day at the post station Kunling. A sudden spell of cold had brought a light fall of snow. The whole landscape was mantled in white. Sitting alone in the cabin of the boat while writing to his family, Jia Zheng suddenly seemed to see a figure emerging from the falling snow on the bank of the river, opposite the bow of the boat.

The man was bareheaded and barefooted, and was dressed in a monk's gown.

Jia Zheng jumped up and hurried over the gangway onto the bank. He stepped up to the peculiar stranger, and was about to ask him who he was and whence he came when, looking more closely, he recognized the stranger. It was Magic Jade.

"It's you, Magic Jade, my darling child," Jia Zheng cried in astonishment.

The stranger remained silent. On his face there was an expression of joy and sorrow.

"How is it that you're here, Magic Jade?" continued Jia Zheng.

The stranger seemed to reply, but Jia Zheng couldn't hear the words. All of a sudden the two other monkish figures came up and stood beside Magic Jade, one to the right and the other to the left.

"Now your earthly destiny is fulfilled," said the other two figures to Magic Jade. "Don't delay, but follow us."

Then Jia Zheng saw the three of them floating lightly upwards together over the river bank. He rushed after them in spite of the danger of slipping on the snowy ground. No matter how fast Jia Zheng rushed after them, he could not catch up with them. Their outlines became more and more indistinct.

Jia Zheng could hear the sound of singing in the distance. But all he could understand were a few disjointed words about "green crag," "great void," and "wandering into the far unknown." The three monks disappeared behind a hill. Far and wide there was nothing to be seen but the white snow and empty landscape.

When his servants had returned to the ship, Jia Zheng told them of his strange encounter a few moments before. They suggested that their master search the whole district for his son Magic Jade, but Jia Zheng shook his head and sighed. He was lost in thought.

"It's strange, very strange!" he murmured to himself. "I saw Magic Jade with my own eyes. I also heard their singing

with my own ears. It was no imagination or empty phantom vision. Now it's clear to me. Magic Jade came into the world with a magic jade in his mouth. That was mysterious enough. We reared this spirit child. Then these two peculiar fellows appeared on the scene. Monks have intervened in his life three times. Once when the boy lay ill, they made him well again with their incantations. Then one of the fellows brought back the lost jade stone and saved the boy from death for the second time. That time I saw him with my own eyes sitting in the reception hall, then all of a sudden he disappeared. Today they have spirited him away. No, it's quite useless to go searching for a spirit."

Jia Zheng reported his amazing encounter with Magic Jade in his letter home, asking that the members should not mourn the lost son any more. As he pointed out, despite the high marks on the exam, Magic Jade had no aptitude whatsoever for the career of an official. To have produced a bodisattva was an honor for the family, and certainly no disgrace.

Now those members of the clan who had been away arrived home one after another: Jia Zheng from his journey to the south; Jia She and Jia Zhen from their exile; and Xue Pan, pardoned and ransomed from his imprisonment.

On the very next day after his return home, Jia Zheng called at the Grand Secretariat, and through him, Jia Zheng was kindly received by the Emperor. His Imperial grace awarded Magic Jade, by decree, a noble title. This honor consoled the Jia family to a certain extent for the physical loss of Magic Jade.

Lady Wang confided tearfully to Aunt Xue, "I don't blame Magic Jade for deserting me. It's my daughter-in-law's cruel fate that upsets me most." This made Aunt Xue's heart ache too.

Precious Hairpin was eating her heart out, oblivious to all around her.

Lady Wang went on, "I was pleased to hear that Precious Hairpin is pregnant. To think it should end like this. If I'd known, I wouldn't have found him a wife or ruined your daughter's life!"

"This was their fate, that's all!" Aunt Xue sighed.

Now a tale of bitterness is told,
So absurd that it's more grief than joy.
Since all of us live in a dream,
Why should we laugh at other's folly?